# Cathy Cassidy

# DIZZY & LUCKY STAR

PUFFIN

PUFFIN BOOKS

Published by the Penguin Group
Penguin Books Ltd, 80 Strand, London WC2R ORL, England
Penguin Group (USA) Inc., 375 Hudson Street, New York, New York 10014, USA
Penguin Group (Canada), 90 Eglinton Avenue East, Suite 700, Toronto, Ontario, Canada M4P 2Y3
(a division of Pearson Penguin Canada Inc.)
Penguin Ireland, 25 St Stephen's Green, Dublin 2, Ireland (a division of Penguin Books Ltd)
Penguin Group (Australia), 250 Camberwell Road, Camberwell, Victoria 3124, Australia
(a division of Pearson Australia Group Pty Ltd)
Penguin Books India Pvt Ltd, 11 Community Centre, Panchsheel Park, New Delhi – 110 017, India
Penguin Group (NZ), 67 Apollo Drive, Rosedale, Auckland 0632, New Zealand
(a division of Pearson New Zealand Ltd)
Penguin Books (South Africa) (Pty) Ltd, 24 Sturdee Avenue, Rosebank,
Johannesburg 2196, South Africa

Penguin Books Ltd, Registered Offices: 80 Strand, London WC2R ORL, England

puffinbooks.com

*Dizzy* first published 2004
*Lucky Star* first published 2007
This bind-up edition published 2012
001 – 10 9 8 7 6 5 4 3 2 1

Set in Monotype Baskerville
Printed in Great Britain by Clays Ltd, St Ives plc

British Library Cataloguing in Publication Data
A CIP catalogue record for this book is available from the British Library

ISBN: 978-0-141-34438-6

www.greenpenguin.co.uk

MIX
Paper from
responsible sources
FSC
www.fsc.org    FSC™ C018179

Penguin Books is committed to a sustainable
future for our business, our readers and our planet.
This book is made from Forest Stewardship
Council™ certified paper.

ALWAYS LEARNING                    **PEARSON**

# Cathy Cassidy

# Dizzy

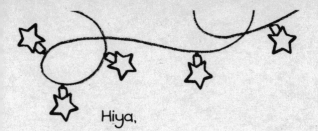

Hiya,

*Dizzy* was my first book, back in 2004 when I was still working as an art teacher and as the agony aunt for a young teen magazine. I loved my work, but I also loved daydreaming and inventing stories, and the stories just got bigger and bigger until they had to be told. Getting my first book published was amazing, and I haven't looked back - after all, once you know that dreams really can come true, the sky's the limit!

These days, I am a full-time writer, but I still live in the Scottish countryside with my husband and two teenage children. We have two cats, assorted rabbits and a mad, hairy lurcher very like Leggit in this story!

The characters and plot in *Dizzy* are imaginary, but little threads and details from real life sometimes sneak their way in. And if you are driving through the Scottish countryside and happen to pass a pretty, ramshackle cottage with a tepee in the garden . . . well, look out for me! I'll probably be in the hammock, soaking up the sunshine and dreaming up another story . . .

Best wishes,

*Cathy Cassidy*    xxxx

www.cathycassidy.com

I never sleep, the night before my birthday.

It's not the usual kind of excitement – I don't get all wound up about whether I'll get a new CD player or a pair of rollerblades or a guitar. It's a guitar, anyway – Dad told me.

I'm not stressed out about a party or a sleep-over or a trip to the ice rink, either. We have this tradition, Dad and me. We stay home with a takeaway and a video. If it's his birthday, Dad picks Indian food, along with something hippy-dippy or all-action to watch, like *Lord of the Rings* or *Star Wars*. When I was little, I used to go for Disney, then soppy stuff like *The Secret Garden* or *Fairy Tale*. This year, we've got Sky TV and I get to have complete charge of the remote control all evening. I'll probably just skip between MTV and Kerrang!, munching pizza as I flick.

Birthdays are pretty cool, I know. It's just that, no matter how hard I try, I can't relax, I can't not care – and I'm always a little bit scared the night before. Every year, I'm up at dawn watching for the postman, because there's one very special card – a parcel, even, sometimes – I just *have* to get.

It's the only day of the year I hear from her.

When I was five, I got a postcard from Kathmandu. It had a picture of a Buddhist temple with a pointy golden roof and weird, staring eyes painted beneath it, and the message was written in three colours of felt pen with loads of kisses.

When I was six, there was a postcard of a donkey with flowers in its mouth, and the postmark said West Cork, Ireland. The next year I got a proper birthday card and a handmade rag doll with pink and purple hair made from fluffy yarn, and a dress stitched from somebody's old tie-dye T-shirt.

On my eighth birthday, there was a postcard from Marrakesh in Morocco, a picture of a grinning Arab girl with armfuls of gold bracelets. The next year I got a rainbow-striped hat with a floppy brim and a postcard of a castle in Wales. I wore the hat every day, till the edges got frayed and the colours ran in the wash. Then I stuck it to my pinboard, along with the postcards and the photos, and it's still there now.

When I was ten, I got a dreamcatcher, a circle

of willow criss-crossed with a crazy spider's web of bright threads and beads. Soft, white feathers hung down either side, with some tiny bells in the middle. The postcard (a spooky stone circle in Wiltshire, this time) told me to hang the dream-catcher over my bed. Its magic web would catch all my bad dreams and melt them away, so I could sleep safe and deep, all night long. Wish I'd had *that* when I was five.

Last year, when I was eleven, she sent a silver chain with a tiny chunk of rose-quartz crystal hanging from it. I always wear it, even at night. There was no postcard that year, just a letter. It's the kind of letter that's difficult to read, even now, but also the kind of letter I needed to have a long, long time ago. It said that she loved me, that she was sorry, and that one day we'd be together again.

I rolled the letter up, tied it with a strand of purple yarn from my moulting rag doll and put it in my treasure box. Then I stuck the envelope to my pinboard, so I could see her loopy, gel-pen handwriting and the postmark, which said somewhere in Cornwall. Not so very far away. But far enough.

I love my mum, but I can't really remember her. Not properly.

There are two photos of her on my pinboard.

In the first, she's standing in the rain on a

pavement in Birmingham, hand in hand with Dad. It's their wedding picture, taken just outside the registry office, twelve and a half years ago.

Mum is tiny and elfin with startling lilac-coloured hair, all braided and beaded and hanging down around her shoulders. She's wearing what looks like a lace tablecloth. It *was* a lace tablecloth, Dad told me. It cost a quid in a charity shop, and she made it into a weird, dip-hemmed number and wore it over a purple sack-dress, with purple and black stripy tights and Doc Marten boots.

Dad looks just as scary. He's so young and skinny and smiley, in patched, worn-out jeans and a vast, black mohair jumper. His hair is dyed ketchup-red, and it stands straight up as if he'd just stuck his fingers in an electric socket.

I'm in this picture, too, hidden away under the lace tablecloth. I'm just a bump, a secret, impossible to see because of the way Mum's holding her flowers (dandelions, along with some orange daisy-things pinched from the local park). All the same, I'm there, and I bet I'm the reason they're standing there in the rain, smiling at the camera and brushing confetti out of their hair.

Five months later, there I am for real, in the second photo. I'm a few weeks old, a small, angry face with black button eyes and a shock of dark hair, dressed in something bright and stripy.

Mum's face gazes up at the camera, looking pale and bewildered, her lilac hair chopped short now, tousled and scruffy. I've looked hard at that picture for signs of blissed-out motherly love and all that happy-families stuff, but Mum just looks lost, unhappy.

She left when I was four.

I don't remember, of course, but by then we'd lived in a bus, a caravan, a squat, a council flat. We toured the music festivals, Mum and Dad selling lentil soup, dreamcatchers, scented candles, handmade earrings. They worked in an organic vegetable garden, a wholefood café, a clog work-shop, a pottery. They signed on the dole and lived on social security and bought me second-hand shoes and forgot to brush my hair so it got all matted and fluffy and made old ladies at bus stops tut and shake their heads.

They tried, Dad said, to give me a name, a family, a future. She tried. *Must try harder*, like my maths teacher says.

When I was four, she ran away with a bloke called Mitch. He was taking a Volkswagen camper van to Kathmandu, and Mum must have thought that sounded better than another ten or fifteen years of wiping my nose and not brushing my hair and reading me stories about fluffy bunnies. She kissed me extra hard one night, and told me she loved me, and in the morning she was gone.

We managed, Dad and me. We stayed in the council flat and I started school and he started college, doing ceramics, which is just a fancy name for pottery. I made friends with Sara and Sasha and Jade, and Dad made mugs and bowls and wiggly-edged plates all glazed with speckly stuff. He also made beautiful models of elves and fairies and sad-faced mermaids, and all of them looked a bit like Mum, but I never mentioned that.

He finished his course and we rented a place with a workshop attached, and after a while he made enough money for us to live on, selling the wiggly-edged bowls and plates to craft shops and the elfy-things to posh shops and galleries. We stopped eating lentil stew every day and progressed to French bread, oven chips and frozen vegetable lasagne, and we were happy. Mostly.

Last Christmas, Dad bought me pink flowery fairy lights, and I draped them all around my pin-board, the board where I've stuck all my postcards, along with the hat and the photos and the loved-up raggy doll.

'Looks like some kind of Hindu shrine,' Dad said when he saw it, and it does, a bit, but that's how I like it.

It's all I've got of my mum.

'Hey, Dizzy! Wake up, birthday girl!'

Dad brings me breakfast in bed on my birthday, every year. And every year, I hide under the covers and pretend I haven't been lying awake, thinking about Mum. I yawn and stretch and wipe imaginary sleep from my eyes.

The room floods with light and Dad lowers a tray laden with birthday breakfast on to the duvet. Each year, it's the same – my favourite, cheese on toast, but with a special birthday twist. Dad always layers yellow cheese over the bread, then shapes a number out of orange cheese and puts it on top to melt under the grill. This year, there are two slices of toast spelling out the fact that I'm twelve. It smells fantastic.

Dad sits down on the edge of the bed. He's skinny and mop-haired, wearing striped pyjamas and an ancient T-shirt.

'Happy birthday, Dizzy,' he grins, giving me a hug.

'Thanks, Dad.'

No more birthday blues. I bite into the toast. Happy.

There's a flower in a jam jar on the tray, and a banana milkshake, and a small, familiar parcel wrapped in blue paper. These days, I'd rather have apple juice or Coke than banana milkshake, but it was my favourite once. I tear off the blue paper and there's another old favourite, a tube of Smarties.

Everything is just the way it was the first time Dad made me a birthday breakfast, when I was five, the first birthday after Mum left. I like it like that. It's a tradition.

We share out the Smarties and Dad brings in my pressies, a couple of small parcels and something huge and guitar-shaped tied up with newspaper and Sellotape. I rip off the paper to uncover the glossy curves, wood the colour of honey and chocolate.

'Dad, it's gorgeous!' I squeal. I strum out 'Happy Birthday', slightly out of tune. My other pressies are the plum suede trainers I admired in town last week and a cool make-up bag stuffed with glittery nail varnishes. Perfect!

I'm all showered and dressed by the time the

post plops on to the mat in the hallway. I flick through the fat, pastel birthday card envelopes, looking for a postcard, a parcel, anything addressed in rainbow-coloured pen in her childish, loopy writing.

There's nothing from Mum.

After school, we pile into the window seat at Dimitri's, Jade and Sara and Sasha and me. We're all school bags, stripy ties and smiles, and Dimitri rolls his eyes as he wanders over to take the order.

'Four Cokes, please,' Sasha says, wafting a fiver.

Dimitri pretends to be shocked. Normally, we order two Cokes and four straws between us, and make them last an hour at least.

'*Four* Cokes?' he asks. 'What's the special occasion?'

'Dizzy's birthday,' Sara tells him. 'Twelve today!'

Dimitri mutters something about hopeless kids, and when the Cokes arrive I laugh, because he's loaded mine up with cocktail umbrellas, ice, lemon slices, even a huge strawberry, all floating in a sea of brown fizz.

We sip and chat and roll up our white shirt-sleeves to compare tans, because it's 18 June and summer is trying hard to burn through the grey city clouds. Sara and I are milk-bottle white, Sasha's freckly and Jade is a gorgeous golden brown, but then that doesn't count, because she always is. We decide to ditch our school trousers in favour of little skirts and ankle socks.

'How is anyone meant to look cool in school uniform?' Jade demands, dragging off her tie. 'Green with puke-yellow stripes? *Attractive*. Very.'

'Although,' Sasha says, dragging the stripy tie from Jade, 'from time to time, they *do* come in handy . . .'

I don't see it coming.

There's a quick scuffle and Sasha has the tie over my eyes. Everything goes black and there's a hand muffling my squeals and more dragging me upright. My so-called mates twirl me round three times, then there's a firm shove in the small of my back and I'm sitting again, tearing at the blindfold as they start singing 'Happy Birthday'.

The tie slides down my face and I look up, pink-cheeked. Dimitri is there, carrying four slices of hot chocolate-fudge cake with ice-cream scoops. The largest slice is stiff with pink birthday candles, flickering dangerously. There are even a few stuck in the vanilla ice.

I laugh and blush and blow out the candles and the café breaks into a sudden round of applause. I love my friends.

\*

'You've got chocolate on your nose,' Sasha tells me later, as we mooch along the street. We've linked arms and the four of us fill the pavement, high on fudge cake and the luxury of having a whole Coke each.

'I love my bracelet,' I tell her with feeling, jangling my wrist while she dabs at my nose with a tissue. 'And the CD, and the posters.' I beam at Sara and Jade.

At the traffic lights, Sara and I wave goodbye to the others and cross over, taking a short-cut through the park.

'Any postcards?' she asks quietly as we pick our way across the grass. 'Anything from . . .'

'Mum? No, not yet.'

'Well, that one from Morocco that time, you said that was late.'

'Three weeks,' I told her. 'I was only eight. I watched for the postman every morning.'

'I know,' Sara sighs.

I also cried myself to sleep every night, stopped eating, stopped talking. Then the postcard came and everything was OK again. Dad said the postal service in North Africa was probably a bit dodgy. It definitely *wasn't* Mum's fault. Not like she'd forgotten, or anything.

'Anyway,' I say brightly, 'Dad's ordering in a

pizza. Three cheese and mushroom. And I can have MTV on all night if I like.'

We leave the park, cross the road. Sara lives in a red-brick semi halfway along the street. The garden's stuffed with violently coloured flowers and the grass is so short it looks like it's been ironed.

'Coming in for a bit?' she asks.

'Nah. Pizza's calling. Thanks for the posters, Sara, I love them. See you tomorrow.'

'See ya.'

I turn away. My chirpy mood has disappeared along with Sara. There's a heavy feeling inside my chest, like I just swallowed a small iceberg and not a vast slab of hot chocolate-fudge cake. Suddenly, I feel a whole lot older than twelve.

Our flat is right down at the end of the road, a tall town house divided into three apartments. We're in the ground-floor one, so we get to use the workshop (which was once a garage) for Dad's studio. I turn into the drive and see a big, grubby van skewed across the flagstones, one front wheel squashing a straggly patch of lupins. Mr Desai from upstairs will have a fit.

It *could* be someone delivering sacks of clay for Dad, although there's no courier logo on the side. The van is mostly red with one blue wing and one grey one. One of the back doors is purple, and someone's scrawled 'wash me' in the thick grime of its window. Lovely.

I let myself into the flat. Dad's left a pile of cards from the second post on the hall table for me, and I take a deep breath before scanning it quickly.

Nothing with her handwriting.

I open the cards, trying not to feel bad. Twenty quid from Auntie Mel, a card with kittens on it from Mr Desai, a book token from Mrs Coulter, my old childminder. If they can remember, why can't she?

I can hear Dad talking to someone in the living room. I hope it's not Lucy, his girlfriend. She's OK, and I'm getting used to her, but I don't really want to share my birthday with her. Birthdays are for me and Dad.

'Home, Dad,' I shout, scooping up my post and pushing open the bedroom door. My new guitar sits proudly on the duvet. Next to it is a little blue camera from Lucy. She let me open it last night, showed me how to load the film, how to work the flash and the little zoom lens. Cool.

I dump my backpack and pull a T-shirt and jeans from the drawer.

'Dizzy?' Dad shouts back. 'Can you come through here a minute?'

I drag off my tie and wander through. It's not

Lucy. Lucy's young and smiley with fair, wavy hair. She wears wafty, trendy tops with fluted sleeves and hipsters with embroidery on them. She wears toffee-coloured lipstick and smudgy eye shadow and she smells of lime-flavoured shower gel.

This woman is older, small and tanned with smiley wrinkles and hennaed hair so short it's practically shaven. She has about a million ear-rings all in the same ear, as well as a stud through her right eyebrow. She's wearing weird stripy trousers that are baggy at the top and tight around the ankles, and a faded vest top with no bra underneath. Yeuchhh.

I can tell without asking she's the owner of the patchwork van, but I can't work out why she's staring so hard at me.

'Dizzy, hi,' she says, and when she grins her teeth look kind of yellow.

'Hi,' I mutter, looking at Dad for clues.

He just stares back, looking shocked and scared and flustered. He's still in his studio clothes, his jeans all streaked with clay, his hands and arms still stained reddish-brown.

'Happy birthday,' she says.

I still don't get it.

'I can't believe how much you've *grown*,' she says. 'How beautiful you are. I can't believe this is really happening . . .'

My mouth feels suddenly dry, and the floor seems to shift under my feet. I look at the tanned, smiley face with the shiny blue eyes and the glint of gold studs. I take a deep breath in, frowning.

'Hello, Mum,' I say.

It's not how I imagined.

I thought she'd be younger, more like her photos. I thought we'd run at each other and hug and hang on forever. I thought I'd be happy, not confused.

Instead, the room gets misty and my cheeks get wet and I need to sit down. Dad comes up and takes my hand, gently, leading me forwards. 'Go on,' he whispers. 'It's OK.'

And then she pulls me close. I don't want to do this, to be here. I'm stiff and wooden, silent, hostile, resisting all the way. 'It's OK, Dizzy,' she says, stroking my hair. 'It's OK.'

I take a ragged breath in, and suddenly I smell it – a rich, sweet, musty perfume from long, long ago. It's patchouli oil, the scent of my childhood.

'Oh, Mu-um . . .'

My body sways against her, my wet cheeks fall against her shoulder. We cling on, and I let the tears come, but I'm smiling, too, because I've waited so long for this moment.

It's like coming home, and I want it to go on and on.

It doesn't, of course. Too soon, she steps back, pushing me to arm's length. I wipe my eyes and nose on my sleeve, and my face feels hot and pink and swollen.

She pushes a strand of damp hair back from my face, grinning. 'Just look at the state of us! Hey, c'mon, sit down,' she says, flopping back on to the sofa. 'We have a whole load of catching up to do. And a birthday feast to plan!'

'We were going to order in a pizza,' Dad chips in. 'Three cheese and mushroom. Want to share, or would you like something different?'

Mum frowns. 'Not pizza,' she says. 'I'm vegan these days, didn't I tell you? No cheese, no milk, no eggs, no honey.'

'Right,' says Dad, looking lost again.

'Besides,' Mum is saying. 'This is a special occasion. Why don't we make miso soup and red bean stew and maybe muesli cake for afters? We can all help. Sound OK, Dizzy?'

'Sure,' I nod, not understanding a word of it. 'Fine.'

'Well, I can ask if they'll do a pizza with no cheese and lots of extra topping,' Dad suggests.

'Pizza's kind of a tradition on Dizzy's birthday.'

'No, no,' I say quickly. 'Bean stew would be great. Honest, Dad.'

Actually, I hate kidney beans, and Dad knows that. Muesli cake sounds more like hamster bedding than food, and I haven't a clue what miso soup is, but if your mum turned up on your birthday after eight years' absence, wouldn't *you* be trying to please her?

'We'll be here all night,' Dad mutters, heading over to the open-plan kitchen.

'So?' she shrugs. 'We'll be here all night. What's the big deal?'

And because my mum has just told me she'll be here all night, and that means she won't be leaving for the next half-hour at least, I hug her again. 'Mum,' I say into her velvet hair. 'I've missed you so-o-o much!'

'Hey, hey!' she laughs, wriggling free. 'I've missed you too, babe. Only don't call me *Mum*, OK? It makes me feel about a hundred and three. Call me Storm.'

I know from Dad that she was christened Linda Caroline Tanner, and when they got married she became Linda Caroline Kerr, but Linda's no name for a punk, a rebel, a New Age traveller.

When I was a toddler, she reinvented herself as Storm. Just Storm. I might do the same thing when I'm older, only I'll ditch Dizzy for something plain and simple and ordinary, like Jane or Ann or Mary.

*Storm*, though. Dad said she chose it because it was strong and brave and unstoppable, but it always makes me think of hailstones, thunder, gale-force winds.

'Storm, then.' The name feels strange in my mouth.

In the kitchen, Dad is boiling a pan of water and washing rice over the sink. He grabs a bag of stir-fry veg from the freezer and heats the wok.

'Need any help?' Storm calls over.

'No, no, you two just relax,' Dad says. 'Everything's under control.'

He tips rice into the pan, tears open the stir-fry and adds it to the sizzling wok. He roots in a cupboard for a jar of curry sauce.

'Is that vegan?' Storm asks. 'Can you check the label?'

'It's fine,' Dad promises, but Storm goes over to check it anyhow.

'All these chemicals and E-numbers,' she says, wrinkling up her nose. 'You should buy organic, Pete. There's just no goodness left in this at all.'

'Tastes good, though,' Dad winks at me.

'Well, it's Dizzy's treat, I suppose,' she concedes. 'Look, if you won't let me help, at least let me contribute something. I think there's some bits and pieces in the van.'

It's weird, because the minute she goes out of the room my heart twists, like it's scared she's leaving me all over again. Dad looks over and catches me chewing my lip.

'Go and see if she needs a hand,' he suggests, and I wonder how he always knows exactly the right thing to say.

Years of practice, probably.

I wander outside and peer in through the van's open purple door. Inside it's a mad, multi-coloured nest of quilts and cushions. All down one side are kitchen cupboards, painted with swirls and spirals and crescent moons. A big bundle of long, skinny twigs lies the whole length of the van's floor. Weirdest of all, tucked into the corner, there's a tiny cast-iron stove with a long chimney-pipe that juts right out the top of the roof.

You could *live* in this van. It looks like Storm does.

Strings of bells are looped across the ceiling, and they jingle as she brushes against them, heaving down a brightly woven shoulder bag and a rolled-up quilt. She reaches under the tiny sink and pulls out a big jar of cloudy amber liquid with a hand-drawn label.

'Scrumpy,' she grins at me. 'For your dad. It'll loosen him up a bit.'

'Right.'

In the house, Storm unrolls the purple quilt and spreads it out across the sofa, making it look suddenly exotic. She sits back down and folds her legs up beneath her, reaching deep into the ruck-sack. 'Carob,' she announces, pulling out a slab of dirt-coloured stuff wrapped up in foil. 'Try it.'

I take a bite. It tastes like soil, only less appealing. 'Excellent,' I nod.

'Now . . . where are they? Ah!' She brings out a small package swathed in black velvet. Care-fully, she opens out the cloth to reveal a pack of cards tied up with gold cord. They're not hearts, diamonds, spades or clubs.

'Tarot cards,' says Storm.

'What are they?' I ask, stroking the bright cards as she swirls them face-down across the carpet. 'What do they do?'

Storm grins. 'The tarot are ancient, fortune-telling cards with a magic all their own,' she tells me. 'Fancy a glimpse of the future, Dizz?'

4

There's a kind of row about whether Storm should do my tarot cards or not. Dad says it's superstitious rubbish and Storm says, in that case, what's the problem? It's just a bit of fun.

She pours him a mug of scrumpy and tells him it's extra-strong cider brewed by a mad old bloke in Somerset. Dad rolls his eyes, but takes a drink anyway, and Storm spreads out the tarot pack and gets me to pick some cards.

It may be just a bit of fun, but when Storm says that my calm, cautious, ordered life is about to change forever, I feel a tingle down my spine. The cards predict adventure, travel, freedom.

'Kids *need* calm and caution and order,' Dad says.

'No, Pete, look at this,' she insists. 'The end of childhood. She's at a crossroads in her life. I see new opportunities, the healing of old wounds. She will choose the path that's least expected.'

'I don't *think* so,' he snorts.

'Dad, please,' I beg. 'Storm, what does it mean? What's going to happen?'

Dad stalks over and knocks the cards to the floor, his face a tight mask of anger.

'Just *stop* it, Storm,' he snaps. 'These are our lives you're playing with here. It's not a game.'

Storm shrugs and gathers up the cards, tying them back safely inside the gold cord and hiding them in the folds of black velvet. 'Did I say it was a game?' she whispers.

We eat vegetable curry and brown rice (no red beans), and Storm says it's lovely, in spite of the bottled sauce. She tops up Dad's mug of scrumpy.

'So,' he asks her coolly. 'What are your plans? Don't tell me you were just passing by, eight years on, and thought you'd call in and say hi.'

'Dad!'

Storm smiles, sadly. 'You're right, of course,' she says. 'I can understand why you're so suspicious. I've hurt you both, I know, but I had my reasons, Dizzy, I promise you. There's so much you'll never know. And there's not a day gone past when I haven't thought of you with love.'

She puts a hand out to stroke my cheek, and instantly my eyes mist over.

'Spare us the heartache,' Dad laughs. 'You could have visited, or phoned, or written.'

But she did write, every year. Doesn't he know how much that meant to me? I know he's only angry because she hurt him, but she hurt me too, didn't she? If I can forgive her, why can't he?

Storm sighs. 'Dizzy and I have a lot of catching up to do,' she admits. 'But, Pete, I'm here because I want to try. I *wasn't* just passing by – I've driven over 200 miles to see my daughter on her special day.'

My heart just about flips over.

The phone starts ringing out in the hall, but nobody moves to answer it. The answerphone clicks on, and I hear Sasha reminding me I need my gym kit tomorrow for the basketball try-outs.

'I want to put things right, make up for the past,' Storm rushes on. 'It's summer now, school holidays and all that. I want Dizzy to come with me for a bit – a break, a holiday, whatever. We can do some mother–daughter bonding, get to know each other properly. We can take in a few festivals, go to the coast, just the two of us.'

'Oh, *Mum*!' I squeal. 'Storm, I mean. I'd *love* that. It's what I've always dreamed of.'

Well, actually, I dreamed that Mum would come home and we'd all live together in the flat, but this is close enough. It's a start.

'*No!*'

Dad slams his plate down so hard it skids across

the floorboards, scattering rice and baby sweetcorn as it goes.

'*No*,' he says again. 'You think you can just stroll back into our lives and hurt us all over again? No, Linda, Storm, whatever you want to call yourself. You *can't*.

'Dizzy has five more weeks of school – she can't just take off and disappear. She has a school concert and a swimming gala and end-of-year tests. You are not going to drag her all over the country to live in some ancient van and eat nettle soup and hang out with losers. No *way*.'

There's a long silence. Storm gathers up the plates, including Dad's, and takes them across to the sink. She runs them under the cold tap and dumps them in the drainer. There's a streak of curry sauce still sticking to one, but I daren't say so.

I look down, and my cheeks burn pink.

'Dizzy?' Dad says.

I glance up slowly, but I can't quite meet his eye.

'Dizzy, maybe when school closes you could go for a week or so. We both could. But not now. Seriously, no *way*.'

Storm pours another mug of cider for Dad. If he doesn't slow down, he's going to be drunk as well as grumpy. I notice Storm is sticking to water. It's probably something to do with being a vegan.

'Let's not argue, Pete,' she says mildly. 'It was only an idea.'

'It was in the tarot, though,' I chip in.

'I don't care if it was in the *Sunday Mirror*,' Dad scowls.

'No rows,' Storm says again. 'I just thought that Dizzy might like to come to this little solstice gathering in Wales, a really magical place, all hills and streams, and only a few special friends. But if your dad says no . . .'

'Don't be making out it's all *my* fault!' Dad roars. 'You started this, Storm. Look, I've said we can meet up some time in the holidays, but that's not good enough, is it? You always have to get your own way. D'you think I don't remember that?'

This is *not* the way it's meant to happen. In my head, Storm comes back all apologetic and sad and says she's had enough of the open road. She starts acting like other people's mums, making chocolate traybakes, picking me up from basketball practice, coming to Parents' Evening.

Scary thought.

I can live with the earrings and the stud and the weird clothes, and I can just about handle the van (she could always get a respray). I can even cope with the carob and the bean stew, but all this fighting *has* to stop. Dad's meant to be pleased to see her. He's spent long enough pining for her, hasn't he? What's going on?

'I've got a maths test tomorrow,' I say quietly, getting to my feet. 'Think I'll go have a look. Don't want to flunk out or anything.'

Dad frowns. 'Dizzy, sweetheart, don't go,' he says. 'What about MTV? And there's toffee popcorn in the cupboard. We're not really arguing, y'know, just talking things through.'

Yeah, right.

Storm follows me out into the hall.

'I'm sorry,' I whisper. 'I don't know why he's being so awkward. He's not usually like this.'

She raises one eyebrow, the one with the stud. 'Do you *want* to come?' she asks.

'Course I do!'

'Then don't worry,' she says. 'Just relax. It's going to happen. Just leave it to me . . .'

It's still dark, but Storm is shaking me gently, dragging me back from my dreams.

'Dizz, *quickly*, we can't hang about. We've got a long way to drive.'

'Hmmm?'

'Dizzy, come *on*,' she whispers. 'You need to pack.'

I sit up, feeling dazed.

'What are you doing?'

Storm upends my rucksack, dumping school books, jotters and gym kit all over the floor. She pulls out the drawers of my dressing table, fishing out socks and undies and T-shirts and jeans, jamming the lot into the rucksack. She scoops up a random mess of bracelets, scrunchies, combs and gel from the top of the dresser, then looks up at the pinboard.

'Hey,' she says. 'Didn't I give you that rag doll?'

'When I was seven,' I tell her, padding across the carpet to stand beside her.

The doll is pinned up by the neck of her faded, tie-dye frock, her fluffy lilac hair thin and grimy now. I called her Linda Caroline, after Mum.

'You kept it, all this time,' she says softly.

I wait for her to see the postcards, the photos, the scuddy old hat, but she doesn't seem to notice them. Maybe they're not all that memorable, except to me.

'Why are we packing? Did Dad change his mind?'

Storm grins at me, her dark eyes twinkling. 'It's sorted,' she laughs. 'All organized, no hassles. I've always been able to wind Pete round my little finger!'

It didn't sound that way last night, but who am I to argue? If she's got Dad to agree I can skive off school for five weeks, it's nothing short of a miracle.

'What did he say? What about the concert and the tests and the gala? Is he going to phone the school? Storm, how did you *do* it?'

She holds a finger to her lips, still grinning. 'Trust me,' she whispers. 'And *c'mon*, pack!'

'OK, OK . . . I just want to see Dad first. Say thanks!'

'Not yet,' Storm hisses. 'It's only five in the morning, he's fast asleep. And he had a skinful last night, I bet he's got a massive hangover. That scrumpy has a real kick to it.'

'Well, later, then,' I frown. 'I'll make him a coffee.'

'Whatever. Just *pack*!'

I wash quickly and pull on purple bleach-dye cords and a stripy top. I brush my hair and plait it into two heavy ropes (when I leave it loose it just gets frizzy and annoying). I pack the hairbrush and root around in the bottom of my wardrobe for a couple of big jumpers, last winter's boots, flip-flops and my new plum suede trainers.

I pocket the twenty quid from Auntie Mel's card, pack my new camera, zip my guitar into its travel case. I hunt down nail scissors, a towel, a big bottle of Orange Zest Shampoo.

Storm laughs. 'Where did I get *you* from?' she says, shaking her head. 'You'll be packing an iron and a first-aid kit, next! We're going to do the festivals, Dizzy – ease up, travel light! And no hair-dryer, OK?'

'OK.'

In the kitchen, the big jug of cider is almost empty. Ouch. Dad doesn't drink much usually, so I bet he's got a really sore head this morning. I put the kettle on for his coffee.

Storm's raiding the fridge for travel snacks. I notice her stash away orange juice, butter, cheese, coleslaw, yoghurts. 'Well, *you're* not vegan, are you?' she says defensively. 'Anyway, Pete won't mind. Hurry up, now, it's almost six – we need to get moving.'

'Right. I'll just take Dad his coffee.'

'Right. But Dizzy, listen – don't make a big deal of it, OK? We don't want him to change his mind. Don't go on about missing him and stuff, it's not like we're going to be away for long . . .'

'No, sure,' I agree. 'But I have to see him, y'know? I have to say goodbye.'

Storm shrugs and goes back to ransacking the fridge.

Dad's room stinks of curry and cider. The air is thick and stale and heavy, and Dad's asleep with the duvet over his head and his feet sticking out over the side of the bed. He forgot to take his socks off.

'Dad? Dad, wake up!' I hiss, peeling back the duvet and shaking his shoulder. He's fully dressed, yesterday's T-shirt crumpled and grubby.

'Gnnnhh?'

He groans and tries to hide under the pillow.

'Dad, Dad, listen,' I tell him. 'I just wanted to say thanks. I can't believe you changed your mind, but I'm so, *so-oo* happy. Thanks, Dad.'

I hug him, breathing in sweat and scrumpy and curry and clay.

'Urggh . . . mouth feels like the bottom of a bird-cage,' he moans. 'That scrumpy's evil stuff. My head . . .'

'Never mind. I made you a coffee.'

He props himself up on one elbow, wincing at the effort. His eyes are all screwed up against the light and his hair is sticking out in clumps. His hand shakes a bit as he takes the coffee, so I take it back again and put it down on the bedside table.

He's looking kind of *green*.

'Good birthday, then?' he says in a wobbly voice, covering his eyes.

'The best ever,' I promise. 'The guitar, then Mum, now . . . this!'

'Hmmfff?'

'Seriously, Dad, you are *totally* the best. I'll never be able to thank you enough. Look, I have to get going, now. You sleep in, take a lazy day, you deserve it. I'm gonna miss you . . .'

Oops. Storm told me not to get all soppy.

'OK, see you later, sweetheart,' Dad says with an effort, burrowing down under the covers again.

I pause in the doorway. I want another hug, a proper chat, a long goodbye, but Dad's snoring gently. I close the door and creep away.

An hour later, we're rattling along at forty-five miles an hour in the patchwork van. My bags and my guitar are in the back, cocooned in quilts, and we're scoffing Mars bars from Hilton Park service station, where we pulled in for a fuel and toilet stop.

'Not exactly vegan,' Storm admits. 'But this *is* a special occasion!'

I'm sitting up front, looking out at the open road over a dashboard draped with tinsel and bells and Blu-tacked seashells. A clump of dried flowers, ribbons and feathers dangles from the roof, swinging from side to side.

We've just turned off the motorway, heading north. The van rattles and coughs like it's tied together with string, and Storm says we're safer sticking to smaller roads in case we get pulled by the police.

'When d'you think we'll be in Wales?' I ask.

'Well . . .'

Storm takes a skinny, handrolled ciggy from her bag and makes a big production of lighting it with a red plastic lighter. She takes a few deep draws.

'Don't mind, do you?' she asks, grinning.

'No, course not,' I say.

'So. Did I say Wales, last night?' she goes on. 'Must be getting forgetful, Dizz. I meant *Scotland*. The solstice festival's in Scotland, up in the mountains. I can't believe I said *Wales*.'

'Doesn't matter.'

'Well, you know, it's just a tiny gathering, just us and some really good friends. Like a little family, yeah?'

I bite my lip. Wales, Scotland, it doesn't make much difference.

'OK, babe?' Storm asks. 'You're kind of quiet.'

'I'm fine. I was just thinking . . .'

'Yeah?'

I frown. 'Well, when I said bye to Dad earlier on . . .'

Storm snaps to attention. 'What is it? What did he say?'

'Well, nothing much,' I admit. 'He was sort of hung-over, like you said. But – well, when I said I was going, he just said *see you later*, like I was off to school or something. Does that seem . . . a bit weird, to you?'

'Maybe he didn't want to make a fuss,' says Storm.

'Maybe.'

'Or – I remember now. He said he'll try and meet up with us in a week or two. Stick around for a bit. It'll be like old times!'

'Oh . . . that's *great*.' I let out a long sigh of relief. 'Where's he going to meet us? When?'

Storm stubs out her roll-up on the jingly dash-board.

'Oh, he said he'd come up to the Tree People

Festival in a week or two. Don't stress, Dizz, I'll let him know where we are.'

A warm, happy glow seeps through my body, and I stretch back in my seat. I can't stop smiling.

'Sorry,' I tell Storm. 'I keep having to pinch myself to remember I'm not dreaming. It's just too good to be true. For a minute there, I started wondering if Dad got mixed up about the holiday, if he agreed maybe when he was drunk and then didn't remember . . .'

Storm rakes about in the glove compartment and drags out an old music tape, squinting at it as she drives. 'You worry too much,' she says, distractedly. 'Pete knows you're with me, and I'm your *mum*, aren't I? What's the problem?'

'No problem!'

She shoves the tape into the cassette deck and a jiggy, rackety noise erupts, almost drowning out the van's roar.

'This afternoon we'll be on a Scottish hillside, with wildflowers under our feet and nothing but blue skies above us. Just you and me, Dizz. No school, no rules, no worries, no hassles, just nature and music and peace and fun. How cool is that?'

Pretty cool.

You learn something new every day, Dad says. Most days, it's French verbs and algebra and the life cycle of the frog, but today is different.

Today I'm learning about the most important day of the whole traveller year, the solstice. It all starts tomorrow, 20 June, and guess what? I'm on my way to a solstice festival to celebrate. The night of 20 June is the shortest night of the year. The sun doesn't set till almost eleven, and then it rises next day at four in the morning.

Storm says that the summer solstice is when the earth's energies are at their strongest. It's a magical night, she says, a night when the curtain between the world of man and the world of nature is at its thinnest. It's a night when dreams come true, when anything can happen.

We're going to take lanterns up to the top of the hill and sing and dance and stay up all night to see the sun rise. I've never done that before.

'Things are changing for you, Dizz,' Storm says. 'I saw it in your cards. It's time to ease up, relax, live a little. Have fun, yeah?'

'Yeah.'

'Anyway, we're *nearly* there.'

The track is so rough and steep and pot-holey, I think the patchwork van will probably collapse and die right here, right now. We're bumping along at ten miles an hour and the engine is howling in pain, but Storm just smokes and smiles and steers the van onwards.

Every bone in my body feels bashed and broken by the time we arrive at the field marked 'car park'. We veer off the track and crash down across the rutted ground, and Storm squeezes the van in among an unruly tangle of ancient buses, vans and cars.

'So,' she grins. 'This is it! Grab your bags and one of those quilts and we'll get moving.'

I look around for nature, music, peace and fun, but all I can see are dusty old junkyard wrecks and a lone sheep peering over the wall at me. I struggle into my rucksack, sling the holdall over one shoulder, my guitar over the other, then try to wrestle a rolled-up quilt into submission. Storm laughs. She drags the quilt-roll off me, flings it over her shoulder and picks up the carrier bags of supplies we bought two hours back in a super-market in Carlisle.

We trail up a smaller, steeper track, through a wood full of tiny, twisty trees with branches that reach out to us like fingers. My legs start to ache and the rucksack drags and the holdall keeps slipping off my shoulder.

In the distance, I hear a slow, soft drumbeat. Thin squeals and dipping voices float down towards us. As we come to the edge of the woods, I see the tepees, three towering canvas structures, surrounded by countless smaller tents.

Bright, ragbag people sit around the clearing, talking, smoking, laughing. A posse of skinny mon-grel dogs scrounge around a scruffy child eating white bread straight from the packet. The smell of wood smoke fills my nose, familiar, comforting.

'I remember that smell,' I whisper.

Storm laughs. 'Well, of course you do, Dizz! You spent the first four years of your life at festivals like this one, didn't you? You're going to love it.'

I don't love it, though, as we walk across the clearing, all eyes fixed on us, interested, welcoming, curious. It's worse than reading out loud in assem-bly, all those faces, a few arms raised in greeting. My heart thumps louder than the drumbeat, and my cheeks flame.

Suddenly, from nowhere, a big black-and-white dog charges straight at us, yelping, squealing, circling around. It jumps up at Storm and she swats it away, laughing, but when it leaps at me I'm terrified. I stagger backwards, dropping my bags and my guitar. Its face is long and thin and hairy, with sharp teeth and slavering jaws like a piebald wolf.

'Leggit!' Storm shouts, and the dog subsides, but not before it's stabbed me in the stomach with its claws. My eyes prickle with tears, and I have to bite my lip to keep them back, bending to rescue my guitar.

'She didn't mean it, love,' a plump, dark-haired woman says, grabbing hold of the dog's collar. 'She's just a big daft pup.'

The dog is still writhing about in excitement, trying to lick my hands. I can see now it didn't mean any harm and I feel embarrassed.

'I'm not used to dogs,' I say.

'You will be,' Storm says. 'OK, Leggit, OK. Bloody pest.'

She drops her bags and quilt on the grass outside one of the tepees.

'This is Tess,' Storm gestures to the plump woman. 'She's known you since you were – oh, well, since forever, I suppose. She made that rag doll you've got at home.'

'Oh!'

It's not much of a greeting, but it's all I can manage. I thought *Storm* had made that doll. I thought . . .

'Nice to meet you again, Dizzy,' Tess says. 'Don't suppose you remember Finn?' She points across the clearing, where a sulky teenage boy in a black hoodie and filthy frayed jeans is standing, hands in pockets, staring. As our eyes meet, he turns away.

'Used to be inseparable, you two did. Still, that was a long time ago. This must all seem pretty strange . . .'

'No, I . . .'

'Hey, Storm!'

A tall man is striding across the clearing, tanned and lean with frizzy fair hair, flecks of gold stubble on his jaw and eyes like chips of green ice. He's carrying an armful of wood, big logs and curving branches that trail along the grass behind him. A small boy; mousy, colourless, follows behind, carrying smaller, twiggy branches.

They ditch their haul beside a vast, central logpile, but Storm doesn't wait for them to come towards us. She launches herself at the man, flinging her arms around him. They kiss, and I have to look away.

'That's Zak,' Tess says. 'She tell you about him?'

I shake my head.

'He's OK,' Tess says. 'The little boy's called Mouse.'

My stomach lurches suddenly, and my mouth feels dry.

'Is he . . . I mean, is Mouse . . .'

'Oh, *no*,' Tess laughs. 'No, Mouse is *Zak's* son. He's only been with us a few weeks, he used to live with his mum. He'll settle down.'

She lets go of the dog's collar and it leaps away, circling Zak and Storm, its tail thrashing. Mouse has disappeared.

I sink down on to the grass, cradling my guitar. My face aches, frozen into a smile. I'm waiting for someone to tell me what to do, how to act. I'm waiting for Storm to remember I'm here.

I wish I'd never come.

7

I lie in my sleeping bag staring up into the tall, tapering roof of the tepee, where the long larch poles cross. Last night the smoke from the fire rose in a thick, choking plume, up and out through the gap in the canvas above me. Now the fire is sleeping, a mound of ash and cinders with a few blackened beer cans at the edge.

A dozen or more people were packed in here last night, laughing, eating, drinking, smoking. They sat around the fire, people with tie-dyed shirts and patched jeans, rainbow sweaters, trailing crinkly skirts, baggy trousers, skintight vests. I didn't have time to be shy.

Tess dished out potato stew from a huge cauldron. I passed round the bread – we used up two whole loaves, plus a slab of cheddar and the bag of supermarket apples Storm had bought earlier. Then cans of beer and bottles of cider appeared and a man with a white beard started playing the fiddle, and the air was thick with songs and smoke and laughter.

It was gone midnight when the party eased up. People stood up, drunkenly, hugging each other good night before lurching off into the dark. A few people just curled up where they were, dragging quilts and blankets out from along the edge of the tepee, even though they had their own tents out there somewhere.

I heard Mouse creep in long after everyone was asleep – everyone but me. I heard him pick his way through the sleeping bodies, a tiny shadow in the dark. He curled up next to Leggit, the skinny lurcher, and pulled a corner of someone else's red blanket over his body. Later, much later, I thought I heard him whimper in the dark, but I can't be sure.

He's gone, now. No Leggit, no Mouse, and the man with the red blanket turns out to be the white-bearded wrinkly with the fiddle. I wonder if he knows he snores? On the other side of the tepee, Storm and Zak lie wrapped around each other, a muddle of arms and legs and patchwork quilt. I can't look at them. It's not like I expected Storm was going to come home and live happily ever after with Dad. Not really. But still, it's hard to look.

My watch says four thirty and daylight streams

in through the pale canvas walls. My guitar hangs from a loop of rope tied round one of the larch poles. The inside of the tepee is draped with cloth, hung with bags, supermarket carriers, four-packs of beer. Yesterday, Storm showed me how to loop, hook and hang my stuff up out of the way.

It's not the first time I've slept in a tepee. Storm says we've done it before, when I was little, at festivals like this. A tepee is a magical place to live, because it's round, it has no corners. Everyone is equal.

They're sleeping soundly, making little fluttery sounds, coughing, snoring. I lie wide awake, stiff and terrified, scared to make a sound.

I don't belong. I want my own bed, my own bedroom. I want my dad.

If I got up now I could walk through the sleeping festival, down the hillside. I could walk along the country lanes until I found a village with a phone box and I could call my dad. He'd come and fetch me, and we'd be home by teatime, curled up, eating pizza and joking about how the tarot is never wrong.

I know I won't, though. I *won't* run away.

Quietly, so as not to wake the muddle of sleepers, I slither free of my sleeping bag. I slept in my clothes and boots, so I stand up creakily, picking a path between the bodies. Accidentally, I kick the fiddle-case, and the old beardy guy sits bolt upright, glaring around fiercely.

'Sorry,' I whisper, but the old bloke's eyes are milky with sleep. He looks right through me.

I duck out through the doorflap, blinking in the thin green light that filters through the trees. The camp is silent. The air smells sharp and new. A few birds skitter through the tree tops, their song drifting down across the empty clearing.

Last night was noisy and hassled and I was way out of my depth, but this morning it's fresh and clean, like anything is possible.

Almost anything.

I wander through the tents, avoiding guy-ropes and empty bottles and the blackened, crackled wood from a dozen cooking fires. Beyond the tents, the woods are cool and green. I step through curls of soft green bracken and my boots crunch twigs, squelch into damp, mossy hollows.

I remember the kids' story about a brother and sister who leave a trail of breadcrumbs to help them find their way back home through the forest. The birds flutter down and eat the breadcrumbs and the children are lost.

I leave no trail.

Instead of a gingerbread house, I find a stream, a tiny, ice-white slash of water, cutting through the trees. The water is fast, pushing past the rocks with a froth of creamy surf. I think of the stand-pipe in the camp clearing where I filled a kettle for Tess last night, and wonder how many of the festival-goers know this is even here.

Some do.

A makeshift den of fallen branches sits by the water's edge. As I creep closer, hardly daring to breathe, I see bracken, moss and black bin bags woven in and out of the branches, as well as feathers, twigs, grass and gobbets of dried mud. Dead matches lie scattered across the ground, among the embers of a little bonfire.

Inside, there's a dirty sleeping bag, a chocolate wrapper and a grey-fur toy mouse, streaked with dirt. A ragged black-and-white heap of spiky hair and bones lies huddled beside it, and two grey eyes blink at me from the shadows, black ears flopping to attention.

'Shhh . . .' I whisper, offering my hand to be sniffed.

The wolf-dog snuffles lazily, painting my hand with a warm, wet tongue before settling itself down again.

The sleeping bag stirs, curling, rustling. A tousled head appears briefly, eyes screwed tight shut against the light, before dipping back out of sight. A skinny arm snakes over the sleeping bag and blackened fingers close round the toy mouse.

Mouse and Leggit have a place all of their own.

I move away quietly, following the water downstream until the den is out of sight over my shoulder. Then I kneel down beside the stream and plunge my fingers into the icy flow, scooping up handfuls of silvery water to splash my face. The cold makes me gasp, and my skin tingles. There's nothing to dry myself on, so the water drips down my neck. A couple of ratty bits of hair, escaped from yesterday's plaits, cling in dark, wet ringlets around my face.

'Bet *that* woke you up.'

I blink, wiping droplets of water from my lashes.

To my right, a huge old oak tree spreads its branches out across the stream. Finn sits astride the lowest branch, his legs swinging. He grins, then looks away into the distance, his face dappled green in the dawn light. He doesn't look like a sulky teenager any more, just a big kid in tattered skate clothes.

'It's freezing,' I say, which may well be my stupidest comment ever. Like a mountain stream was ever going to be *warm*.

Finn rolls on to his stomach and lowers himself down from the oak branch. He hangs for a moment, bare feet peeking out from frayed, baggy jeans. Then he drops and turns to me.

He's older than me, maybe thirteen or fourteen. He's really tanned and his eyes are a surprising blue-grey colour. Jade, who knows about these things, would say he's good-looking. I like his hair, which is dark and thick and matted into dreadlocks, reaching almost to his shoulders.

'You don't remember me, do you?' he says.

'Not really.'

'I s'pose it was a long time ago. We used to meet up at the festivals, your family and mine. Storm and Tess were good mates – still are. You were just a baby, really, but you always wanted to be doing what the other kids were doing. You were always following me, tagging along.'

'Sorry,' I say. 'Must have been a pain.'

Finn laughs. 'Not really,' he says. 'I kind of liked it. You were always asking questions, always listening, like I was the smartest kid you ever met. It made me feel important. I suppose I thought you were kind of cute.'

'Oh!'

'Long time ago, though,' Finn says again, in case I might be getting any ideas.

'Sure.'

'D'you see Mouse up there?' he asks, poking one bare toe into the water. Barefoot, in the woods? Ouch.

'Yeah – he's asleep in the den with that scruffy dog.'

'Right. He doesn't much like the tepee, or the festival. He's missing his mum,' Finn says. He steps into the stream, letting the frayed hems of his jeans soak up water like blotting paper. I can see his toes, pale and bluish, curved around a rock beneath the rushing water.

'Coming in?'

I shake my head. 'No *way*. Too cold – I tried it already, remember?'

'Chicken,' Finn says, kicking an arc of water towards me.

'Don't!' I squeal, pulling at my splattered cords. I take a shaky step towards him, balancing on a shiny rock midstream. I dip the toe of my boot into the water to get my revenge, but the movement wrecks my balance and I slide off the rock into the water, screaming, laughing.

Icy water floods my boots, soaks my socks. My feet slide over the rocks on the streambed, and it's only when Finn grabs at my elbow that I manage to stand upright.

'I changed my mind,' I tell him, as we stagger, giggling, towards the bank.

'Sure,' laughs Finn, 'sure you did. Only next time, Dizzy, remember you're supposed to take off your boots!'

I drag myself up out of the water, boots squelching.

'I will,' I tell him. 'Next time, I'll remember.'

So, I've made a friend. Unbelievably, he's a male friend. Sara, Sasha and Jade would be speechless.

OK, so they might not approve of his dusty, felted dreadlocks or his dirty fingernails or the faint grey tidemark that edges his jaw, but so what? They're not here and Finn is, and right now I need a friend. Especially a friend I've known since forever, even if there has been an eight-year gap in the relationship.

We sit on the bank, with our feet turning blue in the water, and we talk. Finn tells me about his mum, Tess, and his dad, some old Irish hippy he never knew. He tells me about his brother, Niall, who's just finished his A levels and chose to stay home in Lancashire because he's grown out of festivals.

'Will you grow out of them, too?' I ask.

Finn shrugs. 'Right now it's OK. I get to skive off school for a while and bum around the country-side. I'm no crusty, though. I'm not going to waste *my* life sitting in a tepee smoking dope and talking about all the stuff I'll never get around to doing.'

My heart thuds.

'Last night . . . that was *dope* they were smoking?'

Finn laughs. 'You really haven't been around festivals for a while, have you?' he grins. 'Yes, Dizzy, of course it was dope. Y'know, spliff, weed, whatever you want to call it. You were probably half-stoned yourself, sitting in there breathing all that smoke.'

'But –' I struggle to get things straight. 'Isn't it – isn't that *drugs*? Isn't that illegal?'

Finn rolls his eyes. 'Yes, it's drugs,' he says. 'Yes, it's illegal. The papers are always going on about how it's no worse than drink or tobacco, but it's still against the law. Bet you never knew your mum was an outlaw, did you?'

I flop back into the grass. There's a lot I didn't know about my mum. A lot I still don't know. I feel angry, embarrassed, ashamed.

'Look, Dizzy, it's a hippy thing, a festival thing,' Finn says. 'I didn't mean to upset you.'

'You didn't,' I lie.

'I did. I'm sorry,' he says.

I shut my eyes and try not to care. How am I meant to know stuff like this, anyway?

I know about drugs, of course. We've had lessons at school about what to do if your friend offers you something dodgy. You just say no, and you try not to judge them, but it's OK to tell a teacher all the same, because drugs are dangerous, they can wreck your life.

I shudder. Nobody ever told us at school what you're meant to do if your *mum* offers you weed. Well, she hasn't, not yet, but you never know. It could happen.

'Isn't it really bad for you?' I ask at last. 'Dangerous? That's what they say at school.'

Finn frowns, flicking pebbles into the stream one by one. 'Dunno,' he considers. 'Weed's not like the really bad things, heroin and crack and all that. I think they just do it to relax.'

'Do you smoke it? Weed, I mean?' I ask Finn.

'Me? No *way*,' he answers. 'I hate all that. They smoke and they laugh and they talk about all these brilliant ideas they've got. Storm and Zak are always going on about this healing centre they want to set up in India or Spain. Well, they can dream, that's fine. Only they'll never *do* it, and you know why? Because they just smoke and talk and forget it all in the morning.

'I used to believe in the stories, I used to get excited, think we really *would* go to live in a commune on a Greek island or start up an animal sanctuary. It's just daydreams, though. It doesn't mean anything.'

Finn chucks a big, craggy rock into the stream, and we watch the ripples spread as it sinks and disappears without trace. I don't say anything.

'I hate weed,' Finn says. 'It makes you lazy. It makes you sit around dreaming when you could be out there doing something practical to make your dreams come true. I mean, festivals are OK. They're fun. But don't get me wrong – I want more out of life than *this*.'

'Me, too,' I say, although I haven't a clue what I want. It seems to change every other minute, and for now, having Finn like me and not rate me a total loser is pretty high on my wish list.

'It's not like they're doing any harm,' he says eventually. 'Well, only to themselves. They're just turning slowly from New Age travellers into *Old* Age travellers.'

We sit in silence, the stream rushing past us.

'I don't really know Storm at all,' I say, thinking out loud.

Finn looks at me, and I can't read the expression in his blue-grey eyes. It might be sympathy, or understanding, or even pity. 'No,' he says softly. 'I don't suppose you do.'

Then he jumps up, brushing down his soggy jeans. 'I'm starving,' he declares. 'Let's go see if there's any breakfast going.'

Back at the camp, people are beginning to stir.

Little Calor gas stoves hiss beneath battered kettles, blackened pans of baked beans sit heating among the sticks of the morning's newly lit fires. There's a knot of sleepy-faced women chatting beside the tap, and assorted toddlers drift across the grass, eating bread and honey or hunks of cheese while the mongrel dogs hover, ever hopeful.

Finn takes me to the big red family tent he shares with Tess, and there's Mouse, finishing off a tin plate of scrambled eggs, wiping it clean with a wedge of bread. Next to him, Leggit, the black-and-white wolf-dog, is lapping water from a plastic bowl and crunching dog biscuits straight from the carton.

Mouse looks at us warily from big, brown eyes, his face pinched and hostile. Finn ruffles his hair and sits down, but Mouse pulls away, scowling. He shoots a furious look at me, too, dropping his plate on to the grass and edging away from the tent like he can't work out whether to hate us or be scared of us.

'See you later, Mouse,' Tess calls lightly as the small, skinny figure slopes off, disappearing in the muddle of tents.

'I don't think he likes me very much,' I say.

'I don't think he likes *any* of us very much,' Finn agrees. 'Except Tess, and that's probably because she remembers to feed him. And Leggit, because the two of them curl up together at night. He must be feeling rotten.'

'Poor kid,' Tess nods darkly.

Finn dishes up a plate of scrambled eggs and hands it to me, and I wonder if Tess is actually feeding the whole festival or just family, friends, plus assorted hangers on. She cuts big hunks of wholemeal bread, one for each of us. There is home-made jam, Marmite, even butter in a small Tupperware box.

I'm seriously hungry. I've been up since before five, and it's near eleven now. Sleep-ins are compulsory at a festival, Tess tells me.

Leggit, who has been for a quick circuit of the camp, pausing only to wee on the grass outside Zak's tepee, trots up to Tess and collapses happily at her feet.

'Have you had her long?' I ask. 'Leggit?'

Finn shakes his head and rolls his eyes.

'Oh, no, Dizzy,' Tess is saying. 'Leggit's not *our* dog. No, she just comes scrounging around for leftovers. She's Storm's.'

The first signs of life are visible over at the tepee. The fiddle guy with the white beard crawls out through the doorflap, hauls himself up and stretches, groaning loudly. He picks up his fiddle-case and saunters off. Next, a large woman with long, grey plaits emerges, rubbing her eyes, trailing blankets.

I've eaten, downed two mugs of coffee and even managed a wash with warm water, soap and flannel in the privacy of Tess's tent by the time Storm and Zak appear, yawning, outside the tepee. I stare down at my bare feet, my toes threaded with grass and daisies while the waterlogged boots and socks dry out in the sun. I don't want to be like Mouse and Leggit, forgotten, sidelined. I don't want to be disappointed, even though I'm half expecting it.

But Storm shouts over straight away and I look up, grinning.

'Dizzy! Happy Solstice, babe!' she calls, picking her way barefoot across the grass. She swoops down, folding me up in a warm, patchouli-scented hug.

I know I can forgive her anything.

The festival slowly comes to life.

Zak and Finn and a gang of other blokes start moving logs and sticks and branches from the woodpile in the centre of the camp, hauling it up through the woods to the hilltop where the solstice bonfire will be.

All week, Storm says, they've been collecting firewood, picking up fallen branches from the woods, scrounging old pallets and broken packing cases. They have till tonight to build the biggest, tallest, best-ever bonfire on top of the hill.

'Should I help?' I ask, but Tess shakes her head and winks at me. She gives me a basket and asks me to unpack it in the clearing between the tents. I take out garden secateurs, string, glue, old yoghurt pots, sequins, paintbrushes, rusty scissors and a roll of masking tape.

I sit on the grass, baffled. Tess and Storm have gone. A dreadlocked woman with two little girls in neon T-shirts wanders up, smiling. She spreads a blanket on the grass and sits down. 'Gorgeous day,' she says lazily, and I agree. I try not to get worried when the kids start messing with the scissors and the sequins and the yoghurt pots.

The woman with the long, grey plaits appears, carrying a sheaf of coloured tissue paper. 'Want to sort it into different colours?' she asks the neon kids, and they do, making neat piles of soft, fluttery paper, weighting every pile with a stone.

'You're Storm's kid, Dizzy,' the grey-plaits woman says. 'Hi. My name is Amber. My partner's Carl, the guy with the fiddle, y'know? Ever do this before?'

Do what? Sit around in the afternoon sun with a couple of old hippies and a heap of rusty scissors?

'No, never,' I admit.

Two pink-haired women with grubby toddlers in tow amble over, then a thin, dark-skinned man wearing baggy trousers and a blue velvet waistcoat with no shirt underneath. By the time Tess and Storm turn up again, there are a dozen adults and almost as many kids sitting around on the grass.

Tess and Storm are carrying the bundles of long, skinny sticks I saw in the back of the patch-work van. Some are straight and strong, about as thick as my little finger, and some are thin and whippy.

'OK,' says Storm, hands on hips. 'We're going to make willow lanterns for the party. Here goes . . .'

I am now an expert in making willow lanterns. I have the glue-spattered cords and rainbow-stained fingers to prove it, because the dye in cheap tissue paper runs when it's wet.

First you make a pyramid shape with lengths of willow, binding the corners together with string and glue, then tear strips of coloured tissue to paste around the framework until it's covered.

Tess moves in and out of the crowd, leaning over to tighten a knot, pouring glue into yoghurt pots. She quietly rescues the wobbliest lanterns and gives them emergency first aid, until even the smallest toddler has something to be proud of.

Storm makes a lantern of dark blue and violet tissue paper, with a yellow crescent moon curving across one side. The other sides hold small, five-pointed stars filled with white tissue paper and dusted with silver glitter.

'Hey, Dizz, that's cool,' she says about my effort, a plain, lanky pyramid with random patches of red, purple and blue. It's not fancy, but it's OK for a first effort.

Storm helps the littlest kids, her fingers moving quickly, patching holes, replacing scrunched-up tissue, smoothing surfaces. 'You're a star,' she tells one small boy. Or, 'Wow, you must have done this before, yeah? What a natural.'

The children look up at her with shiny eyes, lapping up the praise. I bet I looked at her like that, once, before she went away.

No, actually. I bet I look at her like that *now*.

The grass sparkles with fallen sequins and grains of silver glitter, and eventually a whole crowd of multi-coloured lanterns sit on the grass beside the tepee, drying in the sun.

Tess gets stuck with the job of wiping small, sticky fingers and making endless herb teas for the adults. Storm and Amber put the candles in, a loop of wire hooks them on to a long carrying stick, and they're ready.

Like Storm says, cool.

Tess brings out a tin with a huge, dark, sticky cake in it. She cuts it into loads of pieces, so we all get a bit. It's carrot cake, and it's yummy.

'Is it vegan?' Storm asks, but doesn't wait for an answer. 'Mmm. I needed that.'

She sips herb tea the colour of washing-up water and rolls a ciggy. I look away so I don't have to know whether it's just tobacco or something else as well.

Zak and Mouse come up from the direction of the car-park field, carrying big, wide boxes hidden in bin bags.

'What's that, then?' Tess asks, but Zak just laughs.

'Wouldn't you like to know?' he says, and they march right on, into the woods above the camp, up the hill.

Finn appears with a couple of blokes in tow, hauling amps and speakers and a vast CD player up into the woods. The pink-haired women are making sandwiches from peanut butter and chocolate spread and mushroom pâté. Amber is making a cauldron of punch. I spot empty bottles of vodka and rum behind her tent.

'Loads of fruit,' she says, chopping up apples and oranges and limes. 'For energy. Want to do one for the kids?'

The neon sisters help me concoct a potion of cheap lemonade, Coke and apple juice. It tastes evil.

'Loads of sugar and E-numbers,' I tell Amber. 'For kids who want to stay up all night.'

Amber laughs.

Over by the tepee, Storm is setting out discs of paint, brushes, sponges, a mirror and a bowl of water. She calls over one of the neon sisters, picks up a brush, and paints a sunburst and rainbow on to her face. The other sister is transformed into a butterfly.

Soon, Storm has a queue of kids waiting to get their party faces.

'Come and help,' she calls over, and although I'm terrified and haven't a clue what I'm doing, I pick up a damp sponge and do what she tells me.

'White base, all over the face,' she says, nodding at the small boy at the head of the queue. 'Then a grey edging all round it, light, feathery strokes. A few grey smudges under the eyes and cheekbones. Kyle wants to be a vampire, right, kiddo?'

When I've got the base sorted, Storm moves in to do the fiddly bits and I move on to sponge yellow and orange all over a would-be tiger. I get better, faster. There's no time to be shy, and the kids aren't picky, anyway. They smile, they wriggle, they ask to be turned into cats and lions and witches and flowers.

'What a team,' Storm grins, setting loose her third butterfly of the afternoon. 'Way to go, Dizz, babe.'

We paint for hours, until just about every kid at the festival is bold and bright and beautiful. We charge a pound a face, 50p for arms and tattoos, free for anyone who knows Storm or anyone who hasn't got the cash on them right now. We make £3.50.

We stop for orange juice and Storm paints a curling, sweeping vine with soft, green leaves and tiny blue flowers spiralling round my arm. The brush tickles my wrist, then moves up to flicker softly across my face. When I glance in the cracked mirror, I see green lips, blue flower cheeks, emerald eyelashes spiralling out from around my eyes.

'My turn,' Storm says, presenting her thin, tanned face to be painted. I sponge it purple, adding swirls of pink and white, like the paisley-patterned quilts in the tepee.

The adults are stopping by now, some for a painted tattoo on a cheek or arm or shoulder blade, some for a full-face fantasy, a bird of paradise, a field of flowers, a summer sky.

I see Mouse watching from a distance, his pale face pinched and serious. I wave him over, but he blanks me.

Little girls start to appear with crowns made of willow, wildflowers and ribbon. Tess says they're selling them over by the other tepees, a quid a time. She's got one, a bright halo on her long, dark hair. I dive into the tepee and grab my camera so I can capture first Tess, then Storm.

People are spreading blankets and rugs across the centre clearing, bringing picnic baskets, cool boxes, carrier bags of food for the solstice picnic. A couple of blokes are selling lager, crisps, lemonade, bottled water, chocolate. Another slowly pushes a wheelbarrow laden with slabs of beer and bottles of cider up from the car park.

Tess has changed into a green velvet dress, and Storm appears in a white vest and pink crinkly trousers that billow down to her feet. When she moves, a million tiny bells jingle – she has soft cotton bands stitched with tiny silver bells tied round her ankles.

She scoops the face paints into a bag and heads off up the hill. She doesn't ask me to come. She leaves behind the cracked mirror, a gleam of silver in the yellowed grass. I pick it up.

The drumbeat is back, a low, steady pulse. The beardy guy, Carl, tunes up his fiddle. People sit down to eat and drink, because it's evening now, and the celebrations are about to begin.

The eldest neon sister, now a pink and blue butterfly in a pink embroidered dress, appears at my side.

'Shall I do your hair?'

She slips her hand into mine, and we sneak into the cool twilight of the tepee.

I change into clean jeans and a fresh T-shirt, taking care not to smudge the face paint. She unravels my plaits, spreading the hair out across my shoulders.

'My name's Cara,' she says as she brushes it smooth. 'I'm eight. How old are you?'

'Twelve,' I tell her.

'Can you sit on your hair?' she asks.

'Almost.'

She bites her lip and studies me seriously, like I'm her favourite Barbie doll. Then she pulls off her flowery crown and unknots two of the ribbons from the back, one red, one green. She combs out a slim hank of hair at the front, holds the red ribbon tightly at the top, and tells me to plait. I weave the ribbon in and out, making a long skinny plait, then do the same to the other side.

'I do this for my sister,' she says.

'You're very clever,' I tell her, and mean it. I pick up the cracked mirror and peer into it. I can hardly recognize myself beneath the swirls of face paint. Thick, mouse-brown waves fly out around my face. I will wear my hair loose more often. I look different, older, wilder.

I don't look scared any more.

By the time the picnic's over, it's almost dark. We trail up through the woods carrying lanterns, the drumbeat pounding and the fiddle singing squeakily as we crunch through the bracken and dead twigs. Cara and her little sister, Kai, hang on to my arm, dragging me forwards, pulling me back.

We leap the stream, and minutes later we're out of the woods again, on the hilltop.

'Wow!'

Huge rainbow flags and pennants flutter from tall poles, and a low boom of music floats down towards us from a cluster of rocks where someone has set up a generator, a CD player and a tiny stage made of planks and pallets. Two small dome-tents sit slantwise on the grass, looking like they're about to slide downwards. And on the hilltop stands the bonfire, a towering mound of logs and branches and boxes and splintered, smashed-up wood, silhouetted against the evening sky.

Suddenly the music dies and the drumbeat starts again, building slowly to a loud, thumping beat. A tall figure appears round the side of the hill, carrying three blazing sticks. His face and arms are painted with leaping flames, overlapping colours of red and orange and yellow. It's only because of his hair and his tattered jeans that I know it's Zak.

He lifts the three firebrands high and hurls one upwards, then all three are flying in perfect, swooping curves, through the air and down again to his waiting hands. I see Mouse watching, his eyes shining.

Zak juggles the firesticks higher and higher, on and on, until at last he throws one burning stick after another into the bonfire. As the flames lick gently around the scrunched-up newspaper and dry moss stuffed in among the wood, there's a huge bang behind us and the darkening sky explodes into millions of soft white stars.

'Fireworks!' shriek Cara and Kai, jumping up and down.

*That's* what was in the flat boxes Zak and Mouse were carrying.

There are rockets, fountains, screamers, even Catherine wheels tacked to the flagpoles. Someone's given sparklers to all the kids, and they write their names in the air, drawing zigzags, spirals, stars. The lanterns glow in stained-glass colours and the bonfire is blazing now, a roar and crackle of flames above us.

As the fireworks end, the music starts up again, and Storm swirls past me, a small, skinny whirlwind, grabbing my hand, dancing me round. Cara hangs on to my other hand, and everywhere now people are putting down their lanterns and joining on till there's a big line of people dancing, snaking round the hill, closer and closer to the big bonfire.

Carl runs along the line in the opposite direction, squealing his fiddle, raking the bow back and forth across the strings as his fingers fly. After him come the drummers, then a woman with a guitar, Zak juggling, Amber shaking a tambourine that trails ribbons.

I see a boy playing a tin whistle, his face painted with dozens of curling green leaves, dark, mossy, dreadlocked hair flopping forwards across blue-grey eyes.

Finn.

I dance until my breath is ragged, until we've circled the hill three times at least, until the line is breaking up and Cara and Kai and countless others have peeled away to find a drink, catch their breath, recover.

Those of us who are left drift up to the plank-and-pallet stage, where a CD player is belting out Oasis. For a while it's just Storm and me, our feet stamping a path round each other, our bodies arching, swerving, arms stretched out, fingers splayed, circling each other, laughing, gasping, dancing. Then Zak whirls in and grabs her hands and I back off, slow down and go in search of water.

It costs me a quid for what's meant to be fizzy spring water and turns out to be the warm, brackish stuff from the standpipe down at the camp. At least it's wet. I look for my lantern and find a different, abandoned one. I rescue it and sit down by the stage to watch Storm.

She's like a beautiful, exotic stranger. She's small, lean, brown, her shaven head thrown back as she dances, eyes closed now, lips parted, blissed out. The stud in her eyebrow glints in the light from a dozen tissue-paper lanterns. Her elbows jab and her arms flail as she twists and turns.

She's incredible, electric, unstoppable. Her energy could fuel this whole festival for a week.

The kids shimmy round her and beam when she touches their hair. The men watch her, too, their eyes held captive by her smile. Some of them dance near her, flirting, showing off, and she rewards them with a wink, a grin. Zak lets his hands skim over her face, staking his claim, but even he can't keep up with her. A few minutes later, he's picking up his juggling batons, heading back into the darkness, and Storm dances on.

She's my mum, although I'm not allowed to call her that, and I don't really know her, not yet. But I *will*.

Finn sits down beside me in the dark. 'Like it?' he asks, his face a dark shadow, forest green.

'*Love* it,' I say. 'It's unreal. I didn't know you played the tin whistle.'

Finn shrugs. 'I like music – and at a festival, anyone who plays anything gets roped in. You play guitar? I saw you carrying one yesterday.'

'I'm not very good yet,' I admit. 'I'm learning, at school.'

'Maybe I could show you a few chords.'

'OK, great. D'you play anything else?' I ask.

'Piano, a bit of flute,' Finn says. 'It's what I want to do, music. Go to music college, or start a band, or both.'

'*That's* what you're going to do when you're through with festivals.'

Finn laughs. 'I will,' he says. 'You just wait and see.'

I believe him.

'Your hair looks way better, loose,' he says, sipping a can of Coke.

'Your face looks way better, painted,' I retort.

'Watch it. I asked for that, I s'pose. It's just, you look older, y'know?'

'I know. You look – well, sort of *greener*. Like

you're . . .' I search for something clever to say. 'Branching out?'

'OK, OK,' he says. 'Enough. Let's just *leaf* it . . .'

'Ouch. Truce?'

'Truce,' he agrees.

We wander over to the giant bonfire, watching the flames leap upwards into the night. It's so hot, you can't stand too close, so we sit side by side on a fallen tree, cheeks burning, backs shivery.

'There's baked apples for later,' Finn says. 'You know, with raisins and honey where the core should be, all wrapped in foil. Tess put them in the embers earlier on, fifty or so of them.'

'I like your mum,' I say.

'I like *yours*.'

Before I can interrogate him on the subject of Storm, though, a small, pale-faced child moves round the bonfire in front of us. Mouse is staring into the flames, transfixed, his eyes huge, his mouth open.

He's far too close, but he doesn't seem to feel the heat. As we watch, he picks up a long, charred stick and prods it into the depths of the fire. The burning logs shift, crackling, the topmost branches collapse inwards and a blazing pallet crashes forwards, within inches of Mouse. A fresh wave of flames and sparks flare up, hissing.

'Mouse!'

Finn's on his feet in a second, pulling the stick from Mouse and throwing it into the fire.

'Mouse, that's not safe, pal,' he says, bending down. 'Fire's dangerous, you could hurt yourself. You have to treat it with respect.'

Mouse glares, his bottom lip jutting.

'You scared us, Mouse,' I chip in. 'Those burning branches could have fallen on *you*.'

He doesn't even look at me.

'Want a drink?' Finn asks gently, offering him his Coke. Mouse snatches the can and walks away.

'That kid has a problem,' I say to his retreating back.

'More than one,' Finn agrees.

I'm all partied out. I've danced so much my feet are aching, even though the music is soppy and ancient and sometimes seriously dodgy.

Finn gets to play the tin whistle some more, up on the makeshift stage with Carl the beardy guy, the guitar woman and the drummers. It isn't exactly a band, and it's a million miles from being cool, but it's fun and it's loud and everyone is dancing or watching or singing along.

Later, Finn borrows the guitar and sits on the edge of the stage to sing a few songs I don't recognize. Nobody pays much attention, just me and Tess and a couple of blitzed-looking crusties. I see Mouse, sitting to one side of the stage, his arms round Leggit, his little face pale and intense in the moonlight, watching, listening.

When I look round again, he's gone.

Further up the hillside, a few bodies lie flat out on the grass, staring at the sky or snoring loudly where they've fallen. The music gets slower, softer. The dancing stops. Tess sits by the stage with a blanket wrapped round her, telling bedtime stories to a knot of kids too stubborn or too stoked up on the E-number punch to give in to exhaustion.

Storm sits by the bonfire, watching the stars. She points out the Great Bear and the Little Bear, telling me how the Roman god Jupiter made them when he bewitched a beautiful woman and her son and threw them up into the sky.

'See those bright stars along the tail of the Great Bear,' Storm says softly, 'like a saucepan with a crooked handle? That's the Big Dipper. If you line up the two stars at the end of the Dipper, they point to a big, bright star at the tip of the Little Bear's tail. That's the Pole Star, the most magical star in the sky. You can always see it, anywhere you are in the northern hemisphere. I've seen it in Nepal, and in Morocco. Wherever you are, Dizz, make time to look at the stars.'

'They don't have stars in Birmingham,' I tell her. 'The sky's all orange from all the millions of streetlamps. You can't see anything else.'

Storm ruffles my hair. 'Hey, the Pole Star is *always* there,' she says. 'Even in Birmingham. Even if you can't see it. Might be too bright from the streetlamps, might be too cloudy, but that star is always there. Remember that.'

'I will.'

When the sun finally comes up, it's like someone's spread a bright tie-dye quilt all over the valley below us. The sky is streaked with pink and mauve and soft, pale yellow, and then the sun appears, a big circle of shimmering pink and gold.

'That's it, then, for another year,' Finn says. 'You tired?'

'Mmm,' I say dreamily, but I've gone past tired, past hungry, past everything. My eyes are wide open, gritty, aching. My bare feet are stained green and brown from the grass and mud, because I took my trainers off hours ago to dance, and now I can't find them.

I look at Finn, his face-paint streaked into a mess of smears.

'Your leaves are falling,' I tell him.

'You can talk,' he counters. 'You look like you've had a fight with an extra-large pizza.'

'I wish!'

We mooch around the hillside, looking for my trainers. I find one stranded in the middle of the grass and one, slightly singed, at the edge of the smouldering bonfire.

A convoy of hippy blokes head off down the hillside with the amps, speakers and generator. Clumps of people head back down to the camp, trailing tattered lanterns.

Finn and I wander downhill, picking our way around the diehard revellers who just can't leave. Carl is still playing the fiddle, a mournful salute to the rising sun. Halfway down the hill, Storm and Zak sit sharing a ciggy, squinting into the distance, holding hands.

'Dizzy, babe,' says Storm sleepily as we go past.

I turn back on impulse and duck down to plant a quick kiss on her neck. My mum, human whirl-wind, dancing queen, total party animal.

Her face-paint tattoos are streaked and smudgy, and there are wrinkles around her eyes, across her forehead. She looks small and tired and vulner-able, but the stud in her eyebrow gleams golden and proud.

Down by the dome-tents, Cara's mum is trying to shake her awake.

'Want a piggy-back?' Finn asks gently, and Cara nods, bleary-eyed. He squats down and Cara climbs on, arms hooking tightly round Finn's neck. We go slowly through the woods, splash across the stream. I take a detour to peer into the little den, and there's Mouse, collapsed on top of his sleeping bag, Leggit's hairy face snuffled into his neck.

We reach the camp and Finn finds a last burst of energy from somewhere, galloping down through the trees, leaping guy-ropes and racing around the tents whooping while Cara screeches with delight.

A crusty bloke with bloodshot eyes crawls out of a tent and lets loose a torrent of swear words. Finn skids to a halt in front of him, dropping a deep bow and letting Cara slip gently to the ground.

'Idiot,' Tess says, affectionately. 'People are trying to sleep.'

'But it's morning! Time to get up, get moving, get happy!'

'No,' says Tess firmly. 'Time to wash, eat and go to bed. Don't argue.'

Cara wanders off to find her mum, and Finn and I flop down next to Tess. There's a bowl of warm, soapy water and a flannel, and I wash my face as best I can. Tess takes the flannel and wipes the bits I've missed, then scrubs at Finn's face like he's six years old. He grins at me, brown and shiny and dripping wet.

Tess makes mugs of hot apple juice. We scoff down muesli and chopped bananas, and then I'm yawning, fading fast. I say goodnight to Tess and Finn and drift over to the tepee.

I pause for a moment in the doorway, looking out across the camp. The multi-coloured tents are sleeping now, and it's quiet except for a distant drumbeat and the sound of a dog barking, up in the woods.

The morning light is thin and pink and dappled, like the world is all brand new.

I sleep all day, wake up in time for a bowlful of
Tess's vegetable soup, and then sleep again. Staying up all night is pretty exhausting. The camp is
full of sleepy, lazy people, smiling, smoking, trying
to recover.

The day after, Finn and I scour the hillside
around the embers of the solstice bonfire, filling bin
bags with cans and bottles and rubbish. The bottles
go into one bag, the cans into another, the rubbish
into a couple more. We find dead fireworks, lost
ribbons, sweet wrappers, cigarette stubs, smashed
willow lanterns, scorched jam jars.

'Why are we *doing* this?' I ask, binning yet
another sticky paper cup.

'For the Earth,' Finn reminds me. 'For the
animals, the trees. And because the farmer gave us
a fiver to get it cleared.'

'We've been ripped off,' I tell him.

Finn stuffs one final bag with lost property. Two

watches, a blue jumper, a pair of black lace-up boots, size ten, a purple suede jacket, a silver bracelet, five plastic cigarette lighters, a squashed mobile phone, a child's cardigan, a spotty scarf, a wallet with seventeen pounds and twenty-four pence plus a cashpoint card inside.

'What'll we do with it all?'

'The lost stuff, we spread it all out on a blanket back at the camp for people to claim,' Finn explains. 'If it's something valuable, they'll maybe give us 50p to say thanks. I'll sell the lighters on for 10p a go . . .'

'You're selling people back the stuff they lost the night before last?'

'Sure.' Finn shrugs. 'If they were *that* bothered, they'd have gone back up yesterday to look. We're providing a service, aren't we?'

We leave the lost-property bag in Tess's tent. We drag the rubbish, tins and bottles down through the copse of hazels and past the car-park field. We haul the rubbish bags along a farm-track and leave them knotted by the farmer's big wheelie bins, then set off to the village with the sacks of bottles and cans because Tess says there are recycling skips just behind the primary school. She's given us some cash and a shopping list, too, so we can get some supplies in the village shop.

It's a long walk, especially with heavy, clanking

bin bags. When we get to the village, a few locals give us funny looks, and I try hard not to care, because I'm with Finn and he clearly doesn't.

We find the bottle bank and drop bottles through the holes marked 'clear', 'brown' and 'green', and listen to them smash and clink. Then we stuff squished-up cans into the can bank.

Finn wipes his hands on his tattered jeans. 'Shopping, next,' he grins.

There is a post office and a general store in the village. When we go into the post office so I can choose a postcard for Dad, everyone goes quiet and watches us. I pick a pretty mountain view and pay for it quickly, pink-faced.

'Why are they so . . . funny?' I ask Finn, when we get outside again. 'It's like they've never seen kids before.'

'Probably haven't,' Finn says. 'Not crusty kids, anyhow. There's never been a festival here before, and people get all stressy and think you're going to start nicking things and pushing drugs to the local toddlers. Take no notice.'

'But I'm not . . . a *crusty* kid,' I protest.

Finn looks at me, his grey eyes laughing. 'No?' he says. 'What are you, then?'

I bite my lip.

I'm wearing yesterday's T-shirt with a big, brown stain down one side from a beer can that dripped when I was recycling it. My jeans are dusty with bonfire ash, and there's a sticky bit on one leg where I dropped my bread and honey earlier. My new plum trainers are black with mud and dust and grass-stains. I brushed my hair this morning, but there's a breeze today and I know it's all frizzy and wild, the way it gets when I don't plait it. And, worst of all, after breakfast, I allowed Cara to draw a flower on my cheek with her felt-tipped pens. I never even checked it in the mirror.

'I'm just me,' I say sadly. 'I'm Dizzy.'

'OK,' shrugs Finn. 'That's good enough for me.'

Inside the general store he dredges out Tess's shopping list and starts piling up a basket with white bread and milk and cheese and pasta. I drift off into the next aisle looking for teabags, then stop short. Ahead of me at the till is Mouse, with Leggit behind him sniffing around in the fruit and veg.

'Don't let your dog touch the veg, pet, it's not hygienic,' the woman at the till is saying, as Mouse puts a can of Coke, a box of matches and a handful of penny sweets up on to the counter.

'You don't have enough money,' she frowns, scrabbling through the change in his palm. 'You'll have to put the Coke back. How about one of these instead? They're cheaper.'

She turns away to reach down a small plastic bottle of fizzy pop.

I'm about to call out and tell Mouse we'll treat him when I see his hands dart out, stuffing chocolate bars into his trouser pockets, scooping up the sweets and matches. The woman turns back just in time to see him fly out of the shop like a small tornado, Leggit at his heels.

My jaw drops open, horrified.

'Stop!' yells the shop assistant. 'I *saw* that! Come back!'

She looks like she's about to sprint off down the street after him, but then she spots me and Finn and her mouth sets into a hard, furious line.

'Is he with you?' she demands. 'You saw that, didn't you? He nicked a load of chocolate! Bloody travellers. Everyone said this festival would be nothing but trouble.'

Finn marches down the aisle and dumps his basket on the counter.

'He's not with us, no. In fact, I never saw him before in my life. But I'll pay you for the stuff anyway – will two quid cover it, d'you think?'

The woman rings up our shopping with a face like thunder. She takes Finn's money, including enough to cover what Mouse nicked. Finn peels off a couple of plastic carriers and we pack the shopping in silence.

'Running wild,' she mutters. 'Where's the parents, that's what I'd like to know? Drunk, I bet

– or worse. You try to be nice, but what do you get? Thieving kids and scabby dogs slavering all over the fruit and vegetables. Shouldn't even *be* in the shop. It's disgusting.'

'Want me to pay for that, too?' Finn asks, pleasantly.

'Hmphh. Suppose not. Just tell them people up at the festival to keep that kid away from here, OK?'

'No problem,' Finn beams. 'Have a nice day, now!'

The door swings shut behind us. The village street is still bright and sunny, the cottages still postcard-perfect, but it feels cold and hard and unfriendly now.

'That was awful.' My voice sounds all thin and wobbly. 'That woman was *horrible*. How did you manage to stay so polite?'

'Part of the training,' Finn shrugs. 'People judge you when you're a traveller. They think you're dirty, they think you're scum. I used to get upset and angry, but Tess taught me that staying cool is the best way to handle it. Show them that you're as good as anyone.'

'I know, but Mouse . . .'

'Stupid kid,' Finn says. 'If he's going to nick stuff, he could at least try not to be seen.'

'*If* he's going to nick stuff . . .?'

My head is reeling.

'OK,' Finn says. 'It's wrong, I know, but Mouse is a pretty messed-up kid. He steals. It's a fact. He'll not stop just because I ask him to.'

'Do Storm and Zak know?'

'Course they know,' Finn laughs. 'Everyone knows.'

'Oh.'

We're nearly out of the village now. An old man stops digging his vegetable patch to give us a long, icy stare, and Finn retaliates with a cheery wave, flicking back his dreadlocks for effect.

'Don't you hate it, though?' I ask. 'People staring, people thinking you're dirt?'

'I used to hate it, yeah. But now it doesn't seem to matter so much. *I* know who I am, where I'm going. That's what matters. If someone chooses to think I'm rubbish just because I've got funny hair and scruffy clothes – well, so what? They don't even know me, do they?'

'No, I suppose not.'

We walk back along the lanes, swinging the shopping bags. I try to imagine what it's like to be a full-time crusty kid, with tangly hair, dirty fingernails, raggedy jeans. I try to imagine a whole lifetime of being frowned at by shopkeepers, teachers, silver-haired grannies.

'You can't really blame them, thinking the

worst,' Finn adds. 'It's because they're scared. They really do think we're all no-good, thieving, drugged-up hippies.'

'But it's not *like* that.'

Finn gives me a long, hard look.

'OK, it *is* like that. But it's not *horrible*. Is it?'

'You asking me, or yourself?' Finn laughs. 'Mouse better hope word doesn't get back to Zak about this. The poor kid has had enough upsets. He's missing his mum, he doesn't want to be here in the first place . . . Tess reckons the stealing thing is a cry for help.'

'He's trying to get some attention,' I suggest.

'Yeah, only the kind of attention Zak's likely to give won't exactly help. He scared him half to death last time.'

We walk for a while in silence, while I take this in.

'What happened to Mouse's mum?' I ask then. 'Is she ill or something?'

'Something,' says Finn, shortly.

'You mean she just left him, like – like Storm left me?' I blurt out.

Only worse, I think, because Mouse didn't have a dad around to bail him out. Instead, he got carted halfway across the country to stay with a dad he probably couldn't even remember and a stepmum he'd never met.

Tough deal.

'His mum didn't *want* to leave him,' Finn says carefully. 'She couldn't help it. She's got . . . big problems. She can't really look after herself, let alone him.'

'But why?'

Finn kicks up a cloud of dust and gravel as we turn off the lane and on to the steep farm-track.

'I suppose you might as well know. Mouse is here because his mum is a junkie, OK? A heroin addict, a smackhead. And right now she's in rehab, in London, trying to get clean.'

I stare at Finn, my eyes wide, my mouth dry.

What do you say to that?

Dear Dad,

I've been at the festival for five days now, and it's brilliant! We're sleeping in a tepee, which is weird – I think I prefer my bed at home. On Tuesday we're moving on to another festival, and Storm says you might be meeting us there. I can't wait to see you. I'm missing you loads. See you soon.

   Love,
      Dizzy xxxxxxx

'What's that, then, Dizz?' Storm asks as I put down my pen.

'It's a postcard for Dad.' I scan quickly over the lines, trying to decide if Storm will mind that I've put I'm not crazy about the tepee, or that I'm missing Dad. I decide she won't.

'Can I see?'

I hand the postcard over and she reads it quickly, eyes narrowed.

'I'll post it later,' I say lightly. 'I forgot to get a stamp.'

The people in the post office were so icy I only just managed to pay for the postcard without getting frostbite, so going back for stamps is not something I'm looking forward to.

'Want me to do it, babe?' Storm says. 'I'm going down to the village anyway. Zak's doing a crystal-healing session on Jim Dean and he needs peace and quiet. Keep Mouse away from the tepee, won't you, Dizz?'

'No problem. And thanks, Storm.'

Crystal healing is Zak's thing. I know he takes it seriously because nobody's allowed near the little wooden box where he keeps his crystals, and nobody's allowed near the tepee when he's working.

Crystal healing is an art, Storm says. Zak's little chunks of crystal are full of earth energies, and Zak's healing hands help to channel the energy and create deep, healing powers. It also costs twenty pounds a go, so Jim Dean, who looks like a sleepy skeleton with long hair and a beard, must take it seriously too.

'He's got gout,' Finn whispers. 'Every time he drinks too much, his foot hurts like crazy.'

'Can Zak *cure* that?' I ask, eyes wide.

'Doubt it,' Finn grins. 'But Jim'll have less cash to spend on booze.'

I stifle a giggle, and Storm turns back to look at me, frowning.

'Tell you what,' she says. 'Any other postcards you want to send to Pete, just give them to me and I'll get them posted. I can add my own messages on the end, say hi, y'know?'

'OK. Thanks, Storm. But I'll be seeing Dad soon, anyway, won't I?'

'Sure,' she says, with a slow, easy grin. 'Sure you will, babe. *Soon.*'

When Storm gets back from the village later, all hell breaks loose. I have never seen her angry before.

She marches through the campsite, her face pale with fury. She chucks her rucksack on the grass and shoves Tess out of the way rudely when she tries to remind her about Zak's crystal-healing session.

I put down my guitar, jump to my feet. 'Storm? Mum? What's wrong?'

Storm ignores me and heads straight for the tepee, dragging up the doorflap and hooking it to one side. 'Zak!' she bellows. 'He's done it again. The little git has done it again.'

Tess, Finn and I rush over to the tepee and catch sight of Jim Dean, wearing nothing but a pair of orange boxer shorts, lying flat out in the middle of the floor. A line of little crystals is balanced all along his spine, and Zak's healing hands hover mysteriously above his head.

'Storm,' says Zak tightly, 'not now. Whatever it is, it can wait. I'm in the middle of a *healing . . .*'

'It – can – *not* – wait,' snaps Storm.

Zak's hands drop down to his sides, and Jim Dean leaps up, wrapping himself in a tie-dye sarong. Crystals scatter as he moves, all over the floor.

'Just about done, anyway,' he says, grabbing his T-shirt and limping past us out of the tepee.

'So . . .?'

'It's Mouse, isn't it?' Storm explodes. 'He's only gone and nicked a kid's scooter from the village. He's already been barred from both the shops for stealing stuff – apparently, he was away with a tenner's worth of chocolate, yesterday.

'What's wrong with him? Can't you control him? Can't you *do* something? If he shows his face in that village again, they'll have him strung up!'

'Trouble,' Finn whispers. 'Big trouble. I'll go look for Mouse. Maybe we can get that scooter back to the village before things get any worse.'

He slips quietly away. Tess puts a hand on my sleeve, and together we take a few steps backwards.

Zak looks flushed and angry.

'How d'you know it's him nicked the scooter?' he's saying.

'How many seven-year-old thieves d'you think we've got up here?' Storm roars. 'Come on, Zak, wake up. Small, skinny, filthy kid with matted brown hair and a big black-and-white dog at his heels. Who else is it going to be?'

'He's had a tough time,' Zak says lamely.

'He'll have a tougher one, soon, if I get my hands on him,' Storm snaps. 'If you don't get him sorted out soon those villagers will have the police up here. We're lucky they haven't already.' She stares at Zak for a long moment, her eyes blazing, then she seems to slump, her anger gone.

Tess takes my hand and leads me out of the tepee, letting the doorflap drop behind us. 'Don't worry, love,' she whispers. 'It'll blow over. She lives up to her name, sometimes, that's all.'

'What about Mouse?' I ask, my voice shaky.

'Little idiot,' Tess says, softly. 'We'd better find him, quick, before Zak does.'

Mouse is in big trouble.

OK, that's nothing new. Trouble and Mouse go hand in hand. He's a thief. His mum is a drug addict. His dad ignores him.

That suits Mouse. It's safer being invisible, only today he's not quite invisible enough, and Finn finally tracks him down. He hides out in Tess's tent eating cake and slurping apple juice, while Finn and I trek down to the village with the stolen scooter.

Finn looks straight ahead, wheeling the scooter right down the centre of the main street. He doesn't flinch when a couple of kids point and laugh at him, or when a knot of women outside the post office break off from their gossip to stare, stony-faced. I do, though. My cheeks flush crimson and I try to hide behind my hair. We leave the scooter outside the shop, because we don't know who it belongs to and there's no way we can ask.

'We found it,' Finn says to the silent street. 'And we've brought it back. OK?'

The hard-faced women shake their heads in disgust, and a small boy blows a loud, squelchy raspberry before bolting for safety.

Finn goes into the shop and buys a couple of Cokes, while I hover behind him, terrified. When we come out again, the street is deserted and the scooter is gone.

'Bloody Mouse,' says Finn, tearing at his ring-pull.

'He didn't mean it,' I whisper, although I think he probably did. 'At least you brought it back. They're bound to be mad at us, aren't they, the villagers?'

'Just a bit.'

Back at the festival, the music has stopped, the mood's gone flat. A few people are packing up, talking about moving on.

Zak is shouting at Mouse. You cannot have a row in a tepee without half the campsite hearing it.

'Even Mouse couldn't hide forever,' Finn says.

Storm and Tess are sitting in the last dregs of sunshine, sipping herb tea and looking sad. 'Zak gets so cross,' Storm says helplessly. 'Poor little Mouse.'

I wonder if she's somehow forgotten that she got cross first, that *she* got Zak all wound up. I wonder if she's forgotten all the awful things she called Mouse.

Maybe.

'C'mon, Dizzy, babe,' she says then, flinging an arm round my shoulder. 'Let's go cool things down, yeah?'

'Dizzy can stay here,' Tess says. 'No hassle.'

'No, Tess,' Storm says firmly. 'Thanks, but this is a family problem, y'know? We're all in it together.'

I blink, remembering a whole raft of family problems Dad and I had to sort alone, while Storm was hanging out with her hippy mates in Kathmandu and Marrakesh. We weren't all in it together then.

But this is a *different* family, of course. Maybe Storm values it more.

Tess and Finn shoot me a sympathetic look, but nobody argues. Even I get the message that there's just no point. Storm sweeps across to the tepee and propels me inside. Zak stops, mid-rant, and glares at us, then drops his gaze to Mouse.

'Oh, I give up,' he says heavily. 'You're a no-good, lying, thieving little toe-rag and I'm sick of the sight of you.'

Mouse tries to look defiant, but a huge tear rolls down his grimy cheek. His lip quivers.

'Zak, what chance has he had to learn right

from wrong?' Storm argues. 'Poor little mite, he never had a hope. We can help him forget the past, learn new ways.'

'How can we help him when he's never here?' Zak bursts out. 'The kid's half wild, isn't he? Well, you stay around *me* from now on, Mouse. You do as you're told. You eat here, sleep here, help out. Is that clear?'

Mouse nods, mutely.

'Dizzy, you'll look out for him, won't you, babe?' Storm says. 'Keep him right, check he's in at night, keep him out of trouble? Keep him out of our hair?'

I swallow. This sounds like a full-time job, with overtime.

'Well, you might as well do *something* to earn your keep,' Zak snarls. 'What are we, a bloody orphanage? A holiday camp?'

I freeze. Zak glowers at me, and suddenly I suss that as far as he's concerned, I'm about as welcome here as an outbreak of the plague.

'Zak, honey,' Storm says sweetly, stroking his cheek, his hair. 'Dizzy's a *good* girl. She'll keep an eye on Mouse. And I can claim money for looking after her. We'll be one big, happy family.'

Zak laughs out loud, but there's no warmth in his laugh. I decide that I don't like him, not one little bit.

'It's not for long,' I say in a small voice. 'Dad's coming next week, isn't he? I could always ring him now and explain . . .'

'Nah, don't bother,' Zak says coldly. 'He'll come and get you, won't he? Or maybe he'll join the big, happy family, too. The more the merrier, eh, Storm?'

Mouse edges closer to me. He's still scowling, his brow knotted, but he slips his hand into mine. It feels small and light, like you could snap the bones with a single squeeze.

'Your dad'll be here next week or the week after,' Storm says to me. 'No need to ring him, worry him. We *want* you here, don't we, Zak? We need you here. Don't run out on us just yet, please, babe?'

Zak sits down against a bank of velvet cushions, and the anger seems to drain away from him. Storm stays close, smoothing his hair.

'Look, I didn't mean to shout, Dizzy,' Zak says. 'It's just been a well-stressful day, yeah? Storm's right, we need you. Just help us get Mouse back on track, OK? Stay another week or two. More if you like. Really.'

I nod, feeling numb.

'It's OK,' Storm says softly. 'It's OK. We can be a family.'

Mouse looks at me, his eyes wide. For the first

time since I came here, I begin to understand. He's like me, Mouse. He never had a family, not a proper one. Not the mum, dad and 2.4 children kind. It's like we both got given a jigsaw with half the bits missing, and had to make a picture anyway.

His mum let him down, big-style, just like Storm did me. We may not like each other, Mouse and I. Not yet. But we both know that playing at families is not a game.

Storm scrapes stale breadcrusts with the last of the peanut butter, and we sit together round the tepee fire and eat. It tastes awful and it's not even filling, but we're not about to complain. Zak and Storm sit up smoking and talking, and in the distance I can hear Finn playing the penny whistle and, later, an owl hooting in the darkness.

When I'm woken by Mouse's whimpering cries, I know it's very, very late. I struggle up on to my elbows, peering out across the tepee.

'Not again! Can't you shut him up?' Zak growls.

Leggit barks raggedly, then subsides to a whine.

'For God's *sake*!'

I reach out into the darkness and touch the rough blanket Mouse has rolled around himself. I shake him gently. 'Mouse, wake up!' I hiss.

There's a long shudder, and the whimpering stops.

'It's OK,' I whisper. 'Just a nightmare.'

Mouse squirms, crawling closer in the dark. I let my arm fall round him, pulling him near. Leggit snuffles round and curls against his shoulder, her raggedy tail tickling my face.

Mouse smells of chocolate and peanut butter and fear. Sometimes, in the dark, I hear him sniff. I don't have to touch his face to know it's damp with tears.

Mouse is scared. I know it, I feel it and I understand.

I'm scared too.

We spend all day taking down the tent and the tepee, packing stuff away, rolling canvas, carefully lowering the huge larch poles and lashing them on to the roof rack of the patchwork van. The festival field looks sad and scruffy, covered in yellow and brown blotches where tents and tepees once were. There are only a handful of tents left, a few stragglers too lazy or too chilled to pack up and go.

Storm asks Tess to drive Mouse and Leggit and me to the next festival. Zak's going to drive the patchwork van at night, so it'll be less noticeable, less likely to be stopped by police. He ties a huge tie-dye rag on to the jutting larch poles, just to make sure the van definitely qualifies as Weirdest Vehicle in the Entire Universe. If I was a police patrol, *I* wouldn't stop it. I'd report it to the FBI as an alien spaceship.

Everyone hugs, and Storm asks Tess to save them a good space at the Tree People Festival. Tess promises. Then the first big drops of rain start falling, and we sprint for the car. Storm and Zak stand in the car-park field getting soaked to the skin, waving. Then the car judders round a bend in the track and they're gone.

The wipers swish across the windscreen and Tess peers out over the road, frowning, scooshing through puddles and swerving to avoid the occasional frog. Finn is in the front seat, fighting with a fold-out map that's threatening to take over the whole car. Mouse and Leggit and I are squashed in the back, bags and bedding wedged in around us.

After a while, we stop in a grey, drizzly town to invade the launderette. Tess hauls out bin bags of dirty washing and we pack four machines to bursting point. It's not just Tess and Finn's stuff – I spot Zak's tie-dye shirts, Storm's stripy trousers, a few mud-caked T-shirts that have to belong to Mouse, and loads of my jeans and tops and undies. Clean clothes!

Tess winks at me, pours in washing powder, sets the machines and checks her watch. 'Shopping,' she says. 'OK?'

We find a supermarket and Tess fills a trolley to overflowing, not just bread and rice and cheese and beans, but hot chocolate and fresh pineapple and strawberries and cheesecake and Hi-Juice apple squash. Then we go back to the launderette to drag the washing into the driers.

I bought a postcard in the supermarket, so I scribble a quick message while we wait.

Dear Dad,

I'm writing this in a launderette in the Scottish borders – never thought I'd miss our washing machine or the iron, but I do! We'll be at the Tree People Festival by nightfall. Storm says you'll be joining us there soon – I can't wait! Missing you like mad.

Dizzy xxxx

PS Tess, Finn and Mouse say hi. And Leggit the lurcher!

Tess offers to post the card, but I remember what Storm said and stick it in my pocket to show her first. She might want to add a few directions to the festival for Dad.

By the time we've folded the clean, dry clothes, packed them back into bin bags and stuffed them into an already bulging car, everyone's starving. It's way past teatime. We head for the chippy, because Tess says we deserve it, and anyway, she won't want to be bothered cooking once we get to the Tree People place.

Tess and Finn have fish 'n' chips, I have curry

and chips and Mouse has chips with fish, potato scallops, a battered sausage, a mini pizza, a pineapple fritter, beans, bread rolls and every kind of ketchup. His hand sneaks out to nick a Twix while the assistant's back is turned, but Tess slaps his knuckles sharply.

'I'd have bought it for you if you'd asked,' she says briskly. 'Too bad. You don't steal while you're with us, Mouse. You just have to *ask*. We don't rip each other off, and we don't rip off others either. Got it?'

Mouse nods, staring at his boots.

'Sorry,' he mumbles after a minute, and Tess grins like she's just won the Lotto, then ruffles his hair.

We dodge through the rain and pile back into the car, where Leggit waits on the driver's seat with her head out of the partly open window, dripping wet. When we get in, she ricochets around the car with delight, snuffling at our faces, sitting on our chips.

Tess heads out of the town and on along the little, twisty lanes. The car reeks of vinegar and curry sauce. Mouse gives the battered sausage to Leggit, plus a good quarter of his chips. He wraps the leftovers carefully and stashes them away for later.

Finn drips tomato ketchup all over the map,

Leggit puts a paw through the centre of East Kilbride and Mouse falls asleep, his head against my shoulder. We drive on through the rain.

It's almost dark by the time we arrive. We drive under a vast white banner that says 'Tree People Festival' in fancy letters, on to a huge field dotted sparsely with tents and edged with a fast-running river. We're early, Tess says. The festival doesn't start properly until the weekend.

Our headlamps rake across Amber, trailing across the field in an orange cagoule and a pointy Peruvian hat, carrying water. She tells us she's camped down by the river with Carl, the neon twins and their mum and a whole raft of others I've never even heard of. Tess parks up a little way back from the semi-circle of tents, headlights blazing.

Pitching a tent at night in the pouring rain is no joke. Amber and Tess wrestle with the inner tent while Finn slots together the curving framework. Mouse and I hang on to the flapping corners of the waterproof shell, while the others hammer in tent-pegs, trip over guy-ropes and tug at knots. The rain streams down my face and drips inside my collar.

By the time I've hauled the bedding from car to tent, I'm drenched to the skin. Finn and Mouse are off walking Leggit and checking out the toilet block, which is rumoured to have a hot shower. Tess throws me a towel and tells me to get changed and into my sleeping bag. I do as she says, feeling soggy, exhausted, too tired to care.

Mouse and Leggit explode into the tent, dripping. Leggit shakes herself all over me, then stretches out, making a wet patch on my sleeping bag. Mouse shrugs off his anorak and rolls a quilt round himself, fully dressed. His hair is plastered flat against his head, and I dry it gently with the towel.

Finn arrives with water and Tess fires up the Calor gas, handing out mugs of hot apple juice. We sip our drinks by torchlight, except for Mouse, who's asleep already.

It's more of a sardine can than a four-man tent, but we're so tired nobody cares. I wake briefly, deep in the night, to the low, rumbling rattle of what has to be the patchwork van and the bright sweep of its headlights. Then the engine stutters into silence and the headlamps die, and although I listen out hard for Storm and Zak, there's only silence in the dark blue night. I roll over and sleep.

The rumours are true. There *are* showers in the Portakabin toilet block. I beg 10p pieces from Tess and stand under the hot streams of water to wash away a week of grime. The water runs grey as I scrub at the shadows of Cara's latest felt-pen tattoos, shampoo my hair twice and slather on conditioner. Every few minutes the water fizzles out, but I feed more money into the slot until someone banging on the shower door drags me down from heaven.

Outside the Portakabin, Finn is waiting, his own hair damp from the men's shower, his feet bare on the rain-wet grass. 'Thought you'd washed yourself away,' he grins. 'So *that's* what you look like, clean. I'd just about forgotten.'

I flick him with my towel and he runs away, dodging through the tents and cars and battered-looking vans that are scattered across the site. Some of them make the patchwork van look almost smart. Almost, but not quite.

There's no sign of life inside Storm and Zak's van, but Tess is up, setting out cereal and strawberries and milk. Mouse, who prefers a healthy breakfast, is halfway through the chocolate spread, and Leggit has snaffled last night's leftover chips, including the paper.

'I like it here,' I announce.

'Because?' Finn prompts.

'It's beautiful,' I say. 'The river, the trees, the mountains in the distance. But mainly it's because we've got hot showers, bin bags full of clean clothes and loads of food. Plus, I know some of the people this time. I'm getting the hang of it, y'know? And Dad's coming soon!'

'Not that you're sick of us or anything!' Finn laughs.

'No way! But Dad'll stick around for a bit, maybe. That's what Storm says.'

'I didn't know your dad was coming,' Tess says. 'It's *years* since I've seen Pete. When's he due, then?'

'I don't know,' I admit. 'But he's definitely coming, Storm said. Soon.'

'Right. Funny she never mentioned it – I thought it was just you. Still, it'll be great to see Pete. Like old times!'

Tess attacks the chocolate smeared around Mouse's face with a wet flannel, managing to clear some of it before he ducks away.

I'll have to pin down Storm about exactly when Dad's coming. I'll have to make sure he knows where we are, and how to get here. I know he's going to love it, seeing old friends like Tess and Finn, meeting Mouse and Leggit and Zak. Well, maybe not Zak.

I hope Dad comes soon. I miss him like mad.

Dear Dad,
There's loads going on here! I've done workshops in paper-making and felt-making and drumming! I've eaten falafel in pitta bread and deep-fried tofu fritters and sushi rolls with sour pickled vegetables and seaweed. I've had my hands painted with henna, helped to carve a giant totem pole and learnt to weave friendship bracelets. Come soon or you'll miss all the fun!
    Big hugs,
        Dizzy xxxx

It's a great festival.

There are stalls selling hats from Nepal, itchy jumpers from Peru, tin mirrors from Tunisia. You can buy wind chimes made of seashells and bracelets made from old silver forks, the prongs curled round in little spirals. There's soap made from dandelions and shampoo brewed from boiled-up twigs.

Everyone's doing *something*.

Storm puts a sign on the patchwork van, advertising tarot readings. A steady stream of hippies drift by each day and part with cash to hear her tell the future. She tells them about tall, dark strangers, travel overseas, a new baby, a new career, a dream come true. One day, I hear her telling Amber that she's at a crossroads in her life, that she'll take the path that's least expected.

'The tarot never lie,' she tells Amber.

I frown, trying to remember the things she told me.

'Can Storm see into the future?' I ask Tess later. 'Is it real, the stuff she says? Do the tarot ever lie?'

Tess laughs.

'The tarot's a great way to make money,' she says. 'Everyone wants to know the future. Will we be happy or sad, rich or poor, loved or lonely? I don't know, pet, I'm the wrong person to ask. I gave up on fairy-tale endings a long time ago. You have to make your own luck in this life.'

'Does *Storm* believe it?' I ask.

Tess shrugs. 'Hard to tell, with Storm. Mostly, she tells you what you want to hear. She doesn't mean any harm – it's just the way she is.'

'Just a way to make money,' I repeat.

'Pretty much,' Tess says.

Did Storm really see adventure and travel in my

cards, or did she just say it because it suited her plans? I have to trust her, don't I? Like Amber does, and all the others who queue up to part from their fivers in return for a little bit of future.

Anyone foolish enough to hand over their cash to Zak, however, deserves everything they get – and what they get, in my opinion, is fleeced. The tepee is out of bounds between midday and four each day, when Zak has his crystal-healing sessions. Big deal. I mean, it's not like we'd want to watch, is it?

Every night there's music and dancing and drinking. Every night the tepee is crammed with crusties, thick with smoke, awash with cider.

Mouse and Leggit and I start sleeping in the patchwork van. It's quieter, it's got mattresses and you don't get drunken revellers stumbling over you in the middle of the night. Every night, Mouse and I crash out on separate bunks, formal and polite. Every night, when it's still and dark and quiet, Mouse burrows in under my quilt and we snuggle up. He's so small and skinny you hardly notice him. After a while, I get so I can't sleep properly unless I know he's there.

Is this what it feels like to have a brother?

Mouse doesn't scowl so much these days, and Finn drags him into the shower occasionally, so it's possible to see his tanned, freckly skin beneath the grime. He smells faintly of chocolate, which can't be bad.

If you walk up past the main festival field, cross the lane and follow the river into the hills, you come to a place where a long, white ribbon of waterfall crashes down into a deep, silver-blue pool. The water roars and foams and the pool is icy cold, even on days when the sun is hot.

An old horse chestnut tree hangs over the water, and you can climb right up into its branches and disappear into a cool, green world where the leaves brush your skin like dry fingers.

It's our special place, Finn and Mouse and Leggit and me. We come here when we want some peace, away from the festival noise and hassle. Sometimes, Cara and Kai hang out here, too, and occasionally Tess and Storm come up to swim, but mostly it's just us. When we've had enough of music and juggling and bonfires and boozed-up hippies, we come here.

Mouse can't swim. Finn and I stand for ages in the icy pool beneath the waterfall, towing him about with a hand beneath his chin, getting him to relax and float or kick his legs like a frog. His body is stiff, one spindly leg always trailing the bottom as a safety net. He's not a natural. Without the hand under the chin, he would sink like a stone, but he won't give up.

When he's had enough of the water, Mouse crawls out and sits on a rock to dry out. He practises his juggling with three velvet beanbags Tess made for him, and he's getting really good.

He throws sticks for Leggit to fetch, skims stones, builds dams. He climbs up beside the roaring waterfall, clinging to rocks that are slippy and green with slime. He makes a rope-swing in the horse chestnut tree and swoops across the pool, his feet skimming the surface.

Sometimes, when he thinks we're not looking, he gets out a box of matches and strikes them, one after the other, letting them burn right down until the flames lick his fingertips. He stares at the flame, mesmerized, then drops them into the water. Whenever I catch him, I take the matches away and give him a lecture, but Mouse just shrugs and the next day, or the day after, he'll have another box of matches and the whole spooky game starts again. He looks fearless. Anyone who hadn't heard him cry in the night would think that he was.

I'm happy here, but there's just one problem. We're six days into the Tree People Festival, and there's still no sign of Dad. When I ask Storm what's happening, she gets all evasive and grumpy.

'How do *I* know when he'll turn up?' she says. 'He said he'd be here, so he'll be here. Or maybe he'll catch us at the next place, who knows?'

'What's the next place?' I ask.

'I don't know, Dizz. There's a gathering down in Somerset, there's Womad in Reading . . . or we could head over to Yorkshire for the Green World Festival. Can't you just stop worrying about your dad?'

'But how will he know where to find us?'

'I'll let him know, Dizzy, OK? Come on, you need to stop hassling him and relax.'

'You did remember to post my cards? The one from the launderette and the one I bought from the Greenpeace stall?'

'*Yes*. I'm sure. Look, Dizz, take some advice. Don't pester your dad. Ever think he might be enjoying some time on his own?'

I frown, because that's one thought I really haven't hit on before. Could she be right? Could Dad be making the most of his time out from being a single parent?

'I just miss him,' I trail off sadly. 'I just wondered when he'd be here.'

'*I* don't know, Dizzy, what am I, a fortune-teller or what?' she huffs.

'Well . . . yes.' I nod at the faded sign on the door of the patchwork van, which says 'Tarot readings, £5'.

Storm rolls her eyes. 'I guess you still believe in Santa Claus, too. Grow up.'

She turns her back and walks away, and my eyes prick with the injustice of it all.

Later, up at the waterfall, Finn sits with his back against the horse chestnut tree, playing my guitar, soaking up the sun. He is showing me new songs, busking songs.

'When you play in the streets, you need to grab people's attention pretty quick,' he says. 'You don't want them to walk past. Sad songs are good, old songs.'

He plays 'Hey Jude', 'Wonderwall' and 'Yellow'. His voice is soft and strong, his brown fingers long and graceful as they pick out the chords. It sounds professional.

'Worth 10p?' he asks.

'Nah. I'm saving up for a Cliff Richard CD,' I tell him.

Finn pulls a mock-hurt face and hands over the guitar. I've been practising loads this holiday, and I launch into the chords for Robbie Williams' 'Angels'. I make no mistakes, but Finn is a slave-driver.

'Sing,' he says. 'Go on.'

I start off with a thin, reedy wail, then settle into it a little. I can do it as long as I focus on the guitar and refuse to look at Finn. He's bound to be laughing. I remember how Jade and I got thrown out of the primary school choir, aged eight, for talking too much. Or was it because I had a rotten voice and they didn't know how to tell me? I've never been sure.

'Not bad,' Finn says, and when I peer out from behind my veil of hair, he looks serious. He's definitely not laughing, anyway. 'Try again.'

So I sing it again, and Finn gets his tin whistle and tries out a few sounds. He works up a soft, flutey trill to go with the chorus.

'A winner,' he says. 'Didn't know you could sing. We'll clean up!'

'Clean up where?'

'In town, when we go busking. You can get a bus in if you're up early enough – the bus stop is down the lane, by the crossroads. There's one in every morning, another one back late in the afternoon. Fancy a day out?'

I look at my toes. A day in town would be great, but what if it's the day that Dad turns up? I've waited so long already I can't risk missing him.

'Problem?' Finn asks, gently.

'No. No problem,' I lie. 'It's just – I don't know if I fancy busking. I'd be too scared to sing in front of people. And who'll mind Mouse and Leggit while we're away?'

'We'll take them with us,' Finn says. 'Mouse'll love it. We can busk a bit – you don't have to sing if you don't want to – then we'll grab some lunch and hit the beach. I thought you'd like it.'

He leans forwards and tucks a corkscrew strand of hair behind my ear. His blue-grey eyes look into mine, seeing past the excuses. 'I thought you could maybe find a phone box and ring your dad,' he whispers.

I fling an arm round his neck and hug him tight. It's different from hugging a girl. Finn smells of long grass and waterfalls and warm skin. His matted hair feels surprisingly soft and heavy under my fingertips.

'It's OK,' he whispers into my neck. 'I promise, Dizz, it'll be OK.'

I'm up at seven, crouching outside Tess and Finn's tent, tugging on a length of damp string that snakes through the grass and disappears inside the tent through a tiny gap in the door-zip. I tug again. There's something heavy on the other end, and then there's a grunt and the string goes loose and I know Finn's awake. The string is his alarm clock, tied round his big toe.

By the time he crawls into the patchwork van, Mouse and I are slurping Weetabix and soya milk.

'Hi,' he says, his eyes sleepy, his dreads sticking out at right angles.

I remember how weird it was, yesterday, to touch those matted snakes of hair. Then I blush, and try to forget.

'Hi,' I say briskly. 'Breakfast's ready.'

Finn scoops up his bowl and flops on to the bunk where Leggit is lying, upside down, long legs pointed towards the van roof. She catches a whiff of the cereal and scrabbles back to an upright position. Her head rests on Finn's shoulder, brown eyes fixed on the bowl, a sliver of white fang showing. Finn reaches up to the cupboard and pours some dog biscuits on the floor for Leggit to hoover up.

It takes half an hour to walk down to the bus stop, fifteen minutes more before the tiny, ramshackle coach appears. Mouse sticks his tongue out at a staring passenger. I clutch Storm's fringey purple scarf, looped around Leggit's collar instead of a lead. She barks in excitement as the door swoops open.

'Bringing that dog on? You'll have to pay half fare for it,' the driver says gruffly.

'No problem,' says Finn, stepping forwards with the cash. The driver stares at Finn's bare feet for a long moment before ringing up the fares.

We bundle Leggit on to the bus and shove her into a seat. She writhes around and finally settles down in the aisle. Every time someone gets on or off, they have to step over her. The bus clatters around the countryside for ages, picking up a man in a business suit from the end of a farm-track, two backpackers wilting under the weight of their rucksacks and a trio of old ladies with matching nylon cardies and shopping trollies.

By the time we shudder to a halt at the bus

station in town, it's just past nine. Ayr is buzzing. Shops are opening up, cafés are dragging tables out on to the pavement. It's going to be hot, and it's going to be busy. A perfect busking day, Finn says.

Finn, Mouse and Leggit take a trawl down the main street, looking for a good place to settle. I go looking for a phone box.

'Want us to stay?' Finn asks, but I wave him away.

I stand in the phone box, stacking up my 20ps neatly. I cough, pick up the receiver, check outside to make sure there's no queue. I push a coin into the slot. It feels weird ringing home from a musty phone box in a strange town. I wish I'd asked Finn to wait.

My fingers tremble as they push the buttons, and the ring tone sounds extra loud in my ear.

The receiver clicks and clears and a woman's voice says, 'Hi! Lucy here.'

*Lucy.* Dad's girlfriend.

I hold the receiver away from my face. What's she doing there? Where's Dad? Lucy never stays overnight at the flat. So what's she doing there so early, what's she doing answering our phone like she's done it a million times before?

'Hello? Is there anyone there?' she says. 'Who *is* this?'

I put a hand over my mouth, squeeze my eyes shut and let my face fall against the cool metal of the telephone. I try to remember to breathe.

'Hello?' Lucy says again. 'Dizzy, Dizzy, is that you? Please speak to me! Don't hang up! I'll just get your dad, he's in the shower . . .'

I hear her calling 'Pete, Pete!' in the background. The receiver slips through my fingers, dangling on its long silver cord. I remember what Storm said yesterday. *Maybe your dad is enjoying the break, Dizzy. Ever think of that?*

I press down the button to cut off the call, and replace the receiver with a shaky hand.

It's just gone nine, and Lucy is at the flat while Dad's in the shower. I can't kid myself. She stayed over. She never did that while I was there, but now that I'm not . . . Maybe she'll move in. Maybe they don't miss me at all.

That's why Dad hasn't come – because he's busy playing house with his girlfriend, taking a break from me. He's having fun. He'll come and get me, sometime, sure. Definitely before the new term starts. But right now, he's in no hurry to trade his freedom for parenthood. He's happy. Without me.

There's a sharp rapping on the phone-box door.

'You all right?' a woman calls, her pink face too close to the glass.

I push out of the booth, past the woman. My

throat prickles with hurt. I feel stupid, idiotic, crazy for worrying about my dad, for stressing out over whether he had the right address for the festival, whether Storm put a first-class stamp on my postcards. For missing him.

I want him to miss me back, to rescue me from the patchwork van and the lazy, aimless, muddy world of festivals and travellers and soya milk and stale bread with little patches of green mould.

Too bad. It's not going to happen.

I find a big department store and drift in, hunting down the loos. I fill a sink with cold water and splash my face, drying it on my T-shirt. A woman with a mop and bucket, cleaning the cubicles, tries not to stare. I rake a comb through my tangled hair and hold my head high.

Outside, I follow the sound of twanging guitar strings and find Mouse, Finn and Leggit installed in an alcove outside Marks & Spencer, tuning up. They've spread a stripy rug across the pavement and Leggit is stretched out like a small, spiky-haired antelope. Mouse sits dreamily, licking a huge ice-cream cornet adorned with chocolate flakes and two colours of sticky sauce.

'OK?' Finn grins.

'Don't ask.'

Finn, who knows when to push it and when not to, doesn't.

We warm up slowly, with Finn on the tin whistle, churning out folky tunes and Irish ballads and ancient hippy songs from the land that time forgot. Mouse sets Finn's black sunhat at the front of the stripy rug to collect the cash. A shopper hurls in 10p, then a toddler drops in some coppers. Finn relaxes, gets into the music. The hat fills slowly.

I nip down the street to WHSmith and buy cans of Coke, water for Leggit and a *Beano* for Mouse. Strolling back, I notice the way Mouse is sitting, sad-eyed, shoulders hunched, pale and small and skinny. Every mum that passes him looks back, looks worried, digs into her purse.

'Have you done this before?' I ask him.

'Course,' he says. 'Loads of times, with Mum. Only without the music.'

'Oh.'

Begging.

Sometimes, Mouse makes me feel about a hundred years old.

I hand him the *Beano*, break open the Cokes, pour water into an empty ice-cream tub from the gutter for Leggit. We settle in for the morning.

The streets fill up with tourists, Mouse flicks through his comic listlessly and Finn runs through his list of surefire winners, strumming the guitar or letting me play while he sings. Cash drips steadily into the hat.

People smile as they walk past, a few kids stop and watch, a middle-aged woman gives us a two-pound coin and tells us 'Stand by Me' is her all-time favourite song. A stern-faced bloke gives us a large tin of Chappie, 'For the poor old dog'.

'She's meant to be thin,' Mouse protests. 'She's a lurcher.'

I get brave and try 'Angels' with Finn on tin whistle, and for a whole three minutes I manage to blot out the phone call and Lucy's bright, simpering voice and the fact that Dad's not coming, not any time soon. Like I care.

Then Mouse spots a couple of policemen over the road, and we grab our stuff and melt into the crowd of shoppers. We've made almost twelve quid! Mouse waits while Finn and I dive into a bakery. We buy sandwiches, crisps, pop, chocolate, custard doughnuts.

'All set, then,' says Finn, outside. 'Let's find the beach!'

Mouse whoops and his whole face lights up. He wraps Leggit's scarf-lead round his wrist and skips off along the pavement. I spot his *Beano* in the gutter, dip down to retrieve it. 'Mouse,' I call after him. 'You forgot this!'

'Don't bother,' Finn says, snatching the comic away and dropping it into a wastepaper bin. 'He won't miss it.'

'He might,' I argue, but Finn fixes me with a sad, grey-eyed glance.

'He won't,' he says firmly. 'Didn't you notice? The kid can't read.'

Finn asks directions to the beach, and we cut down a series of side streets until we see the seawall and a vast, rolling slash of deep-blue ocean. Mouse is silent, his eyes huge, nostrils flared. He looks like he could explode with excitement.

'Look,' he whispers to Leggit. 'That's the beach! That's the *sea*!'

'Have you never seen the sea before?' Finn asks.

'Of course. *Loads*,' Mouse says, scornfully. 'Don't think Leggit has, though.'

Finn and I exchange grins.

We trip down the steps to the beach, stumble through the soft, silvery sand. Leggit squirms, slithering free of the fringey scarf. She sprints off down the beach, zigzagging wildly through the football games, sunbathers, kids with buckets and spades. Down at the water's edge, she finds a huge piece of seaweed and shakes it about violently, then charges up to Mouse and drops it at his feet.

'*Sea*weed,' he says, amazed.

Finn, barefoot and wearing skate shorts, is already paddling through the shallows, chucking driftwood sticks for Leggit to chase.

Mouse and I pull off our trainers and socks, roll up our jeans. The soft sand is hot, it squidges through your toes, tickles your feet. Mouse runs down to the water's edge, shuts his eyes and lets the tide wash over his feet. I've never seen him look so happy.

We turn to the right, trailing along the edge of the sea until we find a quiet bit of beach, away from the picnics, the swimmers, the deckchairs. We spread the stripy rug, tip the picnic out of its bag, bask in the sun.

'Is this why they're called *sand*wiches?' Finn asks, after Mouse skids to a halt beside him, spraying his egg mayonnaise.

'Sorry,' says Mouse, then laughs when he sees that Finn isn't cross. When he smiles, he's almost cute.

We eat till we're stuffed. Leggit has a roast chicken triple-layer with salad, plus one of the custard doughnuts. Then she skitters back to the water's edge, where Mouse is building a sand-castle studded with mismatched shells and circled with stumps of driftwood.

'He's happy,' I say.

'Yeah.'

Mouse draws zigzags in the wet sand with a stick, digs a moat round the castle with his bare hands, drapes seaweed from his ears and roars at us like a sea monster. He runs in circles with Leggit, wades fully clothed into the sea up to his waist and staggers out, dripping. His wet, brown limbs are crusted with gold, his damp hair dusty with sand.

Mouse looks like any other kid on the beach – maybe a bit skinnier, a bit scruffier, a bit more nervous. But he's having fun, and I know and Finn knows that it's an awful long time since Mouse had fun.

'So, what did your dad say?' Finn asks at last.

I drop down into the sand, close my eyes. In the distance, a baby is crying, and the sound of an ice-cream van drifts down from the street.

'Change of plan,' I say lightly to the pale-blue sky. 'He's not coming, now. Not till the end of the summer.'

'What happened?'

'Oh, y'know. He's taking some time out to be with his girlfriend, Lucy. She's really nice. He says that I might as well make the most of my time with Storm. Enjoy the summer, that kind of thing.'

Well, that's what he'd have said if I'd given him the chance. If I tell Finn I hung up without even talking to Dad, he'll march me down to the phone box and make me ring back, just to be sure I haven't jumped to the wrong conclusions. I can't do that. I've spent eight years knowing my mum abandoned me when I was four. I won't get through another day if I think Dad's ditched me, too. He's entitled to spend some time out with Lucy. It doesn't mean he doesn't love me any more.

'You OK with that?' Finn watches me from under the brim of his black cotton hat.

'Sure, why not? Lucy's cool. And I'm having fun. Getting to know Storm. It's *good* for me and Dad to have some time apart.'

'Is it?'

If Finn doesn't stop looking at me, I'm going to cry.

'Yes,' I say defiantly. 'Yes, it is.'

I roll over on to my front and stare down at the sand. Crying is a bad plan. It'd only make the sand wet.

'Custard doughnut?' Finn suggests, offering me the box. 'Seriously wicked. Go on – Leggit recommends them.'

I laugh, lifting out the last custard doughnut. It's soft and sweet and soggy, and slightly gritty with sand. It tastes great.

We have to drag Mouse away from the beach.

'Come *on*,' Finn threatens. 'We'll miss the last bus. We've been here all afternoon.'

'Just a bit longer?' Mouse whines.

'No way. We told Tess we'd get shopping – y'know, bread and fruit and chocolate spread. If we don't go now, we won't have time!'

'*Please?*'

Neither of us have ever heard Mouse say please before. For anything. Finn sighs, defeated.

'Half an hour,' I tell Mouse. 'Then we really, really have to go. Promise?'

'Promise.'

We make the bus station with seven minutes to spare. The bus is in, half-full, the driver reading a newspaper.

'Time for a quick ice cream?' Finn says, and we tie Leggit to a lamp post and duck into the nearest sweetshop. Finn picks out two Magnums and orders a cornet with flakes and strawberry sauce for Mouse. He pays. The man at the counter frowns.

'Nice day,' I say, trying out a Finn tactic.

'Hmmph,' says the man, moving over to guard the open door.

Mouse has drifted down to the back of the shop. He trails Finn's rucksack, half-full of seaweed, pebbles and shells, behind him. His fingers stray over the packets of blow-up lilos, beach balls, buckets and spades. He strokes a pair of red rubber flippers and a snorkel.

'Come on, Mouse,' I hiss. 'Gotta go. Can't miss that bus.'

I step out into the sunshine, Finn on my heels. Then Mouse bursts past us like a small explosion, the rucksack on his back.

'Quick,' he shouts, halfway up the street. 'Run! Run! Leggit, c'mon!'

'Oi! Stop!' shouts the shop man. Finn charges past me, and in the confusion, Leggit drags herself free of the lamp post and hurtles off after them. My heart thumps and my mouth feels like sawdust. I want to run, I try to run, but my legs are like jelly.

Two Magnums and a huge cornet lie melting on the pavement.

'Finn!' I shriek, but then the shop man grabs me by the hem of my T-shirt. If I was brave enough, I'd bash him with my guitar.

'Back inside, young *lady*,' he says sneerily.

'Finn!'

I look over my shoulder and see Finn bowl up level with Mouse, grab him round the waist and whirl him round. Leggit is leaping about wildly, crashing into shoppers and tourists, and yelping hopelessly. Behind them, I see the bus shudder to life and crawl slowly out of the bus station.

The shop man marches me back inside. A couple of shoppers stare.

'OK, Jan, ring the police,' the man says gruffly. 'I'm sick of this. The police, OK?'

The shop darkens briefly as Finn appears in the doorway, with Mouse in front of him.

Outside, Leggit is scoffing down the last of the ice cream.

19

Everyone stares as we troop through the shop into a dingy backroom office. I wish I could hold my head high, like Finn. No, actually, I wish the floor would open and swallow me up. My face is so pink you could toast marshmallows in the heat from my cheeks.

Leggit skids into the room just as the door slams shut, her face sticky with ice cream. The shop-keeper snorts in disgust. 'Sorry now, aren't you?' he says to us, nastily. 'Well, too bad, it's too late for that. Put that bag down – I'd like the police to see what you've got in there.'

We stare at the rucksack Mouse is carrying, the bag he stuffed with bits of driftwood and stuff from the beach. The bag he's hanging on to for dear life. It's fuller, heavier than it should be. It doesn't take a genius to figure out why.

'Oh, Mouse.'

He drops the rucksack and flings his arms round

me. I hold him tight. Finn looks at me over Mouse's head, eyes wide.

The shopkeeper tips the contents of the rucksack out across the floor. Along with the grey toy mouse, the driftwood, feathers, seaweed, there are learn-to-swim armbands, a blow-up beach ball, a water pistol, goggles, a yellow plastic spade, six boxes of matches, four Mars bars and a disposable camera.

'Forget to pay for a few things, did you?'

'It was a mistake,' Finn says. 'We can sort it out.'

'Yeah, when the police get here,' the shopkeeper says. 'I've seen it all before. Buy something small, try to distract me while you let the little kid do your dirty work. Bloody cheek. It's *stealing*, you know!'

'I know,' says Finn sadly.

'Empty your pockets,' says the shopkeeper.

The police arrive while we're turfing out bus tickets, chewing gum, fluff, shells, loose change. It's the same two we saw when we were busking. One of them rolls his eyes, and I know they've recognized us, too.

There's a long conversation about whether the shopkeeper is going to press charges. 'They may only be kids, but they're still criminals,' he says.

'Right. Well, certainly, shoplifting is a very serious affair,' the red-haired policeman says. 'We'll be taking these characters down to the station, and of course we'll be calling their parents in.'

'But?'

'But the boy who actually stole the goods – well, he's just a kid,' the policeman says. 'Have they taken stuff from you before?'

The shopkeeper stares at us for a long, long time. 'No,' he admits at last. 'I've never seen them before. You can tell from their accents they're not local. I mean, just *look* at them. Dirty, stinking hippies.'

'That's quite enough, sir,' the podgy police-man says. 'Come on, you lot. Let's get you down to the station and get hold of your mums and dads.'

We get to ride to the station in a police car. Leggit leaves sand and smears of strawberry sauce all over the back seats. The policemen lecture us about stealing, along with threats that next time we risk a court case, a fine, a police record.

'I know,' Finn says. 'We're very sorry. Mouse didn't know what he was doing. It's not his fault. I think he thought I'd already paid, and I didn't realize . . .'

'Sure,' says the red-haired policeman. 'Just don't let there be a next time.'

'There won't be,' I say. 'Will there?'

'No,' Mouse whispers.

Once we're at the police station, things get complicated. We tell them our names, and they think it's a wind-up.

'Finn, Dizzy, Mouse?' the policeman says. 'Mouse, as in Mickey? C'mon, son, you can do better than that.'

'It's his name,' Finn shrugs. 'Really.'

'OK. Mouse. Mouse what?'

But nobody knows Mouse's surname, not even Mouse himself. At least if he does, he's not saying. It gets worse. Our address makes no sense to the policemen. We live in a van, a tent, a tepee, somewhere in the South Ayrshire hills.

'It's the Tree People Festival,' Finn explains.

'Right,' says the podgy policeman. 'Great. And is there a mobile number where we can contact your parents? No? Thought not. Oh, well.'

So we drive back to the festival in the back of a police car. No sirens, no handcuffs, no blue flashing lights, just us and two policemen who are probably hacked off they have to drive out into the middle of nowhere when they planned simply to ring our parents and get us picked up from the police station. We've probably ruined their evening. Then again, they haven't exactly done great things for ours.

We drive in beneath the Tree People banner and across the rutted field. Travellers blink sleepily at the car, or stare, hostile, curious. One bloke drops a spliff into the grass and grinds it underfoot. A man dressed up with stilts and face-paint blows giant soap bubbles at the windscreen.

The police car gets stuck in a maze of tents, and we get out.

'We'll be OK from here,' Finn says. 'Thanks very much.'

'What am I, a taxi service?' the red-haired policeman laughs. 'Nice try, kid. We need to see your parents. Now.'

We weave through the tents and stalls, taking the scenic route to the tepee. No sign of Tess, Storm or Zak.

'OK,' says Finn. 'This is it.'

He nods towards the tepee, points towards the doorflap.

'This?' asks the podgy policeman.

'Yep.'

They step inside, we follow.

The tepee reeks of joss sticks and some kind of incense that's been sprinkled on the fire. Tess, Storm, Zak and an assorted bunch of crusties are sitting around, drumming out a low, hollow beat and singing a wailing, hippy chant. Just an average evening at the festival, then.

Storm leaps to her feet, terrified. Zak stubs out his spliff and follows.

'What's wrong, man?' he says. 'Mouse? You been in trouble again?'

Tess stands up and starts ushering the drummers out of the tepee. 'Everything's fine, we just need some space,' she tells them. 'We'll get this sorted. Gentlemen,' she turns to the policemen. 'Can I offer you something to drink? Tea? Coffee? Elderflower cordial?'

The policemen sip coffee with soya milk and tell Tess, Zak and Storm that they need to keep a closer eye on us, make sure we understand the difference between right and wrong.

'We *do*,' Finn says. 'Honestly, officer. It was all a mistake.'

'The little kid isn't so clear, though, is he?'

'He had a rough start in life,' Zak says. 'A lot to cope with, y'know? But he's getting better. He's getting some real values here.'

The policemen exchange quick glances, but they don't say anything. Storm looks nervous and pushes her dope tin out of sight, under a cushion.

'Discipline is what he needs,' the red-haired policeman is saying. 'Clear boundaries, routine. Supervision.'

'Yes, of course, officer,' Tess says. 'It won't happen again.'

'If it does, then it's just a matter of time before the social services get involved,' the policeman warns. 'If they consider he's not being looked after properly, they could even take him into care. I'm not saying it'll happen, but it's something you should be aware of.'

'It won't come to that,' Tess says firmly.

'No *way*, man,' Zak echoes.

'Let's hope not.'

The policemen go, picking their way through the tents and campfires, stared at by small scruffy kids and glowering crusties. Someone has painted a rainbow on the bonnet of their car. The podgy policeman shakes his head and wipes it off with a large white hanky.

'Take care,' calls the red-haired one, as they drive out across the rutted field. 'Stay out of trouble.'

'We will!' I shout, and we run after the car, waving. Even Mouse.

Staying out of trouble is tough, though, because right now we're up to our ears in it. Bringing police on to the festival site is bad news. How many spliffs and tins of dope are there on site? How many vans or trucks without road tax or insurance, with dodgy tyres or an out-of-date MOT?

It's lucky they weren't interested in anything apart from us, that they didn't get mad about the rainbow on the car. They were OK. All the same, there'll be a row, a showdown, a slanging match. It was Mouse who messed up, but Finn and I were in charge and we blew it. We forgot for a while that Mouse is trouble. We thought we could trust him when we should have known better.

Back at the tepee, Storm is stressing out. 'We have to go,' she's saying to anyone who'll listen. 'They'll be back, they'll bust us for drugs and find something wrong with the van and they'll take

Mouse away . . . you heard what they said. We have to move on, now.'

Tess hovers at the edge of the tepee, watching the drama, trying to stay out of it. Quietly, she puts an arm round Mouse.

'Not *now*,' Zak says. 'Not yet. We'll take a day or two, pack up slowly, decide what to do next. They won't be back. Chill out.'

'Now,' says Storm. 'We have to go now. Did you give them Pete's address?' she asks me, her face pale. She looks older, somehow. Anxious.

'No, we just said we were staying here, at the festival.'

'That's something, then. Pete would go mad if he knew. He'd say I wasn't looking after you properly. He'd say I was letting you run wild . . .'

Maybe he would. Maybe I am. But Dad doesn't know, because he's busy having fun with Lucy, watching slushy films on Sky Box Office and eating takeaway pizza, or whatever you do on grown-up dates. If he was bothered, he'd be here by now, wouldn't he?

'Who cares what Dad thinks?' I tell Storm, stroking the soft, velvet fuzz at the back of her head. 'It wasn't like that, was it? We're OK. Aren't we?'

Storm smiles, but her eyes are distant. She pulls away from me and starts running around the tepee, rolling up quilts, piling up cushions, folding rugs.

'Look, Storm, we're not going now, OK?' Zak argues. 'We'll move on if it makes you happy, first thing tomorrow. But not now. It's getting dark. This doesn't make sense, Storm. There's no need.'

'There's every need. I've got a feeling. Really. A bad feeling. It's time to go, Zak. *Please*.'

Zak takes a deep breath in. He rakes a brown, skinny hand through his long, fair hair and his green eyes swoop over Finn and Mouse and me. He looks seriously hacked off.

'OK,' he says at last. 'OK. But we can't take the tepee down in the middle of the night, can we?'

'Leave it,' Storm says. 'Let Amber take care of it for a bit. Carl's got a truck, they can stash the larch poles in that. They're going down to the Blue River Camp in Somerset, we can meet them there.'

'But that's not till August . . .'

Storm stops packing and looks directly at Tess. 'We could stay at your place,' Storm says. 'We could stay at the cottage, just for a week or so, on the way down. Couldn't we? Tess?'

Tess ruffles Mouse's hair. Like me, like Zak, I know she'll agree to anything to put the smile back on Storm's face. 'Course you can,' she says. 'You know that. No problem. We'll all go, shall we? Finn?'

'Yeah,' Finn agrees. 'We'll all go.'

His fingers squeeze mine in the shadows of the tepee.

'OK,' Zak says finally, defeated. 'OK.'

It's chaos then. We pack the van, stuffing in bags and boxes and rucksacks and quilts. We take down Tess's tent and pack up the car. Then we sit around drinking herb tea with Amber and Carl to talk about leaving the tepee with them and meeting up down south. Dozens of people file in to hug us and wish us well. Cara gives me a daisy-chain necklace.

It's midnight before we set off, Tess's car first, the patchwork van rattling along behind. We lurch slowly through the field, passing out beneath the faded Tree People banner and into the lane. The red tail lights of Tess's car disappear in the distance and we're alone, me and Mouse and Leggit squashed into the back of the patchwork van, Zak and Storm up front.

It seems like a million years since we sat in the sun on the beach at Ayr, since we paddled in the salt water and ate custard doughnuts flecked with sand. Mouse snuggles up against my shoulder. I lean back, trying to stay awake by watching the road, sliding into sleep all the same.

When I wake, we're parked in a pool of light on the edge of a service-station car park. We stumble out of the van, use the loos, then trail into the all-night restaurant. We spot Tess and Finn in the far corner, scoffing chips and beans. We wave. Zak orders two black coffees. It's four in the morning and the smell of fast food makes my stomach growl.

'I'm starving,' says Mouse. 'Can we have chips? A Coke, even?'

'Seen the price of it?' snaps Zak. 'No chance.'

We slump into a booth alongside Tess and Finn. Storm looks around the café, checking out the other diners. A lorry driver eating egg and chips, a sleepy family huddled over huge baguettes, a lone woman sipping coffee and staring at a chocolate muffin.

Finn slides out of his seat just as the lorry driver leaves the café. He scoops up the leftover chips and a plate of untouched bread and butter, bringing them back to us. 'Early breakfast?' he says.

'Isn't that stealing?' Mouse asks, amazed.

'No,' says Tess. 'Not really, because the man already paid for that food. He just didn't eat it all. I think it's more like . . . recycling.'

I open my eyes wide, and Finn winks at me.

The coffee-and-cake woman gets up to leave.

'Chocolate muffin, anyone?' Tess whispers, and Mouse is off like a shot to rescue the abandoned cake before anyone can clear it away.

We sit in the café for over an hour, recycling chips, baguettes, scones and fresh fruit salad, before a tired-looking assistant in a red waistcoat notices and asks us to leave. Mouse, a natural at this game, snaffles a serviette full of abandoned sausages for Leggit on the way out.

We drive off into the drizzly pink dawn, singing.

21

I imagined a chocolate-box cottage with roses round the door, but Bramble Cottage is pure hippy heaven. There are roses round the door, sure, but also nettles taller than I am, and a cool-eyed billy goat (Cedric) chewing mouthfuls of sweet peas. There are chickens in the vegetable patch, eggs under the hedge and frogs croaking in the pond. A large tabby cat is asleep on top of the compost heap.

A grey-haired woman in a dressing gown and slippers comes out along the garden path, snipping flowers and eating toast and jam.

'Mum!' Tess shouts, and flings her arms round the woman. I watch Finn hug his gran and I'm stabbed with jealousy, homesickness, loneliness. I want Dad. Right now, I'd even tolerate Lucy. Maybe.

Instead, I have to make do with Storm and Zak, and I wonder why it's not enough. I thread a hand through Mouse's. He's looking as lost as I feel.

It's hard to resist the atmosphere at Tess's place, all the same. Storm and Zak must be regular visitors here, because they park the van in the 'usual place' under the apple trees and start making it homey right away, hanging wind chimes from the lowest branches and spreading rugs and quilts out across the grass.

'This is better,' Storm says, flinging herself down on to the grass, gazing up at the soft blue sky. 'We're *safe* here. We can just hang out for a while, chill, rest, get sorted for Somerset.'

'No money to be made,' Zak says, sulkily.

'Stop stressing,' says Storm. 'We can sign on. We don't need much.'

'Just as well.'

Finn's brother, Niall, a six-foot version of Finn with a black Mohican, black nail varnish and a pierced tongue, makes a huge veggie fry-up and we squash in round the scrubbed pine table in Tess's kitchen and eat until we're stuffed. Finn's gran wafts about the place in crinkly skirts with bells on, a purple bandana wrapped around her long, grey hair. I'm beginning to forget what normal people look like.

I'm beginning to forget a lot of things.

Hi Dad,

Thought I'd better let you know we've moved again. We're at Tess's place now, Bramble Cottage, for the next few weeks. I'll get Storm to put the proper address on the bottom of this card, in case you want to get in touch or anything. It'd be great to see you, if you're not too busy. And Lucy, of course. I'm still missing you – hope you haven't forgotten me.

Love,

Dizzy xxxx

There's a tree house in a rickety old oak behind the cottage. It's a simple tree house, no roof, nothing fancy, just a wide platform of smooth pine planks with a rail running round the edge and a frayed rope-ladder dangling.

Mouse loves it. 'I'm sleeping here,' he says.

'No way,' I tell him. 'It's too high, too rickety, and there's no roof . . .'

'*I* used to,' shrugs Finn.

A couple of nights later we're holed up there, the three of us, wrapped in quilts and sleeping bags, sipping hot apple juice from chipped tin mugs. Jam-jar lanterns swing from the branches, dropping thin pools of light around us.

Leggit whines and howls so much that Finn has to haul her up the swinging rope-ladder, too, a skinny bundle of wriggling bones and sticky-up hair. She sits with her head over the rail, listening to the goat rooting about in the bushes below.

'I like it here,' Mouse says into the darkness.

'Me, too,' I tell him.

'Me, three,' Finn says.

'We can see *everything*,' Mouse says.

I lean back and gaze up through the leaves, looking at the stars. It's funny how the skies are bigger, darker, when you're in the country. The night is velvet-blue, not neon-orange. I pick out the shape of the Big Dipper and find the Pole Star. I show Finn and Mouse, and explain how it's always there, no matter what. A magical star, like Storm says.

'Magical,' Mouse echoes. Then, 'Nobody can get us here.'

'Who'd want to?' Finn asks, surprised. 'There's nothing to be scared of.'

But maybe, for Mouse, there is.

'Bad people,' he says in a small voice.

'There *are* no bad people here,' I tell him.

'You wouldn't let them get me, anyway,' he whispers.

'No way,' says Finn. 'I'll fight 'em off with a big stick, set Leggit on them, pour boiling oil on their heads. Hot apple juice, anyway. I'll look after you, Mouse, little mate.'

'Me, too,' I echo. 'Always.'

'Always,' Mouse breathes.

His eyes flutter shut and he burrows down beneath the quilt. The grey toy mouse surfaces, clutched in one tiny, grubby hand. I wonder what he dreams about. I wonder who the bad people are.

'Grandad made this tree house,' Finn is saying. 'When we first came back here, when I was seven. For me and Niall. We thought it was the best thing we'd ever seen in our lives.'

'He's not around any more?'

'He died a couple of years back.'

'I'm sorry.'

'It's OK,' Finn says. 'I miss him like mad, but I'll never forget him. He taught me to play the piano, to love music. I had the chance to know him, to know which bits of me I got from him.'

I stare up through the leaves, counting stars. Finn has picked up his guitar, a tattier version of mine, and starts picking out chords.

'D'you ever think about your dad?' I ask.

Finn shrugs. 'He left before I was born. Why should I care about him? He couldn't even hang around long enough to see his own son.'

'D'you think it's a traveller thing?' I ask. 'You know, all this stuff about freedom and fun and moving on?'

Finn frowns in the darkness. 'Maybe, some-times,' he says. 'Mostly, though, I think it's just a *people* thing.'

Finn's picking out the tune to an old Linkin Park song, 'Somewhere I Belong'. I've never heard it before, but when Finn plays it, it's the best, the saddest song in the world.

Does *anyone* know where they belong? I used to think I did. I belonged with Dad, in our flat in Birmingham. I belonged with my mates, messing about at school, drinking Cokes in Dimitri's caff, sunbathing in the back garden, talking on the phone till all hours. Then Storm turned up and took me away, and now I don't belong anywhere.

'I used to dream Storm would come back,' I say. 'Then she did. It's what I always wanted, only now I'm not so sure. Is that ungrateful?'

'Nah,' Finn laughs. 'Your life just turned upside-down. You're bound to feel mixed up.'

'I thought I'd see her more, get to know her more. I thought we'd make up for lost time. I thought she'd want to know about . . . well, *me*. And she doesn't. She really doesn't. Sometimes I think I'm only here to babysit Mouse.'

'You're *not*,' Finn says. 'But . . . babysitting Mouse isn't so bad, is it?'

We look over at Mouse, the scrap of brown hair sticking out from the rolled-up quilt, the outstretched arm flung over Leggit's skinny neck.

'No, it's not bad. It's not bad at all.'

Finn puts down the guitar and leans an arm along the tree-house rail. '*Some* people care,' he says. I can feel him looking at me in the darkness, and I have to turn away.

'I think your dad cares, too,' Finn says eventually. 'What happened the other day when you rang? What did he say to upset you? You've spent weeks looking out for him, writing postcards, talking about him. Then one phone call and it's over. You'd think he's dropped off the face of the earth.'

I'm cold suddenly. I hug my knees, pulling the quilt closer round me.

'His girlfriend answered. It was only nine o'clock and his *girlfriend* answered. She never used to stay, when I was there. It felt like I'd been forgotten.'

'Dizzy!' Finn says, pulling one of the skinny plaits that hangs down by my face. 'Who could ever forget *you*? What did you say – what did *he* say?'

'Nothing. I didn't say anything. I hung up.'

Finn sighs. 'There's a phone here,' he says. 'You can ring him now. Tomorrow. Whenever.'

'Whenever,' I agree. 'Not just yet. Maybe we both need a break from each other? Him to be with Lucy, me to be here. Hey, will you play that Linkin Park thing again?'

Finn picks up the guitar and shifts position. I watch him lean in, long fingers teasing out the tune. His voice is a whisper, hardly daring to sing the words out loud. I join in with the bits I know. When he finishes, I know where I belong, and it's here and now, with Finn and Mouse and Leggit. The rest doesn't matter.

Finn hangs the guitar from a branch and stretches out his legs. His bare feet are pale in the darkness, dappled with shadows as the leaves above us shiver. One foot reaches out and prods my leg, and I catch it, hanging on to the lean, skinny shape of it. My fingers notice the rough, calloused skin on his heel and sole, the smooth skin above. I count his toenails, five little slivers of ice in the moonlight. I notice he's stopped struggling, but still, I'm slow to let go.

'Did anyone ever tell you that you have drop-dead gorgeous feet?' I ask.

Finn laughs out loud.

'No,' he says. 'Nobody ever did. Only you, Dizzy. Only you.'

It's happening again.

Eight years ago, Storm left me and went to Kathmandu with a man called Mitch. It's not Mitch, now, it's Zak, and it's not Kathmandu, it's Goa, some hippy place in India.

'Wow,' Storm says, her eyes wide. 'Wow. We're going to India, Dizz! How cool is that?'

A letter has turned up at Bramble Cottage, redirected from Zak's parents' place in Kent. It's from Zak's brother, Josh. From India. Josh has just bought a big beach house near Goa, in India. He wants Zak and Storm to come out and help him turn it into a spiritual healing centre, where hippy tourists can come to learn yoga, meditation and how to balance small chunks of crystal along their backbones. Zak, naturally, will help with this bit.

'I could do aromatherapy massage,' Storm says.

'You could if you learned it first,' Tess points out.

'How hard can it be? It's just a few oils and a bit of a back rub, isn't it? And I'm sure I could teach yoga and t'ai chi. On the beach!'

'He's talked about it before, but I never thought he'd do it,' Zak is saying. 'What a chance! And he needs me to make it work. Me and you, Storm.'

'All of us,' Storm says dreamily, flinging an arm round Mouse and me. 'What a life for the kids, growing up in the sun, walking barefoot in the sand, learning Urdu or Hindi or whatever they speak over there . . .'

'Right,' says Zak, frowning. 'The kids, too?'

'Of course, the kids too,' Storm laughs. 'We're a family, now, aren't we? We have to stick together.'

'Sure,' says Zak. 'Sure.'

Mouse takes a long drink of cold milk and wipes his mouth.

'No,' he says.

'No?' Storm falters. 'What d'you mean, no?'

Mouse shrugs, drains the milk carton and slips quickly out of the kitchen. I run after him.

We sit on the tree-house platform, swinging our legs. Finn, keeping a respectful distance, is riding his BMX in and out of the bramble bushes below, with Leggit galloping behind.

'I won't go,' Mouse says fiercely. 'They can't make me.'

'No, they can't,' I agree, but I'm not sure. Maybe they can? 'I'm not going, either. Not to *India*. I don't want to leave Dad.'

'I don't want to leave Mum,' Mouse says.

'D'you miss her much?' I ask.

Mouse shrugs. 'A bit. Sometimes.'

We look down through the leaves as Finn does a wheelie.

'She went away,' Mouse says sadly.

'She couldn't help it,' I tell him. 'She was ill. She'll get better, then she'll be able to look after you again.'

'Think so?'

'Know so.'

'Why did your dad dump you?' Mouse wants to know.

'He *didn't*. Your mum didn't, either. It's just – the way things happen. I'm spending some time with my mum, you're spending some time with your dad. Just for a while.'

Mouse frowns. 'And then I'll go back?' he asks.

'Yes.'

'But not yet?'

'No, not yet. And we're not going to India. No way.'

Beneath the tree house, Finn skids off the BMX and lands barefoot in the brambles. 'Ouch!' he yells. 'Leggit, that was your fault!'

'When I do go back to Mum's, I'll miss you,' Mouse says quietly.

'I'll miss you, too,' I tell him.

'Dizzy?'

'Mmm?'

'Are you – are you my sister? Kind of?'

I put an arm round him and he doesn't flinch away. 'I think so, Mouse,' I say. 'Kind of.'

Of course, we're not going to India.

It's not because of Mouse's mum, or my dad, but because the tickets cost £500 and children have to pay full fare. Zak says that's crazy, and Storm says, never mind, Mouse and I can come out later, once they're settled in.

'We'll just go and suss things out,' she says. 'Then, when we start earning, we'll send for you. OK, Dizz?'

But I know it's not going to happen. I'm not going to live in India, thousands of miles away from Dad, from my mates. I'm going home. Only not just yet. I'll wait till Mouse's mum is able to look after him again. *Then* I'll go.

'The kids are very welcome to stay with me for a bit,' Tess says.

'Of course,' Finn's gran chips in.

'Just for a short while,' Storm promises.

'No hassles,' says Tess.

They book the flight over the phone. Zak produces a credit card to pay for the tickets.

'Where'd he get *that*?' I whisper to Finn.

'He's loaded, Dizz, didn't you know?' Finn tells me. 'He's from a well-posh family, went to private school and everything. He and Josh, the brother, inherited a whole packet last year from some rich uncle.'

I whistle through my teeth. 'I thought they were just crusties,' I say.

'They are. Only I think they're kind of *upper* crusties.'

I think of the mouldy bread Zak made us eat, the way we had to recycle food in the service-station café. I remember him moaning about having two extra mouths to feed, even though it's always Tess who gets the shopping, makes the food, gets the clothes washed.

'Unreal,' I say.

'Tell me about it,' says Finn.

Dear Dad,
Just wanted to let you know that Storm is going to India. She might not be back for a while, so I wondered if maybe I should come home now? I'm staying with Tess and Finn and Mouse, so I'm OK,

you don't have to worry. I wish you'd write, Dad,
or ring or just come and get me. I miss you so
much.

Dizzy xxxxx


The day before they fly, Storm hennas her hair.
She mixes a paste from hot water and foul-smelling
green powder, then plasters her skinhead crop and
wraps her head in cling film and towels.

'Now you,' she says.

'Me?'

'C'mon, Dizz!' she teases. 'Live dangerously!'

So she combs through my long brown curls,
softly, slowly, carefully. She doesn't tug, she doesn't
pull. She eases every knot and tangle loose, then
smears the warm green paste over each section of
hair. I close my eyes. This is what it's like, to have a
mother. Someone to comb the tangles from your
hair, your life.

Later, we sunbathe in the strawberry patch,
eating fat, ripe berries and wiping the henna
drips from our ears and necks. Niall has built a
barbecue from old bricks and bits of chicken wire,
and he's cooking tofu and sweetcorn and veggie
kebabs in a haze of smoke. Tess is weeding in
the veggie garden, Zak is reading a crystal-healing
book and Mouse is trying wheelies on the BMX.
Inside the cottage, Finn is playing the piano. The

sound drifts out of an open window like the sound-track from a dream.

It takes an hour to wash the henna paste off my hair, another hour to dry it in the sun. Storm's hair is a fuzz of crimson velvet, mine a deep, russet shade like falling leaves, and shinier than I've ever seen it.

'Beautiful,' she says, looking at me. She roots around in Tess's sewing bag to find embroidery threads in moss green, scarlet and gold, to braid into a hair wrap. Her fingers weave through my hair quickly, gently.

'I'll remember you like this,' she says, and I know that she's saying goodbye.

Storm and Zak are gone, to a pink-walled villa on a scorching hot beach on the other side of the world. They promised to phone, to write, to send for us soon. That was three weeks back, and we're still waiting.

The patchwork van sits abandoned on the drive, a 'For sale' sign in the window. Zak tried to get Tess to buy it, the night before the flight to Goa, but she said she'd stick with the car.

'See if you can find someone who wants it,' Zak said. 'Ask for £500. And when you see Amber and Carl, ask if they'll buy the tepee. Should be worth £700, but try for more. You can send me a cheque. It'll pay for the air fares.'

Tess is sorting stuff out, tying up loose ends for Storm and Zak. It's just that there are a couple of loose ends that can't be neatly tidied away.

We stay at the cottage, Tess and Finn and Mouse and me. Tess says it's easier, less hassle than going on with the festivals. Nobody minds. Leggit chases chickens and barks at the goat and digs up the lettuces Finn's gran has planted. We're happy.

'Have you spoken to Pete lately?' Tess asks one evening. 'Did he say when he wants you back?'

'Oh, any time before school starts,' I say carelessly. 'He's not really worried. I'll ring him in a week or so.'

'Do that,' Tess says. 'Tell him to come up and stay for a few days, catch up on old times. I'm sorry he didn't make it up for the Tree People Festival.'

Finn is watching me carefully to see what I'll say. I say nothing.

'He does know where you are, doesn't he?' Tess pushes.

'Sure. I've sent him postcards, loads of them. Storm said she'd stick a letter in with the last one.'

'She did post it?' Tess frowns.

'I *think* so.'

'I hope so,' Tess says. 'I *really* hope so. Maybe I'll drop him a line myself, OK?'

'OK.'

'Ring him,' Finn says to me, later, when we're outside watering the veggie plot.

'I can't.'

'Why not? He might be worried. Does he know that Storm's done a bunk?'

'I said so on my last postcard,' I shrug.

'Ring him,' Finn says again.

'I'm scared.'

'What of?'

How do you explain it? I'm scared that Dad has forgotten me, that he's busy having fun, making the most of his freedom. I've sent him five post-cards. He knows how much I've missed him, but still he hasn't come to get me. Which has to mean that *he* hasn't missed *me*.

He knows that Storm's gone away, so why hasn't he come to rescue me? Not that I *want* to be rescued.

'*Dizzy*,' Finn says, exasperated.

I don't want to go home because it would mean leaving Mouse, and he needs me. And it would mean leaving Finn, and *I* need him. If there's such a thing as a family, we're it. Home-made, second-hand, tacked together from leftovers, but family all the same.

I stick my tongue out at Finn and he sprays me with the hosepipe, and Mouse thunders down through the cabbages on Finn's BMX to come and join in the fight. It doesn't end till we're all soaking wet, and, sadly, the cabbages are done for.

It's Finn's birthday soon.

I haven't any money to buy a present, but Tess

lets me root through her bag of scrap fabrics and I cut up a length of old blue blanket to make him a new guitar strap. In the mornings, while Finn is practising his piano or playing the guitar up in the tree house, I work on it. I fold the thick blue wool into a long, skinny rectangle. I snip a tiny hole at one end and sew a bright red shoelace to the other. Tess digs out her embroidery threads and shows me how to make stars and spirals out of satin stitch and chain stitch and little French knots.

We've built a bonfire on the lawn, and Mouse asks me if he can juggle firesticks in the evening, especially for Finn. 'Juggle, sure,' I tell him. 'Finn will love that, and you're getting really good. But not firesticks, Mouse. It's too dangerous.'

'Zak did it,' Mouse protests. 'He had those batons that were on fire, and he juggled with them. I want to do that for Finn.'

'No *way*, Mouse. Zak is much older than you. He's been juggling for years and years, and he knows that you have to treat fire with respect. It's a grown-up thing, Mouse, honestly.'

'*I* treat fire with respect,' Mouse argues.

I remember the way he is around bonfires, the way he strikes matches and lets the flames lick around his fingertips. Respect isn't the word that springs to mind.

'I *like* fire,' says Mouse.

Exactly.

'No firesticks,' I say firmly.

Mouse twists his face into a scowl, jumps on Finn's BMX and ploughs off through the flower beds.

Niall is planning a barbie for the evening, and Tess is going to make sponge cake and home-made ice cream and lemonade with real lemons.

'D'you want anyone over, on Friday?' she asks Finn. 'Kids from school?'

'No, thanks,' he answers. 'Jon's in France all summer and Danny's staying with his dad in Chester. I'm not bothered about the others.'

'OK,' Tess says easily. 'Anything special you want to do in the day? We could drive down to Lancaster to the pictures, whatever. Your call!'

'I'll think about it, OK?' Finn says.

That night, in the tree house, he asks if I'd like to take a picnic to the beach on Friday. Just us. My eyes widen. Is that 'just us', as in me and Finn? Or 'just us', as in me, Finn, Mouse and Leggit?

'The beach? I didn't know we were that near the sea. You kept that quiet!'

'It's a bus ride,' Finn shrugs. 'And it's not a touristy beach like the one at Ayr. But it'd be cool, all the same.'

'No, seriously, I'd love that.'

There's a rustling sound from Mouse's sleeping

bag, and he peers out, sleepy-eyed, over the top.

'Yeah, cool,' he says, yawning.

Finn looks embarrassed. 'Hey, thought you were asleep, little mate,' he says. 'Thing is, Mouse, I was thinking that maybe just Dizz and me would go to the beach. Take some time out, do teenage stuff, y'know?'

Mouse frowns. 'No,' he says. 'No, I don't know.'

Finn rakes a hand through his felted hair. 'Well, it's not really your kind of beach, Mouse,' he sighs. 'No ice cream, no tourists, nothing flashy. It's just dunes and mud and gullies and rocks. Pretty boring.'

'No, it sounds *great*,' Mouse argues.

Finn rolls his eyes. He's wavering. He doesn't like to hurt anyone's feelings, and he definitely doesn't want to hurt Mouse. 'Look, Mouse, little mate . . .' he begins.

'I think Tess needs you here, Mouse,' I say gently. 'Aren't you in charge of the bonfire? You have to make sure it's finished, show Niall how to edge it with rocks, get it started. Tess'll be relying on you.'

Mouse stares at me, his eyes huge. Then he looks at Finn. He's sitting up now, his hair sticking up in tufts. His lower lip trembles.

'You don't want me, do you?' he says.

'It's not that we don't want you . . .'

'You *don't*,' Mouse says. 'You think I'll get in the way. You think I'll spoil things. People always think that.'

Finn looks angry. 'No, Mouse, seriously. I just want to spend some time alone with Dizzy, OK? On my birthday,' he says. 'Is that too much to ask?'

'Don't *want* to go, anyway. Sounds rubbish.'

Mouse struggles out of his sleeping bag and dives for the rope-ladder. He drops down into the bushes and crashes off into the dark. Leggit crouches on the platform, whining, then leaps down to follow.

'OK,' sighs Finn. 'That went kind of wrong, didn't it?'

'Kind of.'

'Shall I go after him?'

'Better let him calm down.'

Finn is silent, staring out into the dark.

'I guess he'll get over it,' he says.

Mouse sulks all week.

On Friday morning, he tucks a king-size Mars bar under Finn's pillow and sneaks away.

'Think I'm forgiven?' Finn asks, showing me.

'Hope so.'

I give him the guitar strap, wrapped in tissue paper.

'Wow!' he says, stroking the embroidered patterns. 'Dizzy, it's amazing! I love it!' He unclips the old guitar strap and ties the new one on. He tries it for size, strums a few notes, does a little dance.

'Look, no hands! Oh, Dizz, this is cool.'

He puts down the guitar and for a minute I think he's going to hug me, but Mouse appears, and he gets hugged instead. 'Thanks for the choccy, little mate,' Finn says. 'My favourite.'

We pack towels and swimsuits and apples and peanut-butter sandwiches. Tess drives us to the bus stop and waves us off.

'Don't get into any trouble,' she says.

'Mu-um!' says Finn. 'As if!'

It feels weird without Mouse and Leggit. We sit side by side on the bus, fiddling with bus tickets, looking out of the window. Finn unwraps the birthday Mars bar, breaking it in half.

'Breakfast, Mouse-style,' he grins.

I laugh, and take a bite.

We get off at a road-end in the middle of nowhere, and walk down a steep, skinny lane. The sun warms our backs. I wish this summer would never end, but it's almost the end of August. It can't go on forever.

'Back to school, soon,' I say gloomily.

'Don't! I'm fourteen now,' Finn sulks. 'School gets serious. Revision, exams, acres of course-work.'

I think of green stripy ties in the grey Birmingham drizzle, the boiled cabbage and disinfectant smell of school corridors.

'I don't want to go back.'

To my old school, my old life, my old self.

'I know. Wish you didn't have to. You could come to my school, maybe.'

'Maybe,' I shrug, but both of us know it's not going to happen. Tess is already pretty stressy about being left with Mouse and me. The day before yesterday she wrote to Dad, and she's been in touch with the social services in London, too, trying to find out about Mouse's mum.

'D'you like school?' I ask Finn.

'It's OK,' he shrugs. 'It's just one of those things you have to get through. You just find a way of making it work for you.'

'Did you ever get picked on?' I ask.

'Sure, in Year Seven,' Finn admits. 'I had long hair – it wasn't dreaded, then – and Niall's old hand-me-down uniform. I was always getting hauled up to play piano in assembly. *So* embarrassing. There was this group of older lads – they couldn't work out if I was a wuss or a weirdo. They used to knock into me in the dinner queue, hack me at football, push me on the stairwells. Call me names and stuff.'

Finn frowns, remembering.

'What did you do?'

'I got into a scrap in the middle of a footy match, gave one kid a black eye. I got suspended for a week. They never touched me after that.'

'You were suspended!' I cry, outraged. 'Didn't you explain? Didn't you tell them about the bullying?'

'Didn't see the point,' Finn shrugs.

'You're crazy,' I scold him. 'What did Tess say?'

'She wasn't exactly overjoyed.'

We climb a farm gate and trail up across a

steeply sloping field. The farmer has just cut the grass for hay and rolled it into bales. It smells like heaven.

'It's not so bad now,' Finn says. 'My music teacher introduced me to this kid Jon, who's really into drumming. We worked out that we liked the same music, so we started jamming together. My mate Danny joined in on bass guitar, and we had a band. Spider Pie. We get to play at end-of-term concerts, that sort of thing. We're kind of louder and janglier than the teachers like, but it's better than hammering out the tune for 'Go Tell it on the Mountain' in assembly every week, y'know?'

'I know. I'll watch out for you on the Kerrang! channel.'

'Do that!'

Finn stops to pick a thorn out of his foot.

'D'you wear shoes to school?' I ask.

Finn raises an eyebrow. 'Of course I do. What d'you take me for, a rebel or something?'

'Something,' I laugh. 'I just can't imagine you in Nike trainers and a stripy tie.'

'Trainers? Who said anything about trainers? My school shoes are sixteen-hole Doc Martens with lime-green and black striped bootlaces. And I *always* wear my tie. Round my wrist – or to tie my hair back.'

I laugh, trying to imagine.

We're almost at the top of the hill now. I'm hot and tired. 'Where is this beach?' I ask. 'Outer Mongolia?'

'Patience,' Finn says. 'And remember what I said to Mouse. Don't expect anything fancy.'

We climb up over the brow of the hill and there it is, at the foot of the slope. A wide, shimmering curve of turquoise water, a streak of sludge-coloured mud, a jigsaw of gullies and rock pools.

'Wow.'

It's not pretty, but it's a beach – and we have it all to ourselves.

'Race ya!' Finn shouts, and we're flying down the hillside, arms spread wide, hair streaming out behind us. We crash into the wall that borders the field and clamber over, breathless. The grass thins out, turns scruffy, then gives way to big rocks and patches of mud.

I take off my trainers and pick my way over the stones. Finn is way ahead, balancing on slabs of slimy stone and peering into rock pools crusted with barnacles. When I catch up, he has his feet in the water, a pale golden crab edging sideways over his toes.

'Eeew!' I squeal.

'It tickles!'

'Poor crab,' I sympathize.

'Cheek!' Finn nudges me and I slip, one foot

landing in the pool next to his. I yelp. The water is freezing, and I pull my foot out. The crab darts away under a rock.

'You scared it,' Finn says.

'*You* scared it.'

Finn pulls a face, and I pull one back, laughing. He goes on looking at me for way too long, and I have to look away before I do anything sad and dorky, like blush.

We wade out along the gullies and channels, kick our way along the water's edge.

'It's *cold*!' I screech.

'It's gorgeous! Don't be so chicken!'

We push and shove and splash each other, until at last we're not fighting so much as holding hands. Finn's palm feels big and rough and warm, wrapped round mine. We splash through the cool, clean water, feet sinking into soft mud, toes scraping against sharp-ridged shells. Long scarves of seaweed tangle round our ankles like fine, emerald hair.

'D'you ever wish you could just stop time?' Finn asks. 'Keep things frozen, the way they are?'

'Sure,' I whisper. 'Before real life gets in the way again.'

He squeezes my fingers, and we break apart. Suddenly, I can breathe again.

'Let's beachcomb,' I say. 'Find something to take back for Mouse.'

We walk up to the tideline and scour the ribbon of driftwood and rubbish for hidden treasures. We rescue a clutch of long, white feathers, nuggets of dusty, jewel-bright seaglass and the shell of a giant crab, complete with claws.

'He'll love these,' Finn says, packing them carefully away inside his rucksack. 'Y'know, with Mouse, it's kind of like having a little brother all of a sudden. I like it!'

'I know. Me, too. It's like we're a family, somehow, the three of us.'

Finn frowns, kicking at a tangle of frayed blue rope, an empty plastic pop bottle. 'I don't want to be your brother,' he says darkly. 'I don't feel that way. Not like your *brother*.'

'I know.'

And I do, suddenly. In the family we've invented, Finn and me are *not* brother and sister. His hand snakes out to capture mine again, and I don't pull away. We walk on.

Round the tip of a jutting headland, we find a tiny, sheltered cove of soft golden sand. Beyond, the fields slope upwards, green meadows scattered with wildflowers. It's a tiny, secret beach, half-hidden between the hills.

'Hey!' Finn shouts, delighted. 'I don't remember this. It's amazing!'

'It's a magic birthday beach,' I tell him. 'Just here for one day. At midnight it disappears.'

We drop our backpacks and run out across the hot sand. The grains stick to our muddy feet, spray out behind us. Finn stretches his arms wide, whirls round a couple of times. He spins in the soft sand, arms outstretched, until he keels over and collapses. He looks up at me, grinning.

'D'you remember when we were little?' he asks, breathless. 'We used to spin round and round till we fell, and we called it the Dizzy Game. Remember?'

'I think so . . .'

I know the Dizzy Game, of course I do, from sunny days on the school field with Sasha and Sara and Jade. I just didn't realize it came from a time *before* school, when Finn and I were first friends.

If Finn isn't too shy to hurl himself round in circles until he staggers, screaming, and crashes into the sand, then I'm not. I spread my arms and turn, slowly at first, then faster and faster, out of control. The world spins away and my feet lose their hold on the earth and I'm squealing, staggering, stumbling.

Then the ground shifts and comes up to slap my back, my head. I lie in the soft, golden sand as the world spins round me, and I remember why I used to love this game. It makes everything go away, until there's just you, your head reeling, your heart thumping. Real life churns on, the earth tilts, the sky dips.

I grab handfuls of sand to get a hold of myself, but the grains run away through my fingers. The hot sun presses me down. A hand brushes past my outstretched fingers, weaves between them. Finn. We lie still for a few minutes, fingertips touching, waiting for the world to stop.

Then Finn is struggling upright, dragging me with him. I stumble against him, laughing, and his hands cup my face. He looks at me for a long moment, and then he's kissing me.

It's not like I imagined. His lips taste of salt and sand and happiness. They're soft, so soft. We break apart and we can't stop staring at each other, wide-eyed. He brushes sand from my cheek, my hair.

The world keeps on spinning, with or without the Dizzy Game.

The bus drops us off at six, and we hear the music as we turn into the lane, see the lanterns twinkling up ahead. There's a smell of wood smoke and barbecued tofu.

As we push open the gate, Leggit leaps forwards. Someone's made her a collar of willow and flowers, and she jumps up at us, trailing ribbons and licking the salt from our skin.

'Finn! Dizz!' Mouse calls out from the tree house.

'Hey, Mouse! We did some beachcombing for you.'

Mouse is wriggling down the rope-ladder, bounding towards us through the flowers. He watches as Finn unwraps the parcel of treasure, reaching out to touch the soft white feathers, the seaglass, the crab shell.

'Cool,' he breathes. 'Will you take me, next time?'

'Sure,' I tell him. 'Next time.'

'We missed you, little mate,' Finn says.

'Did you have your Mars bar?'

'Long gone, Mouse. But much appreciated. The best prezzie ever.'

Mouse flashes us a smile. 'The best is yet to come,' he tells us. 'Just you wait and see!'

Then Tess is calling us, and Finn's gran, and Niall, and Mouse melts into the background, eyes bright, smiling his secret smile. The barbie is ready, and we stack our plates high with charred sweetcorn, tofu burgers, veggie kebabs. Someone's brought the CD player and speakers outside, and Niall removes a Bob Dylan CD, feeding it instead with Finn's favourite clashy, trashy nu-metal sounds.

Finn's opening presents now – a new hoodie, a pair of baggy jeans, a couple of piano music books, a beautiful, handpainted bodhrán drum. It's like a big, wide tambourine with weird Celtic dragons painted on the skin. Finn holds it flat against his body, flicking the drumstick over it in a fast, furious beat.

We sit round the bonfire and eat and laugh and talk. It gets dark, and Finn pulls on his hoodie, while Tess hands round sparklers. I dip mine into the bonfire flame and watch it fizz, then write *Dizzy* + *Finn* into the darkness, so fast that nobody could ever know. Except Finn, who catches my eye and draws a heart in the air between us.

Mouse tries juggling the sparklers, but Tess says it's dangerous and threatens to take them away. Instead, Mouse puts on a juggling show with three velvet beanbags, tossing them higher and higher in the bonfire's flickering light. He throws them at Niall, who flings them back in a quick volley. Mouse doesn't drop a single throw.

'*Could* have done it with fire,' he says, to prove a point.

'Maybe,' I tell him. 'But I'm glad you didn't. Nothing could have been better than this, Mouse.'

'Think so? *That* was nothing. You'll see.'

I pull a face, then turn back to the bonfire. I notice Finn's BMX ramp pulled up way too close to the edge of it, flames licking the wood. I kick it, managing to knock it a few inches backwards. 'It's a bit black around the edges,' I shout to Finn, who shrugs. It's only a home-made thing, so I guess it doesn't matter.

'Mouse again,' Tess sighs. 'He was riding the BMX up and over the bonfire, earlier, again and again. Before it was lit, obviously!'

'He's getting pretty good!'

'Sure,' Tess says. 'He's got a skill, definitely. Like with the juggling. And he'll try anything – he just doesn't seem to get scared at all.'

'Maybe,' says Finn, joining us. 'Or maybe he's just scared of different things.'

'Maybe. Better go get that cake organized, anyhow,' Tess says.

A minute later she's in the cottage doorway, shouting for Niall. 'Quick! Niall! That wretched goat's got loose again, it's in the kitchen! Give us a hand!'

Niall runs off towards the house.

'Wonder if she was in time to save the cake?' Finn muses. 'Last time Cedric got in the house, he ate a bowl of ice cream, my Year Eight physics textbook and Gran's cardigan. Scary.'

Finn's gran is sitting on a log at the other side of the bonfire. She looks tired, dreamy. She doesn't notice when Finn edges closer to me, when his hand slides over mine. 'Today was brilliant,' he whispers into my hair.

I let my hair fall forwards to hide my flaming cheeks. I can't think of anything to say. Suddenly, typically, the CD player stops and Niall isn't there to keep it fed with discs, to plug the long, heavy silence.

'Hey!'

We both jump.

'Watch me!'

Mouse is behind us on the grass, waving, grinning, a tiny, skinny figure astride Finn's BMX.

Something looks odd about it. Then I realize —
there are sparklers stuck all round the wheel rims
of the bike, jutting their fuzzy, crackling fire into
the clear night air.

'Looks cool, Mouse,' Finn starts to say, but the
words die on his lips as Mouse pedals forwards,
hammering down the slope and across the grass.
The sparklers leave a trail of silver as the wheels
spin.

He's heading straight for the ramp, the bonfire. He's been practising all day, hasn't he? Before
the bonfire was lit, obviously. Only there's no
obviously with Mouse. There never has been.

*That was nothing. You'll see.*

I'm starting to see, Mouse. I am.

I open my mouth to scream, but it feels like it's
full of sand. No sound comes. Finn's gran is on her
feet on the other side of the bonfire, her face white.
Leggit starts to whine.

Mouse flies straight at the ramp, up and into
the bonfire. The bike hovers, high above the
flames, and Mouse tries for a bar spin. He's going
to make it. He spins the handlebars, and the wheel
turns quickly. And then it stops, and the bike is
dropping, down into the fire.

'There's a branch in the wheel!' Finn gasps.

Mouse is pushing himself away from the bike,
leaping away from the flames. He can still make it.

Then the bike is gone, and Mouse falls after it, down into the bonfire.

And into the silence of the stopped CD player comes his scream, loud and thin and ugly.

It goes on and on and on.

26

Everything happens slowly, then everything happens fast.

Finn pulls up the hood of his jacket, drags the sleeves down over his hands and runs into the bonfire. He claws at the burning branches, hauls the bike to one side. And then he's falling backwards on to the grass, with Mouse in his arms.

Tiny flames curl all along Mouse's jeans, his sweatshirt, but Finn rolls him over and over, holding him close. He smothers the flames with his own body, and then he lets go, rolls away.

Mouse is still, silent.

Finn's gran is there suddenly, dragging the hosepipe. She pours water over Mouse's blackened clothing, dousing him, soaking him. His little body jerks and shudders.

'*Don't!*' I yell at her. 'It's hurting him! Are you meant to do that?'

'Get Tess,' she says to me. 'Tell her to call an ambulance.'

I hesitate. There's a stink of burning rubber from the bike, and the smell of burned fabric, and something worse. It could be hair, or skin.

'*Quickly!*' screams Finn's gran, and because I've never heard her raise her voice before, I push back my terror and run up to the house.

Tess appears in the doorway with a huge sponge cake studded with lit candles. Behind her, in the hall, Niall is scuffling with Cedric.

'Isn't it great?' Tess beams. 'D'you think he'll like it? Dizzy? What's the matter, Dizz?'

'The bonfire – Mouse fell – Finn – we need an ambulance . . .'

Then the stench from the bonfire fills my nostrils again, and I turn away into the bushes and retch.

Tess runs down to the bonfire, dropping the cake on to the path. Niall rings for the ambulance, then puts an arm round my shoulders and leads me back down to the others.

Mouse lies curled on the grass, his face white, his eyelids flickering. Finn's gran kneels beside him, offering sips of water. Leggit skulks nearby, cringing and whining. She pushes Mouse with her long wolf's muzzle, her big pink tongue, and his hand uncurls to touch her.

He doesn't look too bad. Until he turns his head, and I see what the fire has really done. I turn away, sickened.

Finn lies a few feet away, hunched over, Tess bathing his feet and legs with a rag soaked in water. Then I realize that the rag is a piece of her skirt, torn roughly from the rest.

'Oh, Finn, Finn,' she whispers. 'Your poor feet.'

I can't look at Finn's feet, his beautiful, bare feet that ran through white-hot embers and leaping flames to rescue Mouse. Instead I look at his face, scrunched up in pain, wet with tears.

There's a small, dark shape on the grass at the bonfire's edge. An old toy mouse, slightly blackened now. I pick it up, my fingers shaking.

The ambulance takes Mouse and Finn and Tess, and Finn's gran takes the car with Niall and me. We drive through the night and end up in the Specialist Burns Unit of a big hospital, miles away. We sit in a corridor that reeks of bleach and fear, waiting for news. Tess is hollow-eyed, grey with pain.

'It's my fault,' she whispers. 'I should have *known*. All day he was practising with that BMX, flying up the ramp, leaping the bonfire. I should have known. I should have guessed.'

'How could you?' Niall soothes. 'It was a crazy thing to do.'

'His face,' Tess breathes. 'His little face, all down one side. And Finn's feet. Oh, God, how many times have I told him to wear shoes?'

'Mum, don't,' Niall says. 'It's nobody's fault.'

But it is, of course.

OK, Mouse was crazy to try the jump. It was a risk, but it nearly came off. If he hadn't tried the bar spin, if the front wheel hadn't tangled with that branch . . .

If I hadn't kicked the ramp back.

All day he practised, getting everything perfect. And I moved the ramp.

It was *my* fault. I choke back another wave of nausea and let the tears fall. My eyes sting, like they're full of grit.

After what feels like a hundred years or so, an Asian doctor and a little blonde nurse come out to talk to Tess.

'Will they be OK?' she asks, hanging on to the doctor's arm. 'How does it look? Will they . . .?'

'They're comfortable,' the doctor says. 'The little boy has some partial and some full-thickness burns to the head, shoulder and hands, and less severe damage to the chest and back. He will recover, but there'll be scarring. Perhaps, later, we can do some cosmetic work, help to lessen the impact.'

'And Finn?'

'Some damage to the hands and wrists, but nothing serious. It's his feet we're concerned about. It's too soon to say how well things will heal, but again, there will certainly be scarring.'

'But they'll be OK?' Tess asks again. 'Won't they?'

The nurse smiles sadly. 'Yes, Mrs Campbell, they'll be OK. Now . . . is there anyone I can call for you? How about the boys' father?'

'Oh, no, we're not together any more,' Tess murmurs. 'And Mouse's dad's in India. Although I suppose perhaps his mum should know . . .'

The doctor frowns. 'The littlest boy . . . he's not yours?' he asks slowly.

'No, no, he was just staying . . . for a while . . .'

'And his dad is abroad? Where is his mum?'

'She's ill,' Finn's gran says. 'She's in London, somewhere, in a clinic. My daughter's been helping out.'

'I see. And what relation, exactly, are you both to the little boy?'

'Well,' flounders Tess. 'No *relation*, exactly.'

'I see.'

'Somebody had to look after them,' Finn's gran says anxiously.

'*Them?*' says the nurse.

'Well, you know, Mouse and Dizzy.'

The doctor looks at Tess, then me. 'Dizzy,' he

says. 'The sister of the little boy who fell in the fire?'

'Yes,' I say.

'No,' Tess corrects. 'Not exactly. She's just staying with us. Her mum is in India, her dad's in Birmingham.'

'I see.'

They turn away.

'Social services,' the nurse whispers, when she thinks we're out of earshot.

A little while later, they lead us through to see Finn and Mouse. They're sleeping, sedated, the nurse says. Finn looks OK, but looking at Mouse is like seeing a TV report from a war zone. Cling film stuff swathes one side of his face, hides his hands. I reach into my pocket for the skanky toy mouse, tuck it in under the covers, softly.

It's just past nine in the morning when we get back to Bramble Cottage. The sun streaks through the apple-tree branches, still strung with jam-jar lanterns, long since dead. The bonfire still smoulders on the grass, a low mound of grey ash and charred logs. The blackened skeleton of the BMX lies half-in, half-out of the embers.

On the path, a broken china plate marks where Tess dropped Finn's birthday cake. There's no trace of the sponge, jam, cream or candles.

'Goat probably had it,' says Niall. 'Lucky thing.'

The cottage door stands open, the way we left it. The tabby cat lies stretched out in the hallway, basking in a patch of sun.

'Bed,' Tess says wearily. 'All of us, and in the house, Dizzy, not the tree house. We need some rest if we're going to see the boys later on.'

'OK.'

Inside the cottage the phone begins to ring, and Tess wanders off to get it.

'Pot of chamomile tea?' Finn's gran suggests. 'Settle us down?'

We can hear Tess talking in the other room.

'You don't think it could be the hospital?' I ask.

'No, no. Stop worrying,' says Niall.

But when Tess comes into the kitchen, our eyes swivel to her. She tries to fix her face into a happy shape, but it doesn't quite come off.

'Dizzy . . .' she says slowly. 'That was your dad.'

The doorbell rings and rings, somewhere far away. It hauls me out of sleep and I sit up, wearily, rubbing my eyes. It rings again.

Sunlight streams in through thin red curtains, and the bedside clock says just before midday. The walls are covered in black-and-white posters of sulky LA punk bands, and a pair of Doc Martens with lime-green stripy laces sit under the desk. Finn's room.

The doorbell rings again, and I run across the landing, down the stairs. I see dark shadows through the front door's coloured glass.

I open the door, still rubbing my eyes.

'Dad!'

I fling myself at him, and he lifts me right up off the ground like he used to when I was little, swinging me round and round. We come back down to earth, hanging on tighter than ever. I bury my face in his neck and there's a funny, snuffly sound that means he's either laughing or crying.

I don't care which. He's here.

We don't let go, not for a long time. When we move apart, there's a wet patch on my hair where it lay against his cheek, and his eyes are damp and blurry, just like mine.

Dad looks different, somehow. His dark hair is grey at the temples, his face kind of grey and sad. There are lines etched across his forehead that never used to be there. It's like I haven't seen him for ten years, not ten weeks.

'You came,' I say, and my voice comes out all husky and ragged. 'At last, you came!'

A flash of what looks like pain crosses Dad's face. 'Oh, Dizzy,' he says sadly. 'Of course I did.'

Behind him, looking neat and pretty and wonderfully familiar in a blue top and embroidered jeans, is Lucy. She looks uncertain, anxious, but her lips twitch into a nervous smile. Over her shoulder I see the blue Mini pulled up on the driveway. Cedric is hovering by the front wheel, sniffing thoughtfully.

'Lucy,' I say.

'Dizz.'

She hugs me, just a quick, light hug. I hug her back. Behind me, Tess is coming down the stairs, a crocheted shawl wrapped round her nightie.

'Pete,' she says. 'Long time no see. Look, come

in, both of you. Just let me call the hospital, then we'll talk. Get to the bottom of this mess.'

I take them through to the kitchen, put the kettle on.

'How is – Finn, is it? Tess's son?' Dad asks. 'And the other little boy? How did it happen?'

I turn away. 'It was Finn's birthday. Mouse was showing off, trying to impress us. He tried a BMX jump right over the bonfire, but one of the wheels got tangled and he fell in. Finn pulled him out.'

'How awful,' says Lucy.

Dad nods, a hand over his mouth, forehead creased. He's thinking that it could have been me.

'Someone moved the ramp,' I say into the silence. 'That's why he didn't make it. He had it all worked out, but someone moved the ramp.'

Dad looks at me. 'No, no, Dizzy,' he says slowly. 'It was a dangerous thing to do, that's all. If it hadn't been the ramp, it'd have been something else.'

'He should have checked it,' says Lucy.

'He's only seven.'

'Ah, Dizz.'

Tess sweeps into the room, trailing the shawl.

'So?' Dad asks. 'How are they? Any news?'

'Better,' she admits. 'They're resting. We can visit later.'

Tess sits down, heavily. 'Anyway, Pete, um . . . Lucy? It's good to see you. Find us OK?'

Dad just stares. '*Find* you OK?' he says, shakily. 'Not really, no. It's taken ten weeks, hasn't it? This whole thing has been a nightmare. Not one word until your letter.'

'I had no idea, Pete,' Tess says. 'Believe me, until you rang this morning I really had no idea.'

I put three mugs of herb tea and an apple juice on the tabletop.

'You knew I was here, though, right?' I say. 'Storm said she'd keep you posted.'

Dad closes his eyes, takes a couple of deep breaths.

'Keep me posted?' he says at last. 'That's a joke, Dizzy. I've been looking for you since the day after your birthday, the day you took off. Nine weeks and six days. I can tell you the hours, the minutes, the seconds, too. I thought I'd never see you again.'

'Sit down, Dizzy,' Tess says gently.

I sit.

'It looks like Storm wasn't totally upfront with you when she said she'd asked your dad about this holiday . . .'

'Holiday!' Dad rasps. 'Kidnap, I call it! Don't defend her, Tess. Storm is in big trouble, this time. She's gone too far. Too far.'

'But you *knew* I was coming,' I argue. 'Storm said you were fine with it. And I told you myself, that morning, when I was saying goodbye . . .'

Dad drops his head into his hands. 'No, Dizz,' he says sadly. '*No*, you didn't. I was pretty hungover, but I know I'd have remembered if you told me you were running away with your mum for the summer. I . . . I thought you were going to school . . .'

Lucy reaches a hand out to cover mine. 'He started to worry when you didn't come home that afternoon,' she says. 'He rang Jade and Sara and Sasha, but of course they hadn't seen you. Then we went to the police . . .'

The *police*? My heart is thumping.

*Storm, Storm, what have you done?*

The story unravels. The police talked to Dad, decided that it was a pretty sure thing I was with my mum. They put me on the Missing Persons list, but they didn't do much about tracking me down. I was with family, they said. It wasn't a priority.

Lucy drove Dad to Wales in the blue Mini and they searched every festival, every open-air concert, every scrap of countryside.

'I wasn't in Wales,' I tell them. 'I was never in Wales. It was *Scotland*.'

'Right,' Dad sighs. 'Clever girl, Storm. Later on,

the police told us that a traveller girl meeting your description had been picked up for shoplifting in Ayr. By the time they realized and went back to look, she – you? – had gone.'

'It *was* me,' I tell him. 'It was. But I wasn't shoplifting.'

'Unreal,' Tess says. 'All that fuss about moving on, packing up in the middle of the night. Storm *knew*.'

Dad shrugs. 'We drove up to Scotland and searched ourselves, but nobody had heard of you, or Storm. Or if they did, they weren't saying.'

'Did you ring, one day?' Lucy asks suddenly. 'Then hang up?'

I nod, red-faced. 'I don't know why. I was scared. I got confused. I'm sorry.'

Lucy looks at me for a long time. She knows why I hung up. Because I was jealous, hurt, stupid. But if she can read my mind, she must know how sorry I am. Mustn't she?

'Doesn't matter, now,' she says softly. 'We've found you.'

'I sent postcards,' I remember suddenly. 'Five postcards. Didn't you get them?'

Dad's eyes widen. 'No, not one. Are you sure you sent them?'

I'm silent. I wrote them, and, each time, I handed them to Storm. *Let me add my own little message*, she used to say. Or, *I'll post it when I'm in town. No trouble.*

'I gave them to Storm.'

Dad drains his coffee mug and puts it down, wearily. 'So,' he says. 'Where is your mother? Where *is* Storm?'

Tess stands up, wrapping the shawl tightly round herself. 'When I sent the letter, I kind of assumed you knew,' she says. 'And then, when you rang this morning, I realized things were all wrong, but I just didn't know how to tell you.'

'Tell me *what*?'

'It's Mum,' I say. 'She's not here any more. Not for three, four weeks. She's gone to India.'

28

We stay on at the cottage for a while. Each day, I go to see Finn and Mouse in hospital. I get so I don't flinch when I see the shiny patches on Finn's feet, the shimmery cling-film dressings on Mouse's head and hands and shoulders.

Finn is well enough to sit in a wheelchair and scoosh along the corridor to see Mouse. His feet are still painful, but they're healing well.

'Guess I won't go barefoot in summer, any more,' he says.

'Guess not.'

Mouse is chirpier than you'd expect.

'I nearly made it, didn't I?' he says one visiting time. 'It was a pretty good jump, wasn't it?'

'Mouse! You could have been killed!'

'Nah,' he says. 'Next time, I'll do it for sure.'

'No next time, Mouse,' I tell him gently.

'No?'

'No,' Finn says sternly. 'No way.'

Mouse shrugs.

I take a deep breath and tell Mouse about moving the ramp. 'It's my fault, isn't it?' I ask him. 'My fault it went wrong?'

'How far did you kick the ramp?'

'Not far, it was heavy. A few inches?' I spread my fingers, guessing at the distance.

Mouse shakes his head sadly. 'Shouldn't have made any difference,' he says. 'It was a perfect jump. It was just that branch that got in the way. Maybe I shouldn't have tried the bar spin?'

'Maybe you shouldn't have tried any of it!'

Mouse grins. 'It was for you,' he says. 'For you and Finn.'

Finn reaches out and tweaks his ear, the one that isn't cocooned in cling film. The one that isn't burnt. 'I know, Mouse,' he says. 'I know, little mate.'

'I nearly made it,' Mouse says again.

'Yeah, you nearly did.'

But nearly isn't good enough.

A nurse comes to change the dressings, and we glimpse patches of weird, puckered skin on Mouse's neck and cheek and ear and hands and shoulders. The nurse says the scarring will fade, but it won't go away. Mouse looks in the mirror and pulls a face. He doesn't look too bothered.

The whole time Mouse is in hospital, the nurses

and social workers are trying to work out what to do with him. They contact the detox clinic in London. The doctors there say his mum is getting better, but she's still not well enough to look after him. With difficulty, they get a message to Zak in Goa. He rings the hospital and speaks to the doctors, rings the social services and speaks to Mouse's case worker. Finally he rings the cottage and speaks to Tess.

Tess waves us through to the living room and puts the call on speakerphone, so we can hear what he says. We watch as she goes over things one more time for Zak.

'I'm so sorry it happened,' she says. 'We're all sorry. The doctors say he's doing well.'

Things are at a difficult stage with the healing centre, Zak says. There's so much work still to be done to get it up and running, and Josh is relying on him. Coming back to England is kind of awkward right now.

'Couldn't Mouse just stay with you a bit longer?' Zak asks.

Tess has to explain about the social workers. 'They're not all that happy about the situation,' she says. 'I've said he can stay here, of course I have. But it's not that simple. Zak, if you don't come back and get him, I think they might take him into care.'

'No, no, they won't do that, surely,' says Zak.

We lean against the sofa, watching Tess.

'I think that they will,' she tells him.

Zak is silent for a while.

'I suppose he could come out here,' he says at last, grudgingly. 'Only there's nobody to watch out for him, really. I'd just worry about him being safe. Unless Dizzy could come out to keep an eye on him?'

Dad grabs the phone from Tess. 'Dizzy *can't*,' he says crisply. 'Dizzy has school to go to, a life to live. She can't go chasing to the other side of the world to babysit your son. He's *your* responsibility, poor little kid. Can you put Storm on the line?'

'Storm can't come to the phone right now.'

'No, I *bet* she can't.'

Dad hands the receiver back to Tess, trembling with anger.

Zak starts asking whether Amber and Carl have paid up for the tepee yet. Money's a bit tight in Goa, he says. Could Tess chase up the cash for him?

Tess stares at the telephone, speechless.

'Who is this creep, anyway?' Dad asks out loud.

'Hello? Tess?' Zak is saying. 'About the money. Is anyone there?'

'Hi, Zak?' Tess says. 'I have to go now. Give my love to Storm, and tell her Dizzy's safe with her dad again. And, Zak, give Mouse a call at the hospital, yeah? He'd love to hear from you. OK?'

She puts the phone down, and rests her head in her hands.

'Poor Mouse,' says Finn's gran. 'D'you think he'll ring?'

'Maybe,' says Tess.

He doesn't, of course.

Finn's out of hospital first, but I'm well away by then, back in the drizzle and gloom of Birmingham.

We keep in touch, with letters and phone calls. Tess and Finn see Mouse just about every day. They say the doctors are pleased with his progress, but it's November before he's finally discharged. A social worker is taking him to London, to a foster family near the clinic where his mum is staying. He'll get to visit, maybe, when she's a bit better.

Dad and I travel up north to say goodbye. Tess and Finn meet us at the railway station, and we drive to the hospital together through the thin November sunshine.

Mouse is waiting for us in the hospital foyer, his new social worker standing guard. We wave and hug and then stand around, awkward and embarrassed, not wanting to say goodbye.

Mouse is clean and neat, but the smile has gone. His cheeky, flashing eyes are dull and quiet, his face closed, sullen. The burns are way better, and his hair has grown back to a stubbly crew cut. It looks weird, like the clothes they've given him to wear, all trackies and sporty, label stuff.

'Can we have some time?' Tess asks the social worker. 'On our own?'

The social worker, a young man with gold-rimmed specs and a toothy grin, says he'll wait. 'Not too long, mind. It's a long drive to London, hey Mouse?'

Mouse scowls. A *very* long drive, I think.

We go outside, the social worker trailing at a distance. He finds a bench and sits down, watching us. Dad hangs back too, while Tess, Finn and I walk out across the grass with Mouse.

'Hang on, Mouse,' Finn says suddenly. 'Got a surprise for you!'

He runs off towards the car park, still limping a little.

'We'll miss you,' Tess says into the silence. 'We'll ring, see how you're settling in.'

Mouse looks away.

'It's not for long,' she says brightly. 'Your mum will be well enough to look after you, soon. And you'll be living nearby, they'll take you to visit her. That'll be good, won't it?'

Mouse kicks at a stone, scuffing up some turf on the toe of his new trainers.

'I'll miss you,' I whisper.

His eyes snap up to mine, blazing. 'You promised,' he says, his lower lip quivering. 'You promised you'd look after me, you and Finn. You said you wouldn't let the bad people get me! You said!'

I fling my arms round him and hug him tight. 'I won't, I won't, I never will,' I tell him. 'I promise, Mouse, never!'

When we pull apart, he looks at me so sadly that I wonder if Mouse's 'bad people' really are the lowlifes and the thieves I imagined. Maybe not. Maybe it's not that simple. Maybe they're the people trying to help, like the nice social worker with the trendy specs and the wide grin, sitting on a bench with his newspaper.

'It'll be OK, Mouse,' I tell him.

He nods, trying for a smile, acting brave.

'They washed my mouse,' he says, holding out a pale, battered, unrecognizable toy. 'He's not the same any more. D'you want him?'

'Really?'

'Really. So you won't forget me.'

'Oh, Mouse, how could I?'

I take the toy mouse, anyway. It's still kind of scorched all down one side, from the bonfire.

'Hey, watch out!'

We turn just in time to see Leggit racing towards us, a streak of black and white, tail waving like a flag. She circles Mouse, yelping wildly, then leaps up and topples him on to the grass, licking his face, making muddy pawprints on his new grey sweatshirt.

'Leggit! Bad girl! Hey, hey!' Mouse laughs, and he hugs her, ruffling her raggedy fur, patting her skinny ribs. He hangs on for ages, hiding his face in her fur, and when he comes up for air, his cheeks are streaked with tears.

'Got something in my eye,' he says gruffly.

'Yeah, I know, little mate,' Finn says, dragging a sleeve across his face. 'Me, too.'

So I'm back in the land of stripy school ties and maths tests and shared Cokes, of hot showers and takeaway pizzas and Sky TV. I walk around the flat barefoot, letting my toes sink into the soft carpet, wishing it was cool grass, hot sand, scratchy shells. I open windows and breathe in exhaust fumes, pollution, the thump of a ghetto blaster from across the road.

After Christmas, Lucy moves into the flat. I don't mind as much as I thought I would.

She fills the bathroom with fruity shower gels and scented candles and soap that smells like coconut ice. When Dad's working late in the workshop, we watch slushy films and eat toffee popcorn and do each other's hair. The models he makes of elves and fairies and sad-faced mermaids all start to look a bit like Lucy. It's OK.

Jade and Sara and Sasha pump me for information about Finn.

'Are you in love?' Sasha wants to know. 'Or was it just a crush?'

I laugh. 'Don't know about love. It's just – he's my best friend. Apart from you guys, of course!'

Or maybe even including.

'Did you kiss him?' Jade demands.

'Like I'm gonna tell *you* that!'

'You did! She did!' Sara squeals, and they collapse in hysterics, making kissy-kissy noises and fluttering their lashes.

One day, when I'm feeling brave, I show them the pictures I took with the camera Lucy gave me. There's Tess, in a flower crown, looking up from the Calor gas stove outside the tent. There's Zak, juggling batons in the veggie patch at Bramble Cottage, and Storm, her face a swirl of pink and purple face paint, sticking her tongue out at the camera.

And there's Finn, cradling my guitar on the sand at Ayr beach; Finn sitting by the waterfall; Finn's face, close-up and crusted with sand, his eyes the same colour as the turquoise ocean.

'He's cool,' Jade says. 'Weird, but cool.'

'Amazing eyes,' Sara breathes.

'And hair,' says Sasha. 'I wonder if he'll be famous one day? And you can say you knew him.'

When we get to the last photo, Mouse and

Leggit cuddled up in the tree house, the breath catches in my throat.

'Funny little kid,' says Jade.

'Cute,' says Sasha, not meaning it.

Sara, who knows how I feel about Mouse, squeezes my arm. 'He's OK, Dizz,' she tells me. 'You said so yourself. Maybe you'll get to go down and see him next year?'

'Maybe.'

Mouse has settled in really well with his new foster parents. He sees his real mum most weekends. She's out of the clinic now, and off the drugs, but she's not ready to look after Mouse again, not yet. I wonder how he feels about that? I wonder if he still has nightmares, cries in his sleep? It's not the kind of thing you can ask on the phone.

He's going to school and learning to read and write, anyway.

'Still practising your juggling?' I asked, last time I called. 'And the BMX stunts?'

There was a silence.

'I've got a GameBoy,' he said uncertainly.

'Oh. Right. That's great, Mouse.'

'Does Leggit miss me?' he asked then, all in a rush.

'Oh, Mouse, of course she does. Who's gonna feed her Mars bars and cold chips when you're not around? She misses you every day. We all do.'

Sometimes, every couple of months, I get a little parcel from Mouse, addressed to me in his foster mum's neat, sloping handwriting – a Mars bar, sometimes squashed, sometimes not. I never really know if it's for me or for Leggit, so we share it, half each.

Leggit lives with us, now.

Tess couldn't keep her because of the way she chased the goat and the cat and the chickens, the way she raced circuits round the garden, crashing through the flower beds, tearing up the lettuce plants. 'I will if I have to, of course, but . . .'

'Why should you?' Dad had argued. 'Storm should have thought. All her life she's left a trail of hurt and mess behind her.'

'Shhh,' Tess said, looking at me. Like it was something I didn't already know.

'Will Leggit have to go to the dog's home?' I asked Dad.

'No,' he'd said firmly. 'No way. Leggit's coming home with us.'

She did.

The spiky, excitable festival dog who stole your chips and knocked you over with her tail is gone forever. Leggit gets brushed every day, so her hair is soft and clean and fluffy. She wears a red leather collar and walks on a lead without pulling. She has two big meals and never scrounges in between.

Dad takes her to dog-training classes, and now she can sit, lie, stay, walk to heel.

She is a reformed character. Just occasionally, when she's lying upside down on the white, fluffy rug by the fire, her legs in the air, I think I catch a glimpse of her wicked, wolfish side. Maybe, when we visit Finn and Tess this summer, it'll surface again.

We're all going, Dad and Lucy and Leggit and me. We've tried to arrange for Mouse to come out, too, but his foster parents aren't too keen. I guess I can see their point of view. They probably think it's some mad hippy commune where kids run wild and dangerous accidents lurk round every corner. How could you ever explain to them that it's the one place Mouse was truly happy?

Dad and Lucy have bought a tent specially – a big, fancy one with two bedrooms and a flashy porch at the front. We're going as soon as school is over, and that's not long, now.

Tomorrow is my birthday.

We're changing the tradition – we're going out for a meal, Dad and Lucy and me, then on to the multiplex to see a film. Things evolve, Dad says. They can't stay the same forever, they change the same way we do.

My room is different, too – the pinboard shrine full of treasures is gone. I packed away the doll, the hat, the postcards. I still have them, but I don't have them on show. I wrapped up the dream-catcher and sent it to Mouse. I reckon he needs all the help he can get, these days.

Now, my pinboard holds the photo of Finn with turquoise eyes, the snap of Mouse and Leggit in the tree house, a whole strip of Jade and Sasha and Sara and me, pulling scary faces, taken at a photo booth in town. Also skewered on are a Mars bar wrapper, a lime-green and black bootlace, a broken daisy chain, a small, faded, slightly toasted toy mouse. Bits of my life, things that make me smile.

A handful of envelopes sit on my bedside table, cards waiting to be opened tomorrow. One from Tess, one from Finn, with a small, hard bumpy shape inside that might be a bracelet. There's a jiffy bag with a London postmark and a Mars bar kind of feel to it, addressed for the first time in Mouse's own big, wobbly writing.

Nothing from Storm. Why am I surprised?

She wrote at Christmas, anyhow, so I guess I can't complain. She sent me a length of sari fabric, purple silk shot through with silver threads. I've hung it at my bedroom window, along with the flowery fairy lights that used to drape round the pinboard.

*Dizzy, babe,* she wrote,

Hope you like the sari. Someone gave it to me, but it's silk, and vegans don't wear silk, so I thought of you. You'd love Goa, Dizz, I wish your Dad would loosen up a bit and let you come stay. We'd have the wildest time. Zak says hi. We're sitting on the beach, listening to rave music, just smoking and watching the stars above a silver sea. How cool is that?

Love,

Storm xxxxx

It's cool, Storm, pretty cool. Maybe I will go, one day.

Maybe not.

I switch the light off, slip into bed.

The breeze rustles the purple silk, and beyond it I see the night sky, mottled orange from the city's streetlamp glow. If Storm looks up from her beach in Goa, she'll see the Pole Star, hanging there in the velvet dark. If Finn looks out of his window in Lancashire, he'll see it, too. Mouse, in London, won't even be looking.

I'm looking, though. All I see is the orange glow, the soft, bruised shimmer of city sky. I can't see the Pole Star, but I can feel it, dream it.

I know it's there.

# Thanks!

To Catriona, who told me to stop daydreaming and start writing – and gave great feedback and advice. To Liam, for putting up with my stressy, can't-do-it moments, and Calum and Caitlin, who endured many dinners of peanut butter on toast and were such excellent first readers. Thanks to Mum, Dad, Andy, Lori, Mary-Jane, Fiona, Helen, Kirsty, Sheena, Zarah and all my brilliant friends – for believing in me, even when I didn't. Also to Dr Gill Russell for help with the starry stuff, and to Dr Shelagh Neil for advice on the medical bits.

Thanks to Tallulah and Roxanne, whose enthusiasm helped me to find the best agent in the world, Darley Anderson, and also to Lucie, Julia and everyone at the agency. Last but not least, thanks to Rebecca, Francesca and the whole fab team at Puffin, for making the dream come true.

Hello!

Watch out world - Mouse is back!

When I wrote my first book, *Dizzy*, a few years back, I got so many emails and letters asking for a sequel I couldn't quite believe it. *Lucky Star* is not a sequel exactly - you don't have to have read *Dizzy* to read this book - but it picks up on the story of one of the original characters, Mouse, now that he's fourteen. Mouse didn't get a happy ending in *Dizzy*, but in *Lucky Star* . . . well, you'll have to see!

Mouse is my all-time favourite character from any of the books, so I hope you like him too! He doesn't go looking for trouble, but trouble has a way of finding him all the same. When he falls for a cool, cute, confident girl called Cat, Mouse quickly finds himself not just in trouble, but in danger too. Can he trust his new friend, or is she playing a cat and mouse game that can only end in tears?

*Lucky Star* is a book about friendship, family, fear - and fighting back against injustice to find the magic in life. I think you'll like Mouse's story - it's a rollercoaster ride of drama, love and glad-to-be-alive happiness, set in the shadowy world of a tough inner-city estate. As for luck - you can find it in the most unexpected places!

Keep reading, keep smiling . . . and follow your dreams!

Best Wishes,

Cathy Cassidy x ✿

cathycassidy.com

Flat 114/9
Nightingale House
Eden Estate
Clapham
London SW1

Dear Mr Brown,

I know how mad you are with me right now, and you have every right to be, but I just wanted to say I am really, really sorry. I just didn't think that you'd get so upset about a little bit of paint, but I know better now, obviously.

I don't even know why I did it, except that I like graffiti art and I honestly thought that the wall by the gym could do with brightening up. I guess I was wrong about that. I know now that you prefer that wall to be grey, and that you really didn't like the stars and spirals and rainbows I sprayed all over it.

I admit that writing 'school is cancelled until

further notice' on the wall was not very clever, even though it seemed funny at the time. I'm sorry that some of the kids who saw it decided to use it as an excuse to go right on home. I am also sorry that my spelling wasn't too good, and I know that was what tipped you off that I was to blame. That and the paint on my fingers.

Well, I want you to know I have learnt my lesson. Dave (you remember Dave – my social worker) says I have messed up one time too many, and I need to wise up and make amends or else my school career will be down the pan.

If you like, I will come in to school and paint the whole lot out with grey emulsion paint, so the wall is back to being plain and dull and crumbly. I would have done that already, except for being excluded and everything. Mum says if you see me any time soon with a bucket of paint, you'll most likely call the police, and I guess she has a point.

Anyway, I have turned over a new leaf. I am not going to tag any more walls, unless they are very neglected and really need livening up, and only then if I get permission from the government or something. I am also going to work on my spelling, seriously. If you are wondering how come my spelling is so good in this letter, it's because I did it on Dave's computer and used the spell-check, as I know that stuff like that matters to you.

I know you said that my future at Green Vale Comprehensive is hanging in the balance, but I want you to know that your little talk the other day has really made me think. I didn't say much, but I was taking it all in, I swear. I will be a model pupil from now on. I hope that you will give me one more chance, and I promise never to spray-paint the school again, no matter what.

Yours faithfully,

Mouse (Martin) Kavanagh, Form 9b

Green Vale Comprehensive,
211 Peter Street,
Clapham
London SW1

Dear Martin Kavanagh,

I must inform you that the school has already gone to great trouble and expense to paint out the graffiti in question, so your offer to do so will not be necessary. I feel that you still fail to grasp the seriousness of your repeated acts of vandalism. If there are any further incidents of this kind, you are likely to be looking at an anti-social behaviour order, as well as a permanent exclusion.

As things stand, you remain excluded until the October break. I hope to see a marked improvement in your class work, attitude and behaviour once the new term begins.

Yours sincerely,

Mr T. Brown

Head teacher

'He's not a happy man,' Dave says, reading the letter from my head teacher.

'Never has been,' I shrug. 'He worries too much.'

Dave shoots me a dark look. 'At least they're letting you back into school,' he says. 'Your letter showed maturity, Mouse. You apologized, took responsibility for your actions. You realized you were wrong.'

I take a bite of Mars bar, and grin.

'Mouse?' Dave asks, carefully. 'You do know you were wrong, don't you?'

'C'mon, Dave!' I say. 'It was hardly the crime of the century, was it? It was a joke!'

'A joke?' he echoes. 'Mouse, your idea of a joke happens to be most people's idea of mindless vandalism!'

'Mindless? C'mon! That wall looked a whole lot better once I'd tagged it – they should have given me a grant for improving the environment or something.'

Dave clenches his teeth, as if he's in pain. He peers at me over the top of his trendy black specs with sorrowful green eyes. 'Mouse, don't you ever learn?' he asks. 'It wasn't easy to persuade Mr Brown to keep the police out of this. You don't need me to tell you what that would have meant . . . you already have a police record.'

'Not a bad one!' I argue. 'Just for tagging a bus stop!'

Dave shakes his head. 'I'm not kidding, Mouse – you can't pull any more stunts like this. Every time things start going well for you, you do something stupid and mess it all up. I'm beginning to think it's a cry for help!'

I just about choke on my Mars bar. 'A cry for help? Are you serious?'

Social workers always think there's a deep, dark reason lurking behind everything you do – some buried trauma that only a psychologist can dig out of you. Bite your nails? You obviously had a deprived childhood. Wear your fringe too long? Must be hiding something. Don't like carrots? Man, you're just about ready for the nut house.

Dave sits back on his trendy black swivel chair, smoothing down his Nirvana T-shirt and crossing his legs in ancient, faded bootleg jeans. He thinks this kind of stuff makes him look cool, friendly, accessible. I think it makes him look like a sad old loser.

'It wasn't a cry for help,' I say. 'It was art!'

'Hmphh,' he says. 'Well. The next time you're feeling arty, buy yourself a sketchbook.'

I laugh out loud. The things I want to say just won't fit between the pages of a sketchbook – they need to be painted six feet tall, by moonlight, with your heart beating fast and your mouth dry with fear.

'Why, Mouse?' Dave asks, giving me this full-on, sad-eyed stare. 'I just don't understand why.'

Dave has this whole range of disappointed, guilt-trip looks he likes to wind me up with, but I refuse to feel bad. I paint on walls because it makes me feel good. That's as much as I'm going to admit – to anyone.

I'm not about to go digging around in the past for a bunch of deep, dark reasons for why I'm not perfect. It's just not up for discussion – all the bad memories are packed away in boxes I'll never need to open again. Start looking at all that and I'd unravel faster than a sweater with a hole in. Seriously – it's just not happening.

Dave shakes his head. 'Out of here, Mouse,' he says. 'Time's up, and we're getting nowhere. At least the school have agreed to take you back after the October break – I suggest you use this time off to reflect. You need to make some changes – and fast.'

I stand up, shrug on my zip-up hoodie.

'Thanks for your support and understanding,' I say brightly. 'It means a lot.'

Dave rakes a hand through his hair, exasperated. 'I'm on your side, Mouse,' he says heavily. 'If I get hacked off with you sometimes . . . well, it's because I care.'

That's a laugh. Dave may act like my favourite cheesy uncle, but he's not. He is a social worker – my own personal social worker. It's his job to look out for me, to keep me out of trouble, even though he is clearly not too good at it. He is paid to care.

The way I see it, that just doesn't count.

I scuff my way out of the office, leaving Dave with his head in his hands. Out in the waiting room, a girl looks up from her magazine as I emerge, a pretty, mixed-race girl with honey-coloured skin and slanting eyes. She smiles at me, a long, lazy smile.

'He is not in a good mood,' I tell her, by way of a warning.

'Is he ever?'

She unfolds her long, tawny legs and stands up slowly, like some kind of schoolgirl supermodel. She's in uniform, one of those posh-school jobs, but she looks cool – she's the kind of girl who could probably look cool wearing a potato sack. Her black beret sits rakishly above a mass of golden-brown hair that falls in corkscrew curls to her shoulders.

She looks exotic, somehow, a world apart from the girls at Green Vale Comp, who chew gum with their mouths open and wear their trousers slung low and their heels slung high. This girl is wearing a little green pleated skirt, knee-length grey socks and flat shoes. You wouldn't think that could be cute, but I'm telling you, it can.

'Wish me luck,' she says, throwing me a wink as she disappears into Dave's office.

'Good luck,' I say, even though I haven't believed in luck since my dad left, back when I was seven years old. For her, maybe, I'd reconsider.

I've seen all sorts of kids in the waiting room outside Dave's office over the years, kids who look lost, kids who look lonely, kids who look rough, tough, bad, sad, mad. I've never seen one like her before, though, a girl who looks like she could wrap the world round her little finger, then put it in her pocket for later. I can't help wondering what her story is – how come she's washed up here, in the Clapham Youth Outreach Unit, with dodgy Dave as her official guardian angel?

One thing's for sure – nobody ever had an appointment to see Dave because their life was going great. Kind of tragic, really.

I've discovered that the best way to tag a wall and get away with it is to look calm, cool and totally relaxed, like you have every right in the world to have a spray can in your hand and a piece of brand-new graffiti art in front of you. Often, people will give you a puzzled look, like you can't really be serious, but mostly they will carry on walking. In London, people don't go looking for trouble.

Even so, I don't often have the bottle to make a hit in broad daylight. It's five, and the street is busy, but Dave kind of got to me a little bit and I want to have the last word. The last picture, even.

I sit down on the steps of the Clapham Youth Outreach Centre, rooting around in my bag for some paint. I mean, you have to be prepared, don't you? In case of emergencies.

I watch the people go by for a minute or two, shoppers and workers and schoolkids, and then I turn to face the dull brown doorway behind me, shake the can and start to spray.

It's an old red can and it leaks a little on to my fingers, but that's OK. I'm not trying to hide anything. It doesn't take more than a minute. A fuzzy little heart shape, two dots for eyes and round, cartoon ears. A nose and whiskers. A mouse – my mark.

Nobody stops me, nobody shouts at me, nobody reports me to the police. I put the lid on my spray can, stand up and stroll along to the chippy on Clapham High Street, smiling.

There is nothing quite as good as hot chips drenched in salt and vinegar and tomato ketchup, especially eaten straight from the paper with paint-stained fingers. I'm halfway along the street and halfway through my chips when a small, scruffy, skinny dog appears at my heels. He trots alongside, looking up at me with liquid brown eyes. He's a grubby white colour with a black patch over one eye, like a small pirate, with a filthy red neckerchief tied round his neck in place of a collar. He's after my chips.

'Hey, pal,' I say, offering the dog one perfect, golden chip. He leaps up and takes it from my fingers, fast and graceful, and I swear I can see him grinning.

I like dogs. I used to have one, once – well, she wasn't mine, exactly, but still. Long time ago now. This dog is smaller, smoother and much, much dirtier. He looks like he hasn't eaten in a week, so I feed him chip after chip as we walk along the pavement together. Then all the chips are finished, and the dog's grin slips. He looks desolate.

'No more,' I explain, scrunching the greasy paper into a ball and chucking it at the nearest bin. I miss. The scrunched-up chip paper lands in the gutter, and a gust of wind steers it out into the road. Like a flash, the dog is after it, ducking between a couple of slow-moving cars.

'No!' I shout. 'Come back! Here, boy!'

Time slows down, the way it sometimes does in dreams or on TV. The dog is in the middle of the road. A motorcyclist brakes and swerves to avoid him. My heart thumps, and I stick my fingers in my mouth and whistle, the way my dad taught me once, a long, ear-splitting call, surprisingly loud.

A girl passing by on a bicycle turns to look at me, her hair flying out behind her in golden-brown corkscrew curls. She's the cool girl, the cute girl, from Dave's office. Her startled eyes are green and slanted, like a cat.

The next second she lands in a heap on the pavement in front of me, the bike beneath her. Spreadeagled on the flagstones, under the spinning bicycle wheel, is the small white dog with the pirate patch.

'Omigod, omigod, I didn't see it!' the girl is wailing. 'It just ran right out in front of me . . .'

She drags the bike to one side, and I drop to my knees beside the little pirate dog. He takes a shallow, gasping breath like he's just hanging on by a thread, then his eyes flutter closed and he lies absolutely still.

I think I've killed him.

Some days have disaster printed all over them, right from the start – quite a few of my days, actually. This one, though, is an all-time low. I reach out and touch the dirty, matted fur of the little pirate dog. My fingers are stained with red paint from the spray can, which makes me look like a murderer.

Beneath my palm I feel the faint quiver of a heartbeat. The dog gives a dramatic sigh and his eyes flutter open. I take a deep breath in, weak with relief.

'I am so, sooooooo sorry!' the bicycle girl is saying. 'You just totally spooked me with that whistle. I took my eyes off the road for, like, one millisecond, and the next thing . . .' A fat, salty tear slides down her cheek.

'S'OK,' I tell her. 'Don't cry. He's alive, see?'

Her misty green eyes connect with mine for a moment. She looks younger now, less confident, wiping her eyes on the back of a blazer sleeve and smudging her eyeliner.

A small crowd has gathered around us. We are blocking the pavement, a fallen bike, a green-eyed girl, a dog at death's door and me.

People lean in around us, helping the girl to her feet, checking the bike over. 'All right, love?' a woman with a pushchair asks the girl. 'Not hurt, are you?'

'I'm fine,' the girl says shakily. 'But the little dog . . .'

'A stray, by the look of him,' says the pushchair woman.

'Best phone the council,' someone else suggests. 'They'll take him away, put him out of his misery . . .'

'Out of his misery?' the bicycle girl splutters. 'You can't!'

They can, though. They're people in a hurry, on their way back from bigshot city jobs or busy shopping trips, home to their perfect little families. They don't have time for this. I keep my palm flat against the warm, dirty-white fur of the little pirate dog, just above his heart. It keeps on beating.

'He's not a stray, OK?' I say, calmly but clearly. 'He's mine. So if you all just want to push off . . .'

'Well!' The crowd around us take a tiny step back. One by one, they edge off along the street, muttering about ungrateful kids and dangerous, flea-bitten mongrels.

We've been abandoned.

The girl looks furious. 'What's wrong with people?' she howls. 'Don't they care?'

'Not especially.' I take off my hoodie, wrap the injured dog in it and stand up carefully, holding the bundle close. 'So what? I don't need them.' I stride off along the pavement, and the girl grabs her bike and follows, weaving in and out of the passing shoppers.

Great. A posh girl in a scary school uniform, trailing along behind me.

I look down at the face of the little pirate dog, pressed flat against my chest. His eyes are closed again, his grin fixed and rigid. His heartbeat is steady beneath my palm, but still, I walk a little faster.

'Where are you going, anyway?' the girl asks. 'If you're looking for the nearest vet, you've missed the turning. It was just back there.'

I stop abruptly, frowning. She's right – I have no idea where I'm going. 'OK. Sorry.' I try for a smile. 'Show me. Please?'

The girl wheels round and turns down to the left, and I follow.

'Is he really your dog?' she wants to know. 'I thought he was a stray too.'

I sigh. 'He's mine now, anyhow. Someone has to look out for him.'

'He might be lost, though,' she points out. 'Someone could be looking for him right now, wondering if he's OK.'

I hold the dog tighter. I don't think there's anyone out there worrying about him, somehow. He's small and skinny and sad, like a ghost-dog. He looks like he lives on the streets, getting by on his wits, chasing chip papers, stealing scraps. He doesn't look loved.

'What're you gonna call him?' the girl wants to know. 'He needs a name.'

'I'll think of one,' I say.

'How about Chip?' she offers. 'Or Patch, or Scruff? Hey, I don't even know your name, do I? Mine's Cat.'

'You're kidding, right?' I say.

'No – Cat, short for Catrin, but only my parents call me that. Cat is better.'

I laugh out loud.

'It's not that bad!' she says, huffily. 'What's yours, anyway?'

'It's . . . well, it's a nickname, really, but everybody calls me it, ever since I was little. It's . . .'

'Yeah?'

'Mouse.'

Laughter explodes from her soft, pink mouth like

the fizz from a can of Coke. 'Mouse?' she snorts. 'Mouse?'

I crack a grin. 'Well, it says Martin on my birth certificate, but no one ever, ever calls me that,' I say. 'Except my teachers and stuff, when they're trying to be snotty.'

'So why Mouse?' she wants to know.

I shrug. 'Mum says it's because I was small and quick and quiet. Or maybe because I have mousy hair and a serious addiction to cheese and chocolate. Either way, I've been stuck with it all my life.'

'Cat and Mouse,' she says, grinning. 'That's cool!'

The skinny little stray is stretched out on the examining table, eyelids fluttering. His coat looks dull and grey under the bright lights, and his ribs stick out like the keys on a xylophone. The vet says he'll keep him in, do some X-rays, run some tests.

'It's not just the accident,' the vet says, frowning. 'He's in very poor condition.'

'I haven't had him long,' I say. 'He was a stray, before. He just came up to me in the street.'

'About twenty minutes ago,' Cat chips in, and I roll my eyes up to the ceiling.

'Ah,' says the vet. 'That makes sense. He's very weak and thin, and in shock, obviously. This leg is quite swollen – the X-rays will tell whether it's a break or a sprain. Overall, I'd say he's been lucky.'

This is one of the reasons I find it hard to believe in luck. A small, scruffy, half-starved dog gets squashed by a bicycle, and I'm meant to be grateful because it wasn't a motorbike or a bin lorry?

'Lucky?' I echo. 'Yeah, right.'

As I speak, the little pirate dog pricks up his ears, raises his head and looks at me intently. His mouth twitches into a shaky grin.

'Lucky?' I repeat, and the little dog beats his tail against the examining table like it's Christmas or something. I turn to Cat. 'See that?' I tell her. 'That's his name. Lucky!'

'Yeah?' she says. 'Well. He probably needs all the luck he can get.'

I stroke Lucky's ears softly, and he sighs and lowers his head again, still grinning. 'So when can I collect him?' I ask. 'Take him home?'

The vet looks puzzled. 'He's a stray – don't feel you have to take him. I'll ring the dog's home, once I've fixed him up a bit. They'll look after him, see if he can be re-homed.'

'No chance,' I say. 'Like I said, he's mine.'

The vet scratches his head. 'That's very commendable, of course,' he says. 'If you're serious, you could call back tomorrow afternoon, see how he is. Take some time to think about it.'

'Don't need to think about it,' I tell him. 'I'll be here.'

'We both will,' Cat says.

'You're certain you can offer him a good home?' the vet presses, looking at me doubtfully. 'Your family won't object?'

It depends what his idea of a good home is, of course. The ninth floor of a high-rise on the Eden Estate might not be exactly what he has in mind.

'I'm certain,' I say. 'And my mum'll be fine with it.'

'It's not quite that simple,' the vet says. 'The dog's home would normally pay his vet's bill, but if you take him, that bill becomes your responsibility. It won't be cheap.'

My heart sinks to the bottom of my battered Converse trainers. Money? It feels like a ransom demand.

'You're saying I can't get him back until I cough up a wad of cash?' I demand. 'What are you? A kidnapper or a vet?'

'Is money a problem?' he asks, and I want to punch him.

'No problem at all,' Cat cuts in, smoothly. 'We'll pay. Thank you for all your help! See you tomorrow!'

She grabs my arm and drags me to the door. I crane my head round for a last glimpse of Lucky, but his eyes are closed now, his breathing slow and steady. He doesn't even know he's been kidnapped.

'What are you on?' Cat hisses, the minute we get out the door. 'You can't go around insulting people like that. We'll get the money, OK?'

'How?' I want to know. 'I have 73p to my name.'

'Rich and good-looking, huh?' she jokes, and her green eyes are laughing. If I didn't know better, I'd think she was flirting with me, but posh schoolgirls don't flirt with kids like me. Do they?

'I'll get the money,' she says. 'Easy. I'll meet you here tomorrow afternoon, yeah? What time?'

I think of Lucky, lying there on the examining table, waiting to be ransomed. 'Half nine?' I suggest. 'Ten?'

Cat laughs. 'OK . . . so that's, like, early afternoon, huh?'

I look at her blazer, her tartan pleated skirt. She'll be in school at ten, obviously, studying French irregular verbs or rainfall in the Kalahari desert, or whatever they do at those posh places. She's not excluded, like me. 'Too early?' I ask, curling my lip. 'Gonna be in trouble at school?'

'No, no . . . but d'you think the vet will have had time to run all his tests and stuff?' She's unchaining her bike from the railings, wheeling it to the kerb. Any minute now she'll cycle right out of my life, and I'm kidding myself if I think she'll turn up tomorrow with a handful of cash.

'Mouse?' she prompts.

I scowl, because there's no way I want her to see how I'm feeling. I find a dog, a funny little pirate dog. I give him a chip and the next thing I know he gets squashed flat by a bicycle, and it's all my fault. OK, I got him to the vet, but I can't get him back without a miracle or a handout. I look at Cat from behind my fringe, trying for a smile, but she's not fooled.

'Ten o'clock then,' she says, pulling her beret down, flicking a curl from her face.

'I just want to know he got through the night OK, y'know?' I tell her. 'It was my fault, wasn't it? With the chip paper and the whistle and everything. I feel responsible.'

'You were trying to help him,' she says. 'We're in it together.'

I like the idea of that. 'OK,' I tell her. 'Thanks.'

She still doesn't move, just looks at me with those big green eyes until I think I might forget how to breathe. I tilt my chin and stare right back, scuffing the pavement with the toe of my trainers.

'Look, Mouse,' she says, eventually. 'We haven't got all night. Are you walking me home, or what?'

Actually, she cycles and I run along the pavement beside her, grinning all over my face. We cut across the park and turn into a quiet, tree-lined street. Cat slows a little, freewheeling, studying me. 'How old are you, anyhow?' she asks.

I think about lying, but I'm small and skinny, so there's not much point. 'Fourteen,' I tell her. 'Year Nine.'

'Me too!' she grins. 'Got a girlfriend?'

My heart thumps. 'Not right now.'

Not ever, unless you count Neela Rehman, who dated me for two whole days back in Year Five, in the days when dating just involved lots of smiling and sharing your Mars bar at playtime. I have a sneaky feeling that might have been the attraction. On the third day, I had no money for a Mars bar, and Neela dumped me. She said she'd fallen in love with that blonde-haired guy off *Blue Peter*, but I saw her later in the week, batting her eyes at Liam Gilligan, who had a bag of chocolate caramels.

'OK,' Cat says. 'Good.'

I grin. 'Yeah? You interested?'

'Might be,' she says. 'Might not. I'll think about it.'

So will I. Sheesh, I'll probably dream about it too.

'How about school?' Cat wants to know. 'Don't you just hate it?'

I think of Green Vale Comprehensive, with its eight-foot fences topped with razor wire, its blank, grey, crumbling buildings. It looks more like a detention centre than a school, or a prisoner-of-war camp left over from the Second World War. My mate Fitz once found an ancient, yellow-paged history textbook held together with sellotape, with his grandad's name in the front, dated 1971. Seriously.

'I go to Green Vale Comp,' I tell her. 'It's a dump.'

Her eyes shine. 'Isn't that the place where the kids carry knives in the corridor and they can't get the teachers to stay for more than a week?'

'Uh? No, no, you're way out. The kids carry iPods and most of the teachers have been there since the Dark Ages. Seriously. It's got a bad reputation, though, I guess.'

'I wish I went somewhere cool like that,' Cat sighs. 'I want fun and excitement, not netball and maths tests and diagrams of the digestive system.'

'You wouldn't like Green Vale,' I tell her. 'Trust me. Fun and excitement are not on the timetable.'

'They would be if I was there,' she says.

That makes me smile. We stop in front of a tall, Victorian terraced house with climbing roses around the front door. 'So,' she says. 'Coming in?'

She wheels her bike through the gate and up the little path, turning her key in the lock. Me, I'm still stranded on the pavement trying to take in the shiny blue front door with a stained-glass picture of a sunrise, the bay windows, the way the red-and-yellow brickwork has been arranged to make a pattern all around the doorway. I count the windows going up. Three storeys.

'It's OK,' Cat says over her shoulder. 'Dad works late on a Thursday, and Mum's at her yoga class.'

Inside, the house smells of freshly ground coffee and furniture polish, and I take a deep breath, letting it all sink in. The Eden Estate smells like burnt tyres and pee in the lifts, and that's on a good day. There's a full-length mirror in the hallway, and I catch a glimpse of a wide-eyed kid with a dipping emo fringe, stripy top and skinny jeans. The back of my hair, razored short, is sticking

up in clumps like I just spent the night in a hedge.
I look shifty, guilty, awkward. I look like trouble.

I haven't a clue what Cat sees in me.

She leans her bike against an antique bookshelf
stuffed with more books than I've ever seen, then
kicks off her shoes and pads through to the kitchen.
'Drink?' she says.

The kitchen is almost as big as our whole flat.
Cat's pouring us fresh orange juice from a fridge
the size of a wardrobe. I can't stop staring. I peer
into the half-open dishwasher, switch the retro radio
CD on and then off again, and sniff at the big vase
of roses in the middle of the kitchen table. Then
I fling myself down on the big red sofa, bouncing
up and down.

'Who has a settee in their kitchen?' I ask, amazed.
'And a telly?'

'Well, we do. Obviously.'

I shake my head. How come some people have
so much?

'Knew you were a rich kid,' I say at last.

Cat looks defensive. 'Not rich,' she argues. 'Not
really. Rich people live in stately homes and have
their own private jets, don't they? They wear
designer clothes and jewels at the breakfast table.
We're not rich, but we're OK, I suppose. Mum
and Dad have good jobs.'

I open a cupboard and find glass jars filled with

funny shapes of pasta, tins of Italian tomatoes, jars of things I've never heard of in my life. I try the fridge, which is stuffed with green salad and Greek yoghurt and weird salami sausages and stinky cheese. 'What are they?' I ask, doubtfully, sniffing at a bowl of what looks like small, shiny animal droppings.

'Black olives,' Cat says. 'Try one.'

'Urghhh!' I have to spit it out into my hand. Cat's family must be loaded. You'd think they'd be able to afford Coke and oven chips and plain old orange cheese, and a rug for the floorboards that isn't threadbare in the middle. Still, I guess they like all that stuff. The rug is probably ancient and valuable, woven in Afghanistan by tribes of nomadic goatherds or something.

'You're rich,' I tell her. 'Don't kid yourself.'

'It's not my fault!' Cat says. 'I didn't ask for middle-class, *Guardian*-reading parents, did I? Everything has to be organic and fairly traded and politically correct. It drives me mad!'

I look out of the kitchen window on to a small garden, lit up in a pool of light. I try to imagine Lucky rooting around the neat flower beds and the green velvet lawn, lifting his leg to pee against the rustic bird table. I can't. My mum would love a patch of garden like this – she'd have the whole thing bursting with colour, dig up the lawn to grow vegetables, train apple trees and jasmine all around the walls.

'I hate this place,' Cat says, her green eyes dark with feeling, and I wonder how she can hate something that seems like heaven to me.

'Swap you then,' I tell her. 'Any day. Life's one big lucky dip, isn't it? You got something cool wrapped in shiny paper, I got the sawdust from the bottom of the barrel.'

She laughs. 'Sawdust? Yeah, right. It can't be that bad. What, d'you live in a cardboard box or something?'

'High-rise block, Eden Estate,' I say bleakly. 'Ninth floor.'

'Wow!' she breathes, which isn't exactly the reaction I was expecting.

Everyone's heard of the Eden Estate – it's a rabbit warren of crumbling high-rise blocks just five minutes walk from here. It might as well be a whole different planet. It's in the paper just about every week. Joyriding, drug dealing, mugging, vandalism – it all happens where I live. At night you can see the helicopters circling round above, like noisy vultures, their searchlights raking through the dark.

'I've never met anyone who lived there before,' Cat says, her eyes shining. 'Cool.'

I roll my eyes. The Eden Estate is not cool – it's a hole, a delapidated, bottom-of-the-pile dumping ground for people who have nowhere else to go. Half the flats are boarded up and derelict, the rest are damp and scummy and falling to bits. People don't choose to live there – they move in until something better comes along, and then they get stuck. It drags them down.

There's a small, stubborn part of me that's proud of the place, though. I've lived there since I was eight years old, and I've survived – just about. Eden made me streetwise, made me tough. It's a mess – but at least it's my mess.

'It's OK,' I tell her. 'Not cool, but you can get by.'

'So where do you live, exactly?' Cat presses.

'Nightingale House, ninth floor,' I say, then stop short. 'Don't even think about visiting, OK? It's dodgy if you don't know what you're doing. I mean it, Cat.'

'You worry too much!' She slides on to the sofa next to me, looking at me closely like I'm some fascinating specimen of insect she has under a magnifying glass.

'I like you, Mouse,' she says. 'You're funny. And cute.'

I try not to panic as she slides an arm along the back of the sofa, because things never got this far with Neela Rehman, back in Year Five, and I'm way out of my depth.

Out in the hallway, the front door slams and Cat jumps across the room like she's just been scalded.

'Cat?' calls a woman's voice. 'Is that you? I thought you'd still be at drama club! I forgot my yoga mat, so . . . oh! Who's this?'

A small, striking black woman stands in the kitchen doorway, eyes narrowed. She looks at me like I'm a lump of chewing gum stuck to her shoe, or maybe something worse.

'Hello. I'm Mia, Catrin's mum. And you are . . .?'

'Just leaving,' I say, standing up quickly.

'His name is Ben,' Cat says quickly. 'Ben . . . Smith.'

I grin. I've never heard of Ben Smith, but he's obviously more acceptable to Cat's mum than I am.

'Well, Ben.' She looks me up and down, eyes lingering on my bird's-nest hair and trailing bootlaces. I feel like I should grab a comb and start saving up for a suit right away. 'I take it you're at drama club together?' she asks.

'Er . . .'

'That's right,' Cat says. 'We're working on a new play, in pairs . . .'

'Oh? What play?' She's looking right at me with dark, suspicious eyes, and my mind goes blank.

'*Shrek?*' I suggest.

'*Hamlet*,' Cat corrects me, but her mum is unimpressed.

'It's, like, a postmodern version of Shakespeare,' Cat gabbles. 'A sort of fusion of two opposing styles. All the main characters are played by trolls and donkeys . . .'

'Yeah,' I cut in, before she has a chance to dig herself in any deeper. 'It was cool. Anyway, Mrs . . . erm, Mia. I have to go now. Nice meeting you!'

'What about your play?' she calls after me, an edge of sarcasm in her voice, but I'm off, hands in pockets, sloping up the garden path, on my way home to a whole different planet.

It's ten past ten, and still there's no sign of Cat. I shouldn't have expected it, really, not after last night. I could see what her mum thought – she looked at me and she smelt trouble, the way other people might smell Tesco Value Shampoo.

Cat'll be in school right now, telling her stuck-up mates about the boy she met from the Eden Estate who'd never even seen an olive before. Me, I'm sitting on the steps outside the vet's with 73p to my name. I have a plan, though. I'm going to go in, see how Lucky is, then ask the vet to give me more time to pay the bill. I'll wash his car for him, or clean out his hamster cages, mop the floors. Whatever it takes. How much can a vet's bill actually be?

'Hey!' Cat is waving from the other side of the road. I fight back the grin that's threatening to take over my face, and get up lazily, hands in pockets.

She's not in school uniform today, and she looks at least sixteen. She's wearing a short black sweater-dress over footless tights, a studded belt hanging slantwise over her hips. A black beanie hat is pulled down over her corkscrew hair. She crosses the road and comes towards me, and I fall for her honey-brown skin and emerald eyes all over again. I don't want her to know that, though.

'What took you so long?' I ask. 'D'you think of a way to pay the bill?'

'Of course,' she says. 'I told you, didn't I? Not a problem.'

We go inside, and the vet lets us go through to the back where Lucky is asleep in a big metal cage. He looks like he's in prison.

'He looks thinner,' I say, but apparently Lucky ate a good meal last night, and slept well.

'He's doing fine,' the vet says. 'We'll do the X-rays later, and fix that leg up. He should be ready to collect at evening surgery, if you're still sure . . .'

'I'm sure.'

'And the bill?'

I don't blame him for being suspicious. I wouldn't trust us, either. 'We can pay now, if you like,' Cat says, bringing out a roll of money.

The vet raises an eyebrow, taps something into his computer, then prints out a bill and hands it over. 'I'm charging you for the X-rays and the medication,' he says. 'But not the overnight stay.

Just don't tell anyone – they'll think I'm a total pushover.'

'Thanks!' I grin, and then I look at the bill and see that it's still £108, so that wipes the smile off my face pretty quickly. Cat doesn't even flinch, just hands over the money with a smile.

'See ya later, kid,' she says to Lucky, and I wink at him, because you can't stroke a dog through the bars of a cage. We promise to be back by seven o'clock surgery.

That's a lot of time to kill, but Cat's ready for the challenge. Twenty minutes later we are squashed together on a tube train, hurtling through the London Underground on the way to Covent Garden.

'It's not like I normally skive off school,' she tells me. The woman opposite gives her a frowny look, and she lowers her voice.

'I'm doing this for you, Mouse,' she goes on. 'Because you're worried about Lucky and you need cheering up. Besides, I have a French test this afternoon.'

'You're all heart,' I say.

'I know. Anyhow, you're bunking off too.'

I laugh. 'I'm not skiving, I'm excluded.'

The woman opposite chokes on her takeaway coffee, but Cat looks entranced. 'Wow!' she says. 'What did you do?'

I lower my voice to a whisper. 'I tagged the wall of my school gym with eight different colours of spray paint.'

'Unreal,' Cat breathes. 'What made you do it?'

That question again. There are a million reasons, all of them true. I thought it would be cool, I thought it would be funny. I wanted to show my art teacher, a wrinkled dinosaur in a tweed suit, that I could draw.

'I was bored,' I say, because that's as good a reason as any.

School – it's enough to make anyone turn vandal. The lessons are pointless and dull, day after day, week after week, year after year, so that in the end you just about lose the will to live. You start dreaming about rebellion, about locking the teachers into the school canteen and force-feeding them lumpy custard while you build a bonfire on the playing fields with every exercise book, every exam paper in the school. Anything, really – anything to kill the boredom, because nothing ever happens at Green Vale Comp.

And then it did, and for five whole minutes I was a king, a hero. In a quiet kind of way, because nobody knew it was me – until Chan noticed the paint on my fingers and pointed out the spelling mistakes and told me to get out of there. I was on my way out of the door, feeling like Van Gogh with a paint can, when Mr Brown grabbed me by the collar and it was all over, my moment of glory, just like that.

'So they excluded you,' Cat says. 'Did the police get involved?'

'No, Dave spoke up for me and the school agreed not to press charges,' I say. 'I had to promise never to do it again.'

'And will you?'

'No chance,' I tell her. 'Caused too much trouble.'

'Yeah?' She sneaks a look at my fingers. They are scrubbed and clean, with just the faintest rim of red around the fingernails.

'Your graffiti days are done?' she checks.

'Definitely.'

'So what about the door of the Youth Outreach Unit, yesterday?' she asks, triumphant. 'A little mouse face, in the corner. I saw it when I was unlocking my bike, and I knew it hadn't been there when I went in. That was you, wasn't it? Had to be.'

'Caught red-handed,' I say.

We get off the tube at Covent Garden, take the lift up to the surface and emerge on to a chaotic street stuffed with tourists and street performers. I'm still trying to take it all in when a tall, dark-haired bloke walks by, flashing us a sparkly-white grin.

'I think I know him,' I say.

Cat rolls her eyes. 'Of course you know him,' she hisses. 'That's Robbie Williams! Don't stare – he'll think you're a fan or something!'

'This place is crazy!'

'You've been here before, right?' she asks. 'You must have!'

I shrug. 'I've heard of it, but . . .'

'Typical,' she says. 'We live right here in London, but when do we ever really explore? That's why skiving off, once in a while, is so cool. You can get to be a tourist for a day. That's what we're going to do!'

We've only gone a few paces when Cat stops, mesmerized by a guy who has sprayed himself silver from head to toe. He stands as still as a statue, while Japanese tourists with fancy cameras take shot after shot.

'Even his nostrils are silver,' she marvels. 'And inside his ears. Do you think he'll ever get it off?'

I think of my own red-stained fingers, and hope that the silver guy used face paint, not aerosol cans. Does painting yourself silver count as an act of mindless vandalism? Probably not. 'Awesome,' Cat says, dropping a pound coin into a bucket at the silver guy's feet. He springs to life, taking a sweeping bow, offering her a long-stemmed silver flower. She takes the flower and blows the silver guy a kiss, laughing.

We move on into the main square. There's a junk market inside a huge, wide building and an outdoor market too, rows of stalls crammed into the courtyard space between the shops. To our right, crowds of people lounge on rows of steps, watching a troupe of acrobats doing handsprings and human pyramids.

Cat is already cruising the stalls, sniffing handmade soaps, tasting samples of fudge. When I approach, the stallholders blank me and move their samples out of reach. Typical. I stand back, admiring Cat's confidence as she chats up the stallholder on a stand selling handmade chocolates, when the breath catches in my throat.

Quickly, carelessly, as the stallholder turns to speak to another customer, Cat picks up a large, ribbon-wrapped box of chocolates and slips it into her bag. It happens so fast I can't quite believe what I've seen. I frown, waiting for her to hand over the money, but she doesn't. She just pops one last sample chocolate into her mouth and moves on through the crowd.

My new friend, the shoplifter.

OK, I knew she was trouble – she wouldn't have been in Dave's office otherwise – but I didn't know what flavour of trouble. There are any amount of reasons why you might end up seeing a social worker. Your life goes out of shape. Your family might be messed up, or missing, or ill. Maybe you're in trouble at school, or with the police. Maybe you steal things.

I used to do it myself, years ago. I took things from shops – sweets, pop, crisps – sometimes because I was hungry, sometimes because I just didn't know any better. I learnt in the end though, and these days I don't take stuff that doesn't belong to me, no matter how tempting it might be.

Cat does. I'm surprised how much this bugs me. I'm sitting on the steps watching the acrobats, when she tracks me down.

'Where d'you go?' she asks. 'I was looking everywhere!'

She sits down beside me. In front of us, one of the performers is juggling beanbags with ribbon tails attached. They make rainbow arcs of colour as they fly through the air. 'Good, huh?' she says.

I blow air out between my lips, unimpressed. 'My dad was a juggler,' I say without thinking. 'He juggled with fire. Better than this lot, by miles.'

'Yeah? What does he do now?'

I shrug. 'Dunno. He never lived with Mum and me – not since I was about two anyhow. I stayed with him one summer, back when I was seven, when Mum was ill. I thought I'd get to know him, but I didn't get the chance. He took off and left me, went to India with his girlfriend and promised to send for me. He never did.'

'Oh, Mouse, I'm sorry.'

Stupid, stupid, stupid. That's what happens when you let the past leak out from the boxes in your head where you've packed it carefully away – people look at you with pity in their eyes, and that's a look I've had enough of. Too late now, though.

'I'm not sorry,' I say, fiercely. 'He was a waste of space. I hardly knew him, y'know?'

Cat looks confused. She has a normal family, after all, even if they are posh. I bet her dad was never a juggler. I bet he never even thought of ditching his kid to run off to India. How could she understand?

'This'll put a smile on your face,' she says gently, taking out the handmade chocolates in their ribbon-wrapped box. 'They're for you.'

'No thanks,' I say.

Her face falls. 'Why not? I thought you'd be pleased!'

'Did you?'

'Mouse, what's up?' she asks. 'What did I do?'

'It's what you didn't do,' I tell her. 'You didn't pay.'

A pink flush darkens Cat's honey-brown cheeks, and her eyes flicker with doubt. 'Of course I did. I –'

'Cat, don't lie to me,' I say. 'I can't stand liars. OK? I saw you.'

'I thought . . . look, it was just a laugh! These stalls must get stuff nicked all the time. They expect it.'

'That doesn't make it right!' I tell her. 'Look, Cat, I don't want you nicking stuff for me, OK? I don't like it.'

Cat pulls a face. 'Sorr-eee,' she says.

'I don't get it,' I say. 'I know you're trouble – you wouldn't have been in Dave's office, otherwise. I'm not judging you, Cat, but seriously, you don't have to steal. You have a nice house, what looks like an OK family. You handed over a hundred quid for that crazy vet's bill, and you didn't even blink. You don't need to steal.'

'I don't even know why I did it. I'm sorry . . .'

'It's wrong. You have to put them back.'

'Mouse, are you crazy?' she yelps. 'I'm sorry I took them, OK? I didn't mean to annoy you. But seriously, no way –'

I grab the chocolates and slide them under my jacket, and walk off into the crowd. When I reach the chocolate stall, I try to look casual, pretending to choose between the prettily arranged boxes. The stallholder watches me, stony-faced. When she turns to serve a customer, I slip the stolen chocolates back on to the tabletop.

'Hey!' the stallholder yells. 'I saw that! What are you doing?'

That wasn't meant to happen. The stallholder is screeching and shaking her fist at me, which seems a little harsh, considering I was replacing a box of chocolates, not nicking one. I don't hang around to argue – I break into a run, elbowing my way through the crowds.

'Stop! Thief!' she shouts, and people turn to stare.

Suddenly Cat appears at my side. She wraps cool brown fingers round my own and tugs me into a quiet side street. We run through on to The Strand, plunge into a crowd of shoppers crossing the busy road. 'There he is!' a voice yells behind me, and Cat drags me down another side street, past walls of shiny plate glass, queues of glossy black cars. She slows to a stroll, tosses her head back and winks at a hotel porter in a fancy coat with a big top hat. He holds open a door and we walk through, and behind us the shouts and hassles fade away.

My feet sink into thick carpet as Cat leads me past a bank of plush sofas and shiny potted palms. 'What is this place?' I ask her.

'The Savoy Hotel,' she whispers.

'Cat!' I hiss at her. 'What are you playing at? We can't –'

'We can! Tea for two, please,' she says, smiling at a stern-faced waiter, who melts visibly. 'Lapsang souchong?'

That last bit sounds like Japanese to me, but the waiter beams at Cat. 'Certainly, Miss,' he says. 'We're not serving our traditional afternoon tea just yet, but I'm sure we can arrange something. If the young man would just remove his hat? We have a dress code, you know.'

He scans my skinny jeans as if looking for holes and rips, but finds nothing. I take off my beanie and he slides his eyes over my chin-length fringe with a despairing sigh. 'Over here, please.' The waiter shows us to a couple of armchairs arranged beneath a big gilt mirror, and we sit down, sinking into the plush velvet.

'We came here for Mum's birthday, last year,'

Cat whispers to me. 'You just have to act confident.'

Acting confident is not an option, but I do my best not to faint in terror as the waiter delivers a silver tray laden with bone-china cups and teapot. Cat grabs a mini-sieve and pours her tea, dropping in a couple of sugar lumps with a pair of silver tongs. Me, I'm all fingers and thumbs. My hands shake as I lift the teacup. I slop hot tea across my jeans and have to mop it up with a thick linen napkin the size of a small bath towel. 'Relax,' Cat whispers. 'Just enjoy it!' I gulp my tea, spilling puddles of it every time a waiter stalks past, but Cat takes her time, nibbling biscuits and pouring herself a second cup.

'Am I forgiven?' she asks, wiping the crumbs from round her lips with the tip of her pink tongue.

'Forgiven?' I hiss. 'You're crazy. You'll get us arrested. Deported, maybe. The police are probably on their way right now . . .'

The waiter glides over and slips the bill discreetly on to a side plate. One thing's for sure, tea at The Savoy is not going to be cheap. 'Gonna do a runner?' I ask as Cat unfolds the bill, and she kicks my shin under the table. I have a feeling that anyone trying to escape without paying would be shot, quickly and silently, with a non-fatal poison dart. You'd wake up in the hotel kitchen, chained to a dishwasher, washing bone-china teacups for the rest of your life.

Cat calls over the waiter, hands him several crisp notes and tells him to keep the change. She hooks her arm through mine and we walk out of a side door, heads high. Cat starts to laugh, and suddenly the whole situation seems so weird and wonderful that I'm laughing too. The doorman doesn't seem to mind, and tips his hat to us with a grin. We head down towards the river, walking hand in hand, looking across the water at the London Eye as it turns slowly in the thin October sun.

'Ever been on the London Eye?' Cat asks.

'No, never.'

'Let's do it then!'

We run down to where a clump of tourists are queuing to get on a river cruiser. Some of them are French teenagers, being herded together by a couple of teachers. Cat edges right into the centre of the crowd, pulling me after her until we are surrounded by French kids.

'*Comment ça va?*' she asks me, in a perfect French accent.

'What?'

'*Oh, mon ami,*' Cat says. '*Ma petit souris.* Shhh!' She puts a finger to my lips, silencing me. The crowd edges forward, and we are carried on to the boat. Nobody asks us for money, or tickets. The

French teachers don't seem to notice they have acquired two extra students.

'Always works,' Cat says, grinning. We stand by the rail and gaze out over the river, the breeze ruffling our hair.

'Sorry about the chocolates,' she says.

'It's OK,' I tell her. 'You're mad, you know?'

'Nah. I'm just trying to take your mind off stuff. Is it working?'

'Might be.'

Later, as we press our noses against the glass of the pod in capsule 17 of the London Eye, Cat takes my hand again. For a moment I forget about the scruffy pirate dog with the injured leg, about Mum and the flats and being excluded, about the stolen chocolates and The Savoy Hotel and the river boat full of French teenagers. I just lean against the glass and look out over the city. It's dusk, and the water looks shimmery and bright, reflecting the glinting lights strung out along the Thames Embankment.

'I could stay here forever,' I tell Cat. 'On top of the world.'

'Me too,' she says, and just for a moment, nothing else matters – nothing at all.

You can't stay on top of the world forever, though. You have to come down, and in the end we did. We took the tube back to Clapham and collected Lucky from the vet, and it turned out that his leg was sprained and not broken, but it was all bandaged up anyhow. He looked more like a pirate dog than ever. All that was missing was the parrot on the shoulder.

I thanked the vet and tucked Lucky under my arm, and the three of us walked along to Cat's house. Time was running too fast, like it always does when you want something to last. We stood at the gate in a little pool of light from the street lamp, and Cat looked at me with her eyes all soft and smiley, like she was waiting for me to kiss her or ask her on a date.

I didn't, though. I knew enough to suss that there'd be no future for a boy from the Eden Estate and a girl like Cat.

We said goodbye and I promised to bring Lucky

round to see her sometime, when he was better, even though we both knew it probably wouldn't happen. And then the front door creaked open and her mum appeared on the steps and called her in, and that was it, over.

When I was eight years old and Mum told me we were moving to the Eden Estate, I thought it would be like paradise. First off, we'd be together again, after almost a whole year of being apart. I'd have been happy wherever we were, but Mum told me we'd be living way up on the ninth floor, with a view clear across London. Our garden would be one big stretch of pure blue sky.

Our block was called Nightingale House. That sounded kind of magical, as if you could fall asleep to the sound of birds singing, but actually it turned out that you fall asleep to the sound of sirens and shouting and people playing their music too loud. Our view was mainly the tower block opposite, but Mum was right, we had our own patch of pure blue sky, and nobody could do much to mess that up, however hard they tried.

Eden Estate is bigger than you'd think, a city inside a city. There are four big blocks, all with wraparound balconies and scabby satellite dishes jutting out awkwardly. There is no colour, no texture except for the peeling layers of grey paint, the endless pebble-dash. The blocks are all called after birds, which was probably some council planner's idea of a joke, because you'd be lucky to catch so much as a one-legged pigeon hanging out around here.

Some nights the place is quiet, almost peaceful, but tonight isn't one of them. There's a smouldering fire in the middle of the pavement, fluttering pages from the *Daily Star* blowing along the kerb like tumbleweed. A shiny Ford Ka sits abandoned in the middle of the road, minus its wheels, one door hanging open as if the driver just nipped out and never returned.

I wonder if Cat would think it was cool? Probably.

Lucky whimpers, sniffing at the air, and I hold him a little closer. He's going to have to get used to this, like I did, but he's a street dog, a survivor. He'll be OK.

We pass a kids' playground where the swings have long since been trashed. A huddle of older teenagers sit crouched on the ancient roundabout, smoking and listening to rap music on a ghetto blaster. 'Hey, Mouse,' one of them calls through the dark, and I wave and keep walking, past Eagle Heights and Skylark Rise.

Little kids on bikes are circling the Phoenix Drop-In, a wooden hut surrounded by a chain-link fence. It's just about the only splash of colour on the whole estate, with its sky-blue walls and fiery spray-paint phoenix mural. Inside the fence is a tiny garden stuffed with bright flowers and veggies and fruit trees trained in fancy patterns along the fence. I did the mural, and Mum does a lot of the gardening stuff – she works at the Phoenix. It's a day centre for recovering drug addicts, so it's not an easy job, but she loves it. She cares.

Outside the lifts in Nightingale House, my mate Chan's little sister and her pals are playing with Barbie dolls. One of the dolls must be Ballerina Barbie, dressed in a tutu and satin ballet shoes. The other is a wild-haired thing in plastic boots and a minidress, covered in felt pen tattoos. Probably Eden Estate Barbie.

The little girls run up to see Lucky, squealing with delight. The lift appears, clanking and sighing its way to the ninth floor, and then it's just a walk along the hallway to flat 114. I pass old Mrs Scully, out with her can of Mr Sheen, polishing her front door in spite of the peeling paint and the fact that it's past eight o'clock at night.

'Hello, dear!' She smiles, and her skin crinkles up so that it looks like a contour map of the Himalayas we once studied in geography, all spidery lines and wrinkles. She looks hard at Lucky. 'Is that my Frankie's dog?'

'No, he's mine, Mrs S.,' I say. 'His name's Lucky.'

'Must need new glasses,' she says, shaking her head. 'Sorry. He's very sweet.'

'Let's hope Mum thinks so,' I say over my shoulder. The doors on either side of our flat are boarded up, but number 114 is painted spray-can red with a graffiti tag of a mouse-face on the concrete floor in place of a doormat.

I hope Mum's going to be OK with this. I didn't mention Lucky to her last night – I wasn't sure how things would turn out. Now, though, it's real. I shrug off my hoodie, wrap Lucky inside it, turn the key in the lock.

'Mum?' I call. She's curled up on a beanbag in the living room, watching TV, surrounded by huge, jungly houseplants that stretch up to the ceiling. The place looks more like Kew Gardens than somebody's flat. The plants are good, though – they hide the damp patches on the wall, the peeling wallpaper.

Mum's small, like me, with mouse-brown hair in an urchin crop, and big grey eyes that always look amazed or happy or hopeful.

'Hi, Mouse,' she says, flashing me a smile. 'Have you eaten? There's pizza in the kitchen. Oh . . . what have you got there?'

I put my hoodie-wrapped parcel down in the

middle of the scratchy nylon carpet. 'A surprise,' I tell her. 'I know I should have asked you first, but . . .'

Lucky sticks his head out of the folds of black fabric, grinning, and Mum's hands fly to her face. She looks horrified. 'Mouse!' she shrieks. 'What the . . . Mouse, what are you doing with Frank Scully's dog?'

A sad, frozen feeling settles in the pit of my stomach. I'd argue, but Mrs Scully's words are still fresh in my ears.

I've been blanking the idea that Lucky might have an owner, but an owner like Frank Scully? That's just too sick. He's one of the estate's small-time crooks, a weasel-faced loser with a drug habit who also happens to be the grandson of the sweet old lady with the Mr Sheen fixation. Scully is bad news.

'Scully's dog?' I echo. 'No way. I didn't know Scully had a dog!'

If he did, surely it would be a Rottweiler or a Staffie. He wouldn't want a skinny little terrier with a pirate patch. Would he?

Mum bites her lip. 'He has a dog now, not much more than a pup,' she tells me. 'And this is it. I recognize the patch over the eye, and the bandana. He brought it into the Phoenix a while ago, told everyone he won it in a card game. Poor thing was starving – I gave it a plate of macaroni cheese.'

Lucky battles his way free of the hoodie and takes a couple of limping steps forward. He looks from me to Mum and back again, but I can't quite meet his eyes.

'Where did you find him?'

'Near Dave's office, yesterday,' I say. 'He got run over by a girl on a bicycle. We got him fixed up – even the vet thought he was a stray!'

'He's not, Mouse. We can't keep him – Scully's not the kind of bloke I'd want as an enemy.'

Nobody would want Scully as an enemy – not many would want him as a friend, either.

'I've been calling him Lucky,' I say. 'Funny, huh? He must be the unluckiest dog in London. How come he was wandering around the streets anyway? How come he was so thin and dirty? That loser won't look after him, Mum, you know he won't!'

Mum looks upset. 'What did the vet say?'

'Just a sprain. He'll be good as new in a few days. If he's properly looked after, that is . . .'

'If,' Mum says.

There's a long silence while Lucky tilts his head to one side and does his best impression of a hungry, homeless, unloved mutt. Mum chews her lip. She's always been a sucker for waifs, strays and lost causes – I can see her struggling to resist Lucky's sad-eyed gaze.

'OK, OK,' she says, at last. 'We'll keep him for a day or two, until his leg's better. Don't go telling everyone – we don't want Scully turning up on the doorstep looking for a fight.'

'Mrs S. recognized him just now,' I admit. 'I thought she was nuts, but obviously not. She said she must need new glasses.'

'How a lovely old lady like that ended up with that thug for a grandson I'll never know,' Mum says. 'Never mind, Mouse. I don't think that'll matter, not if it's just for a couple of days. And it is just for a couple of days, OK?'

'OK.'

Later, wrapped in our fluffiest bath towel and eating pizza, Lucky settles on a big floor cushion under the Swiss cheese plant. He no longer looks as if he's been living in a coal mine.

'Don't get too used to it,' Mum warns him. 'This is temporary.'

Lucky looks up from his pizza crust, grinning, and she ruffles his ears. I reckon she could get attached to him – his grubby bandana is swishing around in the washing machine right now. Everything would be perfect if it wasn't for Frank Scully.

'Scully might be glad to be rid of him,' I think out loud.

'Maybe,' Mum says. 'If we explain it to him gently. The next time he turns up at the Phoenix I'll have a quiet word, see what he says.'

If anyone can talk Scully round, Mum can. She tried to help him years ago, when the Phoenix first opened. He was still in his teens then, on probation for a drugs-related theft, and he came along to the Phoenix every day for a fortnight before his lowlife mates lured him back to a life of crime. Since then, he's been in prison twice, and even his mum and gran have given up on him. I frown. Something, somewhere, doesn't quite add up.

'What's Scully doing hanging around the Phoenix anyway?' I ask. 'He's a dealer, isn't he? Don't tell me he's trying to clean up his act – no way.'

Mum shakes her head. 'Mouse, I know,' she says. 'I don't trust him either. He's been along a few times lately. If he says he wants to change, what can we do? We can't refuse him the chance to try.'

I wince. Letting Scully into the Phoenix is like allowing a fox into your chicken house – asking for trouble. I bet he's only hanging around for a free meal. Or – the thought makes me go cold all over – to push drugs on vulnerable ex-junkies when nobody's looking.

'Don't worry, I'm watching him,' Mum says, as if she can read my mind.

Lucky turns in a circle three times, then settles down to sleep.

'Lucky,' Mum says, thoughtfully. 'Well, let's hope he is.'

My CD alarm crashes into life with My Chemical Romance yelling about the Black Parade. I open one eye, wince and hide under the covers again.

Last year, I had the bright idea of covering up the peeling woodchip wallpaper in my bedroom by using up all the odds and ends of spray paint I had lying around. It looks like an explosion in a paint factory, which is cool most of the time, but first thing in the morning it can be kind of traumatic. All those swirling, clashing colours and patterns are not for the faint-hearted.

A wet nose snuffles against my neck – Lucky. I hug him close and tell him I'll keep him safe from Frank Scully, though I don't have a scooby how. 'I'll think of something,' I promise. 'Trust me.' Lucky sighs and smiles and burrows in under the duvet, and the two of us sleep till midday.

The doors to Jake's workshop are flung wide, with scabby, half-wrecked cars spilling out on to the forecourt. One of them, a rusting Lada, has the bonnet up, and I can see my best friend's trademark baggy jeans as he leans over it, fiddling with spark plugs and bits of wire.

'Hey, Fitz!' I call over, and he comes out from under the bonnet, oil-smeared and grinning.

'Look who it is – the spray-can king of Green Vale Comp!' he says. 'How's it feel to be a juvenile delinquent?'

'You tell me,' I laugh. 'You've had more practice!'

'That's harsh, Mouse,' Fitz replies. 'I'm just misunderstood. I'm a joker, man, yeah? A stink bomb here, a tap left running there, a fire alarm accidentally set off just before the Year Nine exams . . . I'm only acting in the interests of my fellow students.'

'Practically a saint, huh?' I say.

'You got it. You and me, Mouse, we're like silent superheroes, saving the world from boredom, misery and double maths.'

I laugh, leaning up against the Lada.

'Anyway, man, you're busted, right?' Fitz tells me. 'You were seen. Your secret's out!'

'My secret?'

'Don't pretend you don't know. Like I said, you were seen. Jake!' he yells. 'Jake, it's Mouse!'

Jake comes out from the workshop, wiping his

hands on paint-spattered overalls. He's Fitz's dad, although he doesn't look like a dad – he's still pretty young himself. You get the feeling he and Fitz's mum weren't exactly planning a baby, but Fitz came along anyway. Jake wasn't ready to settle down, though. He's never lived with Fitz and his mum and gran, even though he sees Fitz plenty.

It's the kind of cool, matey relationship I always imagined I might have with my dad, only in my case it didn't happen. It's not just that my dad wasn't ready to settle down, he wasn't ready to even live on the same continent as me.

'Come on then, Romeo,' Jake says, flicking me with an oily rag. 'Spill it. Who is she?'

I start to grin. 'Who's who?' I bluff.

'The girlfriend, man!' Fitz bursts out. 'The chick you were holding hands with last night! Jake saw you, Mouse, OK?'

'Comin' out of the tube station,' Jake says. 'I was making a little – ah – delivery, nearby. I waved, but the pair of you were too wrapped up to notice. Young love, eh? Way-hey-hey!'

The two of them smirk and nudge each other, like they just caught me walking along Clapham High Street in lime-green swimming shorts and a pair of flippers.

I hide behind my fringe. 'She's just a friend,' I say.

59

'Just a friend?' Fitz snorts. 'No, no, Mouse, I'm just a friend. Chan is just a friend. You don't hold hands with us, do you? Nope, this chick is not just a friend!'

'Pretty too,' Jake chips in.

I sigh. 'Yeah, she's cute,' I tell them. 'But she goes to a posh private school and lives up Rivendale Avenue in a house with roses around the door. So even if I did like her, it wouldn't be happening, OK?'

'Why not?' Jake demands. 'So what if she's posh? Shouldn't make any difference, mate. You gotta be confident, get out there, grab the world by the throat.'

'Don't go telling him that,' Fitz argues. 'We'll never hear the last of it. Pass her on to me, man, I'll look after her!'

'In your dreams,' I say, and Fitz just grins.

Jake chucks me a couple of newspapers and a roll of masking tape. 'I've got work to do here,' he tells me. 'You helpin', or not?'

'Might do,' I say. I like helping Jake out, especially if I'm trying to earn some cash, and he always gives me his leftover spray cans, which is cool. 'What needs doing?'

Jake points to a big, blue, shiny four-wheel drive in a corner of the workshop. 'Paint-job,' he says. 'From blue to black – needs masking up. Don't bother with the windows, I'm replacing them anyway – just the chrome and stuff. OK?'

I frown at the four-wheel drive. It looks brand new, and hardly in need of a paint-job, especially one to change the colour. I notice that Jake has taken off the number plates, and he's obviously planning to change the windows too. It crosses my mind that this car may not be strictly legal.

'Whose is it?' I ask, wrapping a wing mirror with newspaper, taping down the edges neatly.

'Let's just say it's for a couple of important local businessmen,' Jake says. 'So do a good job, yeah?'

Fitz pulls a face. On the Eden Estate, businessman translates as drug dealer, and/or crook. Jake is a nice guy, but he has some seriously dodgy friends. He manages to stay out of trouble most of the time, but only just.

Fitz chooses not to talk about his dad's iffy mates, or the fact that some of the resprays and repairs he does at the garage may not be strictly above board, so I ignore it too.

Fitz turns back to his spark plugs. 'How d'you meet her?' he wants to know. 'This posh girl? She got any friends?'

'Like I'd let you loose on her mates!' I tell him. 'As if! I met her in Clapham High Street – she ran over this little dog and landed on the pavement in front of me.'

'She fell for you, man,' Fitz laughs.

'Funny,' I say. 'Like I said, Fitz, this relationship isn't going anywhere. She's posh – different. It wouldn't work out.'

'Who cares?' Fitz says. 'Maybe she wants to slum it a bit!'

Maybe she does, but I don't want to be an experiment in how the other half live. Cat's gorgeous, but she's out of my league. 'We took the dog to the vet's,' I say, masking off the front grille. 'I reckoned it was a stray, so I brought it home.'

Fitz ducks out again from under the bonnet, his face a picture of disgust. 'Let's get this straight,' he says. 'You ditched the girl but kept the dog? Mouse, what's wrong with you?'

'Nothing!' I protest.

'You're crazy,' Fitz declares. 'Seriously.'

I chew my lip. 'Well, maybe I am,' I tell him. 'You'll never guess whose dog it turned out to be? Only Frank Scully's, that's all. How scary is that?'

Fitz blinks. 'Very scary, man,' he says. 'You gave it back, yeah? The dog?'

I turn back to the four-wheel drive, folding and shaping newspaper to the side window, so Fitz can't see my face. 'Not yet,' I admit. 'I mean, I'm going to, when the dog's all better and stuff . . .' As I say this, I know that deep down, I have no intention of ever, ever letting Lucky go back to Frank Scully. I'd sooner hand him over to Cruella de Vil.

'You'd better, man,' Fitz is saying. 'I mean, that guy doesn't have a sense of humour . . .'

A firm hand lands on my shoulder, and I just about jump out of my skin. 'A word of advice, Mouse, mate,' Jake says, and his eyes are serious, his grin long gone. 'You're a good kid. I like you a lot, you know that – so listen. Frank lost his dog a week or so back – probably just ran off, he wasn't exactly treating it well, but he thinks someone stole it. If you found the dog, give it back, Mouse. Don't get on the wrong side of Frank Scully. OK?'

I swallow, hard. 'I'll try not to,' I mutter.

Jake shakes his head, his forehead creased and anxious. 'Try hard,' he says.

I spend the rest of Saturday worrying about what Jake said, and most of Sunday trying to find a way to tell Mum about it. In the end, I mutter something about Scully thinking his dog's been nicked, and Mum tells me not to stress, she'll talk to Scully if and when he turns up at the Phoenix.

'I can handle him,' she says. A prickle of fear snakes down my back, because I don't think anyone can handle Frank Scully. He's a madman – Jake just about spelled it out for me.

'I don't want Lucky to go back,' I say. 'I like having him around.'

'Me too,' Mum says. 'But he doesn't belong to us. Let's wait and see.'

I'm so jumpy by Monday, when Mum goes back to the Phoenix, I just about fall off my chair when the doorbell chimes out at midday. Lucky starts barking, his tail waving like a propeller, and I grab his muzzle to shut him up in case it's Scully out there, raging mad and swinging a baseball bat.

'Shhh!' I whisper. 'Whose side are you on, anyway?'

I shut him in my bedroom and walk to the door. It's half-term, so the chances are it'll be Fitz or Chan. I open the door a crack and my heart lurches. It's not Fitz, Chan or even Scully. It's a green-eyed girl with honey-coloured skin and a guilty smile, leaning on her bicycle.

'Surprise!' she says.

I'm not surprised, I'm horrified. I've dreamed about Cat for three nights running. I've replayed every word she said to me, every stunt she pulled. She's cool and funny and she has 'trouble' printed right through the middle of her, like 'Blackpool' through a stick of rock, but she doesn't belong on the Eden Estate.

'Cat,' I say. 'You shouldn't be here.'

Her face falls. 'Well, I am,' she tells me. 'Aren't you pleased to see me?'

'No! Well – yes. But . . .'

'Mouse, aren't you going to let me in?'

Defeated, I stand back as she wheels the bike inside and leans it against a wall of hanging coats. Lucky has escaped from the bedroom and goes crazy, circling her, jumping up, smothering her with kisses when she bends to make a fuss of him. 'Oh, he's all clean and happy!' she says. 'His bandana's good as new! At least he's glad to see me . . .'

'We both are,' I say grudgingly. 'I suppose. I just didn't expect to see you here.'

'Why not? It's where you live, isn't it?'

'Yeah, it's where I live.' Her eyes skim over the tall, jungly plants, the beanbags and floor cushions. I know that even though I barely notice it any more, Cat will be smelling the damp, clocking the peeling wallpaper.

'I found you easily,' she's saying. 'I remembered you said the ninth floor, Nightingale House, and I followed the trail of graffiti through the estate . . . is that spray-painted phoenix on that funny little hut down there yours too? This place is cool. I almost got chatted up by two lads who talked like Ali G –'

'It's not cool,' I snap, surprised at the anger in my voice. 'It's a dump!'

'OK,' Cat says, carefully. 'I just thought . . .'

I shake my head. 'No, Cat, you didn't think,' I tell her. 'You just came wandering through the place like some rich-kid tourist on a package tour to trouble. You came to see how the other half live and you think it's cool and edgy and real, but you don't have to live it! You don't know what it's like. It's not a game – it's not an adventure.'

Her face flushes. At my feet, Lucky whines, looking from Cat to me, baffled, and instantly I feel small and mean and spiteful.

I sigh. 'Look, Cat, forget it. It's not your fault. You were always going to say the wrong thing – there is no right thing to say about a place like this.'

She looks at me from under her lashes. 'Different planets, yeah?' she says. 'I might not understand much about your world, but I come in peace!'

I laugh, and the tension falls away. 'It doesn't have to matter, does it?' I say. 'We can still be friends.'

Cat laughs. 'Friends? Boy, you know how to make a girl feel good.'

I'm smiling then, because maybe I didn't want Cat to see me here, but she's here anyhow. She's here because she likes me, and eat your heart out, Neela Rehman, because I know that this time around the attraction isn't Mars bars. Cat likes *me*.

'Well, show me the view then!' she's saying. 'I bet you can see the whole of London, up here!'

I open the glass door that leads out on to the balcony and we pick our way through the growbags stuffed with lettuce, leeks and flowers, the pots overflowing with herbs and climbers, the fruit bushes, the wilting tomato plants still laden with fruit in a home-made polythene greenhouse. One climber twines all around the doorway, dripping with tiny, starry white flowers, and Cat picks a bloom and sticks it behind her ear.

'Wow. You've got more stuff on this tiny balcony than we have in the whole of our back garden!'

'Mum loves it,' I say with a shrug. 'She'd love a proper garden, one day.'

We lean on the balcony rail, looking out over the courtyard below. The Phoenix is just an angled brown roof from here, its garden a blur of paintbox colours. Opposite, the towering outline of Skylark Rise rises up, with Eagle Heights behind it, blocking out the sun as well as anything you could call a view over London.

'The only good view is looking up,' I say, and we tilt our faces up to the blue sky, where a couple of wispy clouds scud along in the breeze.

'No wonder it's called Nightingale House,' Cat says. 'It makes you feel like you can fly!' I look at her face, lit up with wonder, and I want to hug her. She likes it here – she really, really does.

'I bet, when it's dark, you feel like you're close enough to reach out and pick a star right out of the sky!' she breathes.

I don't like to spoil the dream, but I can't help myself. 'There are no stars,' I tell her.

Cat frowns. 'How d'you mean, no stars?'

I look at Cat, and I wonder if she'd understand. I'd like her to, I really would. I lean back against the doorframe, and another piece of my history slips out of its box, out of my mouth. 'There used to be stars, when I was a kid,' I say. 'In the country, when I was staying with my dad. I knew how to pick out the Pole Star – I thought it was my own personal lucky star. Then Dad dumped me and I moved to London. There are too many street lights, too much orange glow – the sky never gets properly dark here. No stars.'

'They're still there, though,' Cat says. 'My dad likes astronomy. He has a telescope in the attic, and he watches the stars on clear nights. He knows all the constellations. The stars are always there, even if you can't always see them.'

I think about what it would be like to have a dad – any dad, let alone one with a hotline to the stars. I think of Cat's dad, imagining an old guy in a cardigan who looks at the night sky and sees past the street light glow, right up to the skies. A dad would look after you, fix things when they broke, earn money for treats and holidays, buy you a bike for Christmas or a puppy of your own. Most dads, anyhow.

Not mine. All I have left of him is a memory of a man who can juggle with fire, a man who thought it was OK to ditch his son to go and live on the other side of the world.

'I don't believe in all that stuff any more,' I answer. 'My luck ran out.'

We sit on the beanbags drinking lemonade beneath the big jungly plants.

'Where's your mum then?' Cat wants to know. 'At work? Did you tell her about me?'

'A bit,' I admit.

'What did you say? That I'm gorgeous and clever and funny and brave? That you're mad about me?'

'That you squashed my dog,' I tell her.

'That's just so typical,' she huffs. 'You have to pick out my bad points. She'd like me, I know she would. Shall I hang around until she's home?'

'No, no, Mum won't be back till gone six, and this place is bad news after dark,' I tell her. I try not to look shifty – the truth is, I don't want Cat to meet Mum. Her own mum is pretty, polished, brisk, businesslike. My mum is not.

'Will I meet her another time?' Cat wants to know, but I just shrug.

'She likes all this hippy-dippy stuff, huh?' Cat

persists, looking at the Indian floor cushions, the batik wallhanging, the magazine picture of Buddha peeking out from behind the Swiss cheese plant.

'Too right. She used to be a traveller – a hippy, I suppose,' I explain. 'Years ago.'

'What made her settle down?' Cat asks.

Inside my head, I can feel the memories shifting about inside their little boxes. I need to keep the lids on tight, but with Cat looking at me so intently, it's not easy.

'Just life,' I tell her. 'She got ill and broke up with my dad, and things went a bit wrong for us – we're OK now, though. We've been here almost six years – Mum always says it might be a dump if you look down at the ground, but keep your face to the sun and it's all about blue skies and freedom.'

'She sounds cool,' Cat says, and I just smile.

'So, what's the story with that funny little building down there, the one with the red bird graffiti?' Cat asks. 'It doesn't look like it belongs – all that colour, and the garden. Like your mum's balcony.'

How do you explain a place like the Phoenix Drop-In to a girl like Cat? 'It's just a place,' I tell her. 'Nothing special.'

'But . . .'

Right about then, Lucky jumps up and runs out on to the balcony, barking. 'Good guard dog,' Cat says, and we follow him out.

'Crazy dog, more like,' I say. 'There's nothing there, Lucky, OK? All quiet and peaceful. Seriously, most of the time, nothing ever happens here.'

I trail off into silence as a couple of police cars come screeching into the courtyard below, sirens blazing. They skid to a halt beside the Phoenix, and a bunch of policemen leap out, shove through the gate and into the building.

'Nothing ever happens here, huh?'

I don't even bother to answer. All I can think of is Mum – and Scully. *I can handle him*, she said. I suddenly feel sick, like I know something bad has happened. I'm swearing under my breath, pulling on a hoodie, dragging open the door. Lucky runs out into the corridor, still barking.

'Mouse?' Cat is saying. 'Mouse, what's up? Where are you going?'

My mouth is dry. 'You have to go now,' I tell her. 'I'm sorry, but you really do.' I hold the door wide and she wheels her bike out, wide-eyed. The three of us run along the corridor to the lifts.

'What is it? What's happening? What's wrong?'

The lift doors trundle shut and I feel that awful sensation of falling, like everything safe and stable and reliable is crumbling beneath my feet. 'Mouse?' she says again.

'It's my mum,' I say in a low, angry voice. 'She works at that stupid place, OK? And it turns out

Lucky belongs to one of the local dealers, a real headcase called Scully. He's been hanging round the Phoenix lately. Mum was going to tell him we had Lucky . . .'

I can't look at Cat. If I do, she'll see the fear in my eyes.

The lift crashes to a halt and we run out, across the courtyard to the Phoenix. Cat props her bike against the fence and snaps on the lock. 'You shouldn't even be here,' I say, but Cat just tells me to shut up because she is here, too bad, and I must be crazy if I think she's leaving me now.

Suddenly, the doors swing open and two policeman appear, dragging Scully along in cuffs. He sees Lucky, who is hiding behind my legs, shivering, and his cold eyes lock on to mine, face twisting into a weaselly sneer. 'You skanky little thief . . .'

Suddenly he lunges forward and spits at me. A dribble of slime lands on my hoodie. The police retaliate at once, yanking him away, shoving him into the back of the police car.

'Gross,' Cat whispers. She finds a tissue, wipes away the slime. 'You OK, Mouse?' I nod, but I'm shaking, my face tight with anger. The police car roars away.

I pull Cat into the building. It's a bright, open room that looks like a small herd of elephants just passed through it, turning tables and chairs upside down and splattering the walls with something that looks like spaghetti. Maybe two dozen people are inside, some huddled in groups, shell-shocked, some picking up chairs, straightening tables, wiping walls.

'Mum!' I yell. 'Mum!'

She comes running over and folds me into a quick, tight hug. Lucky runs circuits around us, tail whirling. 'It's OK,' she tells me. 'He had a knife, but Luke got it off him and called the police. It's all OK.'

A knife? It doesn't sound OK to me. Mum holds me at arm's-length, smiling, and I notice for the first time the small wrinkles that curve out around her eyes, her mouth. 'I'm fine, really, Mouse.'

'I'm sorry, I'm so sorry,' I say. 'It's all my fault . . .'

Mum's eyes open wide and she shakes her head.

'No, Mouse,' she says. 'This wasn't your fault – it was nothing to do with you, or Lucky. I never got a chance to even mention all that.'

I frown. 'So, what . . ?'

Mum sighs. 'I caught Scully selling drugs,' she tells me heavily. 'To a couple of new clients, Mark and JJ. I asked him to leave, but he pulled a knife on me . . . luckily, Luke managed to get it off him and Julie called the police.'

'Oh. My. God,' Cat breathes, her mouth a perfect circle of amazement.

Mum turns to Cat, dredging up a smile from somewhere. 'You must be Cat. The girl with the bicycle, right? I'm Magi. Look, I just need to finish giving my statement to the police . . .'

She squeezes my arm and turns away again, and Luke, her colleague, a young black guy with trendy horn-rimmed glasses, claps his hands to get everyone's attention. 'OK, folks, the show's over,' he yells. 'We're gonna close for today – business as usual tomorrow. So if you could all just go home?'

Cat looks bewildered.

'That's Luke,' I explain. 'He works here, with Mum. And that lady over there . . .' I point out an older woman with dyed blonde hair. 'That's Julie – the boss, I guess. She started the place off.'

'What kind of place is it?' Cat wants to know. 'I don't get it. What happened?'

So we sit down in a corner and I tell her that the Phoenix, with its brightly painted walls and flower-filled gardens, is a day centre for recovering drug addicts. They come here to hang out, get a hot meal, get counselling, or just talk, read, play chess, help out in the garden. I watch Cat shift uneasily in her seat as she looks around her, trying to sort out the staff from the clients.

'And that creep who spat at you?' she asks. 'Scully?'

'He's a dealer,' I explain. 'A real lowlife. He's been hanging around, making out he wanted to ditch the drugs, when all the time . . .'

'He was preying on those poor people,' Cat breathes. 'You're telling me he's Lucky's real owner? No way.'

'Way,' I tell her. 'And now he knows we've got Lucky. Trust me, that's very bad news.'

Mum walks over, flanked by a policeman and woman. 'Thanks for calling us,' the policeman is saying. 'Let's hope Mark and JJ are prepared to give evidence in court.'

It's a big 'if', but hope jumps inside me. If Scully goes to prison, he can't come after Mum or hassle the Phoenix clients – and maybe we can keep Lucky? Things might just work out after all.

'This is a great project, but you've had your share of trouble,' the policeman continues. 'Maybe Eden isn't the right place for it?'

Mum puts her hands on her hips. 'It's the best place in the world for it,' she says fiercely. 'This is where it's needed most. You know what the rates of drug abuse are. How many known drug dealers do we have here?'

The policeman looks embarrassed. 'We'd love to clean up the estate,' he says. 'But you know yourself, Magi, people around here just don't care.'

'You're wrong,' Mum argues. 'We do. Look, I'm prepared to stand up and be counted, OK? I'll testify against Scully. I saw it all, and I'm not afraid to stand up in court and say so.'

'You sure?' the policeman asks.

Mum's grey eyes are serious, steady. 'I'm sure,' she says.

When I was eight years old, the social services sent me to see a counsellor. I'd been having bad dreams – seriously, the kind where you shout out in your sleep and yell and fight and wake up covered in sweat. Not good. The counsellor spent a whole year trying to get me to talk things through. 'You have to trust me,' she said. 'I want to help. Anything you say to me will stay private, between us two, but it will help me to help you stop the nightmares. Trust me.'

Yeah, right. Why would I trust her? I didn't trust anybody else in my life back then. Adults let you down, told you lies and left you stranded. That's what I thought. That's what I still think, mostly. They pretend that they're trying to help you, but really they just want you to stay quiet, keep out of trouble, out of sight. It makes their lives easier.

Not Mum, of course. She's different. She loves me, she cares, and if she wasn't always around for me back then, well, that wasn't her choice. She was ill and she couldn't be the perfect mum, but still, she tried.

Anyhow, the counsellor tried everything she could think of to get me to open up. She tried role play, she tried hypnosis, she got me looking at funny little ink-spot pictures and asked me what they reminded me of. 'Ink spots,' I said.

In the end, a whole year on, she pretty much gave up on me. See what I mean about adults? That's what they do. She told me that she couldn't help me to deal with the past if I wouldn't talk to her about it, but that there was still one trick we could use to stop the nightmares.

We? I was the one waking up screaming, wasn't I?

The counsellor's idea was that I take my bad memories one by one and fold them up like so much dirty washing. I had to pack each one in its own little box, a box with a tight lid that I could jam on nice and hard. If I wanted to be extra sure, I could tie a bit of rope round each box, or add a padlock, whatever. Then I had to carry the boxes, one by one, to the furthest corner of my mind, a place I'd never normally go to, and leave them there. It wouldn't matter if the boxes got dusty, or covered in cobwebs, because I would never need the stuff inside them again.

I looked at her like she was crazy. There were

no heaps of dirty washing, no boxes, no rope, no padlocks. 'It's make-believe,' she told me. 'Like a game, in your mind. You want the nightmares to go away, don't you?' I said that I did. 'Then try it, Mouse. Please?'

I tried. I packed each sad, bad memory up and put the lid on tight, and carried the boxes to the furthest corner of my mind, and what d'you know? The nightmares stopped. As long as I kept the past boxed up, it left me alone.

Until now.

I am seven years old. It's three weeks since my dad left for India with his girlfriend, Storm. I'm staying with a woman called Tess and her family, in the Lake District. Tess is a friend of Storm, but she's OK.

Today is Finn's birthday – Finn, Tess's son, my idea of a cool, kind elder brother. I have a sister too here – not a real sister, but real enough. Dizzy, Storm's daughter. She's been dumped here too. She knows how I feel, what it's like to wait for a phone call, a letter, a postcard that never comes.

We're having a bonfire for Finn's birthday. I want to do something special for him, something cool, but when I mention juggling with fire, the way Dad does, they shake their heads. Fire is dangerous, they tell me. I'm not scared of fire, but still, I promise. Instead of the juggling, I practise riding Finn's BMX. I set up the ramps until I can swoop down the hill, hammer up the ramps and fly into the air, right over the top of the bonfire they're building for later. I can do it so well that I build in a wheelspin too.

That night, as the fire is blazing, I stick sparklers all round the back-wheel rim of the BMX and light them quickly. I pedal down the hill, up the ramp and into the air above the blazing bonfire before anyone even knows what I'm doing. 'Look at me!' I yell.

It's a perfect jump, but as I spin the front wheel I feel the pull of a branch in the spokes, and the BMX falters. The back wheel falls towards the flames, and I twist my body sideways, shoving the handlebars away from me, leaping away from the blaze.

And then it's too late, because my throat is full of soft, hot smoke and the flames are all around me, cloaking me in gold, licking and sizzling and burning, burning, burning.

Somebody's screaming, and I sit bolt upright, drenched in sweat and shivering. My breath is coming in great, gasping gulps, and I know that the voice echoing through my head is my own. Lucky is whining and nuzzling my neck, and Mum rushes in, bleary-eyed, her hair sticking up in clumps. 'Mouse, love,' she whispers, putting her arms round me. 'It's OK. Just a dream.'

We sit for a while in the darkness, until I stop shivering and my breathing slows. Mum keeps an arm round my shoulder, strokes my hand, and Lucky presses his worried face against mine, and slowly I come back to the present.

I'm here, on the Eden Estate, in a small, scruffy bedroom with my mum and my dog, and the past is over and done with, long gone. 'It seemed so real,' I whisper. 'I could feel the flames, smell the smoke . . .'

Mum sniffs and frowns, and I realize that I can still smell the smoke. I jump out of bed in my T-shirt and pyjama trousers and together we run through the darkened flat. Mum drags open the front door, looks out along the corridor, but everything is quiet. Then we notice Lucky, standing at the balcony door, scratching at the woodwork, whining, scrabbling.

'No way . . .' Mum whispers.

But you don't stand up to the dealers on the Eden Estate, not even creeps like Scully. You don't upset them. Turn one of them in, even if he deserved it, and you'll be punished – big time. The dealers are getting their revenge for what happened to Scully.

The night is filled with the smell of petrol and

a dark, choking smoke that sticks to your lungs, clogs up your nostrils. And down in the courtyard the Phoenix is more than a smudge of colour in the darkness, it's a whole blaze of bright, burning flames, dancing, roaring, flying up in the air like tiny firebirds.

Mum leans on the balcony rail, tears streaming down her face, and Lucky leans against her, whining softly. In the distance I can hear sirens, but they stay far-off and distant, like a broken promise, as we watch the Phoenix burn.

You can shower off the stink of smoke, but anger's not so easy to wash away. Dealers torched the Phoenix last night, because Mum, Luke and Julie dared to call the police instead of letting Scully and his mates walk all over them. They should have known better than to fight back, and now they're being punished for it – along with everyone who needs the Phoenix.

We smelt the petrol on the air, saw shadowy figures running through the darkness below, but the dealers are smart. By the time the police get round to interviewing them, they'll have alibis, witnesses ready to swear they were nowhere near here last night. The locals won't speak out against them – they wouldn't dare. Drug dealers run the Eden Estate, everyone knows that. You cannot fight them, no matter how angry you may feel, because they're bigger, stronger, angrier than you.

I pour myself a bowl of cornflakes, open a can of dog food for Lucky, but I can't shake the sad, heavy feeling that invades my blood like a poison.

Mum is talking to Julie in the living room, their conversation going round and round in circles. They want to get the Phoenix up and running again, but although the place was insured, it seems that there'll be enquiries. It could be months before there's a payout. 'We don't have months, Magi!' Julie is saying. 'Our clients need us. If we go under, so do they!'

'We won't go under,' Mum says quietly. 'We'll fight back.'

I just about choke on my cornflakes. 'Mum!' I chip in, alarmed. 'Don't do anything stupid, OK?'

'Is it stupid to speak out?' she asks. 'Is it stupid to say something is wrong? Besides, there are other ways to fight back.'

'What ways?'

'Quiet ways,' she tells me.

I listen to Mum and Julie, and slowly I come up with some quiet ways of my own.

Outside, the air is still heavy with smoke and defeat. The Phoenix is a mess of charred beams, a thick, dark soup of stinking ash and embers. The fruit trees that lined the fence have shrunk to bony black skeletons, the flowers and vegetables frazzled to nothing. The chain-link fence survives, collapsed and curled and melted, clinging to the blackened stubs of fence posts. I can't stand to look at it.

Lucky trots ahead, on a lead made from plastic washing line, his nose twitching. We walk past Skylark Rise, round to the back of Eagle Heights where Jake's workshop is, and when I see that the rickety doors are open, I cross over and go inside.

Jake is at the back of the workshop, fitting tinted glass windows to the now black four-wheel drive. 'All right, Mouse?' he says. 'If you're looking for Fitz, he hasn't been in today.'

'OK,' I tell him. 'I wasn't looking for Fitz especially – just had to get out of the flat, y'know?'

'Yeah, I can imagine,' Jake says. 'Bad business, about the Phoenix. Your mum OK?' Jake has a soft spot for Mum.

'She's not great,' I say.

'Suppose not.' Jake sighs, stepping back to survey one shiny black-tinted window. 'Make us a couple of coffees, will you?'

I click on the kettle, spoon Nescafé, sugar and powdered milk into mugs. Jake takes a long look at Lucky, who is sniffing his way around the edges of the workshop, tail twitching happily. 'You kept hold of the dog then,' he says. 'Lucky for you

Frank's off the scene for a while. It's not a good idea to go against people like that, Mouse. They make their own rules, you know that.'

'Like burning down the Phoenix?'

Jake sips his coffee. 'That wasn't Scully,' he says. 'Obviously.'

'Obviously,' I agree. 'It was his mates.'

'Be careful what you're saying,' Jake tells me. 'It could have been an accident. There's no proof, no evidence –'

'C'mon, Jake, you know it was deliberate,' I say. 'Everyone knows. It was a revenge attack, because Mum, Luke and Julie dared to call the police on Scully. What were they meant to do, let the creep push drugs on those ex-addicts, right under their noses?'

'I'm not saying it's right, I'm just saying it's the way things work around here,' Jake says. 'You don't rock the boat.'

'What if you do?'

Jake chucks an arm round my shoulder, and for a moment I feel safe, protected, like nothing too bad could happen.

'You know the score, Mouse,' he says. 'It may not be fair, but it's the way things are on the Eden Estate. Let it go, OK? You don't want to go stirring up a load more trouble, do you? Keep your mouth shut. Keep out of trouble.'

'Is that what you do?' I ask.

'It's what I have to do.'

I work all afternoon, helping Jake to fit the tinted windows in the posh four-wheel drive, peeling off masking tape, vacuuming the inside. I try not to think about the 'businessmen' who own the car, or why they want the colour and the windows and the plates changed. I guess I just don't want to know. Jake gives me a tenner and a bagful of half-used spray cans, and I help him lock up. 'Thanks, Jake,' I say.

'Just remember,' he says as I whistle for Lucky. 'Remember what I said.'

'I'll remember.'

I'll keep my mouth shut, keep out of trouble. The problem is, trouble has a way of finding me.

Next day, I walk Lucky right off the estate and along the quiet, tree-lined streets that lead to Cat's house. I want to breathe air that doesn't smell of smoke, walk pavements that are littered with fallen leaves, not rusting Coke cans and broken glass. In these streets, people don't burn things down just because you do something they don't like.

I walk along Cat's road, looking at the shiny paintwork, the bay windows glinting in the sun. I could be any boy, any place, walking his dog. A man is clipping his privet hedge with electric clippers, so neatly you could balance a mug of tea on top and not spill a single bit.

'Morning,' he says as I pass.

By the time Lucky and I have walked up and down four times, the hedge-clipping man is giving us dodgy looks like we might be axe-murderers or hedge vandals. I hesitate by Cat's gate, unsure.

Maybe her mum is at home. She wasn't too impressed with me last time, and now she probably knows I live on the Eden Estate, where drugs and violence and trouble are normal, the way hedge-clipping is around here. To get past her, I'd need to turn up with a bunch of flowers and a character reference from my head teacher that says I am a nice, respectable boy with good spelling, great prospects and absolutely no tendencies to spray-paint walls in the middle of the night.

An upstairs window creaks open, and Cat leans out.

'You coming in then?' she wants to know. 'Gonna stand there all day?'

'I'm in a hurry,' I shout back. 'Just passing by, can't stop.'

'Whatever,' she says, raising one perfect eyebrow. 'You've been "just passing by" four times in the past ten minutes!'

'These streets all look the same,' I huff.

'Yeah, right. Hang on, I'm coming down . . .'

I sit on the doorstep with Lucky. His tail beats back and forth through the air like a windscreen wiper. Cat grins, opening the door wide. She looks amazing, in a stripy sweater-dress and big black boots, her hair in a bandana. 'Yup. You're in a real hurry, I can see that,' she says.

'Well,' I say carelessly. 'I mean, I didn't call specially, or anything.'

'Sure you didn't.'

We sit together on the squashy settee, sipping Cokes while Lucky slides his nose into the top of the cream enamel swing-bin and snaffles a bit of cheese rind. French stuff, I bet. He'll be digging out the olives next.

'I heard about the fire,' she says. 'I'm really sorry.'

Last night's paper lies on the kitchen table. *Phoenix in Flames*, the headline blares. I lean over, slowly reading the rest.

Police and fire services were called out at three this morning when a day centre for recovering drug addicts caught fire on the notorious Eden Estate. The Phoenix, yesterday the scene of a dramatic arrest, burnt to the ground before fire services reached the scene. Streets leading into the estate had been blocked with torched and stolen cars, in what may have been a deliberate attempt to prolong the blaze.

Petrol cans found near the scene suggest that the blaze was arson. Although nobody was hurt in the fire, locals feel it is unlikely that the Phoenix can rise from the ashes this time.

'I couldn't believe it,' Cat is saying. 'I wanted to see you, speak to you, but Mum and Dad were practically standing guard . . .'

'The estate's not such a great place to be right now. You're better off staying away.'

'Is that what you want?' Cat asks.

'It's not what I want,' I say, frowning. 'It's probably what you should do, though. I'm just telling you.'

'I don't like being told what to do,' Cat says. 'By anybody.'

We sip our Cokes in silence.

'Who'd do that, anyway?' Cat wants to know. 'Burn down a place that's trying to help people?'

I laugh. 'Drug dealers run the whole estate, Cat – Scully's mates. We're not meant to fight back.'

'D'you think the police will find them?'

'Probably not,' I admit. 'No proof. Nobody's gonna grass up the dealers – they're too scared.'

'That's terrible!'

I shrug. 'Tell me about it.' My eyes flicker up to the framed photo on the far wall, some old wrinkly black guy with smiley eyes and a dodgy print shirt. 'That your grandad?'

'It's Nelson Mandela,' Cat says, rolling her eyes.

'Yeah?' The name sounds familiar. I think there's a community centre named after him, maybe, or a primary school.

'He's only one of the greatest freedom fighters that ever lived!' Cat exclaims. 'He stood up for the black people of South Africa, fought so everybody there could be treated as equal. He had courage and determination. He's a hero!'

'OK. What happened to him?'

'He ended up being President of South Africa!'

I frown, and my brain struggles to remember. 'He's not the guy who got stuck in a prison way out on some island for twenty-seven years, is he?'

Cat looks shifty. 'I never said that being a hero was easy. I expect old Nelson thought it was worth it in the end.'

'You don't get many heroes on the Eden Estate,' I tell her.

'There must be something we can do to get people fighting back,' Cat insists.

'You sound just like Mum – she's got all these ideas for getting the Phoenix back in business, for fighting back in a quiet way . . .'

'Well,' Cat says. 'At least she's doing something!'

'Oh, I'm doing something too.'

Cat's lips twitch into a grin. 'Yeah? What's that then? A graffiti protest?'

I shrug. 'It's what I do best, isn't it? As Mum says, there's more than one way to fight back, and sometimes the quiet ways are the most effective. I've got it all planned out.'

Cat snakes an arm along the back of the settee,

and I feel her fingertips moving softly over the nape of my neck. Suddenly every nerve ending in my body is tingling, and my breathing seems kind of shallow, as if I'm holding my breath.

'D'you ever take someone with you, when you go out tagging?' she asks.

'Not . . . not usually,' I say. 'It's easier on your own. Faster, safer.'

'Maybe,' Cat says. 'Wouldn't it help if you had someone to keep a lookout, though? Watch your back?'

'Your mum's not exactly crazy about me,' I say. 'I don't reckon she'll let you sneak out at three in the morning to go to the Eden Estate.'

'But if I could?' Cat pushes. 'If I could get away, would you take me?'

No, my head tells me. Cat is trouble, and trouble is something I have more than enough of already. It's the last thing you need on a graffiti hit, especially on the estate. Looking out for yourself is hard enough – I don't need the hassle of looking out for someone else.

'Maybe,' I hear myself say. 'You any good at spelling?'

'Brilliant,' Cat tells me. 'Top of the class.'

That figures. 'Well, my spelling's not so good,' I tell her. 'Maybe you could help out. Wear a hat, gloves, scarf, dark clothes. And running shoes.'

I get up abruptly, walk across the kitchen, away from those soft, smooth fingertips on the nape of my neck, making my senses go crazy.

'OK,' Cat breathes, her eyes all lit up. 'I'll be there. I'll say I'm sleeping over at a mate's – someone nice and respectable. No problem.'

'It's not a game, Cat,' I say, and I'm not just talking about the graffiti.

She laughs, green eyes dancing. Lucky has jumped up on to the settee beside her, and her long tawny fingers are stroking his fur now. 'Oh, Mouse,' she says. 'Of course it's a game. Don't you know that? Everything is.'

Cat stands on the doorstep of the little, ivy-covered house and waves as her mum drives away. She chats for a minute to a pretty Asian girl, then her friend closes the door gently and Cat turns back towards the street. Lucky and I slip out from the shadows and Cat just about jumps out of her skin.

'What took you so long?' I grin.

We fall into step together. 'OK?' I ask. 'Your parents weren't suspicious? Your friend won't grass you up?'

'Aditi's cool,' she says. 'She won't tell. Relax.'

We walk through the darkening streets and into the Eden Estate. Cat slips her hand into mine as gangs of kids on bikes whirl round and round in the dark. A dozen lads have made skateboard ramps from old wooden boards propped up on breeze blocks. They rattle up and down, making clunking turns and swooping ollies, lit up by the blazing headlights of a clapped-out car parked squint in the road, pumping out skate rock at full volume.

'Mouse, man, you gonna introduce your girlfriend?' Fitz yells from the edge of the group. 'Or are you scared of the competition?'

'When you get fed up with him, give me a call,' Chan adds.

'Not gonna happen,' Cat shouts back, laughing. Fitz and Chan grin, going back to their ramps. They are impressed with Cat. Who wouldn't be?

We head on, past Eagle Heights and Skylark Rise. Psycho Sam, a big bloke from the first floor on Nightingale House, walks past with his two Rottweilers, scowling. He's had a grudge against Fitz, Chan and me since we broke a window with a badly aimed football, back when we were eight. Cat laughs when I tell her the story.

We come to a halt where the Phoenix used to be.

'Whoa,' Cat whispers, taking in the charred wreckage. Then her eyes pick out a clump of jewel-red flowers poking up through the ashes, green stems bright against the dusty grey. Further back there's another clump, and another. 'The flowers!' she gasps. 'I don't get it – how did they survive when everything else . . . ?'

'They didn't,' I tell her. 'Mum planted them, this morning. It's a protest, to show she's not giving up on the place. That there's still hope.' We turn away, towards Nightingale House with its lobby littered with broken glass and cigarette stubs.

'Does she know what you're planning?' Cat asks.

'We haven't talked about it,' I reply. 'She knows I'm going to do something, though. She won't try to stop me.'

We scuff our way into the lift, press the button for the ninth floor. Someone has dropped a takeaway carton in the corner, an oily puddle of chicken tikka masala. 'She's OK with me staying over?' Cat presses.

'As long as your parents are fine with it,' I shrug. 'So you can maybe avoid mentioning the fact that they haven't a clue you're here. Yeah?'

'Sure,' Cat says. 'It's cool your mum's planted those flowers . . . it's like new life coming out of the ashes, y'know?'

'I know. She won't let this beat her – nor will Luke and Julie.'

'It's great that they care so much,' Cat says.

We come out of the lift, start walking along to number 114. 'They care more than you'd think,' I say. 'Julie started the Phoenix, six years ago when her daughter died of an overdose. Luke lost his little brother the same way.'

The colour drains from Cat's face. 'Scary,' she says, with a shudder.

'Too right,' I hear myself say. 'I used to lie awake at night, when I was a kid, watching the stars. Even before Dad took off for India, he wasn't exactly looking out for me, but I had this crazy idea that nothing bad could happen if I could just see the stars. I was scared that if I fell asleep then maybe, in the dark, everything would go wrong . . . and I had nightmares, awful nightmares too. I was so sure I'd lose Mum.'

'Magi?' Cat asks, wide-eyed. 'But why would you worry about her?'

I rake a hand through my hair and look at Cat for a long moment. Bit by bit, her wide green eyes are tugging every memory, every fragment of my past from the places they've stayed hidden for so long.

'Because she was a junkie,' I say.

Cat's eyes widen as she takes in the chaotic rainbow that is my bedroom. 'Whoa,' she says. 'It's like being inside the best graffiti picture ever.'

The walls of my room may be crazy, but as your eyes roll up towards the ceiling, there's less chaos, more blue. The ceiling is like a night sky without stars. Cat peers at the threadbare dream catcher hanging above my bed, stroking the feathers. I slide a Fall Out Boy CD into my player, and we flop down on beanbags.

'Tell me,' she says. 'About when you were a kid, watching the stars. About your mum.'

So I tell her the stuff that I never tell anybody, the stuff I don't even let myself think about any more. I thought it was safely packed away, behind closed doors, but the minute I start to speak the memories just keep coming, and Cat listens, silent.

I tell her that Mum got into drugs when my dad left, when I was just two years old. She was pretty cut up about the split, and the drugs were a way of taking the edge off the pain. Pretty soon, of course, the drugs created more pain, more hurt, than the break-up ever had.

'That's what she told me later, anyhow,' I explain. 'As a kid, I just thought it was normal – I suppose I was too young to know better. We lived in squats and scruffy flatshares with other junkies, and Mum did whatever she could to find the money for her next fix. She stole, she begged, she did other things . . .' I trail off into silence. I don't even want to think about it. Cat is looking at me, wide-eyed. I search her face for traces of pity, but find only concern.

'She was still a good mum,' I tell Cat. 'She made sure I had food and clothes and a safe place to stay. I knew I was loved.'

Cat's fingers trace the line of my wrist, the creased skin of my palm. 'It was OK,' I say, softly.

'I mean, of course, it wasn't great, but back then I didn't know any different. When I was seven, everything changed. Mum overdosed – she almost died, and while she was in the hospital recovering, she asked if they could help her get off the drugs. She did it for my sake – she wanted to be there to see me grow up.'

Cat bites her lip.

'I didn't know that at the time, though. I just knew she was ill. I was sent to live with my dad, Zak. He was a hippy – he had a tepee and he travelled around the music festivals with his new girlfriend in an old VW van.'

'He's the one who could juggle with fire,' Cat says, and I remember telling her that, the day she nicked the chocolates in Covent Garden, as we sat watching the street jugglers.

'That's right,' I say. 'He was tall and tanned, with blonde dreadlocks that reached right down his back. I wanted to be just like him, but he didn't even notice I was alive. I was just a nuisance, as far as he was concerned.'

'Oh, Mouse.'

I take a deep breath in. There's too much stuff hidden away in my head. I was crazy to think it would ever stay there. I feel like running through the neatly folded memories, kicking them to pieces, pulling them out into the daylight where everyone can see. Well, not everyone. Just Cat.

'It wasn't so bad,' I tell her. 'Staying with Zak. I got to run wild every day, out in the countryside. I got to eat proper meals and I made some friends – more like family, really. In some ways it was the best summer I ever had – in other ways, it was the worst. I got into trouble pretty much the whole time, but I had fun too. I taught myself to juggle, I went to the beach, I slept in a tree house. I was happy, a lot of the time, but still, I worried about Mum. I couldn't forget the way she'd looked the day she overdosed . . . so still, so pale. Her lips were blue. I thought she was going to die, Cat.'

'So you stayed awake at night and watched the stars.'

'Waste of time,' I say gruffly. 'Everything went wrong anyway. Dad took off for India and the whole summer fell apart. I ended up back in London, in care. I had foster-parents for a year, this very kind, very serious couple, Jan and Paul. I got to see Mum every week until she was well enough to look after me again. Social services found us a place to live, and we've been here ever since. It's not much, but it's ours, y'know?'

This is not something I've ever talked about before, not even with Mum – we've lived through it once after all. We don't want to go back there. I'm quiet, remembering the little boy who slept in a tree house under the stars, wondering if his mum would ever get better or his dad would ever learn to love him.

'Thanks,' Cat whispers. 'For telling me.'

'Thanks for listening,' I say.

For the first time ever, the bad memories don't seem so scary, so dark, as if sharing them has stripped them of their power to hurt me. Cat listens and understands, as if knowing about my past helps her to know me.

Who knows, one day I might even tell her the very worst memory of all.

'I got you a present,' Cat says into the silence, fishing a small, tissue-wrapped parcel out of her bag. 'It was because of what you said the other day, about there being no stars in London. And then I read about the Phoenix and I know it's stupid, but I suppose I wanted you to have something to believe in again . . .'

'A present?'

'I paid for it,' she says, quickly. 'Promise.'

I can't remember the last time anyone bought me a present, when it wasn't my birthday or Christmas or anything. I rip open the wrapping. Inside are three packets of white glow-in-the-dark stars, the kind with a peel-off backing that little kids might stick on to walls and furniture. I start to laugh.

Cat frowns. 'You don't think it's babyish?'

I can't stop laughing, but it's not because I think the present is babyish, it's because it's the best present I've ever had. 'You bought me stars!' I exclaim. 'You actually bought me stars!'

Cat grins. 'Well, there's this little shop, about a hundred million light-years from here . . .'

I hug her quickly, still laughing, and she feels small and light and soft in my arms. Her hair smells of vanilla. I'd like to go on holding her, but that's not a good idea. I know I'd never want to let go.

I step back, tearing open the first packet of stars, peeling off the backing. I jump up on to the rickety chest of drawers to stick them on the ceiling. Cat hands me up some more, and then we drag the chest of drawers all around the room so I can reach every bit of ceiling space.

By the time Mum sticks her head round the door to see what all the racket is, the deep blue ceiling is sprinkled with glow-in-the-dark stars. 'Fantastic!' she breathes. 'It's like your own private galaxy in here, Mouse!'

She switches the light off and the stars blink and shimmer, fading slowly away to nothing, and in the darkness Cat's hand finds mine and holds on, tight.

The first thing I see when I wake is a ceiling full of stars, glinting softly, and my mouth twitches into a smile. I crawl out of bed and dress quickly in old jeans, a hoodie and ancient Converse trainers. My watch reads three minutes past three.

I creep into the living room, Lucky at my heels. Everything is still, silent. Mum's big, leafy plants loom over me as I look down at Cat, curled in her sleeping bag in a pink *Hello Kitty* nightdress, corkscrew curls spread out around her face like a dark halo. I kick her gently with the toe of my trainer while Lucky snuffles her ear.

'Cat! Cat, wake up!'

She groans and stretches in the half-light. 'Ugh, Lucky, don't!' she hisses, struggling to sit upright.

'Bathroom's free,' I whisper. 'Don't take forever.'

She creeps across to the bathroom, emerging soon after dressed in black jeans and jacket. I grin, picking up a rucksack full of spray cans.

'Where d'you get the paint?' Cat whispers.

'My mate's dad has a garage. He lets us wash cars and help out. Mostly, I get paid in spray cans.'

Lucky trails us to the door, glum. 'Not tonight, pal,' I say. 'I want you to look after Mum.'

The lift plummets down from the ninth floor. 'What if we get caught?' Cat wants to know.

'We won't,' I scoff. 'I've never been caught. Not till afterwards, anyhow. And you can act as lookout.'

'Did I tell you I'm shortsighted?' she teases.

'Knew there had to be a reason you were hanging out with me.'

The lift sighs to a halt and we walk out across the lobby and into the cold night air. The estate is deserted except for a bow-legged Staffie sniffing around near Nightingale House. Distant reggae beats drift down from a far-off balcony.

'Any CCTV to watch out for?' Cat asks. 'Security cameras and stuff?'

'Sometimes,' I tell her. 'Not now. They smashed them all up before the fire on Monday night. Just stay away from the street lights.'

I've planned it all out in my head, and the first hit is Skylark Rise, a big grey expanse of wall just left of the entrance lobby. I set my bag down, pull my hood up and take out a can of paint. 'OK?' I ask Cat, and she grins back, nodding, watching.

I take a deep breath and begin, spraying the

outline of a phoenix, then filling in the detail of the outstretched wings with crimson and purple. I work quickly, confidently, switching to yellow, red and orange to paint a line of curling flames beneath the phoenix. I look over my shoulder at Cat. 'OK,' I grin. 'My spelling's hopeless, and I don't want any mistakes on this. Spell *phoenix* for me, yeah? Slowly! Then *rising*, OK?'

She spells the words, letter by letter, and the legend *phoenix rising* appears, in a perfect curve above the red bird. 'It's cool,' Cat breathes. 'Whoa!' I chuck my paint can into the bag and we move off, just as a police car swoops in from the main road and makes a slow circuit of the estate.

'Omigod!' Cat yelps. 'They'll see it! They'll know it was us!'

'Keep walking,' I tell her. 'Head down. They won't even notice the graffiti, and if they do, they won't care. The police have more important things to worry about around here, y'know?'

'What if they stop us? Search your bag?'

But the police car has gone, and I'm laughing. 'Nervous, huh?' I ask. 'Don't worry. Just keep your ears open, as well as your eyes.'

I paint a second giant phoenix on to the wall of Eagle Heights, then target smaller areas. I spray a colourful *dealers out* on a bit of low wall beside the kids' playground, again on a row of boarded-up windows and a third time on the corrugated metal shutters of the estate's single shop. *No to drugs* is the last slogan, sprayed in letters three feet high on the wall round the bins at the back of Skylark Rise and all along the lock-up garages that edge the back of the estate.

We share a Mars bar, huddled side by side on the wall beside the garages. It's past five now, and the sky is beginning to lighten, but I want to paint one last phoenix. I pick out a huge, scabby wall at the side of a block called Raven's Crest, start blocking in the shape and adding detail to the wings and tail. I'm buzzing. I use up the last of the yellow and orange paint on flames that swirl up to frame the phoenix, and Cat does her dictionary bit, spelling the words out as I spray *phoenix rising* above the artwork.

'Done,' I whisper. 'What d'you think?'

'I think you're crazy,' Cat tells me. 'You're really talented, you know? And these are going to cause one big stir tomorrow, but . . . well, don't you ever get scared?'

'Scared?' I echo. 'No way! It's the best feeling in the world!'

Right then, a middle-aged couple turn the corner by the flats, walking right towards us. I kick the rucksack of paint into the shadows, turn away, but Cat has a better idea. She slides her arms round me, pulling me back against the wall. 'Shhh,' she whispers, burying her face against my shoulder.

I shut my eyes against the soft, springy ringlets of her hair, listening to the tip-tap of high-heeled boots and the low murmur of voices as the couple pass by. I can hardly breathe, but I don't think it's anything to do with fear.

'They've gone,' I whisper. Cat lifts her head, and her cheek brushes mine. Neither of us makes any move to pull apart. 'Cat?' I whisper again.

Then my fingers slide up into her hair and my mouth finds hers, and we're kissing. Her lips are soft and warm and she tastes faintly of Mars bar, which is not a bad way for a girl to taste, I promise you. After a little while, I break away.

'We should get back,' I whisper.

'We should.'

Then I'm kissing her again, and I can feel the soft, vanilla-scented touch of her hair against my cheek and my insides feel all warm and gooey. I want that feeling to last forever. It doesn't, of course. A police siren starts up somewhere nearby, and we pull apart as headlights rake through the darkness. 'That's all we need . . . time to go!'

I pick up the rucksack and grab Cat's hand and we're out of there, running as fast as we can, laughing, breathless, into the night.

Back at the flat, we sit on beanbags under the big leafy plants, sipping hot chocolate. Lucky is curled up between us, me scratching his tummy, Cat tickling his ears.

'My lookout skills weren't so good towards the end there,' Cat says. 'Sorry about that. Disappointed?'

'No way,' I laugh. 'With you? No way.'

She grins in the half-light. 'Well, I guess that's because you just don't know me very well,' she says, but she's grinning all the same. 'I'm not as perfect as you think.'

'No,' I agree. 'Your spelling's OK, though.'

She chucks a cushion at me and I catch it before it hits the Swiss cheese plant, laughing. 'Who cares about perfect?' I ask. 'I like you anyhow. You gave me stars.'

'I wish I could give you the real kind,' she says.

'You did,' I tell her.

'My dad told me once that every last one of us on this earth is made from stardust,' Cat says softly.

My heart jumps. 'What?' I ask. 'Made of stardust? No way.'

'There's a big scientific explanation for it, obviously,' Cat says. 'My dad likes astronomy and looking at the stars, so he knows all kinds of stuff about them. That's what it comes down to, though. We're made from stars. I like the idea of that.'

'I do too,' I say. 'Your dad sounds cool.'

'He's OK,' Cat says, uncertainly. 'I suppose. He works too hard. He never has time for me.'

I hold up my hand in the darkened room, spread the fingers wide. Skin, bone, blood . . . or stardust? How could there not be magic and hope and miracles in the world, if all of us were made of stars? Cat must have it wrong. There's no magic around here, that's for sure.

But when she catches my hand in the darkness, holding it tight, I'm not so sure. 'Do you ever wish you could go back in time?' she asks me. 'Turn the clock back to when things really were perfect? When you were a kid, y'know, and happy?'

I frown, because the closest I've ever been to perfect is here and now, holding hands with a green-eyed girl who thinks I'm made from stardust. 'The past wasn't such a great place, for me,' I remind her.

'I guess not,' she says. 'Wouldn't you like to go back, though? Do things differently?'

I can tell from the longing in her voice that Cat would, but I also know that there's no going back, no matter what. I shrug. 'Things would still have happened the same way,' I tell her.

'Do you think so?' she asks. 'I'm not so sure. I wouldn't mind trying to make things different.'

She makes a snuffling sound in the dark. 'You OK?' I ask.

'Hay fever,' she says, but I don't think you can get hay fever in October. She's crying. Maybe the past wasn't such a great place for Cat, either.

I find a box of tissues and hand her some, watch as she wipes her eyes. 'Want to talk about it?' I ask.

'Nope,' she says. 'Everyone has their dark secrets, don't they?'

'Maybe,' I say. 'But . . . well, talking about it can help, y'know.'

'Talk then,' Cat says in a muffled voice. 'Tell me about what happened after your dad went away. Did you stay in touch with the people you met, that summer?'

'I tried,' I say. 'When Dad went to India, everything changed. I ended up in London, with the foster-parents I told you about, Jan and Paul. I wasn't much good at letters. I couldn't read or write at all back then – I was learning, at school, but it was tough. I'd get Jan and Paul to write for me, or send pictures I'd drawn maybe. Dad never answered. Not ever.'

Cat bites her lip.

'I got letters back from one friend, for a while,' I go on. 'Dizzy – she was like a big sister to me, even though we weren't related. Her mum was Dad's girlfriend – the one he took off to India with. She rang a few times, and I'd write to her and send her pictures for this other guy, Finn, and biscuits for the dog, Leggit.'

'How come you lost touch?' Cat asks. Her voice seems clearer now, softer, as if getting wrapped up in my past has chased her sadness away.

'It was when I went to live with Mum again,' I say. 'We moved here – I had to change schools and there was nobody to help me with my writing any more. I stopped trying.'

Cat frowns. 'But why couldn't your mum . . ?'

I sigh. 'She can't write, Cat. Not at all.' In the thin dawn light, her face is serious, shocked, struggling to understand. How could she? I bet her mum went to university and everything.

I get up, pad across the scratchy nylon carpet to my bedroom, reappearing with a shoebox and a duvet. I flop down again, wrap the duvet round myself. 'These are the letters,' I tell Cat, taking the lid off the shoebox. 'Four of them. I kept them all.'

'Your friend didn't keep on writing, after you stopped?'

'Maybe,' I shrug. 'If she did, nobody ever passed the letters on. She never had this address, and Jan and Paul – well, they thought all of those people from my past were bad news.'

'Why?'

'They had their reasons. They were wrong about Dizzy and Finn, though.'

'You could get in touch now,' Cat suggests.

'No. I've left it too late – I wouldn't know what to say.'

I reach for the shoebox, lift out a letter from the mess of seashells, friendship bracelets, crystals and festival tickets from long ago. I scan through the childish, curly handwriting. It says that Leggit is going to dog-training classes and Finn sends his love, and have I heard anything yet from India, because Dizzy hasn't, but we're bound to soon, don't worry. Oh, and thanks for the Mars bar.

Across the room, Cat huddles in her sleeping bag. She holds out her hand and I pass the letter over for her to read. Outside, on the balcony, sunrise streaks the sky behind Skylark Rise with shades of pink and peach and purple. I curl up, eyes closed, and fall into sleep.

I wake up to swirling, New Age music and the smell of cooked breakfast. Mum is in the kitchen, singing along to a CD player, clanking pans and sipping coffee. On the other side of the room, Cat groans and burrows down into her sleeping bag, pursued by Lucky.

'Sleep OK?' Mum asks from the open doorway. She doesn't seem to notice that Cat and I went to bed at half ten last night in separate rooms, then woke up fully dressed in the living room. Well, I guess she notices, but just doesn't mind. I clear away the shoebox and the duvet, then wash and pull a comb through my hair. It doesn't make much difference – I still look like I slept in a hedge.

'Breakfast's ready!'

Mum and Cat are tucking into toast, scrambled eggs, baked beans and mushrooms, grinning together. Cat looks bright-eyed and wide awake, like she just spent the night in a five star hotel instead of curled up in a sleeping bag on a nylon carpet. 'This is good,' she says. 'Thanks, Magi!'

'You're welcome,' Mum replies. 'How did it go, anyway? The art project?'

Cat just about chokes on her toast. I shrug. 'OK,' I say. 'You can see for yourself, later.'

'He thinks he's some kind of modern-day Van

Gogh,' Mum tells Cat. 'Only with both ears intact, of course.'

Cat swallows a forkful of scrambled eggs, wide-eyed. This is probably not the kind of conversation she'd have with her mum, a strict but successful lawyer. The first whiff of rebellion and she'd be grounded for the rest of her life. Longer, maybe. Me and Mum have a different kind of relationship, more like friends than mother and son, or maybe just like two people who have come through a lot of bad stuff together and managed to survive.

Later, as I walk Cat back across the estate, Lucky trotting beside us on his washing-line lead, I see Mrs S., Scully's gran. She is on her knees in the ashes where the Phoenix used to be, digging away with a spoon. 'Mrs S., what are you doing?' I ask, dropping down beside her.

Her wrinkled face breaks into a smile. 'Well, I saw what your mother had done, planting those flowers,' she says. 'I thought I'd do the same. I got some lovely winter pansies from the supermarket!'

'Cool,' I tell her. 'You could do with a trowel, though, to plant them.' I take the spoon and scrape away at the ash and soil until a couple of little holes appear, and Mrs S. lifts her plants into place and presses the soil down round them. She takes a plastic bottle of water from her shopping bag and soaks the flowers, then packs the bottle, the spoon and the empty plastic pot away inside her bag. I help her to her feet.

'I'm not the only one, either,' she says, and I look again. Half a dozen new plants are sticking up through the rubble since yesterday. I can't help smiling. In a small way, the locals are fighting back.

'It's a great idea,' Cat tells her. 'Magi's gonna love it!'

'Some of that dreadful graffiti art has sprung up overnight too,' she tells us. 'I don't approve of it, mind, but it shows people are angry about the blaze. Tell your mum that – people care.'

She takes a long look at Lucky, who gives her a winning smile. 'He really does look like my Frankie's dog,' she says. 'But now that I see him in daylight, it's very clear he's yours. That's a good thing, Mouse, what with my Frankie being away for a while. Look after him.'

I swallow. 'I will, Mrs S.,' I tell her. 'Promise.'

Mrs S. turns back towards Nightingale House, then stops and looks back over her shoulder. 'Frankie's not really a bad boy,' she says. 'Tell your mum that, Mouse. He just got in with the wrong people, lost his way.'

'Of course,' I tell her.

I wish I could believe it.

The doorbell rings, and when I open the door
there's a girl in a black net tutu and fluffy black
fairy wings standing on the doorstep. Her face is
painted white, and she has black lipstick and
smudged eyeliner, like an emo panda. Her corkscrew
curls are piled up on her head, tied with black
velvet ribbon, and she's wearing a kid's hairband
with a spangly bat at the front.

'Wow!' I say.

The black fairy looks cross. 'You're supposed to
scream,' she tells me. 'Or shudder, or faint. You
don't just say "wow".'

'Sorry,' I grin. 'You walked across the Eden Estate
looking like that?'

'I flew,' she says, tugging at the black fairy wings.
'Look, I haven't got all night. Trick or treat?'

'We don't usually get people coming round,' I
apologize. 'No treats. Sorry.'

'Nothing?' she says, crestfallen. 'No sweets, no
monkey nuts, no fruit?'

'There's half a tin of beans in the fridge,' I say.

'You're too good to me, Mouse.'

Cat pushes me into the flat, right up against the coatrack. Then she kisses me, and her lips taste of sugar and facepaint. 'Who is it?' Mum calls through from the living room, and we pull apart.

'You did have a treat, after all,' Cat says with a sly grin.

'It's just Cat, Mum,' I shout. 'I'll bring her through!'

'Your lipstick's smudged,' Cat says carelessly, and I glance in the hall mirror just in time to wipe away the smears of black and white imprinted on my mouth.

'Happy Hallowe'en!' she says, giving Mum a couple of penny chews from her black plastic cauldron. 'Can Mouse come trick-or-treating? We won't be late.'

'I suppose,' Mum says. 'Not around the estate, though – it's not safe. And don't be too late . . .'

'We won't,' Cat says, producing a pair of devil horns and a pointy tail from her cauldron. 'I knew you wouldn't be prepared, so I brought these. OK?' I slide the horns on over my fringe and tuck the tail into the back of my drainpipes. 'I didn't forget you,' she tells Lucky, fixing a length of black tinsel round his collar. 'There – perfect!'

'So,' Cat wants to know as we wait for the lift. 'Was it you then? The spray paint?'

'What spray paint?' I ask.

Then the lift arrives, the door wheezes open and I see that someone has painted the whole of the inside a soaring turquoise blue. It's like stepping inside your own, private piece of sky. 'Cool,' I say.

'Not you then,' Cat says. 'I guess someone was fed up with the swear word graffiti and the curry sauce stains. Thought you said people around here just don't care?'

'They don't,' I say. 'Not usually. This is a first.'

Cat raises an eyebrow. 'It's a good sign,' she tells me. 'People are trying to change things.'

We mooch past the Phoenix, where yet more bright flowers and climbers twine amongst the ruins. We get a few shouted insults from the kids down by the playground. Cat just laughs and chucks them a load of penny chews, and they look at us like we're crazy. Outside the estate, things are just as strange. Cat doesn't want to call from house to house, collecting sweets. Instead, she stops gangs of small children dressed up as witches and goblins, handing them sweets and biscuits printed with spiders' webs.

'Why are you giving us sweets?' one small vampire demands.

'I want to,' Cat says. 'It's fun. Tell me a joke or something, OK?'

'Why didn't the skeleton go to the Hallowe'en disco?'

'Dunno,' Cat says.

'Cos he had no body to dance with. D'you get it? No body?'

'Cool,' Cat says, and hands him a jelly snake.

'I think you've got the rules of Hallowe'en a little bit muddled,' I say.

'So what?' Cat grins. 'I like my rules better.'

'I like your rules better too,' I admit, as another small knot of ghouls heads off into the night. 'You're good with kids.'

'I used to be,' Cat says. 'Once. Look, I'm all out of sweets now. We'll go back to mine.'

We turn into her road, Lucky straining at his washing-line lead, trailing tinsel. 'School on Monday,' Cat says. 'Can you believe it? How come we get eight weeks of school for every week of holiday? That doesn't seem right.'

'Kind of unbalanced,' I agree.

'Shall we skive off, go up to town again?'

'Cat, no way,' I tell her. 'You know I have to be on my best behaviour after the exclusion. I promised Mum, and Dodgy Dave.'

'D'you always do what Dave tells you?' she asks.

I laugh. 'Hardly ever,' I admit. 'But he's OK, for a social worker – I don't want to let him down.'

We stop on the pavement outside her gate. 'Let's go in, anyhow,' she says. 'You have to get your treat, I've got it all planned . . .'

'If I see another sweet I think my teeth might melt,' I confess.

'Who said it was sweets? Mum and Dad are out, and it's a cool, clear night . . .'

A cool, clear night? I'm not sure why this matters, unless it means we have to huddle together for warmth or something. The idea of that has me feeling hot all over, then breaking out in a cold sweat.

Cat leads me along the path and into the hallway that still smells of coffee and spices, but this time we don't head for the kitchen. She drags me upstairs. 'Is this a good idea?' I ask, as she steers me along the landing and up a second flight of stairs. 'I can't stay too late . . .'

We're on the second storey now, creeping along a little landing under slanting eaves, past attic rooms. 'Relax!' she tells me. 'We won't be late, anyhow. My parents'll be back at eleven, and you have to be out of here by then or I'm dead meat . . .'

She pushes open a pine door and shoves me into the room, with Lucky at my heels. It's dark inside and Cat doesn't switch on the light, but my eyes adjust and I can see from the light on the landing that this is not a bedroom. It's a study, built into the roof of the house beneath glossy Velux windows that face the sky. Right in the centre of the room is a telescope, a proper telescope, on a stand, like you'd see at a museum or something. It's pointing up at the windows, towards the night sky.

'Oh, man,' I whisper. 'How cool?'

'Thought you'd like it,' she smirks. 'It's Dad's. You can have a look, if you like. On a cool, clear night you can usually see the stars. I wanted to show you that they really are there, even if you can't see them without a telescope.'

I take a step forward, unfasten the lens cap. I blink and swivel the telescope slightly, then gasp as the sky comes into focus. The orange haze has gone, and in its place is a blanket of darkness pierced here and there by tiny, glittering diamonds. Cat was right. Above us is a perfect sky, filled with stars. 'Well?' she wants to know, tugging at my elbow. 'What d'you think? Trick or treat?'

I grin. 'Treat,' I tell her. 'Most definitely, treat.'

Cat brings up mugs of hot chocolate and a slice of French cheese for Lucky, and we sit on the floor looking up at the attic windows, looking past the orange haze to the velvet sky beyond. 'It's like one of those magic-eye pictures,' Cat tells me. 'Once you know what to look for, you can see it.'

'Your dad must know loads about the stars,' I say. 'Is that what he does? Is he a scientist or something?'

'No, no, this is just his hobby,' she says, vaguely. 'He knows lots about it, though. The names of the constellations and all that. He used to show me, when I was younger.'

'Not now?'

Cat shrugs. 'He's too busy, these days.' She gets up and switches on the light, and suddenly the windows to the sky are just two dull rectangles of glass in the slanting ceiling. The telescope looks smaller under the electric light, a spindly thing stranded in the middle of the carpet. The walls are covered with maps and charts, patterns of stars and lines and scribbles.

'What are these?' I ask Cat.

'Star maps,' she tells me. 'They show you how to find the constellations. It's just like with an ordinary map – it shows you where you are in the sky. The one you're looking at is for the constellation of Orion the Hunter – these three stars make up his belt. That's his sword, and that's his shield . . .'

I frown. 'I can't see it,' I admit. 'Looks like someone's been scribbling over a dot-to-dot book without following the numbers.'

'I know . . . but that's what those stars looked like to the first astronomers, thousands of years ago. This shape here is Orion's companion, the Great Dog . . .' Cat points to a chart of dots and lines that looks like a jerky sketch of a lopsided dog.

'Hear that, Lucky?' I grin. 'You've got your own constellation!'

'And a star,' Cat says. 'Sirius – the Dog Star.'

Lucky's tail beats against the carpet, like he knew this all along. I sit down, leaning back against the desk. 'A star map, to help you find your way around the night skies,' I say. 'Wish I'd known that when I was sticking up those stars at home the other day.'

Cat rolls her eyes. 'What, are you gonna peel

them all off again and arrange them like this?' she scoffs, nodding at the charts. 'I didn't have you down as someone who followed the rules, Mouse. Why don't you make your own stories up?'

'I suppose,' I say.

'That's what I do,' Cat says. 'I have my own theories about the sky, my own version of a star map. Ever see that Disney film, *The Lion King*?'

I nod. I remember seeing it on video, not long after I moved in with Jan and Paul. All that stuff about fathers and sons really upset me, coming just after Dad took off for India.

'Remember how the lion king tells Simba he'll always be there with him?' she says. 'In the stars? Well, that's kind of like what I believe too. That people who are special to you are always with you, even when you can't see them any more. Like when someone's dead . . .'

'. . . or gone away,' I finish for her.

Cat is silent for a moment, sniffing a little in the darkness. 'What I'm saying is, they never really leave you,' she says softly. 'They live on inside you, no matter what. You can forget the names those old astronomers gave to the stars, call them whatever you want . . . names that mean something to you.'

'So I could call the Dog Star Lucky, not Sirius,' I say.

'That's right. Each one of us can have our own unique star map, our own constellations and star names. That way, we're never alone.'

She looks so sad, so lost, that for a moment I want to hold her hands and tell her that she'll never be alone, because she has me now. I just don't know if that's enough. Her green eyes are misty, and she wipes a hand across them, impatiently. 'Stupid face paint,' she says, smiling. 'Gets in your eyes.'

'Yeah?'

'Yeah.'

I move up beside her so that my arm can curl right round her, and she turns her head so that her cheek rests against my fringe. 'I wish I could grab you a bunch of real stars, Mouse. I would if I could.'

Then we're kissing, and I feel like I'm floating, way, way up in the night sky, a hunter called Orion with a belt made of stars and a dog at my heels. I could be anywhere, nowhere, and then suddenly I come hurtling back down to earth with a bang. Cat's fingers trace along the line of my jaw, creeping higher.

I grab her wrist and hold her still. 'No,' I whisper.

My heart thuds. I'm not sure that Cat is ready to handle this: my secret, the darkest memory of all.

'What is it with this fringe?' she says, huffily. She

pulls free of my grip and strokes my hair softly, blowing against it with warm, sweet breath. I close my eyes and wait, my heart thumping, and sure enough her fingers push up through my fringe, raking it back from my face. I feel her stop, I feel her freeze, and suddenly my chest is so tight I can barely breathe.

'Oh, Mouse,' she says.

Her fingers touch my cheekbone, my temple, my ear, the stretched, puckered skin that nobody ever sees. She doesn't flinch. It's like the flutter of a bird's wings, a butterfly kiss.

'What happened?' she asks.

I shake my head, but Cat just rests her mouth against the ruined skin and her fingers slide down my face as the hair drops back down to hide the scars. After a while, I can breathe again, and finally I tell her about how it all happened, how that summer ended, long ago when I was seven.

Dad went off to India, leaving me behind with an ache where my heart had been. Was I so unlovable? Finn and Dizzy didn't think so. They believed in me, and in return I idolized them.

The nightmare is still fresh – it always will be. Finn's birthday, a bonfire party, my plan for a dramatic leap over the flames. I wanted to show him I could do it, and instead I wrecked his birthday, his life. When the branch caught in the wheel of the BMX, I fell down into the fire, and Finn ran into the flames to rescue me, getting burnt himself in the process.

I'll never forgive myself for that.

We stayed together in the hospital for weeks afterward, Finn racing about the corridors in a wheelchair because his feet were burnt and bound up with cling-film stuff to help them heal. My burns took longer to fix. I'd been wearing a T-shirt and my arms, shoulder and neck were burnt, but the worst damage was on the right side of my face, my cheek, my temple, my ear.

Nobody could see the hurt inside, but the scars on my face were clear enough. Luck? That's when I stopped believing in it, end of story.

I looked in the mirror six weeks after the accident and I saw the ridged skin, dark and angry as if it was burning still. When I was eleven they did some skin grafts – Fitz and Chan called me Frankenstein for a while, which was probably designed to toughen me up. It did, a bit.

'There was me thinking you were dead vain because you wouldn't let me mess with your fringe,' Cat says.

'Yeah, right,' I tell her. 'I was probably the first emo kid in London. I've had the fringe since I was eight years old, and I'll still have it when I'm eighty.'

'I like the fringe,' Cat says. 'But you don't have to hide stuff from me.'

I frown, because I'm pretty sure that Cat's hiding something too. Her faraway eyes, the tears that have nothing to do with hay fever or face paint. How much do I really know about her? Not a whole lot.

'I told you my secret,' I say. 'How about yours? You told me everyone has their bad memories, secrets hidden away. So tell me.'

Cat laughs. 'I don't have a secret,' she says.

'No?'

'No. Nothing dark and tragic, anyway. Maybe I said that, but . . .'

'Cat, tell me,' I say. 'It helps to share things, I promise.' This is something I'm only just starting to realize, but all the same, I know it's true. Bringing those bad memories out of the dark takes away their power to hurt you somehow.

Cat sighs and huffs and hugs her knees, silent for a long moment. Then, when I think there's no way she'll ever open up, her sad green eyes lock on to mine.

'I have a brother,' she says at last. 'Josh. He's – ten years old. And he's been ill, very ill, for a long time. But – well, he's better now, and he'll be coming home really, really soon.'

I open my eyes wide. 'Cat,' I say, honestly shocked.

'I didn't even know you had a brother. What's wrong with him? How long has he been ill?'

She just shakes her head, as if she can't trust herself to speak. 'Ages. Years, really. I don't want to talk about it – I just wanted you to know, OK?'

I put an arm round her shoulders, stroke her hair. 'It's not fair, Mouse,' she whispers. 'He's just a little kid. Kids aren't meant to get sick.'

'No, they're not,' I say. 'They're really not.' We sit for a while in silence. It feels like Cat has handed me something special, worth more than stolen chocolates or glow-in-the-dark stars. She's given me a piece of herself. She's not just a beautiful, daring, posh girl any more. She's Cat, acting tough and putting on a brave face when inside she's hurting for her little brother. She snuffles in the dark, wiping a sleeve across her eyes.

'But it's all going to be OK now,' she says brightly. 'Like I said, Josh will be home soon, and we can be a family again. Sorted!'

'I hope so,' I say.

Cat jumps up suddenly, picking up the hot chocolate mugs. 'It's getting late,' she says, suddenly anxious. 'I don't want Mum and Dad to find you here.'

'I'll say I was helping you with your homework,' I grin.

'No, no, you'd best just go. Seriously.' We pad down the stairs together, and suddenly Cat grabs hold of my belt and untucks the forgotten devil's tail, holding it up. 'Sure you're not a bad influence?' she asks.

'Certain,' I tell her. 'That'd be you.'

We hug in the hallway while Lucky sniffs around at our feet.

'Thanks for telling me your secrets,' she whispers. 'And thanks for listening to mine. It helps, y'know?'

'I know,' I say. 'It can't be easy for you, but you know I'll always listen, if you want to talk. Thanks for telling me about the star maps too. You're up there, on my star map. OK?'

Cat laughs. 'What am I, a fleck of light from a faraway galaxy?'

'Something like that.'

I can't tell her the truth, can I? I can't tell her that in my sky, she's the brightest star.

19

Going back to school after an exclusion was never going to be easy, but at least the October break has given people other stuff to think about. Most people, that is.

'You're a hero,' Fitz tells me as we slouch into school. 'A legend. They'll be talking about your graffiti hit for years to come, man.'

'Yeah, right,' Chan says. 'The spelling, the paint on your fingers, the mouse tag in the corner . . . crazy.'

'Thanks, Chan,' I tell him. 'Don't hold back now. Tell it like it is.'

Chan shrugs. 'Just saying.'

The long wall where I painted my graffiti masterpiece has been repainted in flat grey paint, as if it never existed at all, but I had my moment of glory. I saw the kids' faces as they clocked the explosion of colour, the swirls of pattern, the wild, wonderful, glad-to-be-alive graffiti. I smile just thinking about it, my heart singing inside of me.

Mr Brown ambushes me as I slope along the corridor. He hauls me into his office and sits down behind a shiny wooden desk the size of a pool table.

'Those are not school trousers,' he growls, eyeing my skinny black jeans.

'They're *my* school trousers, Sir,' I reply politely.

Mr Brown sighs. 'Kavanagh,' he barks. 'I'd like to believe that you're sorry for the senseless destruction you caused to this school last term. Your letter led me to believe that you were ready to turn over a new leaf. Is that correct?'

Hmmm. I have a feeling it might take more than a new leaf – more like a whole tree. 'Yes, Sir,' I say.

'Good, good,' he says. 'You may not believe this, Kavanagh, but I'm on your side. I want to make Green Vale a better school, a place where teachers and students work together to achieve the very best they can . . . I can't do that without your help.'

I smile and nod and pretend I have a clue what he's talking about.

'I'll be expecting a good report from your teachers on behaviour, attitude and effort,' he goes on. 'You haven't had the best of starts in life, Kavanagh, but don't throw your future away on vandalism and stupidity. Make something of yourself. Show us what you're made of.'

I look at my fingers, spreading them wide. Skin, bone and blood, or stardust?

'You've been given a fresh start – I hope you realize just how lucky you are. Well?' he concludes, narrowing his eyes. 'Is there anything you've been thinking about? Anything you'd like to say to me, in the light of all that's happened?'

I feel like a rabbit caught in the headlights. There are lots of things I'd like to say to Mr Brown – I'm just not sure he's ready to hear them.

'Kavanagh?' he prompts.

'OK,' I say brightly. 'About the wall by the gym . . .'

'Yes, yes?'

'I think you were wrong, that's all. That wall needs some colour. This school needs some colour, and that really shouldn't be a crime. Sir.'

Mr Brown's face turns a startling shade of pink, and his eyes look as though they may pop out of his head. He runs a finger around his collar, as if it's choking him, and his mouth opens and closes, a bit like a goldfish. I can tell he is not impressed by my speech. Slowly, it dawns on me that he wasn't asking for my views and opinions at all. He was waiting for another apology, or for me to thank him for his lenient approach. Oops.

'Well, Sir,' I say, briskly. 'I'd better be going. Don't want to be late for class!'

New leaf? Yeah, right.

Once again, school swallows up my life. It's just the same – sour-faced teachers, grey, crumbling classrooms, stodgy school dinners that lie in your belly like cold gruel.

Then something weird happens. In art, Mr Lewis shows me a vast six foot canvas at the back of the classroom, behind the partition where the art books are. The rest of the class are drawing a still life of dusty wine bottles, in between hurling paper planes about and discussing last night's *Eastenders*.

'It's for you,' Mr Lewis says. 'You like working large, don't you? Let's see what you can do with this.'

I frown. 'Why?' I ask.

'Not my idea,' he grunts. 'Mr Brown thinks you've got something to say, and he wants to see what it is. Brushes and paint, mind, none of that aerosol rubbish.' He stalks away.

I look at the paints and brushes arranged by the sink, then at the big, blank canvas. I don't want to paint on a bright, white background. I am used to peeling bus shelters, pitted brickwork, bleak grey concrete. Mr Brown is wrong. Without those things, I have nothing to say.

There's an old armchair in the book corner, and I sink into it, out of sight behind the shelves. I take a bite of Mars bar and open a book on Van Gogh. I don't read much, but the pictures in this book tell their own story. They're all about colour, about being alive. I read a caption that says Van Gogh sold just one painting during his lifetime. He gave another to a friend, who used it to patch up a hole in his chicken shed.

Maybe it's not so weird for artists to be misunderstood.

Mr Lewis peers round the partition to see what I've done, and looks smugly satisfied that I'm eating chocolate with my feet up on the bookshelf. 'Hmphh,' he says.

Next art lesson, I drag the armchair round so that it sits in front of the big, white canvas. I stare at it all lesson, while the others draw wine bottles, wondering if I have anything to say, and if so, how to say it.

In the third art lesson, I start to draw. I draw a boy, as tall as I am, with a sad face and a Green Vale uniform and a small pirate dog at his heels. Mr Lewis appears and tells me that the legs are too long and the hands are too small. He drags a full-length mirror over from the corner and props it against the bookshelf, and I look and check and fix things up.

Then I start painting, and that takes weeks. I mix black and white acrylic to make a hundred shades of grey, and paint grey skin, grey lips, grey hair, grey clothes with grey folds and creases. Everything is dull and monochrome, like a black-and-white photo in a long-ago album. It takes a whole lesson just to paint one hand, to get the light and shadows just right, to make it look real.

'Interesting,' Mr Lewis says.

When I start on the background, a clashing, crashing explosion of rainbow colour that drips and smudges and splatters over the black-and-white boy, Mr Lewis smiles. I've never seen him do that before. Ever.

Fitz and Chan come up to the art room one lunchtime to check out the painting.

'Spooky,' Fitz says. 'But good, man.'

'You think?'

'You've let all that red drip on to the figure,' Chan points out. 'And what about all those splodges and splatters?'

'It's meant to be like that,' I say. 'Can't you tell?'

Chan pulls a face. 'I'm not really the arty type,' he says.

'I didn't think I was,' I admit. 'Not like this, anyhow. But I want to do another one now – a colour figure with grey all around it, and broken glass and barbed wire and stuff.' As I talk, I wonder if I can actually stick those things on to the painting, like a collage. Maybe graffiti art isn't the only way to say stuff, after all?

'You've gone all highbrow,' Fitz says, thoughtfully. 'It's Cat's influence. Has to be.'

'I don't think so,' I say.

'Still don't know what she sees in you,' Fitz says. 'Pretty, posh girls don't usually go for dates involving chip shops and dog-walking. Posh girls like class. You know – picnics, music, champagne, fireworks. I've seen it on the telly.'

'Yeah?' I grin. 'Last week you were telling me to treat her mean to keep her keen.'

'Well, yeah,' Fitz admits. 'You have to find a balance between the two.'

'Cat's different,' I say. 'She doesn't care about that stuff.'

She's too busy worrying about Josh, for starters. He still isn't home, and every time I ask about him she changes the subject. I have a feeling that maybe things aren't going quite as well as she thinks.

At least things are quiet on the Eden Estate – Scully hasn't reappeared and a trial date has been set for January, which means that maybe he really will go down this time. Lucky isn't missing him, that's for sure – and even Mum has stopped reminding me that Lucky isn't really our dog. It's like he's a part of the family now.

'Romance,' Fitz announces with a flourish, waving a withered old sunflower from the display on the bookshelf in front of my face. 'That's what you need, Mouse, mate. Posh girls like that sort of thing.'

'All girls,' Chan chips in. He has five sisters, so I guess he'd know. 'They like moonlight, and flowers, and surprises.'

Well, Cat likes surprises all right, I know that.

'Where am I going to get picnics, music, champagne, fireworks?' I ask.

'You'll think of something. You gotta make an effort,' Fitz counsels. 'Or . . .'

'Or what?'

'You'll lose her,' he says.

So I plan my surprise, and Fitz and Chan roll their eyes and tell me it's not classy enough, but they agree to help, all the same.

'Wow,' says Cat. 'Wow.'

We are having a picnic on the roof of the only bus shelter on the Eden Estate. A rickety ladder, twined with tinsel, was leaning up against the bus shelter when we arrived, but it's gone now, so we'll have to jump back down. I've spread a couple of old picnic rugs and some pillows across the corrugated steel and set up Fitz's ghetto blaster in the corner. Already, Lucky has snuggled down between us, sighing, as if he lounges about on bus-shelter roofs every day.

'When I was a kid, that summer in the country, there was a tree house,' I tell Cat. 'It was brilliant – you could lie out at night, watching the stars. There are no trees on the Eden Estate, though, so I got a bit of a thing about bus shelters.'

'You're crazy,' Cat laughs.

'You're not?'

I rummage around under the picnic rugs and bring out a bunch of red roses, only slightly wilted. Mr Lewis used them as his still life earlier today – I had to pick chewing gum off one of the roses, and shake pencil sharpenings out of the others.

'Mouse, they're lovely!'

'You like it?' I ask her. 'All this?'

'I love it. We can see everything . . . and nobody even knows we're here!'

She snuggles down against the slanted roof, peeping out over the top. Eden is looking especially gorgeous tonight. Last week someone – not me – painted a vivid sunrise on the long wall opposite, and overnight a scattering of stencilled silver stars sprang up on the cracked concrete around the old playground.

The Phoenix ruins are stuffed with plants, and flowers have started to appear all along the footpath that snakes through the estate. It's almost December, but it's still mild and there've been no frosts. Some of the flowers have been scuffed up, but most are still there. They make old ladies smile and little girls bend down to pick them, and day by day there are more.

'Did your mum do that?' Cat wants to know. 'With the flowers?'

'No. Could be anybody – or lots of people,

maybe. It's like someone looted a garden centre – actually, knowing this place, maybe they did?'

'The copycat graffiti is cool too,' Cat says. 'And the lifts . . .'

Cat and I added metres of silver tinsel to the spray-painted lifts just last week. Eden Estate is changing. It started as a few flowers, a protest about the torching of the Phoenix, but it's turning into more than that. It's about the people turning a sad, grey dump into somewhere less grim, less scary.

A couple of women wander up to the bus stop. We stay quiet, grinning, but although one of them wonders out loud where the music is coming from, they assume it must be from one of the tower block balconies. When the bus comes, a blaze of light sweeping through the estate, they get on without a backward glance. It's only when an old man glances out from a top-deck window that we're spotted. Cat blows him a kiss, and his startled face has us snorting with laughter as the bus swoops off into the night.

A moped putters to a halt below and a carrier bag appears on the edge of the bus shelter roof. Chan's uncle is a pizza delivery man. I ordered cheese and pineapple, with Coke instead of champagne, and Mars bars for afterwards.

'You thought of everything!' Cat laughs. She spots the tail end of my school tie dangling from a pocket where I stuffed it earlier. 'What's this, a tie? If I'd known we were dressing up, I'd have worn my party dress!'

'I like you as you are,' I tell her.

Cat hooks the school tie round my neck and reels me in. 'You too,' she says. 'You're very cute in a tie. Wish I went to your school.'

'You don't, Cat. It's a dump.'

'A cool dump, though,' Cat argues. 'At our school, nothing exciting ever happens. You could die of boredom in assembly one morning and nobody would even notice for hours. It's that exciting.'

'Hmmm,' I say. 'I can see how that might be difficult for you.'

'Maybe I'll ask for a transfer, turn up at your school one of these days . . . that'd be a laugh. Or you could come to mine.'

'Thought you said it was all girls?' I frown.

'It is,' Cat grins. 'Trust me, they'd love you.'

We duck down as a gang of kids swagger past, laughing and clowning around just inches from our heads.

'How's Josh?' I ask, quietly, once the kids have gone. 'Is he any better? I was thinking, if you want, I could come in and meet him. I know how rotten it is to be stuck in hospital –'

'No,' Cat says.

'No?'

'I don't want you to see him like that,' she says softly. 'They're doing more tests before they let him home, but it's just a temporary setback. He'll be home soon – you can meet him then.'

I shrug. 'OK.'

'He'd like you,' Cat says.

'I'd like him, I bet.'

We finish our pizza. In the distance, I can see three shadowy figures moving about in the darkness. One of them gives me a thumbs-up sign – Fitz.

'All that's missing is the stars,' I tell Cat.

'Well, even you can't organize that.'

'You think?'

We look up at the dark, velvet sky, and right on cue, there's a soft, whooshing sound and the darkness explodes into a fountain of tiny white diamonds.

'Oh!' Cat gasps. 'Fireworks! How did you . . .'

I put a finger to her lips as another shower of stars erupts, followed by a couple of rockets, complete with wailing sound effects. Lucky leans against me for reassurance, but he's got used to fireworks – all through November, the kids on the estate have been setting off bangers and rockets every chance they got.

More fountains of light and colour appear, blurring and sinking into the night sky like drops of bright watercolour on wet paper.

In the light from above, I can see Cat's face, tilted up towards the sky, her lips parted, smiling. On the ground, a couple of kids on bikes and a couple walking a dog have stopped to watch the show. On and on the fireworks go, colours drifting, stars fading into nothing, sparks of silver and gold raining down to earth. When it's finally over, there are a few ragged claps, a whistle of approval from the kids on bikes. Cat hugs me.

'Thanks,' she whispers. 'That was the coolest thing, Mouse. The best night ever.'

Lucky and I walk Cat home, then slouch back across the estate just after eleven. It's quiet now, with a soft drizzle starting to fall, and we're mooching past Eagle Heights when suddenly, Lucky sits down in the middle of the footpath and refuses to move. I tug his washing-line lead, try to reason with him.

'C'mon. What's the problem? You can't just stop!'

I tug on the lead again, but Lucky digs his heels in, leaning back stubbornly. He has never been disobedient or awkward before. His eyes look wild and anxious, and his grin has slipped into a lopsided grimace.

'We're nearly home,' I tell him. 'Come on!' The air smells of fireworks, but I can't see anything that would spook Lucky. The estate is quiet – unusually quiet. 'Lucky, come on!'

Still he won't move. I bend down and pick him up, but he struggles, his little legs scrabbling against me as if trying to escape from an unseen enemy.

'Shh,' I tell him, holding him tight as I walk on.

Suddenly there's a movement just ahead of me, and a rough voice calls out, 'Hey, stupid!'

I keep walking, head down, a little bit faster, but a stooped, scrawny figure steps out from the shadows, a can of beer in his tattooed hand. 'Hello, Mouse,' says Scully. 'Long time no see.'

'I thought . . .'

'That I was still in the nick?' he sneers. 'Well, I was, of course, thanks to your mum. But I'm out now – I got bail. And I'm not happy, Mouse. I'm not happy at all.'

I take a step back, but Scully grabs on to my sleeve. He's right up in my face, his eyes bloodshot, his chin dark with stubble, snarling. He's stronger than he looks. I can feel his breath, sour and stale against my skin, and I remember that this guy carries a knife. Lucky is crying now, a high-pitched whimper, his whole body wriggling and writhing to get free.

'Thief!' Scully hisses, and a fleck of spit lands on my cheek. A couple of kids walking past keep their eyes firmly on the gutter, keen to stay out of trouble. I don't blame them. I'm keen to stay out of trouble too, yet here it is, staring me in the face.

'D'you hear me?' Scully yells. 'D'you freakin' hear me? You nicked my dog!'

'I didn't,' I argue. 'I found him, on Clapham High Street. He was in an accident. I knew he wasn't mine, but I thought I'd hold on to him for you, while you were away . . .'

Lucky stops struggling and lies still in my arms, like he knows I just betrayed him. Scully grabs on to his neckerchief, and the little pirate dog bares his teeth, shuddering so hard his whole body shakes. Whatever I told Mum, whatever I said to Scully, there's no way I can give Lucky up. I just can't.

'I can keep hold of him, if you like,' I say, my voice calm and low. 'Till everything's sorted out. You don't need the hassle of looking after a dog, not at a time like this.'

Scully leans into my face. 'You're right, kid,' he snarls. 'Times are bad. Still, my mates have had a gentle word with a couple of the witnesses – Mark and JJ – and it turns out they don't remember much at all about what happened at the Phoenix. They've withdrawn their statements. That's good news, yeah?'

'Yeah,' I echo, dully. 'Good news for you.'

'I reckon your mum might be better off keeping her mouth shut too. She really doesn't want to get mixed up in a court case. Messy business. You can tell your mum that, from me.'

I swallow, nodding. 'I'll tell her.'

'I bet you've got to like my dog,' Scully says. 'While I've been away. Maybe you'd like to keep him?'

'Yes. I'd like that.'

'I wouldn't miss him,' he says. 'Lousy little mongrel, always whining and moaning. Nothin' but trouble. But he's my dog, see. I have a responsibility.'

Scully laughs. He wrenches Lucky from me and drops him on to the pavement, where he darts behind my legs, whimpering. 'Let's see, shall we? Let's see where the little rat really wants to be? We'll let him choose.'

I stare down at Lucky, and he gazes back at me, terrified.

Scully takes a step back, into the shadows. 'C'mon, stupid,' he says, his voice cold and hard. 'C'mon, boy.'

Lucky steps out from behind my legs, takes a step towards Scully. 'Lucky, here,' I say, but he doesn't seem to hear me. He slinks forward, his body hunched, shivering, like he's walking to the gallows.

'OK, stupid,' Scully says. 'OK.'

And finally I get it; Stupid is Lucky's real name.

'Lucky!' I plead, but the little pirate dog doesn't

look round. He walks right up to Scully, who jabs him with the toe of his trainer and makes him yelp. Lucky runs behind him, cowering.

I don't get it. I don't understand why any dog would go back to someone who treats him like dirt. 'Push off then, kid!' Scully yells. 'Your little mutt don't want you any more, OK? He knows where he belongs. And don't forget to tell your mum I'm out – and I'm watching her!'

He chucks his empty can at me. It hits my leg, spilling dregs of stale beer down my jeans. I stand still on the pavement, staring at Lucky. He stares back, lost, shivering, his eyes huge. He's not grinning. He may never grin again. Then he turns after Scully and disappears into the night.

There's a light on in Jake's workshop and I hammer on the door until he unlocks it, opening it a crack. 'Mouse?' he says, frowning. 'What's up, kid?'

'Can I come in?'

Jake holds the door wide and I slip inside. 'So. Girlfriend like the fireworks?'

I nod woodenly, but the rooftop picnic seems about a million years ago. All I can think about is Lucky – how he abandoned me to be with some thug who calls him Stupid. How I abandoned him.

'I've got a problem,' I blurt out. 'A big problem, Jake.'

'Yeah?'

'Scully,' I say.

'Ah.' Jake puts the kettle on, spoons out dried milk and coffee. 'I heard he was back.'

It all pours out then, about the threats to Mum, about Lucky choosing Scully over me. 'Why did he do that?' I demand. 'Why would he leave me for that jerk? I've never been mean to him. I've made sure he was fed, walked him twice a day, let him sleep on the end of my bed. So why?'

Jake shrugs. 'Dogs are loyal,' he tells me. 'Scully had Stupid – sorry, Lucky – from a pup. Dog probably felt like he didn't have a choice.'

'Scully doesn't even care about Lucky,' I say.

'Maybe not,' Jake agrees. 'But he's Scully's dog – you knew that right from the start. I'm not saying it's fair, Mouse, but there's not a whole lot you can do.'

I blow on my coffee, drinking it slowly. I think about Lucky and Scully and I think about me and my dad, and I wonder how come the people who are supposed to love and look after us can sometimes let us down so badly. Like Lucky, I know I'd go to Dad in a minute if he picked up the phone and asked me to, or wrote, or turned up out of the blue. He won't, though. He doesn't love me enough, and there's nothing I can do about that.

Maybe it's better that way.

'Scully's going to get away with it, isn't he?' I ask. 'The drug-pushing, the knife threat, all of it.'

Jake sighs.

'I don't know, Mouse,' he says.

In the lobby of Nightingale House, a couple of strings of icicle lights have appeared, draped across the ceiling. It looks cool, and it's dimmer than the strip light, so you can't see the peeling paint or the empty fag packets in the corner. An hour ago, they'd have made me smile, made me think that things were changing for the better. Now, I know that things will never change.

Up on the ninth floor, I turn the key in the lock at number 114. It's a moment before I realize that Mum is sitting in the living room in the dark, under the leafy plants. I switch the light on.

'Mum?' I say. 'Are you OK?'

She looks up, arranging her face into a smile that doesn't fool anyone.

'Jake just rang,' she says, her voice sad and heavy. 'He told me about Scully – and about Lucky. I'm sorry, Mouse.'

I sink down beside her. 'I'll get Lucky back,' I say. 'I have to.'

Mum bites her lip. 'I think maybe you should leave it. We've known all along that Lucky was Scully's dog. Try taking him back and you'll make even more of an enemy of Scully – and Mouse, we really don't need that.'

I have a feeling it's kind of too late for that. 'He told me to say he'd be watching you,' I say. 'Already his mates have got Mark and JJ to take back their police statements – that means you're the only witness, Mum. People would understand if you chose not to go to court. Nobody'd blame you . . .'

'I'm going to testify,' Mum says calmly. 'It's the right thing to do.'

I feel cold all over. If Scully's mates decide to have a 'talk' with Mum – well, she's not the kind to back down easily. And that spells trouble.


A handpainted paper banner emblazoned with the words *reach for the stars* has been draped across the school corridor, just along from Mr Brown's office. Wonky stars snipped from gold foil paper are collaged across it, plus a sprinkling of silver glitter. This is odd. We are not usually asked to reach for anything at Green Vale Comp, unless it's a plate of chips in the school canteen or a rope swing in the gym. Stars? Yeah, right. Looks like Mr Brown has finally lost it.

'Kavanagh!' yells the man himself, through the

scrum of early morning pupils. He is waving his arms around like a drowning man, and his face has that desperate, manic glare that all teachers at Green Vale develop after a while.

'What've you done now?' Fitz asks, impressed. 'Sounds like trouble!'

'Where's your tie?' Chan asks.

'Dangling from a bus shelter roof on the Eden Estate,' I snap. 'OK?'

I couldn't find my tie this morning, but that's the least of my troubles. I'm trying so hard to hold it all together today that I really don't think I can face a telling off from Mr Brown. I keep on walking.

'MARTIN KAVANAGH!' he roars again. 'I want to see you! My office, breaktime!'

'Everything OK?' Fitz asks, as we file into class. 'You seem kind of touchy.'

'I'm fine,' I snarl. 'Just leave it.' I can't even get my head round what happened last night, let alone explain it to Fitz and Chan. Not yet, anyway.

'Girl trouble,' I hear them mutter. 'Miaow!'

At breaktime, I hide out in the art room to avoid Mr Brown, then slouch over to the Learning Support Unit. This is the low point of my week. It's where they put the kids who don't speak English too well yet, or the ones like me who have dyslexia and problems with reading, writing and spelling.

Our regular teacher has been off work for months with stress-related depression, so we have an endless stream of supply teachers instead. Sometimes they are keen and well-meaning. Mostly they couldn't care less.

Three Polish girls in the corner are playing Junior Scrabble, which is kind of educational, only I think they're playing it in Polish. Kiran Jamal is drawing rude pictures on the desk, and Ceri Lloyd is touching up her peach-coloured lipstick. The supply teacher pretends not to notice, even when paper planes and chewing-gum wrappers sail above his head.

I slump across the table, doodling stars and spirals across a worksheet illustrated with cartoons. It looks like it was designed for a six-year-old, and I bet most six-year-olds would have it finished by now too. I've barely started. So what? My life's a mess, and one unfinished worksheet won't make a bit of difference.

There's a loud knock on the door, and everyone turns to look as a girl walks in, a pretty, mixed-race girl with ringlet curls and slanting eyes. She's wearing a short black skirt, a little white shirt and a Green Vale Comp tie with the end all frayed and worn, exactly like the one I lost last night. My jaw drops so far it just about hits the tabletop.

It's Cat.

She gives me a little wave and winks and grins, and the boys at the back gawp and make wolf-whistle noises under their breath.

'Can I help you?' the supply teacher asks.

'My name is Catrin Thomas and I just started at Green Vale today. I'm supposed to be working here?'

'Oh? I'm afraid I don't know anything about that. I don't know –'

'I'll just sit here, shall I?' Cat says, nodding towards my desk. 'Do one of these worksheets, see how I get on. Yeah?'

'Sit with us,' the boys at the back leer. 'We can show you everything you need to know! Stay away from Kavanagh, he's weird.'

'Just my type.' She smiles sweetly and slides into the seat beside me. 'Surprise!' she says.

Surprise? It's that, all right. I try to dredge up a smile, but fail. My chest feels tight, and my hands have clenched into fists. It's not a good surprise, that's for sure. 'What are you playing at?' I hiss.

'Schools,' Cat says. 'Isn't it obvious?'

'You're wearing my tie,' I accuse.

'Well, they weren't going to let just anyone in, were they? I had to look the part. You wouldn't believe the trouble I went to pull this off. I had to fake phone calls from my mum, and from the education authority in Cardiff –'

'Cardiff?'

'We just moved here from Cardiff,' she says sweetly. 'At the weekend. All my files got lost in the post.'

'Do you go to drama club, or a support group for compulsive liars?'

'Acting, lying, it's all the same thing,' Cat says. 'Anyway, I'm here. Cool, huh?'

'No,' I say through gritted teeth. 'Not cool. I told you, Cat, I'm trying to stay out of trouble – I don't need this.'

'I'm not causing trouble,' she says airily. 'Just having a laugh. What're you doing in this class, anyhow?' She lowers her voice. 'I mean, it's not like you're thick, is it?'

That hurts. 'Thanks a bunch,' I say. 'But apparently I am. My spelling's bad, my reading's worse, and writing gives me a headache.'

'This'd give anyone a headache,' Cat replies. 'They'll be dancing on the tables, next.'

'You wanted to see what it was like.'

'I know.' She grins. 'It's even better than I imagined. Our place is the opposite – super-strict. Sneeze in class and you get detention for a week.'

'Funny how well you're adapting.'

'Isn't it? Maybe I'm just born to be bad. So. What're you doing?'

She picks up the cartoony worksheet. Her eyes widen a little when she sees the questions, but she doesn't say anything, and I can feel my skin flush crimson. Is she laughing at me, or pitying me? I don't know which would feel worse.

'You're dyslexic, aren't you?' she says to me. 'Lots of people are. My friend Naomi . . .'

I don't want to hear about Cat's friend Naomi. I pick up the worksheet, scrunch it up into a ball and skim it across the classroom. The supply teacher looks nervous, but doesn't say anything. I look at the clock. Five minutes till lunchtime. I don't know if I can survive it.

'It took me forever to track you down,' Cat is saying, brightly. 'I went to maths, French, history, chemistry . . .'

I hide behind my fringe, scowling.

She frowns. 'Aren't you even a little bit glad to see me, Mouse? I thought you'd be pleased. I thought this would make you laugh!'

'Did you?'

'Don't be mad at me, Mouse,' she says.

The bell goes, and kids stampede for the door. I grab my bag and try to lose myself in the crowd, but Cat is running along behind me. 'So,' she asks me. 'What happens at lunch?'

I don't even want to think about that. Fitz, Chan, Neela Rehman, the rest of the kids in my class – and

Cat, eating turkey twizzlers and pretending it's cool. It doesn't bear thinking about. Help me, I think. Please.

A firm hand grasps the back of my jacket and pulls me up short.

'Kavanagh,' Mr Brown says. 'Finally. My office now.'

Sometimes, help comes from the most unexpected places.

I sit across the desk from Mr Brown. 'No tie today, Kavanagh?' he asks.

I could tell him it was stolen by a psycho posh girl who is in the school canteen right now, impersonating a Green Vale pupil and asking the dinner ladies if they have Camembert cheese and fairly traded chocolate pudding, but a few dregs of loyalty linger on.

'Lost it,' I say.

'I'm impressed,' Mr Brown says.

'Uh?'

'Not about the tie,' he says, hastily. 'No. It's the effort you've been making to stay out of trouble, and the wonderful things you've been doing in art. Mr Lewis has nothing but praise for you.'

'He does?'

'He does. And I have to say I agree. You have an unusual talent.'

'Who, me?' I can feel myself sitting up straighter, taller.

'Yes, you,' Mr Brown says. 'What's more, I feel I may have underestimated the depth of your feelings with that whole graffiti incident. I've reread your letter and I can see that you raised some very real criticisms. What seemed like an act of vandalism at the time may have been, in fact, a cry from the heart.'

He's crazy. Teachers get this way, sometimes, especially at this time of year. Stress, school dinners and endless school reports have scrambled his brains.

'You made a valid point with your graffiti protest. I don't approve of the way you made it, but you were right. This school needs more colour. That wall needs more colour! A mural, perhaps? Something tasteful – perhaps a countryside scene? You're the expert, of course. I thought you might find time to draw up some designs over the Christmas break?'

I blink.

'Green Vale has always been a school where pupils are encouraged to reach for the stars,' he says. 'This is your chance to do just that!'

I really scare Mr Brown then. I jump up and give him a high five, tell him he's not the stuffy old loser everyone says he is. Then I'm out of there, sprinting off along the corridor, jumping up to drag down the paper banner as I go. It falls to the ground behind me, curling itself around Mr Brown's feet. Amazingly, he doesn't seem to mind.

At least one thing is going right today.

My fingers are gritty with silver glitter from the banner, like they are made of stars. I might even put Mr Brown up on my star map – a distant star, obviously, in a far-off galaxy. But still.

The minute I get to the school canteen, though, my mood crashes. Cat is at a table with Fitz, Chan and a whole bunch of Year Nine lads. She's laughing, flicking her hair, flirting shamelessly with Lee Costa who is perched on the table beside her, eating her chips.

She sees me and waves, winking cheekily. Suddenly, I'm not hungry any more. I turn round and walk away, but Cat is right behind me. 'Wait up,' she says. 'What did he want with you, the Head? Are you in trouble?'

'No,' I say shortly. 'You are.'

'What?'

'You don't belong here,' I snap, though it's clear from what I've just seen that she's settled in pretty well.

She slips a hand into mine, but I shake her off. 'Mouse, what's wrong?' she asks, genuinely baffled.

I stop walking and turn to face her. Last night, holed up on the bus-shelter roof watching fireworks explode above the Eden Estate, I felt closer to Cat than I've ever felt to anyone. Today, it's like I never knew her at all.

'Why did you come here, Cat?' I ask. 'To laugh at me? To see what school is like if you don't have rich parents and endless cash? To land me in trouble again? To flirt with my friends, sneer at the scabby desks and scruffy classrooms?'

'It's not like that,' Cat says in a small voice.

'So what is it like?' I demand. 'Oh, what's the point? I'm sick of your stupid games. Go away and leave me alone.'

I think she might cry, but instead her eyes flash with anger and she pushes past me, shoving her way through the double doors and marching out across the playground.

'I want my tie back,' I yell after her. She just drags it off and drops it on to the concrete playground without a backward glance.

'Sheesh,' says Fitz from behind me. 'Great move, Mouse. You've really blown it now.'

## 23

I never used to have a girlfriend and I never used to have a dog, but now, without them, I am lost.

I feel bad about Cat. She wasn't trying to wind me up, but the sight of her flirting with Lee Costa was just about the last straw. I got mad, and I said stuff I shouldn't have said, and she walked out of my life. It's probably a good thing. She doesn't need a boyfriend from the Eden Estate, especially one who is sad and scared and has enemies like Frank Scully.

All the same, I miss her.

I walk up and down her street about a dozen times that night, and again the night after. She doesn't come out, but on the third night, her mum pulls back the curtain and gives me a long, hard stare.

I give up then, pretty much. Looks like I'm destined to be a no-dog, no-girl boy. I try to walk away, but walking away from Cat is not easy. I get about halfway down the street, come to a halt at a bus stop and look back at her house. If she'd just come out, then maybe I could explain, tell her why I acted so mean. Maybe.

I have a quick look around, then haul myself up on to the bus-stop roof. The view is better from up here, but it's dark and cold and there's a soft drizzle starting to fall. I've just about given up hope when I spot a bicycle whirling along towards me, ridden by a sad-faced girl with coffee-coloured skin and ringlet curls.

I jump down off the bus shelter roof. 'Cat!'

She skids her bike to a halt and the dynamo lights fizzle and fade. 'You,' she says, coldly.

'Nice to see you too. Look, Cat, about the other day . . .'

She shrugs. 'I'll get over it. You're not so special.'

That hurts.

'You walked past my house about a million times last night,' she comments. 'Why didn't you call in?'

'Didn't think you'd want to see me. Why didn't you come down?'

'Same reason.' Her mouth twitches into a smile. 'You look terrible.'

'Of course I do! I've lost you, I've lost Lucky and there's a knife-wielding maniac on the loose out there with a grudge against my mum . . . I've had better weeks.'

Cat's eyes widen. 'What?' she says. 'What are you talking about? What maniac? Where's Lucky?'

We lean against the bus stop and I tell her the whole sorry story. 'Scully doesn't want Lucky,' I explain. 'He just wants to hurt me – and Mum. What if he does something bad to Lucky, just to spite us?'

Cat bites her lip. 'Look, Mouse, this isn't right. We have to get Lucky back!'

My heart leaps, but I know it's not that simple. 'That'll just make Scully madder than ever,' I say sadly. 'Lucky is his dog . . . well, he thinks so, anyway. No. It's awful, but we have to let Lucky go.' Even as I say it, I feel a stab of pain inside. Letting Lucky go is against every instinct I know.

'We can't!' Cat protests.

'If we take Lucky back, Scully's going to go crazy,' I say. 'He's already had a go at the other witnesses, scared them into withdrawing their statements. I don't want him to start on Mum.'

Cat looks let down, as if I just sold my best friend into slavery. Well, maybe I did. I don't know what to do with the mess of anger and frustration and hurt that's bubbling away inside me. I want to kick through plate-glass windows until the pavement glitters with splintered glass, punch a wall until the skin on my fist is mashed and bleeding. I want to yell and swear and curl up and cry.

I don't do any of that, of course. Cat slips her hand into mine.

'What a mess,' she says.

I'd feel better if I could at least see Lucky out and about around the estate, but it's like he has vanished off the face of the earth. Fitz and Chan ask around a bit for me, but nobody's seen Lucky – or Scully – for days.

'Word is that Scully's gone away for a while,' I tell Mum. 'He must be lying low.'

'That's good, isn't it?' Mum asks.

'I suppose.'

I can't stop worrying, though. I just need to know that Lucky is safe. On Friday, after school, I see old Mrs S. carrying her shopping towards the lift, beneath the twinkling icicle lights, and I run up to help.

'Oh, Mouse, thank you,' she says. 'Those bags were heavy! I've been getting a bit of shopping in for my Frank.'

'Right,' I say carefully. 'I heard he was back.'

'Yes,' she says, beaming. 'It was all a mix-up, Mouse. He's not really a bad boy.'

I bite my tongue. Scully has been trouble since the day he was born, I reckon. He may wriggle out of the drug-pushing charge now that he's 'persuaded' the witnesses to back off, but everyone in the Phoenix saw him threaten Mum with a knife. He won't get away with that, surely?

'I've already made some cakes,' Mrs S. is telling me. 'My Frankie has always had a sweet tooth. He's bound to be round to see his old gran.'

We step out of the tinselled lift. 'You haven't seen him yet then?' I press.

'No,' Mrs S. admits. 'He's been over in Luton, the last few days, seeing his mum. He'll be back soon, though – today, perhaps. I want to be ready.'

She turns the key and steps back to let me into the flat. In the lounge, the table is spread as if for a child's party, with plates of iced cakes wrapped in cling film, wilted sandwiches cut into neat triangles and a bottle of lemonade. It looks like Mrs S. has been ready for Frankie's visit for a while.

'I can make some fresh sandwiches now,' she says, taking the shopping bags from me. 'Thank you, Mouse. Would you like some cake? There's plenty!'

'No, no, it's OK,' I tell her. 'Mrs S. . . . well, I hope you don't mind me asking, but did Scully – I mean, Frank – take Lucky to Luton, d'you know? My dog? It turns out he belonged to Frank after all. He – um – took Lucky back, and I miss him, and I just want to know that he's OK.'

'Your dog?' she echoes. 'Oh dear. My Josie didn't say anything about a dog.'

I frown. 'Right. OK,' I say. 'I expect someone around here is looking after Lucky then.'

Mrs S. looks doubtful. 'Maybe,' she says. 'I hope so. I'll have a word with Frank for you, when I do see him. He's just not cut out to look after a dog – his temper gets the better of him.'

My heart sinks to the soles of my converse trainers. Where the heck is Lucky, if he's not with Scully? And what does she mean, about Scully's temper getting the better of him?

'When will Scully – I mean Frank – be back?' I ask.

Mrs S. looks vague. 'Oh, sometime soon, I expect,' she says. 'Today or tomorrow, or maybe the day after. He's bound to come and see me, the minute he can. I'll ask about the dog, I promise.'

'Well, great,' I tell her. 'Thank you.'

Back at the flat, Mum is draping fairy lights round the Swiss cheese plant, singing to herself. 'Bit early, aren't you?' I ask. 'It's not even December till next week.'

'I know, I know, but I thought it might look nice . . . I've had a bit of good news, Mouse.'

I don't want good news when all I can think about is Lucky, alone maybe, hungry, unwanted, unloved. 'Yeah?' I ask.

'Yeah!' Mum grins. 'Julie's been in talks with the council all week, and it looks like they're going to fund some improvements on the Eden Estate . . .'

'Improvements?'

'General repairs, for starters,' Mum explains. 'Which has to be good, because let's face it, most of the flats around here are in a pretty dismal state. It's not just that, though. They're going to build a children's nursery, a youth club and a day centre for senior citizens, down where the Phoenix used to be. And they're going to lease one of the new buildings to us, so that the Phoenix can carry on helping to fight back against the drug problems here on the estate. We'll be back in business, Mouse! Isn't that fantastic?'

'Great,' I say. 'Really, Mum, it's brilliant!'

'We won't just be a small-time charity, working alone,' she tells me. 'We'll be working alongside the council, with proper support from the social services and the health authority. The Phoenix is going be bigger and better than ever!'

I force a smile. 'I'm really glad,' I tell her. 'You've worked so hard on this project, you and Luke and Julie. It's great the council can see that – that they're prepared to help.'

'There's a scheme like this in Liverpool, apparently, where the council are working alongside an anti-drugs charity to clean up a troubled estate,' Mum says. 'So far, the results have been really positive. Julie thinks we should go up north, take a look at how that project is going – get an idea of how we can make it work here.'

'Great,' I echo. Mum turns back to the fairy lights, singing under her breath. For the first time in weeks she looks really happy, her face alive with plans for the future.

'We'll still have a garden,' she tells me. 'The council loved that idea – they want to make it a big community garden, a focal point, with the buildings clustered around it. It's all about creating a sense of identity and belonging for the people here on Eden – helping them to feel part of a community. I've got so many plans!'

I smile, and Mum doesn't notice that it's a thin, sad kind of a smile. Now isn't the time to tell her what Mrs S. said about Scully's temper, or ask about where Lucky can be. She's had enough doom and gloom, lately. I don't want to spoil her optimism.

'Got homework,' I say, dragging my rucksack through to my room. Mum doesn't even raise an eyebrow, although it must be the first time in living memory I've admitted to having homework, let alone threatened to actually do it. I shut the door and flop down on the bed, looking at the ceiling of stars. I think of Mr Brown's mural idea, of the banner with its gold-foil constellations. I think of the council's plans to drag the Eden Estate out of trouble with a coat of paint, a new youth centre and a community garden, to turn it into a place where people can hope.

Then I think of Lucky, whimpering, lost, forgotten already by the bloke who thinks he owns him. If he's not in Luton with Scully, where is he? Curled up in the corner of some lowlife's flat, cringing, scared? He's not OK, I know he's not. I can feel it inside, a sad, sick feeling in the pit of my belly.

Mum's dreaming of a brand-new Phoenix, a brand-new Eden. Me, I'm still stuck in the real world.

Next morning, Saturday, I'm washing cars for Jake to help pay him back for the firework display. I have a date with Cat for later, but even the thought of that can't cheer me up. I barely slept last night, thinking about Lucky. I know – I just know – that he's in trouble.

Fitz and Chan arrive. They know about Lucky and Scully now, so I fill them in on what Mrs S. said yesterday. I explain that Lucky is not with Scully, and how Mrs S. thinks Scully isn't suited to keeping a dog. 'That's his own gran talking,' I remind them. 'If she thinks that, it must be bad.'

'Creep's not fit to look after a stick insect, let alone a dog,' Fitz says.

'You don't think he'd have left Lucky alone?' I wonder out loud. 'Forgotten about him, maybe?'

Jake looks across from the car he's working on, frowning. Fitz lowers his voice. 'Nah' he says. 'He'll have left him with a mate, most likely. We could take a look around, try and find out.'

'Yeah?'

Chan narrows his eyes. 'We can say we've started a dog-walking business,' he says. 'We can pretend we're making lists and rotas for the business, find out about every dog on the estate.'

'Nice one,' Fitz grins.

Jake straightens up, wiping his hands on an oily rag. 'It's not a game,' he says to us. 'Don't go stirring up trouble, OK? I mean it.'

Fitz shrugs. 'We're not doing nothin' wrong,' he says. 'Just getting some facts together. Wassup with that?'

'Don't mess with Frank Scully,' Jake insists.

'We won't,' Fitz says. 'Scully's not here anyway. We'll stay out of trouble, OK, man?'

Fitz and Chan head off, and Jake rolls his eyes. 'Like kids playing at spies,' he huffs. 'Seriously, Mouse, you have to forget about this dog.'

'I can't!' I burst out. 'Not until I know if he's OK or not. Why would Scully nick his dog back and then disappear and leave him behind? It doesn't make sense. I'm worried.'

Jake pushes a hand through his hair, leaving a couple of streaks of grime on his forehead.

'Lucky was mine,' I explain. 'It's not my fault that he was Scully's first. I care about him, OK?'

Jake sighs. 'The dog's all right,' he says.

'You don't know that!'

'I do,' Jake says. 'All right? Scully's got some business deal, down Luton way. He couldn't take the dog, but Lucky's safe, take my word for it. You can relax.'

I open my eyes wide, but Jake can't quite meet my gaze.

'You knew?' I ask. 'You knew he was safe, all this time?'

'I can't get involved in this, Mouse, mate,' Jake says. 'Forget I said anything, yeah?'

I can't believe what I'm hearing. 'Forget?' I echo. 'Jake, you know how worried I've been about Lucky. Now you're saying you knew all along where he was?'

'I'm not saying that,' Jake snaps.

'But you knew he was safe. You knew he was being looked after, fed, cared for. You could have told me!'

'Mouse, mate,' he says through gritted teeth. 'I've said way more than I should have already. Just drop it. You've got cars to wash.'

He walks away, holes up in the little office and slams the door behind him. I can see him through the glass, hunched over the desk, working through a mound of paperwork. His jaw is set, his face angry, but I can't tell whether he's angry with Scully or with me, or maybe even himself.

I head for the sink, fill a fresh bucket with warm

water and add a capful of carwash, grab a sponge and a squeegee and a chamois leather. I wash four cars, one after the other, but it doesn't quite kill the anger, the sense of betrayal. How come Jake knows so much, anyway? I dig out the chrome cleaner and start scrubbing at the chrome trim, polishing so hard I can see my reflection in the silvery surface. Jake comes up behind me, quietly. 'OK,' he says. 'OK, Mouse. I'm sorry.'

'You should have told me, Jake.'

'I know, Mouse, mate,' he says. 'It's complicated, but yeah, I should have told you. Scully's out of order on this.'

'Is he your friend?' I ask, my mouth curled into a sneer. 'Or just a business associate?'

'Don't matter,' Jake tells me. 'Do you want this blasted dog back, or not?'

My heart leaps. 'Yes,' I say. 'You know I do!'

Jake chews his lip. 'Mouse, you have to keep quiet about this,' he says. 'If Scully ever finds out I helped you . . .'

'He won't,' I promise. 'I won't tell anyone, not ever!'

Jake sighs. 'He'll know anyhow,' he says heavily. 'It ain't rocket science. We're gonna have to lie low for a bit, the pair of us.'

'Whatever,' I say.

He walks back to the office, opens a locked

drawer and pulls out a small silver key on a knotted loop of string. 'Come on then.'

We head out across the courtyard, walking down towards the lock-up garages. 'Scully wanted a guard dog, not a pet,' Jake tells me. 'Something fierce, something tough. Then he won Stupid in a card game. It seemed perfect, only the pup grew up small and skinny and about as fierce and tough as ice cream and jelly. Scully wasn't pleased. He didn't treat the dog well – said he was trying to toughen it up.'

Not treating a dog well . . . I try not to think about what that might mean.

'Then Stupid – Lucky, I mean – ran away. Everyone knew it was because he'd treated the dog so badly, but Scully tried to make out the dog had been stolen. Maybe he even believed it himself.'

We're in the lane of lock-up garages now, walking over broken glass, between rows of ancient, ramshackle garages.

'I'm only doing this because I think it's wrong, OK, to leave him alone like this,' Jake is telling me. 'Scully was only meant to be gone overnight, but the deal's taking a while to sort out –'

'Where is he?' I ask, my heart thumping. 'Where's Lucky?'

'I went in and fed him, yesterday, OK?' Jake tells me. 'I've got a spare key, y'see. I swear I wouldn't have let him stay there another night, Mouse. It's wrong. It's cruel.'

Jake stops beside one of the lock-ups, fits the little silver key into the lock. I think I hear a faint whimpering sound, and then Jake is pulling the metal door up and over our heads.

It's dark inside the garage, and it takes me a moment to focus. Down at the back, behind a posh blue car and a tower of piled-up boxes half-hidden in canvas tarpaulin, Lucky is tied to the wall by his washing-line lead. He has pulled so hard to free himself that the neckerchief has turned into a noose round his neck, almost choking him. He has no food, an empty water bowl, nothing but an oily rag to lie on. There is a yellow puddle at his feet, dog dirt in the corner, the stink of ammonia and fear.

I hate Scully so much right then, I could kill him.

'I had to leave him tied up,' Jake says. 'If Scully had come back and found him untied . . . well, don't matter now, I guess.'

'Did you give him the rag to lie on?' I ask. 'The water bowl?'

'Yeah, but it wasn't enough,' Jake says, sadly. 'I should have done more. I'm sorry, Mouse.'

I'm sorry too. I always thought Jake was someone strong, someone I could trust, but I can see now he's just as scared as the rest of us. At least, in the end, he did what was right. Another day like this and Lucky could have died, maybe, sad and starving and shivering in the long, cold nights.

Jake bends down, slicing through the neckerchief with a penknife. Lucky springs forward, into my arms, and I hide my face against his shivering body. Boys don't cry.

Back at the flat, I make a nest for Lucky beneath the Swiss cheese plant with the twinkling fairy lights. I cover him with my old hoodie, let him lap water from a bowl lifted up to him, take slices of ham from my fingers. He drinks and eats and sleeps a lot, then wakes and gazes at me with sad brown eyes. His lips twitch into a grin.

'He'll be OK,' Mum tells me. 'Thank goodness you found him in time.'

'I couldn't leave him there,' I tell her. 'I just couldn't, Mum.'

'I know, Mouse,' she says. 'I know.'

I told her that I was walking past the lock-ups and heard a whining, scrabbling noise. I pretended I'd been able to force the lock, because I didn't want to dump Jake in trouble. He'll have enough of that on his plate when Scully gets back and finds Lucky gone.

Me too.

'What are we going to do?' I ask Mum.

'Lie low,' she says. 'Stick together. Hope for the best.'

I meet Cat beneath a street light at the corner of her street. 'So, Lucky's back,' she says, her eyes dancing. 'Mouse, I'm so, so glad!'

'Me too,' I tell her. 'But Scully'll go crazy when he finds out. He's still away, so we're OK for now, but things could get very nasty . . .'

'He's on bail,' Cat scoffs. 'What can he do? Besides, you could get the RSPCA on to him. Sick loser. It'll be OK, Mouse, trust me.'

Somehow, I don't think either bail or the threat of the RSPCA would worry Scully much, but I keep my mouth shut.

'Can't wait to see Lucky,' Cat is saying. 'Poor little thing . . .'

'He's much better,' I tell her. 'He was pretty rough at first, but he slept for hours and he's eaten his body weight in ham and sausages and digestive biscuits.'

'I've bought him some Camembert,' Cat says. 'He likes that.'

As we turn in to the estate, we meet Fitz and Chan being towed along by two huge Rottweilers. 'Mouse, man,' Fitz accuses. 'This is all your fault! The dog-walking business was just meant to be a scam, but you try saying no to a nutter like Psycho

Sam. He's signed us up to walk his dogs twice a day from now until Christmas!'

I laugh. 'Think of the money you'll earn.'

'What money?' Fitz wails. 'He reckons it's compensation for the time we broke his window playing footy. Man, we were eight years old! That's harsh!'

'I found Lucky,' I tell them, launching into the edited version of the story I've already told Mum and Cat, the version that doesn't include Jake.

Fitz and Chan high five us, then get dragged off by the lumbering Rottweilers. Cat and I walk between the tower blocks, past the beaten-up kids' playground towards the Phoenix wreckage. I tell her Mum's news about the council's promise to help them rebuild.

'Things are really changing around here,' Cat says. 'It starts with a few graffiti hits and a couple of flowers planted in the ashes, and now look at what's happening!'

'Yeah . . .' I'm looking at something else, though, something just beyond the wrecked Phoenix, a shiny, dark blue VW camper van painted with millions of tiny silver stars.

It reminds me of another van, a clapped-out patchwork-painted VW, a van from the past, from the summer I spent with my dad. It makes me think of Finn, Dizzy and Leggit, of festival nights curled up on a thin bunk, of hot apple squash made from the ancient whistling kettle and drunk scalding hot from spotty tin mugs.

'See that old van?' I start saying to Cat, and then everything goes crazy because a big, scruffy black-and-white wolf-dog is racing towards me across the mud, tail waving like a flag. I don't understand. It can't really be happening, but it is, and my heart hammers so hard you can probably see it through my T-shirt. Cat screams and the big black-and-white lurcher dog launches herself at me, licking my face, twisting and yelping.

'What is this?' Cat is asking, but I'm down on my knees on the concrete, the big skinny dog dancing around me. Suddenly, out of nowhere, Lucky jumps in between us, yelping, grinning, not wanting to be left out. I can see Mum in the distance, grinning, and I scoop Lucky up, hold him tight.

'Feeling better, huh?' I grin. Then I turn to the big, scruffy wolf-dog leaping around me, tail lashing.

'Leggit,' I whisper into her sticky-up fur. 'Hey, hey, Leggit! It's really you! How are you, girl? What took you so long?'

I introduce Leggit to Lucky, and the two dogs circle warily, sniffing, then take off at top speed towards the van, where Mum is standing with a young man and woman. They were just twelve and thirteen that long-gone summer, younger than I am now, but I'd know Finn and Dizzy anywhere.

They were my best friends that summer I was seven, along with Leggitt, of course. My dad let me down, kept his distance and finally ran out on me, but Finn and Dizzy were always there, no matter what. They cared. I thought I'd have them forever, but after the bonfire accident, the summer fell apart, social services stepped in and gradually we lost touch.

Finn is taller, broader now, with dark dreadlocks down past his shoulders, pulled back from his face with a headband. His eyes are blue-grey and his mouth curves up in the biggest grin I've ever seen. Beside him, Dizzy is wiping her eyes, running towards me, whirling me round and round in a tight, tight hug.

'Dizzy!' I choke out. 'Finn!'

'Mouse, pal,' Finn laughs. 'It's so good to see you! We couldn't believe it when we got your letter, after all that time . . .'

My letter? I shoot a sidelong glance at Cat, and she can't meet my eye. Her mouth twitches into a smile.

'It went to Dad's place, obviously,' Dizzy explains. 'They were on holiday, but he passed it on the minute he got back. I couldn't believe it. It was the best surprise ever!'

'Too right!' I grin, and Cat winks at me.

The girl who gave me a handful of stars has just given me back my best friends, and I can't even begin to take it all in.

'We were going to write, but there's so much to catch up on,' Finn is saying. 'It's my brother's birthday tomorrow – remember Niall? He lives in Kent now. We're heading down to see him, so we thought we'd drop in on you!'

'We just couldn't wait,' Dizzy chips in. 'We found the flat OK, but Magi said you were out . . .'

'We came down to the van,' Mum says. 'Not a good idea to leave it parked here unattended. A minute more and the kids'd have picked it clean.'

'This is my girlfriend, Cat,' I tell them. 'And my dog, Lucky.'

'Hi, Cat,' they say. 'Hi, Lucky.'

Everyone is smiling and talking at once, and Leggit and Lucky are skittering around, tails in the air. I have about a million questions, but I don't know where to start.

'Can you stay?' I ask. 'I mean, you don't have to be at Niall's until tomorrow, do you?'

'No,' Finn says. 'We can stay for a bit. If you'll have us, that is!'

'You're very welcome,' Mum says. 'I wouldn't

leave the van here overnight, though . . . it might not be safe.'

'No problem,' Finn tells her. 'We'll stay a while, then head on down to Kent. I promised Dizz a whistle-stop tour of London, so if you want to show us the big city . . .'

'What now?' I ask. 'In the dark?'

'Why not?' Dizzy says. 'It'll be pretty. You can be our tour guides!'

We pile into the camper-van, Mum, Cat, Lucky, Leggit and me, with Finn and Dizzy in the front. Finn fires the engine up, and the whole van shakes and roars like a demented tractor. I frown. 'It sounds exactly like . . .'

'. . . the patchwork van?' Dizzy finishes for me. 'It is. Finn painted it up. We still take it to the festivals, in the summer. We do storytelling workshops, so we get in free!'

I think of the new-look patchwork van struggling over rutted ground, parking up beside a river with tents and tepees all around. Music playing into the night, wood fires burning, children running wild, the way we did at festivals long ago. I can't help smiling.

'Where to first?' Finn wants to know, turning out of the estate and on to the main road. 'Any ideas?'

'A magical mystery tour, yeah?' Mum suggests. 'Take a left here . . .'

'OK,' Finn says. 'We're not fast, but we're reliable. Actually, we're not reliable either, but we do have tea-making facilities . . .'

'I can't believe how tall you are, Mouse,' Dizzy says over her shoulder. 'What are you now, fourteen?'

'Yup.'

'Still into BMX bikes and beaches and tree houses?'

I frown. 'Not exactly. I kind of went off the whole BMX thing after the bonfire, y'know? And I haven't seen many beaches or tree houses, lately.'

'He's more into painting, these days,' Cat says. 'And stars.'

'Stars?' Dizzy asks. 'Remember when we used to look for the Pole Star, that summer? I still think of you, whenever I see it.'

I want to say that I think of her too, and Finn, Leggit, Tess and a half-dozen other people from that long-gone summer. I just grin at Dizzy through the darkened van, and she grins back, and I think she gets the message.

'What about your mum, Finn?' I ask. 'Is she still at Bramble Cottage?'

'Yeah, Tess is still there,' he says. 'And Gran. If you ever want a country holiday, you'd be welcome, Mouse – and you, of course, Magi, and Cat.

London's cool, but if you fancy a bit of peace and quiet . . .'

Finn takes care not to make the offer sound like charity, and Mum smiles in the darkness. She looks happy tonight, like the kind of person who might go for a holiday in the country. I think about the tree house with its roof of stars at Bramble Cottage, and about the veggie garden, the goat, the chickens. I refuse to think about the bonfire, or the BMX, or any of the stuff that happened afterwards.

'Take a right turn just here,' Mum instructs. 'Oxford Circus!'

We rumble past the famous shopping street, grinning at the flashing Christmas lights, the tacky neon Santas. 'Good job none of it's open,' Dizzy says. 'I haven't started my Christmas shopping yet!'

A few minutes later, we're heading for Trafalgar Square, where the giant Christmas tree glints and sparkles in the darkness.

'So, were you, like, childhood sweethearts?' Cat asks Finn and Dizzy. 'I didn't realize. Cool!'

'We weren't together the whole time,' Dizzy says.

'No, she ditched me in Year Nine,' Finn says. 'For some geek who helped her with her chemistry homework –'

'He was not a geek!'

'She got an A in her GCSE and dumped him the next day,' Finn tells us. 'Poor guy.'

'So you got back together?'

'Eventually. I turned up on the doorstep just before her seventeenth birthday in this old crate, and whisked her away to Glastonbury Festival. Haven't been able to shake her off since!'

Dizzy elbows him in the ribs. 'He's been plaguing me, more like,' she says. 'He got a place at music college in Birmingham, so there was no getting rid of him . . .'

'We share a flat now,' Finn says. 'It's a nightmare, but hey . . .'

We drive on through the night, rattling past Big Ben and the Houses of Parliament, talking non-stop, then head for Tower Bridge and the river. Finn parks down by the Thames Embankment, under the strings of fairy lights. This is the place Cat and I walked hand-in-hand after our posh tea in The Savoy, where we caught a river boat and then went on the London Eye. Now, the Eye is still, and the dark ribbon of water glitters with reflected light. A pale sliver of moon hangs above it, a perfect crescent in the dark sky.

'New moon,' Finn comments. 'We should all make a wish.'

But for once in my life, I've got pretty much everything I need. Mum is on one side of me, Cat on the other, Lucky curled up safely on my lap. Leggit, the big skinny wolf-dog, is stretched out at my feet, and Finn and Dizzy are telling me all about the festivals I've missed this summer. Who needs wishes?

Cat yawns. 'Tired?' Mum asks her. 'We can drop you off on the way back. It's a bit late.'

'I've got a key,' she replies sleepily. 'No problem.'

'We'll get moving,' Finn says. 'We can drive on down to Kent, be at Niall's by morning. But now we know where you are . . . well, we'll be seeing a lot more of you. That's a promise.'

Finn starts up the engine and we chug away into the night traffic, a deep blue, starry VW van on its way down to Kent via the Eden Estate. Cat's fallen asleep on my shoulder, her hair brushing my cheek, and Dizzy is telling me that her dad finally got married to his girlfriend, and that she has two new half-sisters. 'Weird, huh?' she says. 'Katie's four, Stella's six.'

We drop Cat at her gate, and I see a curtain twitch as she slides her key into the lock and waves goodnight. I hope she's not going to be in trouble. Finn drives on, finally turning into the Eden Estate. It's quiet, except for a gang of young men in hoodies lurking near Skylark Rise. One of them chucks a stone at the van, and it clatters against the side door.

'Tough place,' Finn comments. 'Don't think they like the van.'

'They don't like anything, that lot,' Mum says darkly. 'But like it or not, this place is changing. It's been sick and ugly and sad, a place where bullies rule and everyone else has to keep their head down. Not any more. People here are sick of being victims – they're learning to fight back.'

We pull up outside Nightingale House, spilling out on to the cracked concrete. Everyone hugs, and I hang on to Leggit for a long time. 'Sure you don't want to leave her?' I ask.

'Not this time,' Finn laughs.

'Good luck,' Dizzy says to Mum. 'With the Phoenix, with all of it, really. I think you're right – you can change things, if you try.'

Then she turns to me, handing me a Mars bar wrapped in star-printed paper. 'Take care, Mouse,' she says. 'Keep in touch. We'll see you soon!'

'Do you ever hear from Storm?' I make myself ask, just as Dizzy turns to jump back up into the cab.

Her face clouds. 'Sometimes,' she says. 'Birthdays, usually. She split with Zak, but you probably know that already . . .'

'No,' I whisper. 'No, I didn't. Is he . . . I mean, what . . .'

'He's still in India, the last I heard,' Dizzy says

softly. 'Scratching a living, hanging out on the beach, getting wasted. Different girlfriend every week, Storm says. You know Zak.'

But I don't, of course. I never did.

The icicle lights shimmer softly as we walk into the lobby of Nightingale House. Lucky starts to whimper. I hold him tighter, glancing around, but the place is deserted. 'Shhh,' I tell him. 'You're tired and it's late and you've had the worst week ever, but everything's fine now, Lucky. Seriously.'

But Lucky knows better than me, because when we step out of the lift on floor nine, it's clear that things are not fine. Things are not fine at all.

Two guys in overalls are trying to patch up what was once our front door. They have patched the shattered glass with board, smoothed the splintered wood. They are replacing the locks.

'No,' Mum says. 'Oh, no.'

A uniformed policeman walks towards us. 'Magi Kavanagh? Martin?' he asks. 'I'm afraid there's been some trouble. A break-in. Some damage . . .'

Mrs S. opens her door and peeps round it, wrapped in a pink dressing gown, her grey hair sticking up in wisps. 'Oh, Magi,' she says sadly. 'Mouse.'

She pulls the door wide and opens her arms, and Mum goes to her. They hug for a long moment, and when they pull apart, both are crying. 'Magi,' Mrs S. whispers. 'I'm so, so sorry. I heard all the commotion, about eleven o'clock it was, but I was scared to go out. I rang the police.'

Mum just nods, shakily.

'You might want to stay somewhere else tonight,' the policeman says gently. 'There's nothing you can do here right now.'

'Please,' Mrs S. urges. 'Stay here. If there's anything at all I can do . . .'

Mum just shakes her head. She squeezes the old lady's hand and steps round the policeman, pulling aside the crime-scene tape. We walk into the flat – what used to be the flat. It's like stepping into a nightmare. The cooker and the washing machine have been torn from the wall and smashed to pieces, and every piece of crockery we have has been broken. Someone has made a pile of the bedding, the curtains, the beanbags, then poured black paint all over them. The bathroom, the hallway and the scratchy nylon carpet have all been splattered too.

On the living-room wall, a single word has been daubed – *stupid*.

We were that, all right, to think we could go against Frank Scully.

'He must be back,' I whisper. 'And he knows about Lucky.'

'Guess so,' Mum says.

What would have happened if we'd been at the flat? Or if we'd gone out with Finn and Dizzy, leaving Lucky alone to recover from the kidnap? I shudder.

'It may just be an act of random vandalism,' the policeman is saying. 'Unless you know of anyone who may have a grudge against you?' Mum looks over her shoulder, but Mrs S. has retreated back to her flat.

'I'm standing witness against a man called Frank Scully in a month's time,' she says softly. 'He's a drug dealer, out on bail. I'm the only witness he hasn't scared off yet. I think he might just have a grudge, Officer.'

'Ah,' the policeman says, scribbling notes. 'That puts a very different spin on things. We'll make some enquiries. Once the boys there have made the flat safe for you, we'll go – we have everything we need for now. We'll call back around midday tomorrow, but I'd advise you both to find somewhere else to spend the night. You can't stay here.'

'It's our home,' Mum says, but the words come out as a sob. 'We're staying.'

The officer shrugs, shaking his head. The overalled guys are packing up now, checking the new lock, handing over a set of keys.

'You're sure?' the policeman asks. 'We'd really advise –'

'Sure,' Mum says. She steers the policeman into the corridor and closes the battered door firmly, taking a deep, raggedy breath. 'Oh, Mouse,' she says.

There isn't a bit of the flat that hasn't been trashed and ruined, that isn't wet with paint or glittering with broken glass.

'Where are the plants?' Mum wants to know. 'My plants!' But the big jungly plants that reached to the ceiling are gone, along with our TV, our toaster, our clothes. Mum picks up the telephone, a mess of wires and shattered plastic, then lets it fall again.

'I can't withdraw my statement, Mouse,' Mum says.

'I can't give Lucky back.'

Mum sinks down into a corner, leaning up against the wall, and I sit beside her, scooping Lucky on to my knee. 'Do you think this is the end of it?' I ask in a small voice. 'Or just the start?'

'I don't know,' Mum says.

I wake to a hammering on the door, and open my eyes to chaos. The flat looks worse in daylight, if that's possible. 'Mouse!' a familiar voice is yelling. 'Magi! Open up. It's me, Jake!'

I stumble to the patched-up door, open it a crack.

'Mouse,' Jake says. 'I heard. What can I do?'

'You can't do anything,' I say. 'Nobody can.'

I let the door swing wide, and Jake comes in. His eyes skim over the wreckage, registering shock, disgust, anger. He goes to Mum and hugs her lightly, as if she's something fragile that might break easily. Maybe she is.

'I had a visit last night from Frank Scully,' Jake says. 'He'd found out about Lucky. I acted dumb, pretended I knew nothing. I had to show him that I still had the key, swear black and blue I knew nothing about it. Don't know if he believed me.'

Mum narrows her eyes. 'You helped Mouse get Lucky back?' she asks.

'I had to,' Jake says, shoulders sagging. 'The dog was suffering.'

Mum looks at Jake with a new respect.

'Anyway, Scully took off in a real rage,' Jake goes on. 'I tried to phone you, but there was no reply. Then I heard the police cars, saw the plants –'

'The plants?' Mum echoes.

Jake takes her elbow and steers her out on to the balcony. The three of us look down on to the cracked concrete courtyard, now strewn with mangled plants, smashed pots, cushions, clothes, bits and pieces of our lives chucked out like so much rubbish.

'I wanted to warn you,' Jake says sadly. 'I just wasn't quick enough.'

'Doesn't matter,' I say. 'It wasn't your fault.'

There's another knock on the door, and Jake goes to open it. This time it's Mrs S. with a tray of tea and toast. 'Oh, my,' she says, eyeing the mess. 'This is going to take some cleaning up. I'd best get my mop bucket.'

'No, really, we can manage,' Mum argues as the old lady bustles away, but Jake just hands her a mug of tea and a slice of toast and tells her not to worry.

'Everyone needs help sometimes,' he says. 'Wouldn't you chip in, if you saw this happen to someone else?' He starts lifting the paint-spattered bedding out on to the balcony. When he has a big pile of it, he heaves it over and the whole lot crashes down on to the concrete below. 'I'll get a skip,' he tells me.

Mrs S. reappears with a fresh apron, a mop, a broom and a whole range of cleaning materials, just as Fitz and Chan appear with their mums. 'Jake said you might need a hand,' Fitz says. 'Man, what a war zone!'

Luke and Julie arrive next, along with a couple

of the Phoenix regulars who've heard and want to help. News travels fast on the Eden Estate, and by mid morning we have more offers of help than we know what to do with. Luke brings a wheelbarrow, and pushes barrowloads of trashed and ruined stuff along to the lift and down to the skip that Jake has organized. The paint-spattered carpet is rolled up and hauled away, bin bag after bin bag filled with rubbish. Slowly, bit by bit, we strip the flat.

Chan's mum rings around on her mobile for dustpans, brooms and mops, and a squad of helpers cleans up the broken glass, the splinters of wood. Mrs S. wipes the walls with soapy water and bleach, and even Fitz grabs a scourer and gets stuck in. At midday, the police arrive again, and Jake touches my elbow lightly.

'Time I was out of here,' he says.

'Thanks, Jake, for all this,' I say.

'Don't thank me,' he says with a shrug. 'Looks like you have a lot of friends.' He winks at me and slips quietly away.

The flat is chaos, with maybe a dozen people scrubbing, wiping, clearing. My CD player is lying down on the concrete courtyard in a dozen little pieces, but Fitz has his own player plugged in, pumping out a lively techno beat to keep everyone working hard. Someone has brought a large can of white emulsion paint, and Julie makes a start on painting out the *stupid* taunt.

'Is there somewhere we can talk?' one of the police officers asks.

Mrs S. invites us along to her flat. She bustles into the kitchen to make tea, and I can't help noticing that the table is still set the way it was on Friday, the same sponge cake wrapped in cling film, looking a little crispy now. Some of the hundreds and thousands sprinkled across the cupcakes have bled into the icing, the colours running like watercolour paint in the rain. Scully hasn't been round to see his gran yet – well, I guess he's had better things to do.

'We've spoken to Frank Scully,' the policeman says, and Mrs S., emerging from the kitchen with a laden tray, flinches at the mention of her grandson's name. The policeman, clearly, has no idea that she's anything to do with Frank. 'I'm afraid he has an alibi,' the policeman explains.

'Surprise, surprise.'

'He was in Luton at the time of the break in,' the policeman explains. 'We know he's been in the area, and a number of witnesses have confirmed that he was with them, at a nightclub, at the time of the disturbance. I'm sorry.'

'Me too,' I say.

'So . . . what happens now?' Mum asks.

The policeman shakes his head. 'We have no prints, no proof, no eyewitness accounts,' he says. 'Frank Scully has a watertight alibi. Unless something new turns up, there's very little we can do.'

Mrs S. is pouring tea into pretty china cups, but her hands shake and she puts the teapot down. 'It's not right,' she says in a quavery voice. 'What happened to Magi and Mouse is criminal, but my Frank wouldn't – he just couldn't . . .'

Mum runs a hand through her hair, embarrassed. 'It's OK, Mrs S., Frank has an alibi. He wasn't here last night, so of course, it couldn't have been him.'

'No,' Mrs S. says.

The policeman takes a sip of his tea, then stands, smiling sadly. 'Well,' he says. 'That's it, really. I'm sorry we haven't come up with anything more conclusive. Mrs Kavanagh – it's great to see the community rallying round to help you, but I have to advise you that whoever did this may still be out there. I don't want to alarm you, but . . . well, just be careful. OK?'

The policeman turns to go.

'Wait,' Mrs S. says into the silence. 'I don't think . . . I mean . . .'

The policeman puts a hand on her arm, reassuringly. 'I'm sure there's really no cause for concern,' he says.

'My Frank wouldn't do something like that,' she repeats. 'I'm sure he wouldn't. But . . . well, he's not telling you the truth, Officer, about where he was last night. He was here, on the estate.'

'What?' the policeman says. 'You saw him?'

Mrs S. sinks down on to a chair, and Mum goes to her, slipping an arm round her shoulder.

'I called the police, you know,' Mrs S. is saying. 'I heard all the racket, and I was frightened, of course, but things went quiet and I looked out into the corridor . . . about eleven, it was. I saw Frank, running down towards the lift. As I say, he wouldn't do a thing like that, but perhaps . . . perhaps he saw someone himself?'

The old lady looks confused, her face crumpled and sad. 'I just don't understand why he'd lie about it, that's all,' she says.

The policeman looks at Mrs S. for a long time. 'Are you sure?' he asks, gently. 'Are you sure the man you saw running towards the lift was Frank Scully? Could you have been mistaken?'

Mrs S. shakes her head. 'He's my grandson,' she says. 'Of course I'm sure.'

The policeman smiles and opens his notebook at a fresh page. 'I think,' he says briskly, 'we've just got ourselves an eyewitness account.'

By nightfall, the flat is looking less like the aftermath of a small hurricane and more like a place to live again. The walls have been painted white, a green nylon carpet has been rolled out across the living-room floor and new mattresses and bedding have been delivered, courtesy of Luke and Julie.

Cat, with a paintbrush in her hand and spatters of white emulsion in her hair, has been around all afternoon – Fitz rang her at lunchtime. 'It's awful,' she whispered into my hair when I first opened the door to her. 'Awful, awful, awful. Scully can't get away with it this time.'

'No,' I said, thinking of Mrs S. with her crumpled face and her pretty china teacups and her iced cakes going stale under a layer of cling film. 'This time, I don't think he can.'

Scully was taken into custody a few hours ago, once Mrs S. had given a formal police statement. I could see Mum taking in deep breaths of air as the police car drove away. Her shoulders relaxed, and the fear and anxiety slipped away from her face, her eyes. 'It's going to be OK,' she told me.

Maybe, just maybe, it is. Psycho Sam, the Rottweiler man, turns up while the clear-up crew are eating fish and chips, and promises he'll cut us a great deal on a new bathroom suite and get it installed next day.

'We'll all chip in,' Julie says. 'Right?'

'Right,' Chan's mum agrees. 'No arguments.'

Mum just shakes her head and shrugs, helplessly, and I know she's feeling the same way I do, overwhelmed with the support and help our friends and neighbours have given us today. I never really felt like I had a family before – it was always Mum and me, against the world. Now I can see that family comes in all shapes and forms. It's like a whole new constellation just appeared on my star map, and together we can tackle anything – even Scully.

There's a banging on the door, and Jake staggers into the flat carrying a six-foot potted palm. Behind him, a delivery guy from the local garden centre lugs in a Swiss cheese plant, almost as big.

'Jake!' Mum gasps. 'You shouldn't have! Oh . . .'

The tears that have been held back all day bubble up to the surface, misting her grey eyes. Jake just grins sheepishly, ruffling my hair, grinning. 'They're just plants,' he says.

To Mum, of course, they are much more than that.

People start drifting off, promising they'll be back next day if anything still needs doing. 'No, no,' Mum assures them. 'We can manage now. We'll be OK.'

I think maybe we will.

Of course, Psycho Sam collars Fitz and Chan for dog-walking duty, so Cat and I tag along for company. We leave Lucky with Mum, Jake and the garden centre man, sipping coffee made with a second-hand kettle, out of brand-new Woolworths mugs.

We head down to the first floor to collect the dogs. 'Here they are,' Psycho Sam says, handing them over. 'Be good, Jordan. Be good, Jade!'

'Jordan?' Cat echoes as we sprint after Fitz and Chan, who are now being towed rapidly along towards the lift. 'Jade? Sam's a big softy, isn't he? I bet these dogs wouldn't hurt a fly.'

'Dunno,' I say, seriously. 'Sam lives next door to a drug dealer. I suppose he reckons the dogs are good security.'

Cat blinks.

'He lives next door to a *dealer*?' she repeats. She stops short, staring back along the corridor, open-mouthed.

'Don't,' I hiss, dragging her towards the lift. 'It's no big thing. Everyone knows.'

'Everyone knows?' she asks, horrified. 'Everyone knows, and yet they don't *do* anything?'

I bundle Cat into the lift. 'What can we do?' Fitz asks, reasonably. 'The Eden Estate is full of dealers. You learn to live with it.'

'But those losers are the people who got Scully into drugs,' Cat says. 'They're his friends, right? They wreck lives. They probably helped to torch the Phoenix. And you guys are OK with all that?'

Jordan and Jade lurch out across the lobby, beneath the icicle lights. They bound out across the floodlit courtyard. 'We're not OK with it, obviously,' I say. 'Fitz is just saying, that's the way things are around here. You get to know stuff.'

'Up on the tenth floor, there are two flats next to each other where a couple of dealers live,' Chan tells Cat. 'Scully's in Eagle Heights, next floor down from me. There are dealers in every block.'

'You know where they live?' she asks, incredulous. 'All of them?'

'Not all,' Chan admits. 'Some, though.'

'Shut it, Chan,' I snap, and he shrugs.

'Just saying.'

It's cold, and the first real frost of the year has blackened and shrivelled the last of the flowers poking up through the ash and wreckage.

'Why won't the police do something?' Cat wails. 'It's crazy! It's wrong!'

'You need proof, man,' Fitz says. 'Nobody wants to point the finger.'

'Well, Mrs S. did,' Cat reminds us. 'She's probably the bravest person around here! If we could get a list together of where the other dealers are . . . mark them, somehow . . .'

'No,' I tell her.

'Bad idea,' Fitz chimes in. 'Haven't you had enough of trouble?'

Sometimes, though, I think that's the one thing Cat will never get enough of. She tugs at my arm, pulling me back as the dogs drag Fitz and Chan out of earshot.

'Mouse, listen!' she whispers, her eyes gleaming. 'If we could just find out who all the dealers are . . .'

'We could,' I say. 'But what's the point? We couldn't go to the police – they'd need proof, and we don't have that. Besides, it would be dangerous, and like Fitz says, we can't risk more trouble. It's not an option.'

Cat narrows her eyes. 'Not the police,' she says, slowly. 'I've got a better idea . . .'

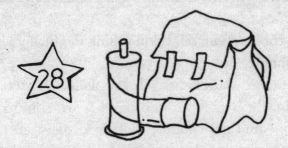

Cat can wrap the world round her little finger. Before long, she's got me convinced that her crazy plan is worth one last risk, one last effort.

'You have to stand up for what you believe in,' she tells me. 'You can't stand by and let bad things happen without trying to stop them.'

I think of Mrs S., who stood up for what she believed in, even though it meant sending her grandson back to prison. The old lady looks crushed, beaten, lately, as if all the hope has been taken away from her. I suppose nobody ever said that doing the right thing was meant to be easy.

'People are learning to fight back around here,' Cat points out. 'They're angry about the Phoenix, they're fed up with being pushed around. Look at what's happening – the lobbies, the lifts, the flowers people have planted.'

'I suppose,' I say, doubtfully.

'We're not going to the police,' Cat promises. 'We're just going to make sure people know exactly who and where the dealers are. We'll shame them, right?'

I'm not convinced. I don't think the dealers have any shame.

'It's too dangerous,' I tell Cat. 'If we get caught –'

'We won't get caught,' Cat says.

It takes us two days to gather a list of the dealers on the Eden Estate. We talk to Fitz and Chan again, picking their brains without letting them know what we're planning. 'The less people know, the safer it'll be,' Cat says, but what we're doing is not safe, no matter how I look at it. We've just got one local thug off our case, and now Cat wants to stir up trouble with a whole bunch more? Bad news.

There are nine addresses, scattered across each of the four high-rise blocks. 'Just nine?' Cat demands. 'I thought there'd be more.'

It doesn't sound so many, but those nine people and their lackeys are responsible for a whole lot of misery, fear and pain. 'Nine,' I tell her. 'Fitz thinks the new blokes along the hall from his place are dodgy, but he's got no real evidence. They've been hanging around, getting pally with some of the dealers, but I think most likely they're just buying stuff.'

'We'll stick to the known dealers,' Cat says. 'We can't afford mistakes.'

I think that this whole idea is a mistake, but I swallow my fear and do my best to make sure nothing will go wrong. We plan our hit for Thursday night, when Mum, Luke and Julie are travelling to Liverpool to spend the following day checking out the anti-drugs charity working alongside the council up there. 'They're getting fantastic results,' Mum explains. 'We can learn so much from them, for when the Phoenix is back on its feet. Things are going to be different here, Mouse, I know they are.'

'When will you be back?'

'Friday night,' Mum says. 'Look, Mouse, I know Scully's safely out of the way again, but still, I don't like leaving you alone, not the way things are right now. Can you and Lucky stay with Fitz?'

'Maybe,' I bluff.

'D'you want me to call his mum, check it's OK with her?'

'No, no, I'll sort it,' I say. 'No hassle.'

Mum has learnt to live with the occasional graffiti hit, but I don't think she'd be as understanding if she knew what we're planning this time. It's better that she doesn't know.

'Don't do anything I wouldn't do,' she says before she goes.

'That gives me a pretty free rein,' I quip.

'Cheeky,' she laughs. 'Seriously, though. Take care of yourself.'

'I will. Don't worry, Mum. And good luck in Liverpool!'

Everything is ready.

It's four twenty-five in the early hours of Friday morning. Cat's parents think she's at Aditi's house, curled up in her *Hello Kitty* nightdress, spark out after a night of French revision and popcorn. Mum thinks I'm at Fitz's place, tucked up in the spare bunk with Lucky at my feet.

They're all wrong. Cat is dressed in an old jumper and ragged jeans, face disguised by a black fleece ski-mask with just a slit for the eyes and mouth. I pull on a black beanie and wrap a scarf round my mouth and nose, but I know that if we are seen, a scarf and a ski-mask won't save our skin.

'Scary,' I tell Cat, and she pulls the ski-mask off, grinning.

Lucky licks his lips and starts to whine. 'Be good, Lucky,' I say in a muffled voice, wondering how he can manage to look worried and disapproving at the same time. 'Don't wait up for us.'

Cat hugs me quickly in the darkness. 'Let's go.'

My heart is racing as we creep along the corridor, ride down in the turquoise tinselled lift and skulk across the courtyard. The estate is deserted and still. My senses are sharp with the adrenaline, but there's a heavy dread in my belly that feels like real fear. If I was the kind of boy who prayed, I'd be praying now, but the best I can do is look skywards, searching for stars. A bright, blinking light falls slowly through the darkness.

'Look,' I whisper to Cat. 'Shooting star! That's good luck.'

She rolls her eyes. 'It's a plane, you idiot,' she says, and when I look again I can see that she's right. Typical.

We start in Skylark Rise, on the seventh floor. Cat pulls on her ski-mask as we leave the lift. The corridor is empty, each scratched and ancient front door hiding nothing but silence. We linger outside number 83, uncertain, and then Cat hisses, 'Go!'

I start to spray, a quick blast of red that blooms like a flower against the dull, grey paintwork and drips down like blood. I step back and Cat uncaps her spray can, painting the words *dealers out* in spiky black letters. Before the paint has even begun to dry, we are back inside the lift, spray cans hidden, hearts hammering.

'One down, eight to go,' I tell Cat.

The second hit, down on the third floor, is just as smooth. Nobody sees us, and within minutes we're back in the lift, clunking slowly downwards. We come out through the lobby, cross towards Raven's Crest, and Cat elbows me in the ribs.

'Look!' she whispers. 'In the playground! They weren't there, before.'

Under the thin orange lamplight, two men are sitting on the battered roundabout, smoking and talking in low voices. The tips of their cigarettes glow red in the darkness. We tug off the scarf and the ski-mask, try to look casual.

'They're not interested in us,' I say, hoping I'm right.

Cat links my arm and we move out of view, into the lobby of Raven's Crest. The third graffiti hit goes without a hitch, and then we move on to the tenth floor. I've just sprayed my burst of red when a door opens along the corridor. 'What d'you want?' a voice asks.

Somehow, I drag up the name of the dealer who lives here. 'Looking for Carlo,' I answer. 'Seen him?'

'Don't you know what time it is?' the voice snaps back. 'People are trying to sleep! Clear off!'

The door slams, Cat sprays her *dealers out* slogan and we're off at a sprint. 'Close one,' Cat says, in the relative safety of the lift.

'Four down,' I whisper. 'Five to go.'

As we cross towards Eagle Heights, I see the figures in the playground, quiet now, still smoking. They make me feel faintly uneasy, as if they're watching us. Inside, there's a party going on at one of our target flats. Loud music booms out along the corridor, and it takes every bit of courage we have to walk towards that noise, but I spray my blood-red mark and Cat scrawls her message, and we're out of there. The next hit is easy by comparison, and now there are only three doors left to mark, all of them in Nightingale House.

'Almost there,' I say, as we come out of Eagle Heights, but straight away my scalp prickles and I look around me. I can smell trouble – something is going on. A couple of dark vans are parked across the way at Skylark Rise, two more down by Nightingale House. As I watch, another dark van slides into the road and turns down towards Raven's Crest.

'Weird,' says Cat.

The men from the playground are watching us, their faces moon-pale in the darkness. 'Kids,' one shouts across to us, his voice steely-cold. 'Go home. You hear me? Get out of here.'

We keep walking, heads down. 'You hear?' he repeats, falling into step behind us, and suddenly I feel cold all over. 'Go home.'

'OK, OK,' I say, trying to keep the fear from my voice. 'We're going.'

We make it to the lift in Nightingale House, wide-eyed. 'What was all that about?' Cat wants to know. 'Something dodgy, I bet.'

'Too right,' I say. 'Let's get this over with, yeah?'

On the tenth floor, our targets are side by side, two smartly painted doors. It should be fast, it should be easy, but my hand shakes as I start on the second door, and my scalp is still prickling with fear. I want to get out of here. I want to get out of here now. 'Cat,' I hiss. 'Leave it.'

Her green eyes blink, astonished, through the slit in her ski-mask. She shakes the spray can. 'Leave it? We're almost there!' she argues.

Suddenly, the lift clanks open at the end of the corridor and a whole bunch of men and dogs come charging towards us. Cat drops the spray can. I grab her arm and try to run the other way, but at the end of the corridor the fire-escape door bursts open and we're just about flattened in the stampede.

'Grab those damn kids!' someone yells.

Someone grabs my hood and yanks me to one side as the half-tagged doors splinter and give way. Men shove their way into the flats, uniformed men with bulletproof vests and guns. Policemen.

'Whoa,' Cat says from under her ski-mask. 'It's a raid!'

'Shut up,' a policeman snarls in her ear, and for once she does. A barrage of screaming, swearing and scuffling erupts from inside the flats, and I feel sick with fear.

A tall, sandy-haired man with breath that smells of cigarettes appears in front of us. 'I thought I told you kids to go home?' he says in that same ice-cold voice I recognize from earlier. 'Now look what's happened. You've got yourselves mixed up in something you really don't want to be mixed up in.'

'We'll go home now,' I squeak. 'Promise.'

The plain-clothes policeman sighs. 'Too late for that,' he says. 'Graffiti vandals, aren't you? And playing a very dangerous game, if you're doing what I think you were doing. I think we'd better take you along to the station, get your parents in.'

Cat pulls her ski-mask off, revealing golden-brown corkscrew hair and wide, anxious eyes. 'Noooo . . .' she says. 'Please. Can't you let us go? This was a mistake, a stupid mistake.'

The policeman raises one eyebrow. 'It's that all right, miss,' he says. 'Boys, take them down to the car.'

29 POLICE STATION

Two policemen walk us down to one of several squad cars that have joined the black vans outside Nightingale House. As we emerge into the cold night air, Cat wriggles and ducks and tries to make a break for it, but the policeman holds her firm.

'You're goin' nowhere, miss,' he says. 'Except for the station.'

As we are driven through the Eden Estate, it's clear that we've chosen the worst of all possible nights for our hit. The police, who for weeks have seemed less than bothered by the estate's problems, have clearly been planning this raid for a while. Outside every high-rise block, the black vans have been joined by police vans and squad cars. Officers are watching each exit, talking into radios, coordinating everything. I wonder if they have the same nine addresses we had. I hope so.

At the police station, we get put in a bare little room with a sleepy policewoman for company. I've been in police stations a bunch of times. When I was a kid, with Mum, once with Dizzy and Finn that long-ago summer, and more recently, of course, for crimes against a bus stop in Islington.

After a long wait, the sandy-haired plain-clothes cop from the raid turns up. He eyes us, coldly.

'We need names and addresses,' he says. 'Get your parents in.'

'My mum's away,' I say. 'Won't be back till evening.'

He raises an eyebrow. 'Other relatives?'

'None.'

'You've been in trouble before,' he says to me, scanning a print-out in his hand. 'Vandalism. Graffiti damage is a serious offence, you know!'

'I know,' I sigh.

'You have a named social worker, David Thomas. I'll call social services, see if they can send someone out.'

'He'll be overjoyed,' I say. Cat squirms with discomfort, and I remember that Dave is her social worker too.

'It may not be him, personally,' the sandy-haired guy is saying. 'Not at this hour of the morning. They'll send someone, though. What about your parents, Catrin?'

'Please don't tell them,' Cat pleads. 'I'm so, so sorry. I promise –'

'We have no choice,' he snaps. 'You were caught

committing criminal damage outside the homes of two notorious drug dealers. Have you any idea at all how dangerous that could have been? You could have fouled up a police drugs raid that has taken us months to plan. It's a miracle you're still here to tell the tale.'

'We didn't know!' Cat says. 'We thought you didn't care about the dealers. You let that creep Scully out on bail, and look what happened!'

I think of Lucky, tied by his washing-line lead in the corner of the lock-up, and Mum, determined to speak out at Scully's trial. I still can't let myself imagine what might have happened if Scully had come calling when we were all at home. Sometimes, when you think nobody else cares, you take crazy risks, to make a point, to make a difference.

'We were only trying to help!' Cat appeals.

The sandy-haired guy shakes his head. 'Remind me to stay well clear the next time you kids decide to help anybody,' he says. 'You could have wrecked the whole operation. We've had plain-clothes officers on the estate for weeks now. We let Scully out on bail because we wanted him to lead us to his suppliers – we've had him tracked, the whole time. What happened to your flat, son, that was unfortunate – but we'd have nailed him for it, with or without his gran's statement.'

I open my mouth and close it again, speechless. The police let Scully out deliberately, so he could lead them to the drugs suppliers? All of the bad stuff that's happened over the last week or so could have been avoided. It's like it was all a game, and one we were never going to win.

'You knew?' Cat asks, frowning. 'You planned this, all the time?'

'And you kids almost blew it,' the policeman says. 'Still . . . you didn't, I guess. I'm going to let you off with a caution, but if I ever see either of you in this place again, I'll be down on you like a ton of bricks. Got that?'

'Yes, sir,' I say. 'Thank you, sir.'

'So. Catrin. Your parents, please.'

Cat bows her head and gives out her mum's name and address, and the policeman scribbles down the information and walks away, leaving us alone with the silent policewoman.

'I am in soooo much trouble!' Cat wails.

I shrug. 'Your parents won't be pleased, but they'll get over it,' I tell her. 'Admit it, Cat – wasn't there just a little bit of you that knew this might happen?'

'No!' she protests.

'Come on,' I argue. 'When you run as close to the wind as you do, you're gonna get caught sometime. They'll forgive you.'

'But you might not!' she bursts out. 'Omigod, I've ruined everything!'

'Cat, shhh,' I tell her. 'We're OK, aren't we? We've got off with a police caution. And it sounds like the raid was a success too, and that's brilliant news.'

'But –'

'No buts,' I tell her. I slip my arm round her and pull her close, and she leans against me, her head on my shoulder, her vanilla-scented hair soft against my cheek. That's how we are sitting half an hour later, when the door swings open again.

Cat's mum comes in, anxious and tired, her face a perfect mask of dismay. Her eyes lock on to mine. 'You!' she says. 'The boy from drama club!'

'Me,' I admit. 'About that whole drama club thing . . .'

But I can't explain, because before I get the chance, Dodgy Dave appears right next to Cat's mum, his hair sticking up in clumps as if he just rolled out of bed. Well, he probably did.

'Mouse,' he says. 'What the . . .?'

Cat's mum flings her arms round her, and then, to my horror, Dodgy Dave does the same. That's taking the whole social worker thing a little too far, I reckon. I take a step back, confused.

Dave puts an arm round Cat's mum, and that's even weirder. The super-keen white social worker and the sad-eyed black lawyer huddle together, like they belong. My head struggles to make sense of it all. Dave Thomas. Mia Thomas. Catrin Thomas.

'I'm sorry I lied,' Cat says huskily, and I realize she's looking at me. She turns back to the adults. 'To you too. We had a plan . . . and then . . .' She runs out of ideas and shakes her head silently, eyes bright with tears.

Dodgy Dave glares at me over his glasses. In all the years I've known him, I've never seen him look this angry. His hands are balled into fists, as if he'd like to punch me, and his voice trembles as he speaks.

'Mouse,' he says. 'Just what in hell have you done to my daughter?'

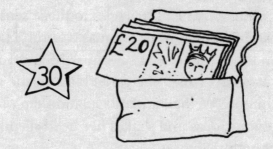

I'm not just confused, I'm numb. I don't understand what's going on, and nor does Dave, by the look of it. He looks at Cat, shakes his head. 'You've been hanging out with this – this delinquent?' he splutters. 'This loser?'

That hurts, coming from someone who is supposed to care about me. It hurts more than I would ever have imagined.

'Dad,' Cat says to Dave. 'Please!'

Dad? Dad? I look at Cat and her eyes slide away from mine, and I realize that she was right. Everything is ruined.

There's a whole lot of fuss and confusion before the police are ready to let us out of there. Dave manages to prove that he is my designated social worker as well as Cat's dad, and finally, after about a million warnings of what might happen if we're ever in trouble again, we are released into the thin, cold December morning.

Dave drives through the early morning traffic in

silence, Cat's mum stony-faced in the passenger seat. Cat reaches for my hand in the back seat of the car, but I pull away, my head a mess of anger and betrayal.

'You lied,' I hiss. 'All this time, you lied. You let me think Dave was your social worker, when all the time . . .'

'I'm sorry,' Cat says again, but the words sound empty, hollow.

'What was I, some kind of charity project?' I ask softly. 'Or were you just slumming it? Notching up some bad-girl kudos with your posh mates? Poor little rich girl, hanging out with the boy from the Eden Estate.'

She just turns her head away.

Back at the house, Dave marches us into the kitchen. 'We need to know what's been going on,' he says. 'Catrin was supposed to be spending the night with a friend. At six in the morning we get a call to say she's in police custody, after a graffiti attack on the homes of known drug dealers on the Eden Estate! She's just a kid, Mouse!'

'We're not kids,' I snap back, defiantly. 'We're fourteen.'

Dave looks at me for a long moment, his eyes weary. 'Fourteen?' he asks. 'Is that what she told you? Catrin is only twelve.'

Twelve? I sink down on to a wooden chair. Cat

won't meet my gaze. In her cheeks, two pink spots appear. 'If I'd told you I was twelve, you'd have treated me like a kid,' she says. 'You'd have seen me differently. Like if I'd told you that Dave was my dad.'

'Well, yeah,' I admit. 'Obviously.'

I'm seeing everything differently now. Twelve isn't old enough to stay out all night on graffiti hits, or to stay over at your boyfriend's place when your parents think you're at a mate's. Twelve-year-olds shouldn't skive school or steal chocolates, and they shouldn't kiss you the way Cat kisses me. Twelve? I rest my head in my hands.

'You didn't know?' Dave asks.

'No, I didn't know.'

'Even so,' he says. 'You must have seen that Catrin was an unhappy, vulnerable girl. You've latched on to her and dragged her down . . . she's been totally out of control, these last few weeks.'

'It wasn't like that,' Cat protests. 'Mouse helped me.'

'Helped you?' Mia Thomas bites out. 'Ha! He's helped you to skip school, flunk your tests, stay out all night doing lord knows what . . .'

'Two hundred quid went missing from my wallet a couple of months back,' Dave tells me. 'I couldn't believe it was Cat, but . . . well, it makes sense now, doesn't it? She's been hanging out on the Eden

Estate with you, spending it on drink and cigarettes and . . . and –'

'No!' I argue. 'Nothing like that, I promise. I wouldn't! I don't smoke, or drink . . . or anything else!'

'You want me to take the word of a boy who can't stay out of trouble for five minutes at a time?' Dave laughs. 'I know too much about you, Mouse. You're trouble. You always will be. Can't you see that?'

I hang my head.

'Dad, Mum, stop it!' Cat cuts in. 'Mouse is my friend. I don't care if you believe me or not, but he has helped me – he's taught me about right and wrong, about friendship, about love.'

'Love?' Dave just about chokes.

'He cares about me,' Cat ploughs on. 'He really, really cares, which is more than you two do.'

I look at Dave. His mouth is opening and closing slowly, like someone underwater. 'Catrin, that's not fair . . .' he says.

'No, it's not,' she snaps back. 'My life has never been fair, not since Josh.'

There's a silence, a long, painful silence. Like an idiot, I try to break it. 'Maybe things will be better now,' I say. 'Now that Josh is well again. Now that he's coming home.'

Dave's face pales, then flushes a slow, dark pink.

Mia Thomas blinks, and her face seems to collapse. She hides behinds her hands, sobbing quietly.

'Josh won't be coming home,' Dave says icily. 'He died, a year ago. Didn't she tell you?'

My stomach turns over. Everyone has a dark secret, Cat once told me. Something buried, hidden, something that gnaws away at them, messing up their head, eating at their happiness from inside. I thought I knew the secret, but it was just another lie.

Cat won't look at me. 'It's like our lives ended then too,' she says to her parents. 'We're all in mourning for a little boy who's never coming back. Never, OK? Don't you see that?'

'We've lost one child,' Mia whispers. 'We don't want to lose you.'

'You don't even notice I'm alive, half the time!' Cat flings back. 'You're so wrapped up in the past it takes something like this for you to see that I'm hurting too!'

'You've been lashing out for a year now!' Dave retaliates. 'We've tried to be patient. We've tried to be understanding –'

'Did you ever try just being there for me?'

'We're always there for you!'

'It doesn't feel like that.'

'Catrin, don't punish us for what happened to Josh,' Mia says. 'We loved him, but we couldn't make him better. Losing him has made you all the more precious to us, but you've been on a self-destruct mission for months . . .'

Cat takes a deep breath. 'I felt like I didn't matter,' she tells them. 'Then I met Mouse, and just for a little while, I didn't feel that way any more.'

Dave sighs, sinks down on to a chair. He looks broken and defeated.

I'd like to tell Dave it's OK, that it doesn't matter that he just called me a delinquent and a loser, but I can't. It matters. My head feels like it's filling up with smoke and lies, splitting in two.

Cat reaches over, touches my hand, but I flinch. I don't know what to think, what to feel. Should I feel sorry for her, or angry that she's lied to me for so long? It's like the last few weeks have been some elaborate game, designed to wind her parents up, catch their attention at last.

She's more messed up than I ever imagined. All the good times, all the special times we shared were based on lies. Did I ever know her at all?

'Cat and Mouse,' I say, coldly. 'That's a joke – and the joke was on me, right? Well, good one, Cat. You had me fooled. You know what, though? Next time you start playing games, remember that other people have feelings too. Other people get hurt.'

'Mouse, that's not the way it was!' she protests.

'That's the way it looked to me,' I say. 'You know what? Forget it. I hope things work out for you, OK?' As I walk away, I can hear Dave calling my name, Cat crying, Mia comforting her. I don't look back.

A cat-and-mouse game can only ever end in tears.

Mouse . . .

Don't walk out of my life. You're my best friend
– more than my best friend, OK? I need you. I let
you down and I lied, but I never meant to hurt
you, I swear. It started off as a game, wanting to
hang out with you – a cool way to wind my parents
up. It didn't stay that way. Pretty soon, you were
the only thing that mattered.

I messed up, big style. I didn't think you'd want
to know if you sussed I was only twelve, or worked
out that Dave was my dad. I was right too, I guess.
Lying about Josh was different. I was trying to fool
myself, really, make out that there could still be
some kind of happy ending. Crazy, right? It's just
that I loved Josh, and I think you'd have loved him
too, and I so, soooo wanted things to be different.

Sometimes, the truth just hurts too much.

Dad said he handled things badly, said things he
shouldn't have said. He won't be your social worker
any more, anyhow – he's got a new job at a youth

project up in Brixton, starting in January. Shorter hours, less stress. We're going to family counselling, which is kind of weird, but Dad says we all need some help to get over the hole that Josh left in our lives. Maybe he's right.

Mouse, I'm missing you like mad. Lucky too. Give him a hug for me, yeah? You were the best thing that ever happened to me, and I let you down, stuffed up, lost you. I guess I only have myself to blame. Dad says it's probably all for the best, because we come from different worlds, but I liked your world, Mouse. I liked *you*.

After Christmas, Dad's taking us away for a few weeks, a proper holiday, somewhere hot and sunny. He says that'll cheer me up, but I don't think anything will ever cheer me up again. I feel so sad.

Please get in touch, Mouse. Please?
Cat xxx

That was four weeks ago. I tore the letter into tiny pieces and let the pieces drift into the waste-paper bin like snow. I wasn't ready to get in touch, I wasn't ready to forgive or forget, or even to understand.

Mum knew something had gone wrong between me and Cat, but she also knew me well enough not to ask too much. 'Sometimes,' she told me,

'You just have to work things out on your own. Think it through.'

Maybe. Sometimes, though, it's easier not to think about things.

Things are changing on the Eden Estate – it's like the whole place can breathe at last. It said on TV that the police raid was one of the most successful ever – hundreds of thousands of pounds' worth of drugs were seized, and a dozen arrests were made on the Eden Estate alone. The bigshot suppliers Scully led the police to were arrested and charged too – the guys who pulled the strings, masterminded the whole business. They didn't live around here, of course. They had posh houses with swimming pools and triple garages filled with fancy cars, all bought with drugs money. These guys were running drugs all over the south of England.

I had to tell Mum how I got tangled up in it all, of course. If I hadn't, she'd have heard from the social services anyhow – I figured it was better coming from me.

'Oh, Mouse,' she said, her eyes wide. 'No way!'

The colour drained from her face, and she was trembling as she pulled me close. 'Of all the nights to go away. Promise me you won't try anything like that again – it was dangerous, Mouse, way too dangerous. No more risks, no more vandalism, no more graffiti.'

I blinked and chewed my lip and finally I promised, and I'll stick to it too. Mum needs me and I need her, and neither of us need any extra hassle. We've had enough of that to last a lifetime.

Scully's trial finally came up, and Mum stood as a witness just like she said she would. Mrs S. stuck by her statement too, and a few other locals came up with evidence that showed Frank Scully hadn't got everybody running scared. He would have faced a good long stretch inside, but you know what? The weasel turned traitor and grassed up his mates, giving evidence against the other Eden Estate dealers.

'He did the right thing in the end,' Mrs S. said. 'My Frank.'

Well, maybe. Maybe he just wanted a lighter sentence, though, and that's what he got, for cooperating with the police. Still, it was three years, so we won't be seeing him around for a while.

'I told him you'd be keeping Lucky,' Mrs S. said to me, after her first prison visit. 'He said that might be for the best.'

'Frank Scully said that?' I asked, amazed. 'Really?'

Mrs S. looked shifty. 'Perhaps not in those exact words,' she admitted. 'I told him, though, that it was time he grew up and took responsibilty for his mistakes. Lucky's better off with you – he knows that. He still listens to his old gran!'

So Lucky became our dog, officially, or as official as anything ever gets around here, and that was one good thing.

Eden won't ever be perfect, of course, but it's better, for sure. Work started on the new community buildings just before Christmas – council workers came in diggers to break up the concrete courtyard, map out the new community garden. Mum was involved from the start – she got the garden centre guy, the one who brought the Swiss cheese plant, to do some designs and donate some plants. Our flat looks like a high-rise greenhouse, these days. The balcony is stuffed with twiggy fruit trees and trays and trays of budding daffodills and primroses just waiting to be planted out.

Jake has been hanging around Mum, lately, making her laugh with cheesy chat-up lines and offers of fancy dates involving nightclubs, cocktails and flash cars. She's not interested. She's spending more and more time with the garden centre guy, talking about hardy perennials and compost heaps and the best varieties of lettuce.

'Women,' Jake sighed. 'They're a mystery, Mouse, mate – every one of them. I've never figured them out yet.'

It's not so hard to figure – Jake's still up to his

ears in dodgy car deals and iffy deliveries, and Mum's not crazy about that. She prefers the kind of date where she can stay out late planting hedging all round the perimeter of the new community garden.

Me, I got wrapped up in the Green Vale Comp mural. Mr Brown wanted something cultural and uplifting, a landscape or a pretty rural scene. I had other plans. I marched into his office on the first day of the January term with a folderful of designs that made his eyes open wide. 'Ah,' he said. 'Not what I was expecting, but . . . well, you're the expert, Kavanagh. I'll leave it to you, shall I?'

He looked terrified when I turned up the next day with a box full of spray cans, but I promised this would be my last graffiti hit ever. It took me weeks, working in school time and out of it. I painted giant swirls of red and yellow and turquoise, silver stars and orange spirals and curling fronds of emerald green. I added a trail of little cat footprints, weaving in and out of the patterns, and Fitz spotted them and raised an eyebrow, smirking.

'So you're over her, huh?' he said.

'Over who?' I asked.

Fitz just laughed. 'Man,' he said. 'You've got it bad.'

*

It doesn't matter whether I'm over Cat or not, though – by now, she'll be over me. She's had a chance to think, a chance to let go, a chance to move on. I had my chance, and I didn't respond, and now it's most likely too late. Who knows, maybe she's better off without me.

I walk Lucky through the estate, hands in pockets against the cold. A couple of flakes of white drift past my face, swirling around in the wind, and I shiver and tug my beanie hat lower.

Cat was trouble, I know. She lied to me, used me, played games with my head, but there was another side to her too. The money she took from her dad's wallet wasn't for drink or ciggies, it was to pay a vet's bill. She bought me neon stars, showed me real ones, stroked the tight, crumpled skin of my cheek and didn't flinch. She wrote a letter to friends from the past I thought I'd never see again, and brought them back into my life. Cat cared.

Flakes of snow are landing on my fringe, stinging my cheeks. Lucky tries to chase the flakes, snapping at them as they fall. It never snows in London, or hardly ever. It feels like magic, like tiny, perfect stars, falling all around. A smile tugs at my mouth, my heart, and even though it's cold I feel like I'm warming up, defrosting, after a long time of feeling numb.

The snow falls faster now, and I stop beside the

fenced-off building site, the abandoned diggers hunched in the darkness. I look up into the navy-blue sky, and I see the snowflakes falling softly, relentlessly out of the darkness.

Beyond the whirling snowflakes, way up above Nightingale House, I think I see a bright star, silver-white, glinting above me, and then it's gone, lost in the gathering storm.

By morning, the whole world is muffled and quiet. The new garden is carpeted with snow, the diggers draped in white. All the ugliness has gone, as if it were never there at all. Lucky is smiling hopefully, his tail beating against the floor.

It's very early, but I pull on a hat, a hoodie, a jacket. I lace up my Converse trainers and slip out of the flat, along the corridor to the lift. Down in the lobby, everything is quiet beneath the twinkling icicle lights, and outside the estate is still and silent.

Lucky launches himself forward and almost vanishes into a snowdrift. He emerges grinning, his tail twitching. My trainers crunch into unspoilt snow as if I am the only boy alive, and I walk through the Eden Estate, catching snowflakes on my tongue.

I try to imagine the place in a year's time. I picture kids playing on a new, revamped playground, mums chatting over their pushchairs outside the nursery, oldies calling into the Day Centre for a cup of tea and a biscuit. The garden will be bursting with colour and life, and the new Phoenix will be up and running, and better than ever. It's hard to see the future, but snow has a way of washing the whole world clean, making anything seem possible.

Almost anything.

Seeing Cat again is going to be the hardest thing of all. I know I've let her down – I wasn't there for her when she needed me. I got angry, and I backed off and walked away. I tried to forget her, but I couldn't.

Some people are just part of your life, whether you like it or not.

There's my mum, who messed up so badly when I was a kid she almost didn't make it through. She did, though, and now her whole life is about helping others to survive, even when everyone else has given up on them.

There's my dad, who didn't really want to know me, but gave me my crooked teeth, my love of colour and countryside and risk-taking. As dads go, he's pretty useless, but who knows, one day I might just save my money and buy me a ticket to India and surprise him. Wonder what he'd say about that?

Bad stuff happens sometimes, and there's not a

whole lot of point in looking around for someone to blame it on. Who's to say my life would have been easier if Dad had been around? I used to think so, but now I'm not so sure. These days, I live my own life and I make my own luck, and that's something I think he'd understand. Besides, if Dad hadn't been so hopeless, I might never have found people like Finn and Jake. Even – don't laugh – Dodgy Dave and Mr Brown. There are plenty of people out there who care, or try to, if you just give them a chance.

Lucky – well, Lucky is my best friend. His lopsided grin, his pirate patch, his murky past . . . I didn't rescue him, he rescued me.

As for Cat, well, I realized a while ago that trust is something you either have or you don't have, no matter what. OK, so she lied to me. So what? I knew everything I needed to know about her anyway. I knew that she was messed-up and lost and lovely, and that all she ever wanted to do was to make the world a better place. She wanted to be loved too, and that's where I let her down.

I walked away from her, and nothing has been worth anything since then, nothing at all. I'm hoping it's not too late to tell her that.

I've left the Eden Estate behind me, and I'm cold now, my feet soaked and frozen as I trudge along the snow-caked pavements. The trees in Cat's road are bare, their branches bowed with snow, and when we get to her house I can see that it's still too early to call on her, way too early. The curtains are closed, the house still and silent.

I push the gate open softly, creating a mini-snowdrift. What if she doesn't want to see me? Four weeks have gone by since she wrote me that letter, and a lot can change in four weeks.

I don't know what I'd say to her, anyway – words have never been my strong point. When I don't know what to say, I say nothing at all. Lucky blinks up at me, tail wagging. I root through my rucksack and my fingers close round a can of paint, a half-used can of red. I take it out, shake it, and start to work.

I've never painted on snow before, but it can't be vandalism because the snow will be gone in a few days' time. That's what I reckon, anyhow. The red paint bleeds softly on to the crisp, white snow and pretty soon I step back and there is a giant heart curving across the snow-covered lawn beneath Cat's bedroom window. I tag a little mouse-face and a cheeky cat-face underneath it, then I whistle Lucky softly and we walk away, leaving two sets of perfect tracks in the snow.

Later on, I'm sitting on the corrugated roof of the bus stop along the road, eating a Mars bar, legs dangling. Lucky is tucked inside my jacket, a long-suffering expression on his face. My bum has frostbite and my legs are like blocks of ice, but I can't give up, I can't go home. Not yet.

An old lady comes along, looks up and bashes my feet with her walking stick. 'Bloomin' hooligan,' she says crossly.

A girl appears in the distance, a cool, cute, skinny girl with coffee-coloured skin, walking fast, slipping and sliding in the snow. She's wearing a little parka jacket with fur round the hood, corkscrew curls of golden-brown hair flying out around her face. Under the parka, I see what looks like a *Hello Kitty* nightdress over black leggings, and on her feet are red fluffy funfur slippers, which may explain why she's slithering around so much.

Lucky wriggles out from my jacket, tail wagging, his face one huge grin that stretches from ear to ear.

'Hey,' says the girl. She looks up at me with slanting green eyes that are wet with tears, starred with snowflakes.

'Hey,' I grin. 'What took you so long?'

# Thanks . . .

Thanks, as ever, to Liam, Calum and Caitlin for keeping me sane and putting up with me – also to Mum, Dad, Joan, Andy, Lori and all my fab family for endless love and support. Thanks to my lovely friends, Sheena, Helen, Fiona, Mary-Jane, Zarah and co. for the pep talks, hugs and chocolate, and to my cheerleading fellow writers, Catriona, Meg and Lisa. Also to Paul for the web support, Martyn for doing the adding-up bits, and John for driving the Dizzy-mobile!

Big thanks to Magi for being a fab first reader and offering lots of great insight, and to my editor, Rebecca, for carefully unearthing the story I'd planned to write all along! Thanks too to Amanda, Adele, Francesca, Kirsten, Emily, Ali, Jodie, Katya, Sara, Sarah, Jennie and the whole team at Puffin HQ for being so brilliant, and to best-ever agent Darley and his angels Julia, Lucie, Zoe, Emma and all at the agency.

The last thank you goes to my readers, whose emails, letters and pictures make all the hard work worthwhile. To know that you love the stories as much as I do means everything to me – you're the best!

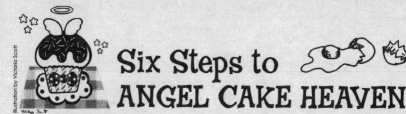

# Six Steps to ANGEL CAKE HEAVEN

Illustration by Victoria Scott
Vicky Scott

## INGREDIENTS . . .

2 ¼ cups plain flour
1 ⅓ cups sugar
2 large free-range eggs
3 teaspoons baking powder
½ teaspoon salt
½ cup butter/margarine
1 cup milk
1 teaspoon vanilla essence

**CHOCOLATE ICING:**
150g butter – softened
250g icing sugar
2 tablespoons cocoa powder
2 teaspoons very hot water
Chocolate buttons or your
    favourite sweets

## YOU WILL NEED . . .

A cupcake baking tray, a mixing bowl, cupcake paper liners,
a wooden spoon or electric mixer, a spatula and a sieve
(Ask an adult to help you use the whisk, preheat the oven and put the cakes in.)

💙 Preheat your oven to 180°C/350°F/Gas Mark 4.
Put paper cases in the cupcake tray.

💙 Put the flour, sugar, baking powder and salt into a
large bowl. Mix well.

💙 Add the butter, milk and vanilla. Beat for 1 minute until
thick and gooey, and add eggs. Beat for a further 1
minute on medium speed then 2 minutes on high speed.

💙 Spoon cupcake mix into tray until ½ to ⅔ full and bake
for 20–25 minutes. Leave to cool on a cooling rack.

💙 For the icing, beat together the butter and icing sugar.
Mix the cocoa powder and water in a separate bowl.

💙 Add the combined cocoa powder and water to the
butter and sugar, beat until smooth and creamy then swirl
over your angel cakes. Decorate with choccy buttons or
any sweets to make your own delicious angel cake treats.

## YUM!

CREATED BY

Candy Cakes

# Indigo's Blueberry Muffins

## GET YOURSELF:

A muffin baking tray and paper cases
300g plain flour
2 tsp baking powder
250g blueberries
2 free-range eggs, lightly beaten
75g caster sugar
110g unsalted butter, melted
½ tsp vanilla extract
250ml full-fat milk

 Preheat the oven to 190°C/375°F/Gas Mark 5 and put the paper cases in the tray.

 Beat together the eggs, sugar, milk, melted butter and vanilla extract in a bowl until soft and fluffy.

 Now sift the flour and baking powder into the bowl and mix it all together, before carefully stirring in the blueberries.

 With a teaspoon, divide the mixture equally among the paper cases. Bake for 20–25 minutes or until the muffins have risen and are pale golden-brown.

# A gorgeous new series by

# Cathy Cassidy

## The Chocolate Box GIRLS

### Cherry:
Dark almond eyes, skin the colour of
milky coffee, wild imagination, feisty, fun . . .

### Skye:
Wavy blonde hair, blue eyes, smiley, individual, kind . . .

### Summer:
Slim, graceful, pretty, loves to dance, determined, a girl with big dreams . . .

### Coco:
Blue eyes, fair hair, freckles, a tomboy who loves
animals and wants to change the world . . .

### Honey:
Willowy, blonde, beautiful, arty and out of control, a rebel . . .

*Each sister has a different story to tell,
which will be your favourite?*

# Cathy's Gorgeous Cherry and Chocolate Cake with Chocolate Sauce

## YOU WILL NEED:

**2 ramekins**
**75g dark chocolate, melted – plus extra for serving**
**50g unsalted butter, melted**
**2 whole free-range eggs, beaten**
**50g caster sugar**
**50g plain flour**
**50g pitted cherries from a can, chopped**
**2 tbsp juice from a can of cherries**
**Butter, for greasing**

Place the chocolate, butter, eggs and sugar into a bowl and mix.

Add the flour, cherries and cherry juice and mix together until smooth.

Grease the ramekins with butter, then spoon the mixture into each until they're three-quarters full.

Cover each ramekin with clingfilm, place in the microwave and cook on full power for 4 minutes, or until risen and cooked through.

To serve, turn the puddings out on to plates and drizzle the melted chocolate on top.

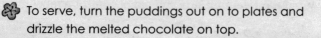

# Cathy Cassidy's

## Rocking Rocky Road Recipe
## — with Marshmallows!

### You will need:
**2 medium-sized bars of milk chocolate**
**A couple of handfuls of mini marshmallows**
**6 digestive biscuits (broken into largish chunks)**
**A handful of raisins (optional)**

♥ Melt the chocolate in a bowl over a pan of simmering water

♥ Once the chocolate has melted, leave it to cool slightly then add the rest of the ingredients and mix well (but make sure that you don't break up the biscuits too much)

♥ Pour the mix into a baking tray, which has been lined with baking parchment, level out and put in the fridge for a few hours

♥ Once the mix has set, tip it out of the tin and cut into squares, make yourself a cup of hot chocolate and enjoy!

*Best Friends* are there for you in the good times and the bad. They can keep a secret and understand the healing power of chocolate.

*Best Friends* make you laugh and make you happy. They are there when things go wrong, and never expect any thanks.

*Best Friends* are forever, **Best Friends Rock!**

Cathy Cassidy's
MY
BEST FRIEND
Rocks!
Enter at:
www.cathycassidy.com
mizz
AWARD

Is your *Best Friend* one in a million?

Go to *www.cathycassidy.com* to find out how you can show your best friend how much you care

Catch all the latest
news and gossip from

# Cathy Cassidy

at

# www.cathycassidy.com

★ Sneaky peeks at new titles
★ Details of signings and events near you
★ Audio extracts and interviews with Cathy
★ Post your messages and pictures